True Lovers' Knot

Ross Naheedy

Copyright © 2019 by Ross Naheedy

All rights reserved. No part of this book may be reproduced, used, or transmitted in any form without the express written permission of the publisher, except for the use of brief quotations in a book review or scholarly journal.

First Edition, First Printing: December 2019

ISBN 978-1-7334747-1-9

N'Vek Inc.
PO Box 643
Plainfield, IL 60544-0643

Publisher's website: https://bellamarc.com

Dedicated to J. S. Bach whose music awakens the senses and M. Chagall whose love for Bella as depicted in his paintings always brings tears to my eyes.

Acknowledgments

I'd like to thank several individuals for their help in creating this novel.

First and foremost, I'd like to thank my wife, Shelley, who read my first draft on a nightly basis as I wrote it. Surely reading such gibberish was trying at times. Her initial feedback was what I needed to make sure I was on the right track, and she helped me keep the story focused on Mehran.

I'd also like to thank my cousin Nazli Nahidi, who read the finished draft and provided me with invaluable feedback. Her words of encouragement and wisdom, along with her suggestions, helped me modify the story in much-needed ways, and the story flows better because of them.

Most of all, I'd like to thank my editor, Francie de Rose. Her fantastic mastery of the English language has been my holy grail throughout this whole process. We may not see eye-to-eye on my over-usage of "thus" – I had 40 instances initially and seven now following her edits, not counting this one. But, she truly is talented when it comes to editing and improving the flow of words, to the point that they sometimes appear lyrical. Additionally, her first edit provided much-needed direction on what was essential and what was extraneous to telling Mehran's story. This novel is 100 times better with her edits than without them. With every iteration, I felt more confident that this work was genuinely worthy of publishing.

Ross Naheedy
November 2019.

PS I encourage you to listen to the soundtrack from this book as you're reading it. Visit https://bellamarc.com to find a link to the playlist for the music referenced in this book.

True Lovers' Knot

Chapter One - April 1996

Mehran was agitated and couldn't be attentive to the conversation that his date, Kirsten, was trying to have with him. He continued to glance between Kirsten and a woman two tables over. The woman's husband was trying to calm her.

"Honey, it's no big deal. It's just water."

"No, it is not! Look at me. I'm soaked, and all because of a stupid busboy who doesn't know how to pour water."

"Ma'am, I am your waiter," said the panicked waiter while offering the woman several linen napkins.

"I don't give a crap if you're the owner of the restaurant. Do you know how much I paid for this dress? And it's all ruined."

She snatched two napkins from the waiter's hand and patted her leg while continuing her belligerence.

"They should demote you to a busboy then. Or better yet, just fire you, since I've seen busboys handle a carafe of water better than you. I mean – are you high? How could you knock over my glass while trying to pour water *into* it?"

The manager rushed over and offered his apologies.

"Mrs. Baker, I beg your pardon. Is there anything we can do for you? We have a private room with a hairdryer and an iron if you'd like. Pam, please show Mrs. Baker to the hospitality room," he motioned to one of the waitresses who had arrived to help.

Mrs. Baker continued to rant. Mehran was having a hard time hearing what she was saying, but he heard something about Mrs. Baker having come to the restaurant for 15 years and never having had something like this happen to her.

By now Kirsten had stopped talking and was looking at the commotion. Mrs. Baker got up and followed the waitress to the private room. The moment she was a few feet from the table, everyone sprang into action. Mehran looked in awe at the speed with which they operated. The manager asked Mr. Baker to push away from the table for a minute while waiters, waitresses and a busboy rushed over with an entourage of clean plates, glasses, silverware, napkins and a tablecloth to replace those on the table. First the busboy quickly stacked the old plates and took them away, while one of the waitresses collected glasses in one hand and folded the soaked tablecloth inward with her other hand, so as to wrap the remaining silverware and napkins. The moment she removed the old tablecloth, the new tablecloth was laid on the table and new glasses were promptly placed down. Next came plates and, finally, the waiter who created this whole ordeal placed clean silverware in the proper places. The entire cleaning and setting up of the table took less than a minute, Mehran thought. Maybe even about 45 seconds. It was as if that's what the crew did during the day, practiced disaster recovery.

Mehran looked at the waiter and saw the despair in his eyes, and instantly Mehran understood why this situation had fixated him. The look. He had seen it 27 years ago, when he was about 4 years old, during a visit to one of his dad's construction sites. Then, as he had just now witnessed the woman tear into the waiter, his dad had torn into and berated a lowly peasant worker. The worker had been doing his job by shoveling dirt from a pile to fill a hole he had previously dug for a sump pump. Mehran had walked over to the hole to see what the ground under looked like. The worker missed the hole when throwing the dirt and the dirt hit Mehran's neck and shirt. At 4 years old, Mehran hadn't had enough sense to brush the dirt away, but instead started crying. His dad walked over to the worker and slapped him hard across the face. Mehran stopped crying and looked at the man who was quietly holding the side of his face with one hand – head down, the man glanced up every few seconds at Mehran's dad, who was yelling and threatening to fire him.

Mehran remembered the eyes of despair on the worker's face, just as he could see in the waiter's eyes.

"Mehran! Mehran! Earth to Mehran!" Kirsten said.

He snapped back from his thoughts and looked at Kirsten.

"I'm sorry, I just got lost for a second."

"Yes, I know. Are you okay?"

"Yes, I was just thinking of this one time – eh, never mind. I don't want to talk about it now."

He looked into Kirsten's beautiful sapphire-colored eyes and thought about the world of difference a stare can convey. Ten seconds ago he was in agony, his heart feeling the despair he saw a mere 10 feet away, and now his heart found calm and kindness in Kirsten's eyes.

Kirsten tapped her finger on his hand on the table and repeated, "Are you sure you're okay?"

"Yes. I'm fine. Please continue your story about Berlin."

Kirsten wasn't convinced, but she continued. "Okay. Well, I had just arrived in Berlin, West Berlin really, on November 9th, 1989. My friend met me at the airport, we took the train to the city center and then a bus to his apartment near the Bornholmer Street border crossing. We noticed a lot of people gathered there. From the apartment, we could see over the wall and people had gathered on the East Berlin side as well. We decided to check it out and walked the few blocks over. It looked like people were just standing in front of closed gates. We headed to a nearby bar, had a few beers and headed back out around 11 p.m. While we were trying to figure out what was happening, all of a sudden, the gates opened and the crowd from East Berlin just started pouring into the West Berlin streets. It was surreal. In a matter of just minutes a couple of thousand people crossed the border into West Germany, and people on our side started walking over the border to East Germany.

So my friend and I just walked through the crossing and onto the other side."

"Just like that? Didn't anybody check any of your documentation?"

"No! They just stood there with their machine guns."

"That was a moment to be remembered, no?" asked Mehran.

"For sure," Kirsten said. "People in East Germany were greeting us like they had never seen anybody other than their own countrymen. You know, the whole thing happened because of a couple of mistakes, right?"

"I did not know that. I guess I always imagined people protested and then tore down the wall."

"No, not at all," said Kirsten. "East Germany was going to allow their people to cross the border, but only after they had obtained proper visas from West Germany. The minister in the meeting where this was discussed missed this small detail. As a result, the media told people that the borders were open for crossing. People showed up at the borders, but border agents didn't know what to do with them. After trying to get clarification from their superiors, they eventually decided to just open the gate at the Bornholmer Street crossing and other crossings followed suit. By that time, the authorities had already lost all control and couldn't contain the people or the border."

"What was it like in East Berlin?"

"Nothing like West Berlin. The old buildings looked the same, but there weren't any stores with merchandise. Bars looked ragged, although everything was very clean. Over the next few days, the East German government started to bulldoze sections of the wall to allow people to move freely between the two countries. By the next summer they removed the rest of the wall."

"Hah! To think Germany united just because a minister wasn't paying attention in a meeting. How ironic is that?"

While Kirsten continued to talk about her trip, Mehran noticed Mrs. Baker walk back. The waiter was standing at their table and apologized again as he pulled the chair out for her. Mehran peered at the dress from afar and couldn't notice anything awry. The manager was at the table as well, and he apologized again and offered them a free bottle of the house wine, a 1992 Merlot. Mr. Baker waved his hands and denounced that it wasn't necessary, but Mrs. Baker made a couple more mean-spirited comments and told them to bring the wine. She also asked for a different waiter.

Kirsten noticed that Mehran's eyes had wandered to the other table again and asked, "Is something bothering you?"

"No," he mumbled. "Well, yes. I just don't like it when people treat others not so nicely."

"It's clear she's a bitch," Kirsten said as she glanced at Mrs. Baker over her shoulder. "I mean, accidents happen."

"Yeah, and to think – I mean, the waiter is probably scared shitless that he's going to lose his job. Or maybe not. I doubt people lose their jobs over just an accident or two. But still, that woman terrified the waiter. I could see it in his eyes."

Kirsten set her hand on Mehran's. "Don't worry about it."

"Oh, I'm not. I'm just glad I don't have to deal with people like her."

Mehran looked over again and almost everything had returned to normal. Mr. Baker was still trying to calm his wife. Mehran, after glancing at Mrs. Baker for the umpteenth time, decided that he'd had enough of her negativity. He turned his attention to Kirsten.

Kirsten was, by most standards, a very attractive woman of 29. She had straight, darker blond hair that was midway down her back, neatly shaped eyebrows that matched the color of her hair, full lips and a narrow chin. Her chin didn't fit the rest of her face so much, Mehran thought, since her face wasn't elongated but not round either. Her ears were nearly flat and sported a pair of small, hanging sapphire earrings that matched the color of her eyes. She had a slender neck leading to her exposed clavicles, which hid under her dress on one end and flanked her suprasternal notch at the other end, leading to a garnet pendant hanging from her neck. Her arms looked perfect with a hint of muscle tone, and a delicate, yet sturdy wrist, adorned with a simple Omega.

This was Mehran and Kirsten's first date, and there was much Mehran wanted to learn about Kirsten. As he glanced over her long, narrow fingers and trimmed nails he thought, *with those fingers, she'd make a great violinist. I wonder if she plays.*

"So, let's change the subject," Mehran said. "Tell me. I noticed some Chopin CDs on your desk the other day. Do you play any instruments?"

"A little bit of piano. In Europe, being able to play an instrument is rather a standard. I played piano for a few years before we came to the States and continued playing through high school. How about you?"

Mehran's thoughts traveled back to his childhood again, this time to his dad's insistence that he learn to play the violin. His dad was a unique individual with an intelligence way above the smartest of people, as long as he didn't succumb to his bad temper. Mehran remembered once receiving a punishment from his dad, although he didn't remember what had landed him on the wrong side that night. His dad played the violin as well and used the bow for the punishment. Mehran ran into his dark bedroom with his dad running behind. When Mehran entered the room, his hand missed the light switch. His father stood in the doorway, lit from behind, looking into the dark room. The first strike of the bow left a sting on Mehran's leg; he ran behind the bed. The next strike of the bow hit the bed, causing the bow to shatter. His father stood still for a while, staring into Mehran's eyes, before walking away. After that, playing the violin hadn't been on Mehran's list of things he liked to do.

"I was forced to play the violin for a couple of years before my parents gave up on me," Mehran told Kirsten.

Despite having hated to play the violin, he thought how fortunate he was to have had the opportunity to play. Yet he was disgusted every time he touched the instrument during the following 2 years. While he believed he had a talent for music, he didn't believe he had a passion for the violin at all.

"I didn't care much for it. It was torturous. Sometimes I wish I had stuck with it, though. I played Tar, a Persian instrument, for a couple of years and was pretty good at it. I probably should've played the drums, though."

To him, keeping rhythm was just as much a rite of passage to Iranian boys as playing an instrument in Europe was for kids. Just like all other Iranian boys, he was a natural-born rhythm master.

He started rapping his fingers and nails on the table in a manner so that only Kirsten and he could hear it.

"This, Kirsten, is the cornerstone of Persian dancing. Before you know it, you'll be hypnotized and belly dancing right over there," Mehran said while nudging his head toward the open space in the aisle between the tables.

Kirsten laughed. It was a combination of what Mehran said, the rhythm he tapped out, his bobbing head, and his eyebrows lowering and raising in unison with the beat. She looked at his neatly combed hair, dull under the light pendant hovering above their table. His looks were completely common, not like the handsome Aussie she had dated for a few months prior to this date. Mehran wasn't tall. As a matter of fact, he looked slightly shorter than Kirsten when she was wearing her heels. He was neither built nor out of shape. His skin was fair, his brows thick, eyes deep gray, cheekbones and chin pronounced, and his four-day-old facial hair was just enough to edge him on the upper part of average. But there was something about the way he talked and acted that more than compensated for his looks, Kirsten thought.

As they sat across from each other at the restaurant, Mehran felt a bit uncomfortable by the long pause in their conversation. After pouring some more Cabernet into her glass, he reached into his pocket, pulled out a penny, laid it on the table, pushed it toward her and asked, "Penny for your thoughts?"

Kirsten picked up the penny, put it in her purse, and said, "I was just thinking of when you stopped by my office with the box of chocolate."

"Oh, my God," Mehran laughed. "I couldn't figure out if my heart was more confused than my brain, or the reverse, so I just stared at the chocolate. I could have taken a rejection just fine, since that's what I came prepared for, but what you did just stunned me."

"Well, I really wanted to have this dinner, but I had to follow company policy. I was pretty certain they'd bend at the end."

"I'm glad they did." He raised his glass.

She raised hers as well and both drank their wine.

Two waiters set down their dinner plates. One left, and their waiter said, "Sautéed Chilean sea bass with fried spinach in wine sauce for the madam." "Australian rack of lamb, medium, with fried spinach in wine sauce as well for sir. Please let me know if there's anything else I can get for you."

Kirsten and Mehran both thanked the waiter, looked at each other, smiled, and waited as the waiter retreated.

As Kirsten cut a small piece of sea bass, she asked, "So, are you Muslim?"

"I was loosely raised with Islam. The years after the Iranian Revolution, taking Arabic was mandatory in high schools, and Islam, or rather 'religion,' was taught throughout my entire studies in Iran. I am, however, an atheist." He finished his sentence before popping a chunk of lamb into his mouth.

"An atheist? That's interesting. I don't meet many people who are openly atheist, let alone one whose apostasy would come with a penalty of death in Iran."

"That's funny. Last I checked, we were in the United States of America where I, as an American citizen, have earned the right to speak my mind."

"How old were you when you left Iran?"

"Well, I came here in 1984 when I was 19."

Kirsten quickly did the math in her head. Mehran was 31.

"How do you know of the death penalty for atheists in Iran anyway?"

"I know a manager in a subsidiary we have back in Geneva." She pointed her fork at Mehran while tilting her head forward and raising an eyebrow to Mehran: "She tells me all about your Middle Eastern stuff."

"Yes, she's right. I wouldn't openly say so in Iran, although it doesn't matter. I cannot go back anyway."

"Because you exited the country illegally and dodged the draft?"

"Hmm. You seem to know a lot about me," Mehran said in an inquisitive voice. "How's that?"

Kirsten thought that she must have confused him. "Don't worry. Being in international banking, I like to keep abreast of what goes on internationally. Once I knew you were Persian, even before I knew we were coming on this date, I updated myself on the situation in Iran and what happened to of-age boys who were eligible for the draft in the 1980s during the war with Iraq. Not too hard to put two and two together."

Mehran smiled. "Okay, Miss smarty pants, how did I get here?"

"Probably on a mule through Kurdistan. You crossed the border to Turkey, flew to a European country, either had a visa waiting for you or waited for one, and flew to the U.S.," she smiled. "Tell me I'm right."

Mehran was amazed. How could she hit the bull's eye on some of the details in his life he didn't think anyone would know of, or care about, for that matter? He thought she must have spent some time studying her date before the actual encounter.

"You're scary," he said.

"I'm smart, not scary."

She took another bite of the sea bass.

"Why do I feel inferior sitting across from you?" he asked.

Kirsten wondered whether she had been over-the-top. Her expression softened. "Mehran. I'm sorry. I think you're misunderstanding my – my boastfulness. It's just because I like to prove that I'm smart and knowledgeable about what goes on around me. I did not mean to offend you."

Mehran made a dismissal motion with his face. "You didn't offend me. It is obvious that you're very smart. You don't have to overpower me on our first date. I have the utmost appreciation and respect for your trying to understand where I've come from. But, you know, as my grandmother used to say, 'Some things are best explained than studied.' You can't just read about places and people. At some point you're going to have to hear of their experiences firsthand."

Mehran thought of his grandmother, who had just recently died of pancreatic cancer. She had taught history to Iranian high school girls for as long as Mehran had remembered. He recalled asking her what she had meant by that sentence, to which she had replied, "The written words can only say so much. Sometimes, if you have the opportunity to sit across from someone and learn their story, it's worth a thousand times more than if you read it on paper."

She was right. How could Kirsten know what he went through on his trip from Tehran, his city in central Iran, to Tereshkova, Turkey? She wouldn't, other than having read a couple of sentences about Iranian boys having to cross the Iranian border on mules.

"So, explain to me what happened on the mule ride to Turkey," she asked.

"Hey! I can't tell you everything on our first date; otherwise there might not be a second one."

Kirsten smiled and took a sip of her wine. She wanted to tell him that there would definitely be a second date but decided to withhold that information until later.

"So, where was your stop in Europe?"

"I stayed in Amsterdam for a few weeks."

"Ooh, tell me you visited the red-light district."

"You can't avoid the red-light district in Amsterdam walking around in a single day, let alone a few weeks."

"So, what did you think of the girls?"

"I don't know. I've been to Las Vegas, and the girls there are a thousand times better than those in the red-light district in Amsterdam. Those girls just looked way too overweight and beat out for prostitution work. The girls in Vegas look top-notch. But I guess if you wanted to lay down and talk to them, the girls in Amsterdam might be more interesting."

Kirsten didn't care for prostitutes but didn't mind them either. She had heard the expression "the oldest profession on Earth," and she believed it. Prostitution was legal and regulated in most of Europe, and most Europeans were used to it being around all the time.

"Did you go to Turkey by yourself or with someone?"

"I was with my dad most of the way. We parted before the actual border crossing, and then we met in Turkey."

"So, did he take you to a brothel in Turkey?"

Mehran laughed. "Not in Turkey, but we talked about it a lot in Amsterdam. He tried to convince me that the red-light district was a good thing to have around. I was a different person back then, though. I suppose I was more moral."

"More moral? This I gotta hear."

Mehran taught for a few seconds. "While we were in Amsterdam, we ate breakfast most mornings at our hotel, and the same young waitress waited on us. My dad always smiled at her, looked her in the eyes and told her that she was beautiful. I argued, to no avail, that my dad was a married man and that he shouldn't be looking at beautiful, young girls."

"Do you think he was into her?"

"I think so. If she had grabbed his hand and taken him upstairs, he would've gone with her. But I didn't appreciate my dad talking about her the way he did."

"Why not? She was pretty, you said."

"Oh, she was. Probably almost as pretty as yourself."

She smiled.

"No, I'm serious. She was quite pretty. Under different circumstances, I would have loved to be with her. I just didn't feel it was right for my dad to be hitting on her. What about my mom? Wasn't he married to her?"

"Could it be that you misunderstood his meaning, and that he was just appreciating the youth and beauty in her?"

"Maybe. When we were in Amsterdam, my dad kept telling me that I should try sleeping with a prostitute."

"Did you?"

"No, I didn't believe prostitution was right. Like I said, I was a different person. I've come a long way since then. I don't look at prostitutes and beautiful waitresses the same way any longer," he smiled.

"How *do* you look at them now?"

"I see beauty where there is beauty. When I see a beautiful waitress, I smile, because her beauty brings a smile to my face."

"I guess you understand what your dad was doing then."

Mehran shrugged his shoulders. "Perhaps. You know when you're a teenager you have these ideals in your head because you're so impressionable by books, movies, music and so on? Tell me. Which teenager hasn't tried being a vegetarian?"

"I know I did," said Kirsten. "It lasted exactly a month."

"That's what I mean. As a teenager you think you can change the world with ideals, and sometimes you stick to those ideals throughout your life. Sometimes you don't. One ideal for me was that inner beauty was the only important quality in a relationship."

"Obviously you don't think that's the case now, do you?"

"I couldn't be in a relationship where inner beauty did not exist, but I would be hard put if that was all there was in the relationship."

Their conversation continued in this way throughout dinner. After Mehran had paid the bill, they left the restaurant and got into the limousine.

"Where to now?" Kirsten asked.

"Remember, we didn't order dessert so that we could have it somewhere else."

"Where did you have in mind?"

Mehran remained silent. The limo was already moving, as if the driver already knew where they were headed. They were each sitting by a door on opposite sides of the limo, as if they were afraid of ruining a good first date. He had his hand on the middle seat, bracing himself for turns, when she put her hand on his. He looked at her. She seemed serious at first, but, within a few seconds, her lips and cheeks lifted into a smile and she squeezed his hand.

"It's a surprise," he said.

Mehran was liking this a lot.

Chapter Two

Kirsten was born in 1966 in Switzerland to a middle-class family and lived much of her life in the outskirts of Lucerne. Her French mother was an avid skier who had studied design management with a minor in the fine arts at Lucerne University of Applied Sciences and Arts, where she had met Kirsten's father, a Swiss. Kirsten's father was going through his graduate studies in architecture at the time. They had fallen in love and married shortly after graduation. Kirsten and her younger sister had been raised in a house where they were bombarded with French from their mother and German from their father. Kirsten's school taught Swiss German and required her to study a foreign language. English should have been Kirsten's obvious choice, but English would have been an easy language to pick up because of its influence on the rest of the world through magazines, television and movies, so Kirsten had chosen French. When Kirsten was 14, her family moved to Los Angeles, California, because of extremely lucrative job openings for both her mother and father in designing the 1984 Summer Olympics swim stadium and the velodrome. Kirsten enrolled in a public high school, where her previous exposure to English quickly led her to become fluent in that language as well.

The positions Kirsten's parents held were only short-term, with no future in sight. In 1983, her father was looking for other ways to advance his career when he was offered a prominent job as a partner at a German firm based in Denver, Colorado, specializing in designing and building commodity office towers in cities around the United States.

Having lived in the United States for 3 years, the family considered their options. Kirsten was 17 at the time, so she participated in the decision as well. They could go back to Switzerland and look for jobs there or take the position in Denver. In the end, Kirsten's decision to study business in the United States put closure to the decision. A couple of months after moving to Denver, Kirsten's mother found a job as curator for the Denver Art Museum.

Kirsten graduated from high school in 1984 and studied business at Northwestern University in Chicago. While she excelled in her studies and was content, a part of her yearned for the culture she had left in Europe. Her intention was to continue her graduate studies in international business. It made sense to complete her graduate work abroad. She decided to study at Université de Genève. She lined up a job at Swiss Bank Corporation upon graduation. Her mastery of multiple languages, along with her sociability, smarts and having lived in the United States, quickly boosted her to her current position of international account manager in the Chicago branch of the bank.

Kirsten first met Mehran a couple of months ago at the bank. He was meeting with Marie, a co-worker. Kirsten had walked over to Marie to ask about a company-wide email from earlier in the day, when she had noticed Mehran sitting in Marie's office. Marie, Kirsten found out later, had checked Mehran's application and noticed that he wasn't married, so she had taken the opportunity to introduce him to Kirsten.

"Mr. Noori," Marie looked at Mehran. "did I pronounce that correctly?"

"Yes, that was perfect, but Mehran will do."

"Mehran, I'd like to introduce you to Kirsten Hostetler, our international accounts manager. She's Swiss."

Marie had winked at Mehran while saying that last part, causing Mehran to mentally revise the sentence to *she's Swiss, available and looking for a date.*

Mehran shook Kirsten's hand. "Kirsten, what a beautiful name. It is a pleasure to meet you."

"And you as well. How's Marie treating you? Anything I can assist with?"

"No, Marie is on top of things."

"Mehran. Is that, Persian?"

"Yes, it is. How did you guess?"

"As our international accounts manager, Kirsten's well-traveled," Marie explained. "And, amazingly, she speaks fluent German, French, and some Spanish."

"And a bit of Italian," Kirsten laughed.

"You must have some Middle Eastern customers then," Mehran replied.

"Well, we have a subsidiary in Switzerland that handles our Middle East accounts. I know just enough people to be useful, and sometimes dangerous," she added jokingly.

Marie turned to Kirsten. "What can I do for you?"

"Nothing. It can wait. It was very nice meeting you, Mehran."

"And same here, Ms. Kirsten," he said with a smile. "Khodahafez!" he said in Farsi, meaning God take care, or goodbye.

"I know what that means!" Kirsten replied as she walked away with her finger wagging.

Later, Marie told Kirsten that Mehran hadn't taken his eyes off of her until Marie had closed the office door behind her.

Kirsten hadn't thought much about Mehran after their first meeting, especially since he hadn't followed through with a call or any indication that he was interested in her. Then one day, out of the blue, he was at her office door with a box of chocolate.

"Mr. Noori! Great to see you again. How are you?"

"Mehran, please, and I'm great. Well, I may be exaggerating a bit. I'm well. How about yourself?"

"Fine, thank you! Would you like me to page Marie for you?"

"Actually, I am here for you."

He extended his hand with the box of chocolate.

"I know it's not the Swiss chocolate you are used to, but I hear this is darn good. It is made right here in Chicago."

"Thank you!" Kirsten smiled. "But to what do I owe this fortunate encounter?" She reached for the chocolate and read the box cover. It read "The Fudge Pot."

Mehran mumbled a bit and then said, "Promise not to get angry?"

Angry? That's odd, Kirsten thought. "I don't get mad easily," she laughed.

"It was the wink."

"The wink?"

"When Marie introduced you to me, she gave me a wink."

"Why that little –"

"Please don't take this the wrong way, but I was wondering if you'd like to go out sometime."

"Oh, that is so sweet of you to ask. I would love to." Kirsten hesitated. "Unfortunately, the bank has a policy prohibiting any employee from dating bank clients."

"Wow. That's harsh. I suppose I could always take my money elsewhere and solve that problem."

"Well, I wouldn't quite do that yet," she smiled with her eyes. Her smile hinted that there may be an out somewhere in the bank clause. "Since I am the international division manager at this branch, I have some pull. I'm pretty sure I won't get in trouble, but would you mind if I check on that and get back to you?"

She could feel the defeat Mehran was feeling. She had rejected his advances without actually rejecting them, or even meaning to. "Until I get to the bottom of that, can you help me get to the bottom of this?" She opened the box of chocolate. Inside, there was a handwritten note: "Hello. This is Milos at the Fudge Pot. This chocolate was cooked on April 19, 1996, so it's best to eat it now! Thank you for your purchase."

"So, they want me to eat this chocolate by the end of the day?" Kirsten asked.

She looked up at Mehran as he stared into the box of chocolate. He must have been ready for a rejection and confused. She took a piece of chocolate out of the box and moved her hand toward his mouth. He opened his mouth, perhaps involuntarily, and grabbed the chocolate with his lips. The tip of her index finger touched his upper lip as she let go of the chocolate. Then she took a piece of chocolate and put it in her mouth, relishing the taste. Not better or worse than Swiss chocolate. Just different, and quite good. He must have enjoyed the taste as well, as he uttered "Mmmm."

Kirsten assured him that she would call him one way or another. She then watched him leave, thinking he was probably disappointed that he did not manage to sweep her off her feet. But she had every intention of going out with him. She remembered what her mother had once said: "Chocolate is a woman's best friend after sex." She had wondered at the time. It wasn't until now that she understood what her mother had meant. She felt a pleasure deep within her, and it wasn't just because of the chocolate. It was the feeling of being elevated. It was the feeling that she was wanted. Chocolate was just a mean to an end.

Later that week Kirsten received an email from corporate HR, letting her know that the company did not have any issues with her dating the bank client, as long as they didn't mix business and pleasure. HR was also appreciative that she had asked. In general, corporate gave her much leeway. She was a star in the corporation, and she knew it.

She picked up the phone and called Mehran to let him know that they were free and clear. Later that night, he picked her up in front of her place in a limo and took her to this nice restaurant near Chicago's North Shore. She thought that he had wanted to impress her by hiring a limo, but his excuse was that he didn't have a car.

Chapter Three

The limo came to a halt at the corner of Armitage and Western. Mehran looked at Kirsten. "Ready for dessert?"

They exited the limo and walked to the sidewalk.

"It's right over here," he said.

Mehran took Kirsten by hand and walked her about 20 paces to Margie's Candies.

"This place has been open for eons. They have the best ice cream in town. But we only have 30 minutes. They close at 11 o'clock. We need to hurry if we want some."

Kirsten was intrigued. She had never been to Margie's.

They sat in a round booth and quickly glanced over the menu. Mehran had been there a few times before and thought their banana splits were to die for, but he couldn't convince Kirsten to go for a "regular" banana split. They ended up ordering The Eiffel Tower, which was close to a banana split anyway. They would have to share the tower, since it was a gigantic creation of ice cream, towering up about eight inches and covered with colorful decorations.

Initially they had sat on opposite sides of the round booth. Kirsten excused herself to use the bathroom while the tower was being made. When she came back, she motioned to Mehran and said in a bossy way "move over," sliding herself right next to him.

"It'll be easier to share the dessert this way," she winked at him.

As they sat and talked while waiting for their order, Mehran could feel her body heat against him.

"Tell me about how you grew up. Your parents," Kirsten asked.

"They wanted the best for me."

"Yes, but you seem completely out of the ordinary. They must have done something differently."

"Different they were. Different than whom, though? Compared to other Iranian parents, I suppose they were still different."

"What's your dad like?"

Mehran paused before answering. "He was an alcoholic. Bad temper. But probably the smartest man I knew at the time."

Kirsten paused, and then asked, "Was he good to you?"

"Yes, I'd say. I had my share of punishments. Probably none I didn't deserve. He had his strong points. He loved the arts and humanities. Our views differed on worthy authors and subjects to read."

"Like what?"

"He read all of Sartre's books and considered himself to be an existentialist."

"That's noble. I believe in that."

"Yeah, but I don't think he fully understood existentialism. For instance, he believed that anybody could be Mozart given the right circumstances."

"I don't know about that," Kirsten responded.

"Exactly. That's why I don't believe he fully grasped the meaning of what he proclaimed to be. Not everyone can be Mozart. Not that I really like Mozart. I actually don't. But you can't make the circumstances right for someone and deduce that he could become Mozart. What I believe existentialism to be is that we are what we make ourselves to be. If I'm a bad person, then that's because of choices I have made up to that point."

"I'd agree with that. But, why don't you like Mozart?"

"He's too blah. There's a reason why when you hear Mozart you can tell it's Mozart, because his style was mostly monotonous. Plus he didn't divvy up his works well."

She started laughing. "What do you mean divvy up his works? He wrote a bit of everything."

"That's not what I mean. He wrote, how many symphonies? Forty-one. Of those, how many are in minor scales? Only two. The rest are all in major scales. I would say he had a prejudice against the minor scale," Mehran concluded.

"Wow! I'd say you were a music snob!"

"I know a little about music."

"So who's your favorite classical composer?"

"I don't think I can really choose just one. There are Mozart pieces I adore, such as the 'Queen of the Night' aria, the 'Quando Avran Fine Omai' aria, as well as his whole 'Requiem.' I also adore Bach, Beethoven and Chopin."

"I asked for classical. Bach wasn't classical; neither were Beethoven or Chopin."

This girl knows her music history, Mehran thought.

"Okay! Technically Bach was Baroque. Beethoven and Chopin were in the Romantic era, although Beethoven did start in the Classical era. But I thought we were talking about *classical* music as the genre."

"We were, I'm just kidding," she laughed. "Who is your favorite composer of all time?"

"I don't know. I would say it has to be Chopin or Bach."

"Really? Not Beethoven?"

"Beethoven has his place in my heart, but I adore the structure of Bach's music and the softness of Chopin."

"What a romantic!"

Kirsten was impressed. She hadn't pegged Mehran to be into music that much and was pleasantly surprised.

Just then, the waitress brought what was supposed to be the Eiffel Tower, but it looked more like the Tower of Pisa because of its slight lean.

"Don't worry. There's a stick in it that'll stop it from toppling," said the waitress. "Here you go, huns."

They each picked up their spoons. Kirsten was the first to attack the monument. She put a spoonful of ice cream in her mouth and acted like she was taste testing. After a few seconds she said, "I've had better."

Mehran gave her a frown.

Kirsten let his reaction set in before she retorted, "I'm just messing with you. It's really good."

She smiled, and he smiled back.

They worked to devour the gigantic creation but couldn't finish it by 11, when the shop was closing.

"God! I feel like a pig!" said Kirsten.

"It was good and worth it."

"No argument here. Definitely worth it."

Mehran looked at the limo. "Maybe we should walk a little of this off before we get back into the car."

Kirsten smiled in agreement. Mehran walked over to the limo driver and spoke to him. When he came back, he took Kirsten's hand in his and started to walk.

"Tell me more about you," Kirsten said.

Chapter Four

Mehran was born in 1965 in Shiraz, Iran, the first child of a marriage between a civil engineer named Barbod Noori and a girl from a prominent family involved in international trade. His mother, Mahtab, and Barbod had met while he was on assignment from the Iranian government in Shiraz, building housing for the poor. Mehran's birth nearly ended Mahtab's life; because of the complications during the delivery, she was told she would not be able to bear more children.

Shortly after Mehran's birth, the family moved to Tehran, the capital of Iran, where Barbod had created a company and entered into business with a couple of partners. Life had, at times, been hard on the Noori family, but gradually they had risen to prominence among the engineering crowd in Tehran. By the time of the Islamic revolution in 1979, they had amassed some wealth and were living prosperously. Given that, life for Mehran hadn't really been difficult at all. He grew up as a privileged child, at times to the point of being spoiled. The clubs his parents enrolled him in, the amenities they afforded him, the vacations, the toys and the violin lessons all contributed to shielding him from the realities of life. He got in trouble often, since he believed that the world revolved around him. He thought that everyone should succumb to his whims and wants. His parents tried from time to time to curb his insolence and freedom. A beating with the violin bow was just one occasion when punishment was doled out. In general, he was the kid that no parent would have wanted to have, had they a choice in the matter. The expression in Iran regarding kids his type, and what his mom would say, was, "He is so crazy and energetic that he'll climb up a straight wall."

Things started to change, however, during Mehran's mid-teens. Several factors were at play: the Islamic Revolution of 1979, living through a turbulent teenage period and Mehran's association with the free-thinkers community in Tehran.

In the few years preceding the revolution, many atrocities by and shortcomings of then ruler of Iran, Shahanshah Reza Pahlavi, were exposed to the general public. Shahanshah, the king of kings, or just plain Shah as was chanted during demonstrations in 1978, had lived lavishly without regard for the people of the country he had ruled for nearly 40 years. Things had gotten bad around 1951 when the parliament chose Mohammad Mosaddegh, a prominent parliamentarian and lawyer, as the new prime minister. Mosaddegh immediately nationalized Iranian oil, which rightfully belonged to the collective people of Iran, kicked the British oil industry out, and over the next 2 years, took over most of Shah's responsibilities and decision-making. However, in 1953, a CIA-led coup overthrew the popular Mosaddegh and reinstated the Shah. The CIA also helped Iran set up its secret service, SAVAK, to suppress political dissent. The communist party, Tudeh, was banned outright. Additional parties were either secretly taken care of or marginalized so that there was no real opposition to Shah's rule.

In the next decade, Shah instituted a series of reforms, branded The White Revolution, and tried to improve rural Iran via land reforms, privatization, creation of literacy and health corps, compulsory education along with reform, and increasing women's rights, among many others. However, most of these benefits were either poorly planned, poorly implemented or sabotaged by the opposition. Even the education reform backfired, since rural farmers were hard-pressed by the diminished workforce due to kids attending school instead of working.

By 1978, Shah was seen as a puppet of the United States. He was debated in higher social circles, and the masses were generally unhappy with the way the country ran. A couple of incidents elevated this tension, including what was at the time the largest-ever terrorist attack in the world that caused the death of 422 people burned alive inside a cinema, and the massacre of Black Friday, when Shah's soldiers gunned down a crowd of demonstrators and killed nearly 90 protesters. After these events, Ayatollah Ruhollah Khomeini, a religious figure previously exiled for 15 years, led revolts and demonstrations while still in exile. In just over 6 months, Shah had fled Iran, and Khomeini was put in authority. Shah moved from country to country, including Egypt, Morocco, Bahamas, Mexico and the United States, for the next 18 months. He eventually died of complications from cancer in 1980.

The revolution also affected the psyche of most Iranians, especially adolescents. Young teens, like Mehran, who may have wandered through a Westernized life in Iran without worries about their countrymen, were suddenly awakened to the realities around them. What shocked Mehran was the condition of rural life in Iran. Mehran had never seen rural life in person. However, through some brief travels and his association with the free thinkers of Tehran, he began to understand that most of Iran's people lived in poverty. And not just poverty. They lived a life of abject poverty, without education and with no way out.

Mehran also noticed the living conditions around him in Tehran. In more impoverished areas of the city, huts for the homeless were made from five-liter oil cans filled with mud, stacked upon each other as if they were bricks to form walls, and then topped with branches and leaves as roofs to provide shelter for a small family. While riding on trains through rural Iran, Mehran noticed that everyone outside of major cities appeared to be homeless just like the homeless of Tehran. As the trains passed through small town after small town, he could count on one hand the number of buildings made out of actual bricks. Children without shoes and shirts would run along the train, not caring if they stepped on a stone, a thorn or glass.

A couple of books were published a few years before the revolution that detailed the atrocities SAVAK had committed toward political prisoners. These books detailed the torture methods SAVAK used in the infamous Evin prison in northern Tehran. There were even hints of assassinations performed by SAVAK, such as that of Samad Behrangi, Mehran's favorite children's book writer. In addition, SAVAK was responsible for all censorship in Iran, including the press, literary works, books, films and even theater.

The combination of his associations with the free thinkers, the books he read, the revolution, and the small glimpse of other people's lives, started to shape Mehran from the spoiled child he had been into a more caring person.

In the years that followed the revolution, life had become difficult for everyone, including teenagers. Iraq started a war with Iran in 1980. War was taking its toll on the country and Iranian people as a whole. Inflation went through the roof. Girls and women were required to cover their arms, legs, chest and hair with dark scarves. Tight jeans, which were extremely popular in the 80s, were banned. Association between girls and boys was strictly forbidden, and arbitrary rules were harshly enforced by the Islamic religious police, or Komiteh. Komiteh members all wore beards, rode on government-owned Nissan Patrol trucks, and were armed with either Heckler & Koch G3 machine guns or Kalashnikovs, locally and mistakenly pronounced Klashinkov. Komiteh often raided parties, weddings and even funerals, to ensure the segregation of sexes. Alcohol was banned outright and Westernization was considered a plague that needed to be wiped from Iran.

Ultimately, it was the mandatory draft that prompted Mehran's parents to consider sending him away from Iran. Under no circumstance were they ready to let their one and only son end up "a martyr of the revolution." Thus, in 1983, after much debate, they decided that Mehran would go to the United States for his college studies. The choice of the United States had been somewhat arbitrary, but two factors dictated the choice: Mehran was somewhat fluent in English from years of private lessons, and Barbod had a few friends in the United States.

Relations between Iran and the United States weren't on the best of terms, however. Late in 1979, a group of radical Iranian students had stormed the U.S. embassy in Tehran and taken 52 American diplomats hostage. The crisis had lasted 444 days, and the hostages were released on Jan 20, 1981, the same day that Ronald Reagan was sworn in as the 40th president of the United States. Much speculation was given to this co-incidence, and many thought that the new Islamic Republic was still in bed with the United States. But the rhetoric between the two countries cast a different shadow. In particular for Mehran, it had become extremely difficult for Iranian nationals to become permanent residents of the United States.

Despite the political climate, Barbod's friends in the United States assured him that there was no issue money could not solve in the country. Luckily, money was one thing the Noori family didn't have to worry about at the time. The family paid U.S. lawyers a nice sum to file applications with universities in a variety of U.S. cities. Those universities gladly accepted Mehran, and his family's foreign money, for enrollment. Permanent residency for Mehran also was guaranteed, but there would be a few weeks between his formal interview with a U.S. embassy abroad and being granted the status of permanent resident.

The larger issue at the time became that of obtaining an exit visa for Mehran from the Iranian authorities. The supreme leader, Ayatollah Khomeini, had encouraged young men to fight for their country and to eradicate the disease that had invaded their land, a reference to Iraq and Saddam Hussein. As a result, boys over 16 years old were expressly forbidden from exiting the country for any reason. All majors exits of air, land and sea were strictly monitored for compliance with the supreme leader's wishes, so the only viable solution to exit the country was through illegal means, on foot across a remote border area.

The question was where to make the illegal exit. Iran is a vast country of more than 600,000 million square miles. At the time, Iran bordered the U.S.S.R, Afghanistan, Pakistan, Iraq and Turkey. Entry into the U.S.S.R. was difficult, since the Soviets usually didn't allow people in without cause. Afghanistan was ravaged by the internal war between the Mujahideen and the Soviet forces. Exit through Pakistan was a possibility, but the border was far from Tehran. Iraq was out of consideration. That left Turkey as the only viable option for exit.

According to smugglers familiar with the area, the best time of year to cross the border was during the final months of winter. It was possible to cross the border during other times, but the chances of getting caught were higher. The border crossing would virtually be guaranteed during most of March due to the season and the Iranian new year, Nowruz. Nowruz always fell on the first day of spring and was followed by nearly two weeks of celebration. The smugglers determined that fewer guards were posted around the border at this time.

It was decided that Mehran would graduate from high school in spring 1983 and leave in March 1984.

Mehran's last year of high school was memorable. He was in love with a girl, Bahar, since May 1982. He called her his girlfriend, surely something to boast about, since most boys didn't have one. The word "girlfriend," however, had to be taken with a grain of salt. Boys did nothing more with a "girlfriend" than talk on the phone or exchange notes. Even exchanging notes was not easy. A location, usually and literally a hole in a wall, somewhere on the street would be agreed upon during a phone conversation. Then, when nobody was on the street, Mehran would leave his neatly folded notes in the designated hole and walk away; he would keep an eye on the site from a distance. Minutes or sometimes hours later, Bahar would make an excuse to her mother that she needed to go to the pantry around the corner. She would cover herself with a roopoosh-roosari, a long jacket-like cover worn over clothes, her neck and head, visit the hole, take the note out and replace it with her own note, and follow through to the pantry around the corner. If Mehran was lucky, he would have positioned himself between the hole and the pantry, to see Bahar up close, twice! The phrase "up close" should also be taken lightly, since it usually meant loitering on one side of a 12-foot-wide street while Bahar walked on the other side. After Bahar bought something from the pantry she'd pass him again. Bahar always had her eyes on Mehran, although she never turned her head his way. The ultimate exchange would be to actually say a sentence or two during the passage, uttered not too loudly, but loud enough to be heard by each other. Bahar would slow her pace when she was close to Mehran to increase the time they had with each other.

It was by chance that Mehran and Bahar fell in love. Prior to the two of them "dating," Mehran was talking on the phone on a regular basis with Bahar's friend, but the conversations were casual and innocuous. Then, on one occasion, Bahar was over at her friend's house and she spoke to Mehran over the phone. A spark ignited during that conversation, the two exchanged phone numbers and they started conversing.

The style of houses and apartments in Iran is very different than traditional Western houses. Building grounds are always separated from each other by shared walls between 6- and 12-feet tall. Apartment buildings have a walled-in yard, usually in the back, typically accessible only by the first-floor occupants. The front façade of a block with apartment buildings would always be flush with the street, each apartment looking different than the two beside it. Bahar was lucky to live on the first floor of an apartment building at an intersection. At times, she would pretend to study in the yard, near a door that led to the street. Mehran would walk the block, and they would see each other through tiny holes in the door; they might even exchange words as he walked by.

This was the love life of a teenager in Iran.

In the first few months of their "relationship," the two were able to talk on the phone into the wee hours of the morning. But Bahar had a very strict mother. After a few months of catching Bahar on the phone, her mother became suspicious of Bahar's activities. Phone conversations were difficult and lasted only minutes. They sometimes ended abruptly when Bahar had to hang up the phone, run to her room, and pretend that she was studying. At times, Mehran was so desperate to hear Bahar's voice that he would call her number, she would pick up the phone, he'd tell her how much he missed her voice and that he loved her, while she would pretend that nobody was on the line, repeatedly asking "Alo? Alo?" *Hello. Hello.* She would hang up after 10 seconds. When her mother would ask who it was, she'd shrug her shoulders, or say, "Mozahem Telefoni." *Prank caller.*

Frustrated with the phone situation, Mehran wrote a four-page single-spaced letter on a legal pad to Bahar's mother and put it in the hole for Bahar. In the letter, he tried being honest with the woman regarding his relationship with Bahar, reasoning that there was no harm in what they were doing. He didn't ask to see Bahar, he asked that he be allotted time to speak freely with Bahar on the phone, limited in length and time by what Bahar's mother would decide. He professed that he was tired of calling their home so many times and staying silent or hanging up when Bahar's mother picked up the phone. He wrote that he'd appreciate being able to politely say hello to Bahar's mother and ask to speak with Bahar.

Bahar balked at the idea during a brief phone conversation, but she was receptive to seeing the letter. After reading it, though, Bahar refused to give the letter to her mother, fearing that the little contact Mehran and Bahar had would end.

Mehran was a distinguished student throughout high school, and technical subjects came naturally to him. He still was in trouble often, though, since he was contemptuous, and life after the revolution didn't leave any room for public insolence. While Mehran was in school and doing well, he wasn't in jeopardy of being drafted, but once he completed school, he was eligible for the draft. Graduation meant house arrest for Mehran, since even going with his parents to a family party and returning at night risked them being stopped at intersections, as was common during the period after the revolution. Questions would be asked, especially about Mehran, his papers, and why he hadn't reported for the draft. With Komiteh's frequent stops of boys on the streets, visits with Bahar were rarer after graduation. It was Mehran's idea that he enroll in Tehran University, even if it meant that he would not be able to transfer any credits when he left the country. The upside was that he would be able to dodge the draft legally while he was studying. He had already passed the college entrance exams with flying colors and had his choice of a major. He enrolled in the college of liberal arts.

Enrolled in college, Mehran stayed in Iran and continued to see Bahar. His visiting opportunities, even though diminished by her mother's suspicions, still existed. Since Bahar didn't have to attend school during the summer and did not have to study, she was given permission to meet some of her girlfriends at a few popular teen spots. Baloot was an ice cream shop that did a brisk business because it was the hang out of many boys and girls in similar situations to Mehran and Bahar. Baloot had been raided many times by the Komiteh, but the young adults continued to use it as a venue to be around each other, despite the consequences. Via a few simple words spoken swiftly, yet softly, by Bahar during a prank call, usually "Baloot at 5" or "Tajreesh at 4," Mehran was told where and when to show up. Then, at the designated places, they would see each other up close and maybe even extend their fingers as they walked in opposite directions, in the hope that they would feel the electricity for the split second the tips of their fingers brushed against one another.

Mehran often compared his love of Bahar to a pressure cooker. Without a proper outlet, the pot would certainly explode. He felt that the letters and occasional conversations on the phone were outlets for the pressure, but it seemed that the outlets were never big enough, leading to more and more pressure buildup. He wondered if this was Bahar's preference.

For instance, Mehran had a close friend, Amir, who had confided in him that he had already slept with his girlfriend.

"How? When? Where?" Mehran had asked.

"Oh, her parents had left the house for a party, and she let me in. It was great!"

"You're lying."

"Believe what you want. Her pussy was so tight, and she couldn't stop kissing me."

"No way! I know her brother. He'd kill you if this was true."

"Dummy! You think she told anybody? She'd never tell."

A part of Mehran felt jealous hearing about Amir's triumph, but another part didn't believe him. Yet another part felt that what he and Bahar had was worth a thousand times more than what Amir had done with his girlfriend.

Doom, however, had its way of interfering with Mehran and Bahar's relationship. One evening, Bahar went out with her girlfriends to a pizzeria; Mehran and his friends sat at the table next to them.

Mehran and Bahar sat at the edge of their tables, positioned to be as close to each other as possible. They talked to each other, as if they were sitting at the same table, while their friends ignored them and talked amongst themselves. Bahar's mother surprised her daughter when she came into the restaurant. She recognized Mehran from his loitering around their apartment, and confronted Bahar in front of her friends. Mehran's legs were coiled and locked in position like a snake, ready to spring to Bahar's defense. When Bahar's mother grabbed Bahar's wrist to drag her out of the establishment, Mehran's legs fired, only for his wrist to be held down by Amir sitting next to him.

When they left, Mehran stormed out, ran to the alley behind the restaurant, put his forehead against the building and cried. *I'll never see Bahar in close proximity again,* he thought. He grew angry at Bahar's mother and worried about the consequences to Bahar and how she might curb Bahar's social life even further. Despite this new limitation, Mehran's love for Bahar grew stronger in her absence.

Mehran spent the summer pining for Bahar. When he went outside with the hope of glimpsing Bahar, Mehran also feared being picked up for questioning by Komiteh. For teenage boys, life had become a roll of the dice.

Mehran didn't think much of being detained, though. A part of him wondered what the big deal was about going to war and dying. *We'll all die in due time, and maybe dying in this war is* my *due time,* he thought. Dying didn't seem such a bad alternative to never seeing Bahar again.

Throughout the summer, Bahar's mother spoke about sending Bahar abroad for studies after she finished high school. This rejuvenated the idea that Bahar and Mehran could end up with each other after all while in the United States, and the fragility of their relationship seemed to fade. In rare opportunities for conversation, they dreamt of how they'd get married as soon as they were both abroad and of age.

Mehran had a choice of colleges to attend in the United States, as well. He applied and was accepted to five major universities in five distinct U.S. cities. In the summer of 1983, Mehran spent time at the Iran National Library in Tehran, reading about each city's characteristics, weather, surroundings and landscape. He knew he wanted to study chemical engineering, and his final choices were University of California Berkeley and Northwestern University in Chicago. His close circle of free thinkers directed him to many books and publications on the student movements in Berkeley during the 1960s and 1970s. On the other hand, studying at the Chemical & Biological Engineering School of Northwestern was, by all standards, a top-notch education.

In the end, however, it didn't matter. Barbod's friends in the United States were all in Los Angeles, comically called Tehrangeles because of the sheer number of Iranians who had settled in Southern California. It was decided for Mehran that he would study at UC Irvine. A part of him was excited to live in California, since it was considered the holy grail for all Iranians moving abroad. The weather was considered nice, although not to Mehran's liking. He liked the weather cloudy and cool. Yet, he thought he would miss the Persian culture less by living among Iranians.

As luck would have it, the potential destination for Bahar was Los Angeles, where her aunt lived. This spark of light convinced Mehran that his father had made the right choice in UC Irvine. His hopelessness disintegrated and enthusiasm took over.

The university Mehran was to attend in fall, Tehran University, was instrumental to the revolution, as well as the demonstrations that led to it. Many demonstrations started at the university and gained momentum on the streets as ordinary people joined the students, chanting slogans that landed many of them in custody and prison.

The street bordering the university on the south was lined with stores of art supplies, musical instruments, calligraphy ink and pens and scientific instruments. Bookstores dominated most of the kilometer facing the university. All kinds of books were usually available, though some were sold underground, literally. Just about any sort of book could be found, from Marx and Engels' and Darwin's *Theory of Evolution* to the holy books of world religions. Mehran spent countless hours drifting from bookstore to bookstore. He loved to browse books he never knew existed.

Despite his intention to become a chemical engineer, Mehran chose the liberal arts program for the few months he attended college in Iran. He thought political science would expand his mind and provide him with critical thinking skills useful in the sociopolitical realm of the world. He also would have a higher chance to mingle with non-technical professors and other students, and he could read books he usually wouldn't. Studies at college, however, didn't turn out as he hoped.

Soon after the revolution, the government started to turn people against each other. Snitching was greatly rewarded, usually in the form of other favors returned, and people began to distrust each other. Keeping one's thoughts to himself was a skill to be learned and perfected. Professors in college were no exception to the new methodology of being turned in to the government for trivial material they used in their teachings or things they said in the classroom. Conversations outside of the classroom were curbed as well, since someone listening might be a snitch. As a consequence, the few months of liberal arts education Mehran received were completely watered down. The syllabi of all university courses were changed to conform to Islam and reflect Islamic values. Left-leaning professors were replaced with lesser qualified faculty based on their beliefs.

It had also become customary for men who wanted to be accepted by the regime to grow a beard. A beard became the symbol for someone who was either already in the government or someone who wanted to be associated with the government.

Classrooms contained many references to the atrocities of the previous regime. Not a day went by when every action of the Shah wasn't condemned. Even the White Revolution keynotes were discarded as having benefited the regime only or considered anti-Islamic. During one lecture in Mehran's "Introduction to the Constitution" class, a woman argued that extending voting rights to women, one of the elements of the White Revolution, was a good thing. The professor argued against it under the disguise that Islam didn't allow it. When the woman asked for references in the Quran, the Muslim holy book, and also noted that the Iranian constitution didn't reference women to be restricted from voting, the professor dismissed the question as irrelevant. He retorted that according to the teachings of ayatollahs, the experts of Islamic studies, women should not be allowed to vote. The same woman argued, on a different occasion, on why the Islamic court system counted the testimony of a woman as only half that of a man's, even though the Quran expressly states otherwise. She quoted parts 3:195 and 4:124 of the Quran in support of her statements. The professor, confirming the statements the student had made, retorted that it is best to leave the interpretation of the Quran to the ayatollahs, and that in testimony in the country's judicial system, it was ruled that two women's testimonies were to equal that of one man's.

Every fiber in Mehran wanted to engage in the conversations and take the side of the woman, but he kept out of the discussions to stay out of trouble and avoid confrontations. To conform became increasingly difficult, though. For someone who had always publicly voiced his opinion, this new life appeared to conflict with every grain of Mehran's being. He read the Declaration of Independence and the Constitution of the United States, in addition to all the amendments, and a big part of him craved to get out of Iran and be in a country where words would not land him in jail. Freedom to write what one believed was unheard of in Iran, neither during the current regime's time, nor its predecessors'. He read about the Watergate scandal and the role journalism played in bringing attention to President Nixon's illegal behavior. Mehran watched the movie *All the President's Men*, and appreciated that the journalists exposing the scandal, even though they were harassed, were under no jeopardy of jail or torture.

A couple of times some things could have gotten very ugly for Mehran. Mehran and a couple of friends planned a trip to Ramsar, a resort city by the Caspian Sea in north of Iran. On the morning of the trip, Mehran was reading *The Mother* by Maxim Gorky while they waited at the city bus terminal. An undercover agent about Mehran's own age casually started a conversation with Mehran. The agent asked about Mehran's life, then his vacation plans and finally his book before presenting his identification card and motioning two armed guards to escort Mehran to a trailer in the terminal's parking lot. Mehran was questioned and a file was created with his name, address and other identification information. His backpack was searched. Luckily for Mehran, the two things he was most afraid they would find, they did not: his deck of cards and a liter of vodka. He had the cards hidden inside a college textbook, one card at a time between pages and spread so as to not raise suspicion. The vodka was triple-tied in strong plastic bags toward the bottom between his clothes. His audio cassettes of the Bee Gees, Julio Iglesias and assorted Western music were confiscated. Some other items found included letters from Bahar, a picture of Bahar, and the libretto to *Koroghlu,* an opera by Uzeyir Hajibeyov, an Azerbaijani classical music composer long dead.

The subject matter of *Koroghlu* was what caught the interrogator's attention. The *Epic of Koroghlu* is about a hero who tried to avenge the death of his father at the hands of the local chieftain by forming an uprising against the unjust rulers of his clan. The interrogator was not familiar with the story, so Mehran explained the libretto in short. While trying to defend the epic story, which had been handed down generation to generation for centuries, Mehran was baffled how his interrogator could not see the irony of questioning him about such a story. Just a few years ago the whole country had done the same to the previous regime.

During the interrogation, a sense of panic overtook Mehran. The interrogator had his address. He assumed the worst and imagined that they dispatched a Nissan Patrol full of Komiteh members to his house. Maxim Gorky's book was the most innocuous of his books. His library at home contained books by Marks, Engels and Darwin – books forbidden by the regime. If any were found, he and possibly his whole family could be in trouble. Alas, in the interest of time and a phone call Mehran needed to make quickly before leaving on the trip, he begrudgingly gave up the libretto. After his release, he left the terminal and walked, frequently looking over his shoulder to make sure he was not being followed. After walking a few blocks in a zig-zag pattern, he found a payphone and called Mahtab.

"Mom."

"Hi! I thought you would be on the bus by now."

He didn't want to worry Mahtab with the details of his interrogation, but he also felt that he needed to warn her.

"Mom, I was under interrogation and just got out. They picked me up because I was reading a book."

"What book? Are you okay? Where are you now?"

"I'm fine, mom. I'm a few blocks away at a payphone. They let me go. But they took down our address."

"They let you go? Did they say anything? Did they take anything of yours? Oh, God!"

"No, mom. They took my cassettes. But in case they show up at our house, I don't want them to find my books."

"What books?"

"They're on my bookshelf on the very bottom shelf. Put them in a box and have Amir pick them up right now."

"Are you sure they let you go? If they let you go, then they're done. They're not going to come here."

"Mom, in case they do. Do this. I have to run back to catch the bus."

"Call me from the telephone station over in Ramsar when you get there."

"I will."

With that out of the way, Mehran ran back to meet his friends. The rest of the trip was fun and uneventful.

Mehran was picked up again by the police during the month of Ramadan, the holy month of fasting. Fasting is one of the Five Pillars of Islam. Fasting Muslims usually get up before dawn and eat a small meal. While the sun is out, they are forbidden from eating or drinking. Then, after the sunset, they eat another meal, usually their dinner. In Iran and most Islamic countries, in respect for Muslims who are fasting, public eating and drinking are strictly forbidden during the daytime in the month of Ramadan; restaurants are closed during the day, but restaurants will open in preparation for Iftar, the meal after sunset.

Due to differences between the sun-based calendars like Gregorian or Persian, and the lunar-based Hijri, the Islamic calendar, Ramadan can fall at any time of the year. The cycle repeats every 33 years. In 1983, Ramadan was during the summer.

One of Iranians' favorite street foods is grilled corn. Corn cobs are cooked directly on top of charcoal without the husk and the speed at which the corn is cooked prevents it from drying up. Once all sides of the cob have a hint of char, the corn is dunked in saltwater and eaten. Mehran was waiting by a street vendor one day in Ramadan. In anticipation of what was to come, Mehran chose a fat corn, stripped it of its husk and was waiting for the Adhan, the call to prayer, marking Iftar, so the vendor could cook the corn. While waiting and talking to his friends, unaware of what he was doing, Mehran broke off a kernel or two of raw corn and popped them in his mouth. A passing unmarked Komiteh car noticed the event and arrested him on the charge of public eating. After picking him up, the car drove around to pick up others eating in public. The unmarked car pulled up to a construction site.

The peasant workers, finished with working all day, were sitting on the curb, each with a loaf of bread in hand. They ate like their life depended on it. The undercover agent exited the vehicle, looked at the workers and shook his head. He realized there was not enough room in the car to take six construction workers. He decided that the foreman was the culprit, since he was the one who bought the bread and gave it to the workers; the foreman was put in the back seat with Mehran, and they made their way to the police station for questioning.

In Iran, major charges like murder often carry a sentence of death by hanging or life in prison. Islamic law also dictates stoning in cases of adultery. Adulterers are half buried in the ground while the public casts stones. A male adulterer is buried waist-deep, while his female counterpart is buried chest-deep. Hand amputations are allowed in cases of theft and robbery, and prison is used for most other crimes.

Minor crimes are usually dealt with via public or private lashing. These crimes include, but are not limited to, being caught at a party with the opposite sex, being caught at a party with music, inebriation, possession of alcohol, possession of minor amounts of narcotics and, as applied in Mehran's case, public eating during Ramadan. The punishment for public consumption during Ramadan, as Mehran was told, was 40 lashes. It wasn't clear to Mehran if the intention of arresting and detaining him was to scare him; he didn't know if the judge would actually dole such punishment upon him. After strings were pulled, Mehran walked away free following a few hours in detention.

This wasn't the first time Mehran's family had pulled strings. During a trip to Nur, a resort town by the Caspian Sea, Mehran and his family were stopped at a checkpoint, commonplace at major intersections in cities and peppered across country roads. Cars were searched for contraband as well as guns and ammo that could be used against the new government. They passed the first two checkpoints without incident. At the third and final checkpoint near their destination, an officer searching the trunk opened the Coleman cooler Mehran's family used to carry fresh food, meat and, of course, vodka.

Barbod was a functioning alcoholic. Despite his drinking problem, Barbod was the sharpest among all his engineering friends, or people in general. But he was dependent on alcohol at nights and on weekends. Several times during Mehran's teen years Barbod had no access to alcohol; those nights left Mehran with scarred memories.

Alcohol was illegal in Iran, but Christians could produce it and consume it in their own homes. Many Christians produced plenty of vodka, the easiest of distilled spirits to make, and sold it at high prices on the black market. Most of the Christians in Iran were Armenian, or Armani as they were called.

To purchase alcohol from the Armanis, you had to know a friend to facilitate and vouch for you. That friend was one you trusted, who assured you that others whose consumption had left them with no ill effects had been purchasing alcohol from the person you were introduced to. Some Armanis went to prison not only because they sold alcohol to non-Christians but also because of their production methods that lead to blindness or death.

Non-Christians might also obtain alcohol from pharmacists, although those quantities were hardly enough to quench the thirst of a nation. In a pinch, though, Barbod was able to acquire drinkable ethanol from pharmacies at outrageous costs.

Yet another source of alcohol was smuggled bottles of genuine liquors and spirits. These typically included Johnnie Walker whiskey and various brands of cognac, since creating them was more involved and much harder than creating vodka.

During the final checkpoint stop, the officer discovered two plastic bottles at the bottom of the cooler and asked what they were.

"You know what they are. How about you just close the cooler and the trunk and let us go," Barbod said.

The officer looked him in the eye, closed the trunk and decided to let them go. His superior watched the interaction, became suspicious and decided to search the vehicle again. After Barbod was questioned, the vodka was confiscated, and Barbod was told to appear in court. Barbod, however, wasn't worried about the loss of his alcohol, since he had an additional two liters of vodka stashed in the windshield washer fluid tank in the engine compartment. That was how critical alcohol was to Barbod.

On the day of the trial, Barbod was accompanied by his lawyer and Mahtab's brother, who had previously had his share of drug-related charges and lashings. The lawyer told Barbod not to worry, that he knew the judge and had already met him regarding the case. Meanwhile, Mehran's uncle offered Barbod pills that would dull his senses if he did receive lashings.

The judge couldn't dismiss the case with the vodka produced as evidence. Citing that this was Barbod's first offense, the judge ordered that Barbod personally pour the vodka down the drain in front of court officers. The judge also lectured him on the law, fined him and dismissed the case.

Barbod knew that the lawyer must have bribed the judge. After he left the court, Barbod asked his lawyer how he did it. "A case of Johnnie Walker," he responded. Barbod would always say later that the worst part of the ordeal was having to pour good vodka down the drain.

Chapter Five

Mehran continued his studies at the University, patiently waiting for his time to exit the country. As months passed and March drew near, the whole family was on edge. After all, their only son was going to leave soon. The pressure took a high toll on Mahtab, since she had become especially close to Mehran in the past 2 years.

In November 1981, Mehran interfered during a fight between Mahtab and Barbod. When Barbod became belligerent with Mahtab and moved to strike her, Mehran stepped in between them and pushed Barbod away. A fight broke out between father and son. The next morning, Barbod proclaimed that there was no place for Mehran in their home. Mehran spent the next month living between his grandmothers' homes.

Mehran did not see his father during that month. His mother, though, visited frequently. Because of Mehran's courage, Mahtab viewed him as a grown man. She would cook him food and bring it over for visits. At times, she spent the nights at the grandmothers' homes to spend more time with her son. Eventually, Barbod agreed to a reconciliation. In December, Mehran returned home. He and his dad looked at each other for a bit. Mehran said he was sorry, but Barbod stopped him before he had a chance to finish his sentence. Barbod opened his arms to embrace Mehran; they both cried.

Mehran could tell that Barbod had changed. It seemed as if he had done much soul-searching during the month Mehran wasn't home. Perhaps he realized that the boy he had been raising was no longer a boy, but a man with his own convictions. Perhaps he realized that he was wrong in the first place to attempt to strike his wife. Whatever the reason may have been, Barbod was a more polite and subdued man after that time.

Mehran himself was no stranger to alcohol. He was raised with alcohol around. On a memorable vacation to the south of Spain, when Mehran was 13, wine was openly served at the ranch they visited. Starting from the moment they got off the bus on the gravel lot, then at the entertainment before dinner, with a family-style dinner at a table of 20 or so of their friends they were on vacation with, and again after dinner, everyone was invited to drink generously.

Mehran had more than his share of wine. He started vomiting in the bathroom and continued to do so on the bus ride back to the hotel. Barbod, who was sitting next to him and taking care of him, had slapped him quite hard a few times. His friends protested that now that Mehran was already drunk, there was no point in slapping him. "I'm not mad at him. I just want him to stay up so that he can enjoy the feeling of drunkenness," Barbod replied.

Mehran also never stopped himself from drinking. A group of Assyrian friends Mehran hung around always seemed to have plenty of booze available for everyone. These friends were older, some much older, including a renowned artist who was in his mid-50s. They were considered the intellectual friends of his time, and conversations with them ran deep, from existentialism, Marxism, imperialism and communism to critically acclaimed movies of the time. Some of these intellectuals were educated in the United States and had formative conversations with Mehran regarding a U.S. education.

One time, when looking through the record collection of the renowned artist, Mehran ran across the American bluegrass genre and performances by Earl Scruggs and Lester Flatt. He had never heard of a banjo, let alone heard a bluegrass tune. The banjo rhythm in the songs fascinated him, so he copied many songs off of the LP's the artist had in his collection. Another set of records he transferred to cassette were those of Chet Atkins, an American country guitarist who was popular in the 50s and 60s.

Mehran lived for and loved music, whether it was the song of the Adhan, the sound of Atkins playing the guitar, the Bee Gees singing

How Deep is Your Love, or Edward Lalo's *Symphony Espagnole.* During his last year of high school, before he left, Mehran was part of a private club that he and his intellectual friends formed to listen to and discuss classical music.

Although he played the violin for only a short time, Mehran's musical sense was strong. He could pick up tunes via ear and play them on his melodica, a small, portable blow organ. He always analyzed the music he was hearing and had a sense for the chords that were being played. He decided if he liked a piece of music by analyzing the music according to chord patterns and the melody; genre was not necessarily relevant. He also excelled at playing the tar, a traditional Persian instrument.

During high school, Mehran was torn between the choices of music he was exposed to. On the one hand, he wanted to listen to everything popular among teenagers. Elvis Presley was always hot among Iranian teens, as were the Bee Gees, American and European disco songs, and such rising stars as Michael Jackson. Less popular were the true rock and heavy metal bands, such as Pink Floyd, Deep Purple, Nazareth and Judas Priest. Even less popular was the traditional Persian music itself. On the other hand, Mehran felt, the chord progression of most popular music was so simple a 2-year-old should be able to follow it. He felt that classical music offered the breadth of chord progressions that would boggle the mind. Listening to the series of six completely unrelated chords at the end of Rachmaninoff's *Prelude in C-sharp minor* was a hair-raising experience for him.

Mehran also enjoyed listening to traditional Persian and Turkish music. As a tar player, he was exposed to centuries-old melodies, his favorite melodies being ones from the Šur dastgāh. The scale for Šur itself was amazing, similar to the Western minor scale, with a couple of quarter tones thrown in. Šur was the most important one of the seven dastgāhs in Persian music and contained the largest number of melodies. Mehran couldn't pin the reason why he liked Šur so much, other than that many of the melodies were haunting. Šur wasn't a "happy" modal at all. Hearing and playing the melodies often evoked complex feelings of sadness and despair. These melodies were a cornerstone of his listening preferences later when he met Bahar in May 1982, when desperation set in during the times they could not see each other.

Chapter Six

Mehran and Kirsten returned to the limo following their long walk.

"So, how often do you travel, Kirsten?"

"It depends. Usually for a few days at a time. Winter months I'm gone more than summer months, since I like to get out of the Chicago cold."

Mehran felt good, since it was May, and summer was nearing fast.

"Okay. I answered this question for you, but I'll ask now. Who is your favorite composer, Ms. Kirsten?" Mehran asked.

Kirsten paused for no more than a couple of seconds before she responded. "I'd have to say Beethoven. His music simply has the best combination of power, romanticism, harmony and originality."

"What's your favorite piece?"

"Hmm, either the *Emperor Concerto* or his violin concerto."

"Ah, *Piano Concerto No. 5* and the lovely violin one. Say what you will about the man, but anybody who wrote just one violin concerto either put everything he had into that one, or after writing the one he figured he wasn't any good at it."

"Funny! Which one do you think is the case?"

"Neither," Mehran smiled.

The limo stopped in front of Kirsten's building. Mehran exited and walked around to open the door for Kirsten, but she already opened the door and was almost out.

"Kirsten, I had a lovely time with you and would love to repeat this."

"I'm not sure if we can do this again."

Mehran was starting to understand Kirsten's playful nature, so instead of his jaw dropping, he bluffed. "Okay. In that case, it was great meeting you," and turned around to walk back to the other side of the car.

"What I meant was that we cannot do the limo thing anymore. Next time we do casual, and we walk somewhere."

He stopped in his tracks and turned around, then slowly walked back. "Then it's a date."

Kirsten smiled and said, "Yes, it is."

He took her hand in his and brought it up to his lips to kiss it while keeping eye contact. They smiled at each other, and Mehran returned to the limo.

As Mehran sat back, his thoughts drifted to Iran.

Kirsten watched on as the limo drove away.

Chapter Seven

By December 1983, Mehran began to get nervous. His future with the girl he loved became uncertain again. Bahar's mother decided that she could not separate from her daughter; Bahar would remain in Iran. Bahar, now in 11th grade, was told to prepare for the national college entrance exam.

Mehran worried about changes to his own life. In a few months he would be cut from his friends and family, not to mention a culture he had lived in for 19 years. Not that he was married to the culture. Though he was raised with all the amenities of a Westernized living, like houses with pools, color televisions and video cassette recorders, he would still be leaving his home country. The thought of leaving everything behind became so overwhelming that at one point, he broke down and begged his family not to send him abroad. But the future for him lay ahead in the United States, Barbod told him. Until the war was over, there was no future for him in Iran. If he stayed, he was as good as dead. Iran, confronted by failure to overtake Iraq and end the war, had resorted to foot soldiers for large-scale offensives. In Operation Fajr al-Nasr in February 1983, Iran amassed 200,000 troops for a land attack along a 40-kilometer stretch in order to take control of major highways east of Iraq. By the end of 1983, an estimated 120,000 Iranians were killed in that offensive. Iran resorted to using human minesweepers. It involved a twisted infantry tactic where the attacker forced an unprotected frontal assault. The frontal assault had always been accompanied by equipment and support in the back, until the Iran-Iraq war, when Iran used humans to clear the minefields.

Mehran often dwelt upon the choice he could still make. He might survive the war and then be a free man, or as free as it was possible to be in Iran. What sort of future would he have in the United

States, without his family? The closest relatives he had outside of Iran lived in Freiburg in southwest Germany, and in Stockholm, Sweden. He even considered going only as far as Turkey to escape the mandatory draft. Then, at least, he would be close to his family and they could visit often. But his future prospects in Turkey wouldn't be as good as in the United States. It didn't help that Mehran was highly sentimental. He loved to think about and dwell on the past. When his family visited the Persepolis ruins outside of Shiraz, he insisted on seeing the place where Mahtab and Barbod had first met.

Mehran had much to accomplish in the little time he remained in Iran. He wasn't confident that store owners in Los Angeles would share his taste in music, so he made duplicates of the many cassettes Barbod owned. He also transferred many of Barbod's LP records into cassettes. This was a time-consuming process; in the end, he amassed a collection of 150 cassettes to bring with him.

Amid his preparation efforts, winter was making life difficult. When heavy snow made the streets of Tehran beautiful, going back and forth to the University was difficult. Buses were packed with people who couldn't drive their cars. Once Mehran stayed the night near the University with a new school and his family at their apartment because of an anomaly in the Persian culture referred to as "tarof."

Mehran mentioned to his friend that he would never make it home due to the traffic and the heavy snow. His friend offered for him to stay with his family in their two-bedroom apartment, and Mehran accepted. The offer would inconvenience his friend's family for the night and was meant as a gesture of goodwill, but Mehran didn't recognize the tarof – a fake offer that was more than the family was really willing to provide – and took the offer as genuine. He stayed the night at the friend's apartment. Mehran should have followed tarof practices and determined if it was genuine by refusing the offer over and over until he was certain that the offer was truly authentic.

In February, Mahtab planned a going away party at their house for Mehran. Telling everyone who was attending the party the reason for the party was another point that needed careful attention. Mehran's family could not afford the news of him being smuggled out of the country to be leaked out, or rather snitched, to a government official. As a result, only the closest family members and Mehran's closest friends knew of what was to come in March. So the official reason for the party was a belated 19th birthday party.

Mehran tried to figure out how to get Bahar to the party. He called Amir, his best friend, on the phone.

"Hello?"

"It's me."

"What's up man? You wanna go to Baloot?"

"No, listen. My mom's throwing a party for my departure."

"You're calling to invite me?"

"No, doofus. You don't need an invitation to show up here. I want to know if Faranak can convince Bahar's mom for Bahar to spend the night at Faranak's place on the night of the party," Mehran explained. Faranak was the girlfriend Amir had allegedly slept with and was a good friend of Bahar. "Then they can both come to the party," Mehran continued.

"I can ask. She's good at lying, so I think it's totally doable."

"Okay. Call her and call me back when she's figured it out."

When Amir called back a few hours later, he told Mehran that Bahar would be able to stay for only an hour. An hour was an hour more than Mehran had ever had with Bahar. Amir and Mehran planned for Bahar to come toward the beginning of the party. That way less suspicion would be raised with her mother and Mehran would have a higher chance of spending most of his time with her.

The party was set for Thursday, February 23, 1984. Thursday is the beginning of what is considered "the weekend" in Iran. Schools are closed at noon on Thursdays and all work is halted on Fridays.

Saturdays are the start of the new week. Guests were told to arrive at 7 p.m., while Bahar was set to arrive at 6:30.

Mehran could not contain himself on the day of the party. The thought of seeing Bahar uninterrupted for an hour was more than he had ever imagined. Amir spent all day with him, running errands for the party. Snow flurries started in the early afternoon, but not enough to accumulate on the ground. Mehran made sure everything Mahtab had asked him to do was complete by mid-afternoon. He took a quick shower, brushed his hair, put on his skinny jeans as was the fashion, put on Pierre Cardin cologne, and watched the clock.

When the doorbell rang at 6:15, Mehran's heart dropped. He walked over to the intercom.

"Who is it?"

"Supermarket delivery, sir."

Aaarrrggghhh! he thought. He went through the front yard and opened the door to the street. It was already dark, but he recognized the supermarket delivery guy, who had five large bags of groceries. Mahtab asked the store to send these over right before the party, since she didn't have enough room in the refrigerator. While Mehran was paying the delivery man, he noticed the lights of a car coming toward them. The car pulled right up to the front door and the driver, Faranak's brother, let Faranak and Bahar out.

"I'll be back at 7:30 to pick you up," he said to Faranak.

Mehran waived to Faranak's brother as he started to drive away. Picking up the five bags, Mehran looked at Bahar and became speechless. Under her breath, Bahar said, "Hi."

Down at the bottom of his stomach, Mehran had a tingling sensation that was actually kind of annoying, but he could also feel his heart tapping the inside of his chest as if it wanted to get out. He felt his temples contract and expand in unison with his heart. He could feel the same rhythm on his fingers, their blood supply cut from the weight of the plastic bags, and he felt a hot flash across his face.

"Hi," he managed to utter.

"Hi. Should we go in?" Faranak asked while raising her eyebrows and tilting her head toward the door.

Mehran gathered himself and moved out of the doorway. Faranak and Bahar went in, followed by Mehran.

"I can't believe you're here," said Mehran.

Bahar looked at him and smiled.

They made their way through the short courtyard and entered the house. Amir was at the doorway of the house.

"Salam azizam," *hello dear*, Faranak said to Amir.

In the house, Mehran quickly took the groceries to the kitchen and returned to the living room.

"Do you want to show us around the house?" Faranak asked.

"Sure. What do you want to see?"

"I don't know. Let's go say hi to your mom."

They walked toward the kitchen. Mehran looked at Bahar, who was walking at his side. He smiled and gently took her hand. She didn't resist. He remembered the last time they were able to hold hands and how he hadn't washed his hand for a week. The thought made him smile. If, for a touch that lasted only 5 seconds, he hadn't washed his hand for a week, what would he do for being able to hold Bahar's hand for an hour? Would he have to chop off his hand and put it in a glass container for the rest of his life, like a memory that should be cherished forever?

"Hello Mrs. Noori," said Faranak.

"Hello dears. Welcome! Welcome."

"Mrs. Noori, this is my friend, Bahar."

"It's very nice to meet you, Bahar. Mehran is a private person when it comes to you; thus he doesn't tell us anything about you."

"It is very nice to meet you, Mrs. Noori," Bahar said shyly, surprised that Mehran had mentioned her at all to his mom.

"Mom, Bahar has to leave in an hour, so I'm going to show her around the house."

Mehran gave them a tour of the house, all the while holding Bahar's hand. He saved his room for last, since that's where he wanted them to stay and to be secluded from the rest of the house.

"Wow!" said Bahar upon entering his room. "It is just like you had described it."

Pictures and posters covered one wall. Some of the photos Mehran had taken himself, some of the pictures were cutouts from magazines, and some were portraits his friends had drawn by pencil, charcoal or pastel for class assignments. One wall framed a large window and had a couple of short bookshelves full of books that covered the width of the wall. One wall contained built-in closets and storage for the room. The last wall was again filled with pictures and posters, but a large rectangular area was empty.

"Why the empty space?" asked Faranak.

"So that he can display the slides he's taken on the wall," Bahar said while looking and smiling at Mehran.

They all sat on the floor to talk. The talk centered on popular music, new stores around the town, how school was for Bahar and Faranak, and the troubles everyone had gotten in with their parents over time.

Guests started arriving at 7, so Mehran often left to greet them but always returned quickly. He felt there was so much he wanted to talk about with Bahar and how her imminent departure in less than 30 minutes would probably be the last time they saw each other up close, until perhaps years from now when their lives would be in their own hands. "Do you want to walk in the yard for a few minutes?" he asked Bahar.

"Sure. Let's go," Bahar responded excitedly.

They snuck out through the back door to the yard. Snow was still falling. Mehran took her around to the side of the house and they stopped under a light on the brick wall.

"Bahar, I love you. I love you more than you will ever know."

"I know. And I love you, Mehran."

"I wish we could be with each other forever. I hate the idea of not being able to see you again in the foreseeable future."

He was holding her hands, one in each of his, their elbows locked at ninety-degree angles, betraying their desire to get closer to each other. She remained silent.

"What will I do without you? This is going to drive us mad if we do not keep in touch, or see each other," he said.

She remained silent.

He paused, thinking about the negativity in what he was saying, and about how he should keep enjoying the moment, how to make the feelings of being with her last for longer than the few minutes they had remaining with each other. He looked up, only to be blinded by the light. When he looked back down, his constricted pupils could not see the wall against which Bahar was leaning, but only her face, her black pullover, and the flakes of snow that fell in his field of view. It seemed like he had tunnel vision. Only her face was in focus. He couldn't decide whether the flakes coming down were taking away from what he was looking at or adding to it. He decided that what he was seeing wasn't complete without the snowflakes and that he liked them.

For the first time in the past two years, he had a chance to actually look up close at the girl he was in love with. Her face, however pretty, wasn't what he had fallen in love with, though. He had fallen in love with the girl as a whole, inside and out. This was the girl that, for the past 2 years, had received countless letters from him, each exclaiming his love for her. Each exclaiming how he would be incomplete without her. Each exclaiming how he would wait forever for her.

He turned his elbows outward while still holding her hands, but now they were closer to each other. He tilted his head down so that he could continue to look in her eyes. "Kiss me. Please," he whispered.

She smiled at him, and kissed him on the right cheek. For the brief moment that her lips had touched him, time seemed to have stopped, as if an internal camera had its shutter speed set to bulb and fired open, trying to envelop the darkness in slow motion and over a long period. Bahar moved her head back. The two continued gazing into each other's eyes. Suddenly they released their hands and hugged each other, neck to neck, head to shoulder, and held each other.

The silence was broken by the sound of a car horn. "This must be Faranak's brother," Bahar said.

"But he's early!"

"I know, but he did drop us off 15 minutes earlier than he was supposed to." She started to move away.

He led her toward the back door, and they entered the house. Once inside, he went to get Amir and Faranak.

Mehran opened his bedroom door and caught Amir and Faranak making out on his bed. Amir had his hand under Faranak's shirt while she had hers on his rump, pulling him toward her, and their lips were locked together.

"Whoa!" exclaimed Mehran, still dazed about what had just happened outside.

"Hey! We weren't doing anything," said Amir.

"Faranak, your brother is here to pick you up."

Faranak got up and ran to the bathroom to fix her hair.

"Nice going, Amir!"

"Yeah, I told you she wants me!"

"I know; I didn't believe you."

"Where's Bahar?"

"She's in the living room, waiting. I'm going to go wait with her."

Mehran rejoined Bahar, and after a few seconds Faranak and Amir returned.

"Your face is red," Bahar said to Faranak.

"I know. It's okay. He won't see anything in the dark."

On their way out, Mehran stopped to greet another guest. He heard another honk of the horn and ran out to catch up with Bahar.

"Bahar – " he said while grabbing her hand. He didn't finish his sentence.

Bahar didn't say anything.

Mehran walked over to the car and thanked Faranak's brother for driving them over. Before Bahar got in the car, Mehran looked her in the eyes. "I will always love you." Bahar got in the back seat next to Faranak and the car pulled away.

"That's it? That was it?" Mehran said in an exasperated voice.

"Yeah, what did you want? A blowjob?" laughed Amir.

"Don't be sick. I don't think about her like that. I just can't believe she's gone forever from my life."

"I always told you. You need a looser girlfriend. One that puts out. Didn't you see Faranak and me and how easy it was for us to make out? You were literally gone for just 10 minutes and we were already enjoying ourselves."

Mehran shook his head in disgust as they walked back to the house.

Mehran couldn't get the thought of Bahar and their time in the yard out of his head. In a way he felt it was the holy grail he had sought for so long, to be able to share such a moment with someone he loved. He wanted so much to go to his room, relax and listen to music, but the party had just gotten started and it was supposed to be a celebration for him. He went through the motions for the next few hours, holding casual conversations with guests about his enrollment in the university and other happenings in his life, but his encounter with Bahar continued to occupy his mind.

When Mahtab lit the candles on the cake that evening, Mehran took a moment to count the candles and realized that he was no longer a boy, but a man of 19, one whose life would be his own, one whose future would be built by himself and nobody else. He looked at all the guests cheering him on to blow the candles and his eyes rested on his father and mother, holding hands. He knew that they wanted the best for him, and perhaps, even though he was now a man, he could use their experiences to his advantage. If they were willing to part with their only son and send him to the other side of the world, then there had to be some merit to the decision. Mehran smiled at his parents and blew out the candles. He was ready to leave, or so he thought.

Chapter Eight

The limo stopped and the driver turned the inside lights on. Mehran snapped out of his thoughts.

"We're back to the apartment, sir," said the limo driver. Mehran opened his own door and stepped out, paid the driver and thanked him for being very patient and accommodating.

Back in the apartment, Mehran couldn't get Kirsten out of his mind. He contemplated playing a CD to take his mind off his family memories but decided that it was too late to risk bothering the neighbors downstairs. Instead, he settled for some easy reading before he fell asleep in his listening chair.

A few days later, Mehran picked up the phone to call Kirsten.

"This is Kirsten."

"Hello Kirsten."

"Hi, Mehran!"

"Is this a bad time?"

"Give me just a second." She returned to the phone a few seconds later. "This is better. I had to close my door. So, what rule were you following when you waited 3 days to call me?"

"The rule that said not to call you too soon after our first date. I had to stop myself from calling you sooner!"

"Ah, the stupid three-day rule. Why do guys always think they should do that?" asked Kirsten.

Mehran was no longer surprised by Kirsten's forwardness. He had learned to expect the unexpected from her. He sidestepped her question and asked, "How are you?"

"Just dandy."

"I wanted you to know again that I had a lovely time on Saturday."

"And me, too. I have been looking forward to this call."

"So, I was thinking we should go to this Somalian restaurant on the North Shore."

"Why not a Persian restaurant?"

"I suppose that's fine. Have you had Persian food before?"

"Never. I've been thinking about it a lot since our last date, and I'd love to try it."

"When would you like to go?"

"The weekend is too far away. What do you say we meet tonight? Around 8?"

Mehran liked where this was going. Kirsten didn't have to be pushed at all. "That sounds great! The restaurant is on Kedzie. It's by – "

Kirsten interrupted him. "Kedzie and Lawrence? I know."

"I thought you hadn't had Persian food before," exclaimed Mehran.

"Persian food I haven't had, but I do know how to look things up in the *Yellow Pages*," she answered.

Interesting, thought Mehran. *She must have spent some time studying my culture*. "You continue to surprise me," he said.

"I warned you to expect the unexpected from me."

"I guess so! I'll meet you there at 8. I'll ride my bike."

"You ride a bike around?"

"Sure do. Why? Do you have a car?"

"I do. I can pick you up."

"You know, in my culture it would be considered odd for a woman to come and pick up a man."

"I thought you were American," she laughed.

"All the same, if it's okay with you, I'd rather bike there."

"That means you won't be able to drink. Are you sure that's okay?"

"Why? Are you trying to get me drunk on our second date?"

"The thought crossed my mind."

"Hmm, get drunk with Kirsten, or stay sober and ride the bike. Geez! Which one do I choose?"

"You choose to have drinks with Kirsten."

"Okay. You twisted my arm. That's fine."

Mehran gave Kirsten his address, and Kirsten said she would pick him up at 7:45.

At 7:43, Kirsten pulled up in front of Mehran's apartment, and Mehran got into the car.

"Wow! Nice wheels!" Mehran said of her BMW M3.

"Thank you. You know, I'm Swiss. I love driving a German-engineered machine."

She revved the engine, popped the clutch and tapped the brakes, squealing the tires. When she lifted her foot off the brake pedal, the car took off like a rocket.

"Okay! Okay! I like my life the way it is," said Mehran.

Kirsten laughed and slowed down.

Mehran wondered why Kirsten always tried to come over the top in their encounters. Perhaps she was trying to show him right away that she wasn't a docile woman. She had gotten the point across pretty clearly, but perhaps she was covering her bases in case he turned out to be a chauvinist. She probably had no idea how far Mehran was from the average Iranian.

"I like this neighborhood," said Kirsten.

"Yes, it's a great neighborhood, with a nice nightlife."

"How long have you lived here?"

"Since 1986."

"Do you own the apartment?"

"No. Just renting."

"You've been renting the same apartment for 10 years?" Kirsten asked in surprise.

"Yeah, why?"

"Tell me again, what is it that you do? Aren't you a chemist?"

"I am. Chemists can't rent apartments?"

"No. I mean, sure they can. I was just wondering why you haven't bought a place but continue to rent."

"I've thought about it. But I like my landlord. He's very fair, and I like the location. Plus, I can move any time I want." Mehran paused for a bit. "What about you? Do you own your condo?"

"No."

"And why don't *you* own it?"

Kirsten laughed. "Because I can up and vanish if I wanted at any time."

She parked a few blocks away from the restaurant. As they walked to dinner, Kirsten took Mehran's hand. "So, what kind of food am I going to eat?"

"Well, I figured that during your investigations about Iranian boys leaving the country and about the culture you would have found out about the food as well."

"Ha ha! I did, but to hear it first-hand from you is what I would prefer."

"Well, like most Middle Eastern food, we eat a lot of lamb, rice and vegetable-heavy side dishes, with some spices."

"Do you cook?"

"Actually, I do."

"An Iranian chef?"

"I wouldn't go that far. I'm by no means a chef, but I can make a mean jambalaya."

"Jambalaya is not Persian."

Mehran turned his head toward her as they were walking. "Why not? Am I supposed to only cook Persian food because I grew up over there?"

"No. But now that I know you cook, I want to eat something you make next time."

Mehran was glad. Their second date hadn't even started and she was thinking about a third date. Once at the restaurant, Kirsten said, "I am going to let you order for me."

"You're going to allow your man to order for you?"

Kirsten thought *My man? Crazy!* and before she realized, she had said it aloud. "Crazy! Don't get ahead of yourself. This is just our second date, with a third date planned for you to cook for me."

Mehran laughed. The waiter came to the table, and Mehran ordered for them.

"I'd like to know about how you escaped Iran," Kirsten said as the waiter retreated.

Chapter Nine

On Thursday, March 8, 1984, two weeks after his birthday party, Mehran and Barbod were ready to leave for Khoy, a small city in northwest Iran, close to the Turkish border. Mehran and Mahtab had many conversations in the days leading up to his departure. Mehran made his mom promise that she'd visit as soon as he had settled in Southern California. They each shed many tears, but Mahtab was thankful that Mehran was embarking on a journey that would define the rest of his life.

The morning of Mehran's departure proved to be even harder than what everyone had anticipated, especially for Mahtab. How does one let her only child leave? "I love you, mom. Thank you for everything you've done for me. I will call you as soon as we're in Turkey," were Mehran's last words to his mother.

With that, he entered the car that was packed with the belongings he would take to his new life in the United States.

Barbod would take Mehran's belongings over the border by himself, while Mehran was smuggled through the mountains. For the actual crossing of the border, their contact had said that Mehran should take with him a small backpack, enough to carry an extra set of clothes and a notebook or a book. The contact also mentioned that Mehran should not bring a bulky coat, since they would have blankets for him to wrap himself in during transport across the border. He also was told to have as much of a beard as possible, since that would help hide his identity. He stopped shaving the day after his birthday party.

Mehran and Barbod drove all day before they reached Khoy. They checked into a local motel and met the man arranging that leg of the trip. They were told that they would spend the night in Khoy, and the next morning they would drive to a smaller town called Chaldoran. They would wait there until the next contact arrived.

The motel had surprisingly comfortable beds, but Mehran could not fall asleep. He tossed and turned for hours. All he could think of were Mahtab and Bahar. Eventually his tiredness got the better of him, and he slept. The next morning they had a small breakfast and left for Chaldoran. The man making the arrangements accompanied them. He said that it should not be more than a couple of days for Mehran to cross into Turkey, but it could take longer if they ran into border guards.

Barbod was worried, but he had been told that the smuggler taking Mehran across the border was the best in the area.

The house they went to in Chaldoran was very small. A cramped yard had a miniature square pool in the middle, probably 3 feet across. Stairs led to a small terrace, and two small bedrooms flanked a hallway leading to a small bathroom on one side and a small kitchen on the other. There were no dedicated showers or baths in the house. Instead, there was a handheld shower in the bathroom that drained right into the squatting pan toilet, something standard throughout Iran. The house belonged to a local teacher, Roshan, whose wife had died during their only child's birth. The child was now in third grade and lived with the man in the house. Mehran was told that Roshan was sympathetic to other parents who didn't want to send their sons to die in the war, because his own son was the only living memory of his wife.

Once Barbod met Roshan and heard his story, he felt more comfortable leaving Mehran. He said goodbye to Mehran and assured him they would meet in Turkey soon. Barbod drove to Bazargan to cross into Turkey and await Mehran's arrival in Doğubayazıt. Mehran wanted to watch Barbod leave from the street but was told that it would be best for him to stay in the house and the yard until the smuggler arrived.

It was early Friday morning. The air was chilly, near freezing. Mehran looked back at the house through the yard and saw a young boy looking through a window that was fogging up from his breath.

"Come on in. I've made hot tea," said Roshan.

Mehran followed him through the hallway door, closed the door behind them and took off his shoes.

"I really appreciate your allowing me to stay here with you and your son."

"Nonsense! It is my pleasure."

Mehran was baffled. There was no tarof in neither what the man was saying, nor in the way he was saying it. The rules of tarof would have dictated for him to say something along the lines of "It's nothing and not worthy of your staying in it." Mehran was pleasantly surprised.

Roshan continued, "What am I supposed to do? Let these bastards send every young man to his death at the front lines?"

Mehran was cautious. Every fiber of his being for the past couple of years had been trained to distrust anyone with such a lofty tone for fear of entrapment. *This man could be trying to lure me into speaking against the regime*, Mehran thought. Mehran remained silent.

Roshan was in his mid-30s, with black hair, a face with pronounced cheekbones, no beard, but a mustache that Stalin himself would be envious of. Everything about him spelled "comrade." He was a teacher, educated and didn't tarof. The age of his child dictated that he had waited before being married, or that he had married but had waited to have children. The fact that he didn't have a beard, but a socialist mustache, spoke Chapters about him as stereotypes went in Iran. The room he led Mehran to had a large bookshelf full of books. Roshan hadn't married again after the death of his wife during childbirth, which meant that he had raised the boy all by himself.

Mehran decided to go with his gut feelings and trust Roshan.

"They certainly are doing that. That's all I read about in the newspapers," Mehran said, as they sat on the ground, Indian style, as was customary in Iran.

Roshan picked up the teapot and the kettle from atop the kerosene heater that was heating the room as well as keeping the tea and the water hot. He poured tea into three small glasses and topped them with hot water. He picked one up and gave it to Mehran. This was yet another sign that the man was not ordinary. Rules of tarof would have dictated that Roshan put the three glasses on a tray and hold the tray in front of Mehran, letting him choose which one he wanted according to the color of the tea. Darker tea meant stronger tea.

"Have you been teaching for a long time?"

"Ever since I finished high school. About 15 years."

"You didn't have to go to college in order to teach?"

"Son, if every teacher around here had to go to college before teaching, there would be no teachers." He took a sip of his tea.

Mehran looked at the boy, who had come into the room but remained silent.

"Yashar, come here. I want you to meet Mehran. Mehran has come all the way from Tehran."

"It's very nice to meet you, Mehran."

"You, too, Yashar. What a beautiful name."

Yashar looked at his father, the man nodded, and Yashar said, "It means 'lives forever.' I was named this so that my mother could live forever. What does your name mean?"

It hadn't occurred to Mehran to ever ask what his name meant. Roshan saw the hesitation in Mehran's face and said, "Yashar.

Mehran comes from Mehr, our seventh month of the year. That, in turn, comes from Mithra, the Zoroastrian divinity of covenant and oath. Mehran means 'the protector of truth.'"

Mehran was in awe. How could a teacher in this rural town have so much information ready at hand, when in all his life, Mehran hadn't thought about the meaning of his own name?

"I can't believe I didn't know what my name meant."

"That's okay. You don't need to know everything, but you just need to make sure you never stop learning."

Mehran looked at the bookshelves and saw books in English, and asked, "Do you speak English?"

"I do, but I probably read it better than I speak it."

"What grade do you teach?"

"I am the teacher for all five grades of our elementary school."

"All five grades? Do you mean that all the elementary school children are lumped together in one class?"

"We live in a small town. We cannot afford to have multiple teachers for different grades. I group the kids according to their abilities. Then I pair students who have already grasped the concept of what I'm teaching with the ones who haven't. So grades don't really mean anything in my classroom. Children get to teach each other."

Mehran thought that was a fantastic way to teach; children in classrooms should help each other. Unfortunately, education in the city was organized much like its Western counterpart, rigid in structure and materials.

"You can't treat all kids equally," continued Roshan. "Everybody has different needs. Some of my kids may need a shoulder to cry on, some of them may need to better themselves in math, some of them may need me to talk to their parents about the importance of education. As a teacher in a rural area, we must be prepared to handle any needs the kids may have."

Mehran sat mesmerized, tea in hand, and listened, as Roshan continued to speak of the life of the children.

"One of our biggest problems is city folks like your parents and friends."

Mehran was taken aback. "Why?"

"Realize that what I say is not directed toward you personally. I don't know much about you, and you are still young. So forgive me for being blunt, since I have always spoken my mind."

"Please. Go on. I want to hear what you have to say."

"The needs of the rich are destroying the future of rural Iran and these children," Roshan explained.

"How so?"

"Take, for instance, your appetite for Persian rugs and carpets. You demand more and more intricate rug work to be done, while not realizing the futures that are destroyed when children whose fingers are small enough, and the only instruments capable of creating beautiful rugs, are forced into neglect and slavery."

Mehran looked at the rug they were sitting on. It looked old. By all means, even in the room Mehran's house servants lived in near the garage, the carpet was in better shape than the one under him here.

"And carpets are just the tip of the problem. Fruits, vegetables, bricks, wheat, rice, cotton. Children are forced to give up on education that's rightfully theirs and a light in their future in order to slave and perform manual labor."

"But don't you think that by picking rice or cotton, the children are helping their parents make a living to sustain their lives?"

"Aha! There lies the problem. The person who you are buying your rice from is not the person who grew that rice. The person who you are buying the cotton from is not the person whose children were forced to pick that cotton. If you were buying your rice from the farmer who grew rice, not only would his children not have to tend the rice fields, but he'd be able to hire workers to help him pick the rice, sell you the rice for the same or probably a lower price than what you're buying it for right now, and still have left enough to expand his farm and buy equipment to help him harvest more efficiently."

"I see what you mean."

"There are issues of logistics. How can a farmer get his rice to you who are a few hundred kilometers away, and still make money?"

"The rice must still be transported and someone will have to pay that cost."

"True," Roshan acknowledged, "but that can easily be fixed with an exchange depot, an organization that is not in business for profit but to play as a middleman, as the broker, between the farmers and the stores that sell you the rice. Even accounting for the cost of the transport and the depot, the farmer would still be doing much better than he would otherwise."

"So what's happening to the difference between the price the farmer is getting paid and what the rice costs people in cities?"

"My dear Mehran," he said, "This is why the rich keep getting richer, and the poor keep getting poorer. There are simply too many middlemen in the production-to-consumption chain. Each is adding a bit to the cost of the rice being delivered to you. By the time the rice reaches you, it is over three- or four-folds of what the farmer was paid for it. All the middlemen who have the means to get the rice from the farmer to you have profited immensely from the deal. It's good for everyone involved except the farmer and the customer."

Mehran sat dazed.

"And here's another issue. The price you're paying for rice may be higher if you were to buy from the farmer in a more direct route, but at least you can afford it. Have you thought about the shoeshine who stands at the corner of the street in Tehran and is willing to shine your shoes for 20 tomans? He has to pay the same price for that rice as you're paying for it, but he came to Tehran because there was no job for him in the rural area, because the farmer couldn't afford to hire him to help harvest the field, because the farmer was getting gypped on the rice, but he struggles himself to earn a living. You see how vicious a circle this is?"

"How come they don't teach *this* in school?"

"Mehran. The truth hurts people with interests in keeping the status quo. Nobody wants to think of the needy, or a broken system. It would be much easier to just look away. The poor don't have the means to fix the system, and the rich don't have an incentive to. As a matter of fact, the rich have an incentive *not* to fix things!" He slammed his fist on the ground.

"So, what's our way out of this?"

"Well, obviously, education is a necessity. Without education, our country is doomed to deplete its natural resources. Do you think once we run out of oil, anybody is going to care about what happens to Iran?"

"Education is a must. We definitely agree there."

"The other thing is a revolution."

"A revolution? But we just had one."

"Not a rebellion against the regime, but a revolution against the status quo. Against the vultures who take advantage of the poor and use them only as a workhorse."

Roshan paused with a look of deep thought on his face and finally asked, "What do you know of Gandhi?"

"Just a little. That he was the leader of India for a while."

Roshan smiled, got up and walked toward his bookshelf. He dug out a book, opened the inside cover, smiled again, and walked toward Mehran.

"I want you to have this," Roshan said as he extended the book toward Mehran.

Mehran thought about offering a tarof and saying that he couldn't take it, but then he thought the man deserved more respect than an empty tarof.

He took the book without saying a word, opened the inside cover, and read *"To My Dearest Roshan on his 21st Birthday. With Love, Solmaz."*

"Solmaz?"

"She was my wife. We had just married."

Mehran looked at the title, *Satyagraha in South Africa*. "What's this book about?"

"It is the story of Gandhi's struggles for Indian rights in South Africa."

Mehran thought, beyond the tarof, that he truly could not take a book Roshan's wife had given him for his birthday.

"I can't take this. I'm sure this book means a lot to you. Perhaps it should go to Yashar someday. I can always pick up a copy when I get to the United States." He extended the book back to Roshan.

Roshan pushed the book back to Mehran. "Solmaz would have wanted you to have this book."

"I don't know what to say."

"Just promise me that you will read it."

"I promise," Mehran said, as he held the book close to his chest.

Mehran and Roshan held many conversations that day. They even played a couple games of chess.

"Chess is a game that expands your mind. Not like card games, which are fun to play but pretty repetitive," Roshan said.

That night they had a simple meal of boiled bulgur, and they all slept on the ground in one room, since the second room did not have a heat source.

Chapter Ten

Kirsten and Mehran enjoyed the Persian food and their conversation immensely. They purposefully didn't finish their meals; they wanted to eat dessert at the restaurant and take home the leftover food.

"Roshan seemed like a very, how should I say, noble man? To offer his house like that was surely very dangerous for him. He could have ended up in a lot of trouble," Kirsten said.

Mehran paused for a moment, savoring the story he had just told Kirsten. What were his chances of meeting such a memorable man like Roshan had the pieces not perfectly fallen in place in his life? Had he fought with his parents about leaving Iran, would he have met Roshan? Would he have met Kirsten? He looked at her, smiled and said, "Definitely. I wish we had more people like him teaching children in Iran. I learned many things from him during my short time there."

Mehran ordered them Turkish coffee and bamiye, a traditional restaurant dessert.

"So, what happened after Roshan's house?" asked Kirsten.

Chapter Eleven

Mehran woke up to Roshan shaking his shoulder.

"Mehran, it is time."

"What time is it?"

"It is 3:30 in the morning."

Mehran got up and put on his jacket. He picked up the backpack, stuffed the book in, and then turned to Roshan.

"Roshan, I want to thank you for letting me stay with you. Thank you so much for the book. I will cherish it."

"Don't cherish it. Read it! And then give it to someone else who needs it."

"I will. And I want to thank you for the illuminating conversations."

"Mehran, don't forget. This is your land. When you get an education, if you can, come back. Your people will need you."

Mehran remained silent. He didn't think he would ever be able to come back.

They embraced, and then Mehran hugged Yashar, who was still rubbing the sleep from his eyes. Mehran stepped from the house.

A Zamyad truck was parked in front of the house, running with its lights off. Mehran met a man who put his hand on Mehran's shoulder and extended his other hand to shake.

"Mehran, my name is Jalil. Let's get in the truck."

They quickly got in and Jalil drove away.

"Will you be smuggling me out tonight?"

"You will be smuggled out, but not by me. I'm just a driver."

"How long will it take?" Mehran nervously asked.

"The route you're taking is not long at all. It'll probably take you 4 or 5 hours before you're in the car waiting for you on the other side."

The rest of the ride they did not speak. Jalil drove the truck on a dirt road leading north until he saw the flash of a light down the road. He flashed his high beam first three times, followed by a pause and one more flash. The light responded by flashing twice, a pause, and then three times, the whole transaction obviously a code. "Be ready to get out," Jalil told Mehran.

Once they reached the position of the flashlight, Jalil stopped the car and someone opened the passenger door.

"Quickly, quickly," a voice in the dark said.

Mehran exited the truck without saying goodbye to Jalil. He made out the face of a mustached man in the reflection of the truck lights on the road.

"Have you ever ridden a horse before?" the man asked.

"Yes, I have, but I don't feel comfortable riding."

"It's okay. I'm Yazdan."

"I'm Mehran."

Yazdan laughed, "I know. Do you have everything from the truck with you?"

"Yes. Just this backpack."

Yazdan crossed the road in front of the truck to talk to Jalil; Mehran got a good look at him. He had baggy cloth pants, a worn blue shirt, a worn long suit jacket, and wore a traditional papaq on his head. He had no beard but wore a toothbrush mustache. Seeing Yazdan's lack of a beard made Mehran wonder why he had been told to grow a beard. Yazdan talked to Jalil for a few seconds and then let out a whistle. A horse came to them from the darkness.

"Come here, Mehran," said Yazdan. Mehran crossed in front of the car. Yazdan reached into a satchel on the horse, took out a beanie hat and a worn overcoat and gave them to Mehran. "Ditch your jacket and put this on." Mehran took off his jacket and threw it in the truck through the open window. Yazdan waved Jalil to go. Then, in one swift move, Yazdan got on the horse and held his hand down toward Mehran. "Hop on."

Mehran used Yazdan's arm to get on the horse behind him. They started riding through the terrain. That Saturday was the eighth of the lunar month and the moon was half full, but it had almost set. Mehran could barely make out a mountain range ahead of them. Besides that, he could not see anything. Yazdan rode the horse very slowly at first.

"Because of the lights from the truck, we have to wait for the horse's eyes to adjust back to the darkness again. I won't be using the flashlight because of that. The horse can see very well in the dark, but his eyes take more time than ours to adjust to the darkness."

After a bit, they started riding the horse faster. It seemed as if the horse had done the routine many times and didn't have to be directed much.

"What we're traveling on is a dry riverbed. Those lights over on our right is Jagandlu, and the other ones over there on the left are Gergereh."

Twenty minutes passed. "The foot of the mountain is just ahead. The horse cannot carry us both up the mountain, so I'll be traveling on foot beside you," Yazdan said.

As they neared the mountain, Yazdan dismounted and walked at a fast pace alongside the horse. They were going up a slight hill. After a bit, the hill plateaued, and they came upon a road.

"We can't take this road right now, because it goes by that settlement over there."

Mehran looked in the dark. "I can't see anything over there."

"Oh, trust me. It's there. Once we bypass the settlement, we'll get on the road, because it's the easiest way to go down the mountain on the other side."

Mehran figured it must have been about 5 in the morning when they passed the settlement and were on the road going down the mountain. Suddenly, Yazdan saw car lights in the distance.

"Quickly, let's get off the road. Follow me. The road drops on the side here, but it's only a couple of meters. It's a good place for the horse to hide."

Mehran got off the horse and went off the side of the road in a steep dirt bank. He slid down the side and they waited.

It took a few minutes for the car to reach their location and then another few minutes before they could not hear the engine any longer.

"Okay, follow me."

Yazdan led them a few meters down by the bank before they moved back up on to the road again. Mehran didn't get back on the horse. By the time they reached the foothill of the mountain on the other side, the sun had lit the horizon and the landscape a bit. Mehran could see several huts ahead of them a few hundred meters. "This part we have to just act normally and pass in front of these huts. It's still too early. Nobody will be up," Yazdan said.

As they were approaching the huts, however, one of the front doors opened and an old man peered out.

"Don't say anything or your Tehrooni accent will give us away. If he says anything, just nod," Yazdan whispered.

The old man stood in front of his hut as the two passed. Yazdan said something in Turkish to the old man, and the old man answered. Mehran thought they had exchanged hellos. They continued to walk. Suddenly the old man went back in his hut and a young man appeared with a Kalashnikov in his hands. He rushed toward them, speaking in Turkish.

Mehran's heart dropped. A man with a machine gun had to belong to the government. Yazdan pulled Mehran's hand to signal him that he should stop. The man and Yazdan started talking, but shortly it sounded like arguing. The young man looked at Mehran. In broken Farsi and in a heavy Turkish accent, he asked, "Shoma ki hasteed?" *Who are you?*

Mehran was afraid to answer, for his accent would give him away. He was also afraid to not answer, since he was asked a question directly by the man holding a Kalashnikov. Mehran looked desperately at Yazdan. Yazdan started raising his voice and continued speaking in Turkish to the man. A couple of other doors opened and two more men exited their hut and got close to them.

The man holding the Kalashnikov pulled out a walkie talkie from his coat pocket and raised a signal. Someone came on and started talking to the man in Turkish.

Yazdan turned back to Mehran. "Don't worry. We will get out of this."

"What should I do?" Mehran whispered.

"You're fine. Don't talk and let me do all the talking."

The man with the Kalashnikov came toward them, said something in Turkish, took the horse's bridle and led it away, leaving Mehran and Yazdan in the middle of the road.

A few minutes passed and Mehran could make out lights from a car approaching from a distance. The lights grew brighter. At about 200 meters away a flashing red light was turned on as the car slowly drove up to them. Leaving the car running, the headlights and the police light on, the driver exited the vehicle, put on his police hat and approached them.

Yazdan started talking in Turkish to the man while holding his hand in front of his chest and nodding his head down, which Mehran recognized as a sure sign of Yazdan sucking up to the man. They continued speaking in Turkish for a bit. Yazdan reached in his pocket and pulled out some paperwork and handed it to the man. The man looked it over as Yazdan continued to talk. The man gave the paperwork back to Yazdan, pointed to Mehran and said something that sounded like a question.

At this point, Yazdan started to move away from Mehran. Mehran was sure that they were found out. He looked at the zeal on the gun-holding man's face. How Mehran wished he was home in bed right now. He looked at Yazdan walking away. Yazdan didn't even look back at him.

When Yazdan reached the officer, he put his hand on the officer's back and seemed to lead him out of the general area they were in. Mehran thought it was a good sign, since the officer didn't appear to be hostile toward Yazdan's hand movement. Yazdan and the officer walked about 50 meters away, stood there and talked. By now the sun was lighting the sky and the area was lit enough to see everyone else who had come out.

After a couple of minutes of talking, Yazdan and the officer came back, the officer made a motion to the Kalashnikov man, and the man released the horse. The horse walked toward Yazdan, who grabbed its bridle, walked toward Mehran, smiled, and motioned with his head for Mehran to follow. The two slowly exited the small village, while all eyes remained upon them.

Once they were a couple of hundred meters from the village, Mehran exhaled deeply. "Oh, I was so scared."

Yazdan laughed. "That? That was nothing. All they want is money. They're too poor to just hand you over to the authorities. This way they make some money on the side and everyone's happy."

"So you had to bribe him?"

"I wouldn't call it so much a bribe as a contribution."

"Has this happened before?"

"Not with these guys, but their boss knows me and I have – well, you need not be concerned with that. We're fine. We are just two kilometers from the border now, but there is no road any longer. You should get back on the horse."

Mehran mounted the horse and they continued on.

"So, where are you going Mehran Agha?" *Sir Mehran.*

"We are going to fly to Amsterdam and then to Los Angeles."

"When you see those pretty girls behind the glass in Amsterdam, be sure to tell them Yazdan said 'Hi'!"

"You've been to Amsterdam?"

"Yes. I've also been to Paris and Frankfurt, too. I like German girls. The girls in Paris are too skinny. I need something to grab on to."

"If you've been to those countries and like those girls, what are you doing here? Why do you continue to smuggle people out?"

"Because I'm good at this, and it pays really well. Do you know how much your father paid to have you smuggled out of the country?"

"$10,000."

"Do you know how many trips I can take back and forth and how many girls I can be with over there with that money?"

"Probably many."

"I smuggle three or four people out every month. I take half and everyone else in my group splits the other half. Take out the occasional bribing I have to do to continue this, and I'm still left with more than $10,000 a month. I live like a king!"

Mehran thought the rationale made sense.

"What are you going to do in Los Angeles?"

"Study chemical engineering."

"Well, when you get rich, Mehran Agha, don't forget us peasants over here," he smiled.

How could he think that Mehran would forget this experience and Yazdan? Mehran had heard horror stories about other boys' adventures while being smuggled out of Iran. Having to walk the terrain on foot for a couple of days and sleeping on rocks with no blanket; getting on their hands and knees in the middle of a herd of sheep and goats with a sheepskin coat on, so as to blend in; having been sexually assaulted by some of the smugglers who were smuggling them out, although that didn't seem likely with a man of 19 years of age. Mehran's experience hadn't even come close to the horrors of some of those boys, but it would nevertheless be etched in his memory forever.

After walking on another hour, Yazdan said, "Welcome to Turkey, Mehran Agha!"

This is it? It looks no different, Mehran thought, after he managed to utter, "Thank you."

"You're welcome! You're welcome!"

By now they had made it to a dirt road and Yazdan mounted the horse in front of Mehran and kicked the horse's ribs with his heels. The horse took off, and soon they met up with a truck on the side of the road.

Yazdan slowed the horse, got down and greeted the driver in Turkish. Yazdan handed him some money and a package and came back to Mehran.

"Okay, Mehran Agha. We're done! This man will take you to your father's hotel."

"Thank you, Yazdan. You made the whole journey very easy."

"No problem, Mehran Agha. Enjoy those Amsterdam girls!"

Mehran watched as Yazdan mounted his horse and turned back to Iran.

The truck ride to Doğubayazıt was uneventful. The driver, a man in his early 20s, looked like a Barry Gibb wannabe, with shoulder-length hair parted at the top. He played Turkish music the whole ride and didn't speak to Mehran.

The dirt road soon led to a highway and in just over an hour, they arrived at the hotel. The man gave the package Yazdan had given him to Mehran and said in Farsi, "Khodahafez!" *Goodbye*.

Mehran exited the truck and went into the lobby, where he found Barbod waiting. Barbod grabbed Mehran and pulled him into an embrace.

Over tea and breakfast, Mehran told Barbod everything that had happened to him since they had left one another.

The next day, father and son took a bus to Ankara. The bus ride was rough and lasted nearly 18 hours, but it was the easiest way for them to make it to a major city with an international airport. During the bus ride, Mehran opened the package he had received in the truck. It included an Iranian passport with his picture in it, stamped with a visa to the Netherlands and an exit stamp dated a few days ago through the Bazargan border crossing in Iran. Other than that, the pages remained clear. The package also included five $100 bills in U.S. currency.

He turned to Barbod. "Wow. This is a lot of money. Why the money?"

"In case something happened along the way between the time I let you go to the time we met again."

"Here," Mehran offered him the money.

Barbod said in a low voice, for only Mehran's ears, "Keep it. Put it in a safe place. Always have cash available. You never know when you will need it."

Once they arrived at the Ankara airport, they walked up to a Turkish Airlines counter, purchased two tickets for Amsterdam, checked their luggage, proceeded to the transit area and awaited their flight.

Once in Amsterdam, one of Barbod's friends was there to greet them upon arrival. They checked into a hotel and scheduled a visit to the American consulate for the next morning.

The consulate visit was uneventful. After a series of questions and answers between Mehran and the interviewer, they were told that it could take up to 30 days before they would be called.

The next few weeks were tortuously boring. Living out of a hotel room was not fun. Since they did not have a car, getting around was not easy either. Though public transportation in Amsterdam was extensive, it was limited mostly to the city.

The few weeks in Amsterdam were painful as Mehran did not have any means of calling Bahar. He continued to write letters, and even mailed a couple of them, but he had no way of knowing how she was doing. The men managed semi-weekly calls to Mahtab that were short and included only brief updates.

Iranians celebrate the new year, Nowruz, on the day of the spring equinox, March 20. The preparations for Nowruz are somewhat elaborate. First, every corner of the home is cleaned and dusted. A couple of weeks before Nowruz, families start growing sprouts, usually wheat or barley, although lentils work as well. There is an elaborate setting called Haft Sin, or seven Ses, for which at least seven items whose names start with 'S' are placed together on a cloth or table. Each item resembles something. Sabzeh, the sprouts, represent rebirth. Seer, or garlic, represents medicine. Seeb, or apple, represents beauty and health, while serkeh, vinegar, represents age and patience. Senjed, the fruit of the oleaster tree, represents love and powdered sumac berries represent the color of sunrise. And finally, samanu, a pudding made of germinated wheat, symbolizes affluence. Many people add other items whose names sometimes start with 'S' though not always, such as hyacinth, coins, candles, mirror, colored eggs, goldfish, rosewater or a book.

The celebration happens at the exact second of the spring equinox. The exact time is known ahead and can fall at any time of the day, since Earth's orbit around the sun lasts 365 days and roughly 6 hours, but it falls on the same second no matter where in the world you are. Families gather around the Haft Sin setting, while radio and television countdown the time. In the old days before most people had watches, radios or televisions, a cannon was fired so that the whole city would know the new year had come. Once the new year has come, family members greet each other with happy new year wishes.

The first family to visit is the elders, usually grandparents. Children are given presents and/or money. Then the visit is extended to aunts and uncles, then cousins and so forth. The visiting process is then reversed and all who were visited, in turn, repay the visit. The process usually ends up as chaos, since visitors may never know whether someone is home. A lot of phone calls are made to prevent mishaps. The visiting process can last up to 4 or 5 days.

In Amsterdam, a couple of days before the new year, Mehran and Barbod met a man on one of the city buses. The man had overheard their conversation in Farsi and had introduced himself as Ali, an Iranian living in Amsterdam. After a brief conversation, Ali understood their situation and invited father and son to come to a gathering for Nowruz. It wasn't home, but it was the closest to their culture in a foreign land that Barbod and Mehran would get.

Eventually, the call came with a summons to the United States consulate. On April 4, Mehran received a temporary green card, with plans for the permanent one to be mailed to his U.S. address. Once they left the building, Mehran and Barbod were jubilant. Mehran was clear to enter the United States. Barbod had a pint bottle of vodka in his coat pocket, which he took a swig from and then offered to Mehran. Mehran grabbed the bottle and took a swig as well. He could finally go to his new home.

Chapter Twelve

Kirsten's wowed face spoke volumes. "That is some story, Mehran. I can't imagine how scared you must have been during the confrontation with the armed man."

"I was, but now that I think about it, they could've just taken me to draft, which is what I wanted at the time anyway."

They enjoyed the Turkish coffee and bamiye dessert. Mehran said, "You know, there are people in Iran who will look at the bottom of a Turkish coffee cup and tell your fortune." He remembered his mother, who always pretended to be able to read futures on the bottoms of cups.

"Really? How does that work?"

"Well, after you're done drinking your coffee, you turn it upside down on the saucer, wait about 10 minutes, and then turn it over to have the fortune teller read your fortune. I have told many fortunes and most have turned out to be correct, you know."

Kirsten laughed. "Okay, Mr. Fortune Teller. I know you didn't, but I want you to do that with my cup."

They finished their Turkish coffees and flipped the cups on the saucers. While they waited, Kirsten insisted that Mehran continue his story.

Chapter Thirteen

When they arrived at the Los Angeles airport and cleared customs, Barbod's friend was there to greet them.

"Barbod!" yelled a man.

"Nader!" Barbod called out.

Barbod dragged two pieces of Mehran's luggage behind him and lead the way while Mehran carried the other two pieces.

"Nader! Hello! Wow. Look at you."

"Look at yourself! Welcome! Welcome to L.A.!"

Mehran watched the two men as they embraced and whispered to one another. When they separated, the man looked at Mehran.

"Nader, this is Mehran. Mehran, this is Mr. Shahab."

"Hello, Mr. Shahab," Mehran said as he extended his hand.

Nader dismissed the handshake and instead went for a hug. "You can call me Nader. Come here boy. It is good to finally meet you again."

"Thank you."

"You may not remember, but we have met before."

"I believe you are right. I do not remember."

"You were 4 years old, and I came to Iran and visited your father. You were living in the apartment in Gisha at the time, on the second floor."

"Yes, that was a long time ago."

"Let me look at you."

Nader put his hands on Mehran's shoulders and held him at arms' length. "He looks just like his mother."

"That he does," Barbod said.

"Well, come! Come! Let's get out of this forsaken airport." Nader led them away.

They traveled on a moving platform, away from the terminal and toward the garage. "So, how was the border crossing? Did it go smoothly?" Nader asked.

"As smooth as one could expect," replied Barbod.

"I'm glad you made it and that you're in one piece," Nader said to Mehran.

"Yes! Nobody is more glad than I," replied Mehran.

"Mehran, I have known Nader since high school. We graduated together and went to Tehran University, except he studied business and I studied engineering."

Mehran nodded.

"So, Nader, how are Pari and the kids?"

"Kids? They're not kids anymore! They're 18 and 17. And, we now have a boy who is 9."

"Wow! Congratulations, Nader! You never told me."

"Well, you know," he said and then whispered to Barbod, "Oops baby."

They reached the car. Nader had a Mercedes 450SL, considered a very posh car in Iran. They put the suitcases in the trunk and in the back seat with Mehran, and then left the airport.

Los Angeles seemed as busy as Tehran. The traffic was just as heavy, and the smog wasn't any better. L.A., like Tehran, is surrounded by mountain ranges. Situated on the West Coast of the United States, L.A. is nestled by the Santa Monica and San Gabriel mountains on the north and by the Santa Ana Mountains on the east. The air is immovable and traps the smog, contributing to air pollution. That is the first thing Mehran thought of after seeing the landscape from the airplane and then driving around the city.

"Los Angeles is a huge city," Nader said. "We live in the southern corner on Huntington Beach," he continued. "Actually, we are not right on the beach but a few blocks away."

They drove on a couple different highways until they exited into what seemed a bit more posh area of the city. Nader drove the streets and finally pulled into a driveway leading to a narrow house. While the house was narrow, just like all the other houses on the block, its facade was larger than the others because of its increased height. It had a dwarf palm tree and a banana tree in its tiny front yard. The spacing between and styling of the houses made it look like someone hastily put a sandwich together, mixing all sorts of layered meat and vegetables. The walls of some of the houses were covered with stucco while some had panel sidings and others had brick. Overall, they appeared to be a hodge-podge of styles, all extremely limited by their width.

"Well, this is it!"

They exited the vehicle and Mehran tried to get the luggage out.

"Don't worry about that right now. Let's go in first," Nader said.

They entered the house and Nader's wife greeted them. "Barbod!"

"Hello, Pari!"

"My God! How long has it been? How have you been? How's Mahtab?"

"She is well, although she probably misses this tokhme sag," *son of a gun,* Barbod said, pointing to Mehran.

"Hello," Mehran said.

"Hello Mehran! I'm Pari! It's very nice to meet you."

"And you, too."

A boy peered around the corner of the room.

"Peyman! Come here and meet our guests."

The boy tiptoed into the room. "Hello."

As soon as everyone had greeted the boy, he disappeared into another room.

"Khejalatiye," *he's shy,* said Pari.

They sat and Pari served hot tea and fruit. They talked for a bit before Pari suggested that they get the luggage and take it to the guest bedroom. With the luggage out of the way, the adults sat back down and chatted the rest of the afternoon, catching up. As Pari started to cook dinner, fragrant smells traveled through the house. Based on the scent, Mehran deduced they were having rice, the staple food of any Persian table, and a couple of Persian stews. When dinner was ready, they took places at the dinner table.

"What about Parisa and Naghmeh?" Barbod asked.

"Well, Parisa is now in college. Incidentally, she is a freshman at UC Irvine," Nader said as he tilted his head toward Mehran.

"That's great. What is she studying?" Barbod asked.

"Pre-law. And Naghmeh, we don't know. She's probably at her friend's right now," Nader said. "Eat! Eat!"

After dinner, Pari took Mehran upstairs and showed him the linen closet and the bathroom with the shower. Pari told Mehran she was glad he would be spending the next few months with them.

That night Mehran could not sleep. Now that he had arrived at Los Angeles, his thoughts went back to Iran. *What is Bahar doing right now? It must be about 9:30 in the morning. Mom is up and about right now. The weather has turned nice, and the flowers are blooming everywhere. Bahar's probably at school in her Farsi class. God, I miss home. What the hell am I supposed to do here?* and the thoughts continued. He tossed and turned in bed until Barbod said, "Go to sleep."

Mehran lay motionless in bed for another hour before sleep took him. He woke up to the sound of the house alarm and it being disabled, and then re-enabled. He heard footsteps on the stairs and then a door close. *That must be Naghmeh,* he thought, and closed his eyes again.

The next morning, Mehran woke up to see the other bed empty. Barbod had already gone downstairs. Mehran brushed his teeth and washed his face.

As he headed downstairs, he heard the men talking about the war in Iran. He entered the kitchen and greeted them.

"Good morning, son," Nader said.

Mehran sat down while Nader poured hot tea for him.

"We were just talking about what will happen with you this summer and everything," Barbod said.

"Oh? I figured I would be going to college," said Mehran.

"Well, not until September. Until then, the plan is for you to stay here," Nader said.

"Thank you for letting me stay in your home," Mehran said.

"Nonsense! No thanks needed. When I needed help, your dad was there for me, and now it is us who will be here for you," Nader said.

"The plan is for me to stay here for a few more days before I head back," Barbod said. "There is a lot of work waiting for me when I return to Iran."

"Don't worry, Mehran. You'll be fine," Nader said.

Mehran thought about how plainly his father had explained his plans to return to Iran, but he also understood that his dad would have wanted to stay with Mehran if he could.

Nader owned a car dealership in South Los Angeles, but he took off the next couple of days to show Mehran and Barbod the city. They went to Beverly Hills, the Hollywood Walk of Fame, Rodeo Drive, Sunset Boulevard, Newport Beach and the UC Irvine campus. Mehran was excited to see the campus where he'd be living for the next 4 years. While there, he met Nader's older daughter, Parisa. She spoke broken Farsi and seemed very nice. She told Mehran that he'd have a great time at the university. She also told him that, given a choice of dormitories, he should choose to live in Middle Earth housing area in either The Shire, or Rivendell, since the dorms were most central and had easier access to the campus.

Back at the house, Mehran got the young boy, Peyman, to loosen up and talk to him. It was several days more before he met Naghmeh. One afternoon when Mehran and the adults were sitting in the family room drinking tea, Naghmeh came downstairs.

"Naghmeh, dear, come and meet our guests," said Pari.

"Hello," said Naghmeh in English and waved her hand.

"Hello, Naghmeh," Barbod said.

"Mom, I'm going to Sara's house," Naghmeh said.

Mehran glanced at Naghmeh and suddenly realized she could easily have been one of the girls in the band Ace of Cups. Dressed in a hippie outfit, complete with round purple glasses, she would have fit the role to a tee.

"Honey, please come back for dinner. We're having guests tonight," Pari said.

"I don't know," said Naghmeh as she walked out.

Pari watched her leave, then looked at Mehran and Barbod. "She has too many friends."

Mehran wasn't certain he liked Naghmeh. He felt it was a judgment call and that he stereotyped the girl. But he thought, if he ever got married and had a daughter, he'd teach her more manners than Naghmeh appeared to have.

That night, the Shahabs entertained many friends. Most were either doctors, lawyers or car salesmen. Most spoke Farsi pretty well. A few guests were about Mehran's age. Booze was flowing freely in a corner of the house, and Mehran grabbed a beer. Beer was something he hadn't gotten to drink often in Iran, mainly because of its low alcohol content and the space it took to smuggle into the country. Smuggling was all about maximizing profits, and carrying "watered down alcohol" wasn't high on the list of goods to smuggle. Mehran and Barbod had actually made their own beer by fermenting non-alcoholic beer, which was readily available in Iran. The fermenting process was touch and go. He remembered the first time they had made it, they had gone on vacation afterward. When they returned, they found half the bottles had exploded because of excess carbon dioxide due to a miscalculation on the amount of sugar that was needed for each bottle. Mehran also remembered making wine with Barbod, purchasing the grapes and stepping on them in the traditional, old-fashioned method, and then letting the grapes ferment for weeks before siphoning them through pantyhose, to catch the sediments, and bottling the liquid. Mehran looked toward the bar area. More than 20 bottles of wine lay flat in a rack, along with cases of beer in a see-through refrigerator. *Ah, the irony,* he thought.

Mehran made his way to the people his own age.

"Hello," he said in English, heavy with a Farsi accent.

A girl from the group looked at him. "Hi. I'm Nikoo."

"Hi, I am Mehran."

"I know. Pari Khanoom told us about you. This is Marjan, and this here is Babak."

They exchanged hellos, and Nikoo continued, "So, Pari Khanoom said you just came from Iran. Welcome. I hear you're going to UC Irvine. What are you going to study?"

"Chemical engineering."

"Cool!"

Cool? Mehran thought. *Why is studying chemical engineering cold?*

"Do you go to university?" Mehran asked.

"I'm studying pre-med at Loyola Marymount," Nikoo answered. "So, tell us. What's life like inside Iran?"

Before Mehran had a chance to start talking, Marjan said, "Oh, I was there last year. They surely live the life over there. I was there for two weeks, and we must have gone to 8 or 10 parties and – "

Nikoo interrupted Marjan, "Yada yada yada! I know you went to tons of parties. But let's see how life over there was for Mehran."

Mehran thought about what Marjan had said. They surely live the life over there? Mehran thought he was far removed from the experiences of most people living in Iran, but how much further would one have to be removed to make a statement like Marjan had just made? Even in Tehran, the capital, one could see that people were busy, trying to earn a living, and that they certainly didn't "live the life." He relented and muttered, "Oh, that is okay. There definitely are parties over there, but – I do not know. It looks to be much different than here."

"Is life as hard as they say it is?" Babak asked.

"Well, that is certainly the case for some people. Actually, that is the case for most people. Most people are poor and cannot afford to have parties or even go to parties."

"That's sad! Life without parties?" Marjan exclaimed. "That certainly wasn't the case when I was there."

Nikoo raised her eyebrows and gave Marjan a stare that caused her to stop talking.

"Forgive her," Nikoo said. "She's lived a sheltered life."

"Oh, I would say I have as well," said Mehran. "However, living over there, you cannot help but wonder how some people make ends meet."

"Have you seen any real poor people?" Babak asked.

"Probably not as many as I should have," said Mehran. And then he thought about what he had just said. *Not as many as I should have, and now I wouldn't even have the chance to see them anymore.* He felt that not only did he miss his mother, Bahar, his family, their home and the streets of Tehran, but now he missed seeing people he didn't even know.

Mehran and the teens continued mingling until dinner was served. Dessert and tea followed.

When Mehran woke up the next morning, he knew this would be his last day with his father for a long time. He was sure Mahtab would come in a month or so, but he didn't know what Barbod's plans were. After Mehran brushed his teeth, he went downstairs and found Barbod drinking tea in the kitchen.

"Sit down, Mehran," Pari said.

Mehran sat for hot breakfast tea with feta cheese, butter and bread.

"Mehran joon," *dear Mehran,* "I can't imagine what you may be feeling," Pari started. "With your father leaving tomorrow and you being here for the first time and not really knowing us that well, – well, I hope you feel comfortable to come to us and confide in Nader and me. We love you, not only because you're our good friend's son, but because you are a beautiful person. I want you to really feel at home here."

"Mehran, I have known Pari and Nader for over 20 years," said Barbod. "Granted that we haven't been together this whole time, but we are true life-long friends, and I appreciate their letting you stay here for the time being –"

"Oh, nonsense," Pari interrupted.

Barbod continued, "and this is a great segue for you into the United States' culture, whatever that may be."

Mehran thought he knew where Barbod was going with the conversation. They had touched on a particular subject during their stay in The Netherlands. He remembered the conversation.

> "Mehran, tell me about what you see here," Barbod asked.
>
> "I don't know. I see girls behind windows, some naked at the top and some all the way, waiting for men to walk in their store and have sex with them."
>
> "What else?"
>
> "What do you mean? I don't know."
>
> "What do you think of their culture? Everything you see here, what does it tell you?"

"Well, by everyone just walking by the windows and not paying attention, for one, it tells me that they're either comfortable with the prostitution, or they're ashamed."

"Good point. It's hard to tell. What about everything else?"

"There's a lot of drinking, there's a lot of people walking around as if they've got a mission to accomplish. They're affectionate in public. I don't know what you're getting at."

"Mehran, what you see here is the culture of this country. This is who they are. They're mostly European, and in this city, they all share pretty much the same culture."

"Okay?"

"Do you know what they mean when they say a melting pot?"

"A pot with butter and other stuff melting in it? What? Is that it?"

"Listen! What you see here is culture. When we get to the U.S., you will see a different thing."

"How?"

"Well, the U.S. really doesn't have a culture. The U.S. is considered the melting pot of the world. What you see in the U.S. is really a little bit of everything."

"Surely they're Americans, no?"

"Not really. In the U.S., many people are of European descent. However, there are pockets of people who are different enough to categorize them differently than everyone else."

"You mean like we distinguish Afghanis in Tehran."

"Yes, pretty much. Except, in Tehran, we only have Afghanis. In major U.S. cities, there are areas for Polish people, areas for Mexican people, Chinese people, Korean people, and so on. Everyone goes to the U.S., but they all congregate around each other and form bonds that do not cross over to other people."

"You mean like Los Angeles and the Iranians?"

"That's an example. What I was really getting at was that, in order for you to immerse yourself in people's culture, you'll have to adapt and change yourself."

"Why? I don't think I have to conform to what others want of me if I've already chosen who I want to be."

"You don't have to conform to others' wishes, but you may have to consider the choices you have to make."

"Why? I am who I am."

"Okay. Let's assume, for instance, that you lived in a society where if you were a man and wore an earring in the left ear, you'd be considered a man who's heterosexual."

"Okay."

"All right. Let's now assume that if you were a man and wore an earring on the right ear, you would be considered a homosexual."

"Okay."

"Would you wear an earring on your right ear in that society?"

The question baffled Mehran briefly, but he soon answered, "If I wanted to, I would."

Barbod looked at him. "Really? It would mean that others can prejudge you to be a homosexual."

"Yes, but *I* know that I'm not. Their judgment is their problem."

"Seriously? You would wear an earring on the right ear in that society and not care about what others thought of you?"

"If they want to prejudge me based on an earring, then that's their problem, not mine."

Barbod seemed disappointed, and it appeared Mehran was, too. Mehran thought his father wanted him to conform to the norms of the society in which he lived, whereas Mehran was disappointed that his father had such shallow views of individuality.

"Eventually, whether you like their culture, or lack thereof, you will have to assimilate. Just remember that eventually only *you* can dictate your future. You will become what you make yourself out to be," Barbod concluded.

That day, Mehran had felt invincible because of what he believed was his individuality. And now, his father was lecturing him about the culture of the United States.

They chatted at the breakfast table for a bit, and then Barbod suggested that the two of them take a walk to the beach.

During the walk, Barbod put his arm over Mehran's shoulder, at times squeezing Mehran's neck with either his elbow, or his fingers. He looked at Mehran often while walking. They made it to the beach, and Barbod suggested they find a place to sit down.

"Mehran, I have some things to tell you."

"Yes?"

"Well, let's first get the essentials out of the way."

"Essentials?"

"Mehran, it's clear that you won't be going back to Iran anytime soon. We will apply for U.S. citizenship for you when it's time, in another 4 or 5 years. That way you won't have any trouble staying in the U.S. There are, however, difficulties with you being our only child and not being able to visit our country because you dodged the draft."

"Okay."

"Let's talk about the worst-case scenario, should the unwanted happen."

Mehran knew where this was going. He mumbled, "Let's not."

"No. What I have to say you need to hear. There may come a time when something happens to your mother and me – "

"Stop it. Nothing is going to happen to you two."

"And we need to be prepared for a time like that. Everything your mother and I have worked for has been for you. You're our only child and, without you, there would be no purpose for our lives and us living. We have had our differences, we have both learned from each other ..."

Tears started to form in Mehran's eyes.

"... and your mother and I are proud of the man you have become. There may, like I said, come a time when we will no longer be around. I don't want to lengthen this talk any more than it has to be. Suffice it to say, should something happen to your mother and me, everything we own has been willed to my brother, Roozbeh. He knows that you are the real beneficiary and that he needs to liquidate everything and move the money over to a place you can access."

"Nothing is going to happen. You'll live longer than me."

"Don't say that. Even if we die of natural causes, we will still die before you." Barbod stopped.

Mehran remained silent. He thought that Barbod was telling the truth. There would come a time, even if he didn't want to think about it, when Mehran would be alone in the world and without his parents.

"Should that time come before your college is over, you and your uncle will work out the details."

They both remained silent.

"Your mother and I are sure you will continue your life without any issues. Such is life, son. You will be strong and continue on, marry a beautiful girl and have children."

Tears were rolling down Mehran's face. He imagined a life without his mother and father and, even though he would be thousands of kilometers from them, he wasn't sure he'd be able to go on.

"I love you, baba," he said.

"And I love you, Mehran. I remember when you were born and I held you in my arms. I never thought I would be sitting on a beach in the United States of America and having such conversations with you. But the fact that I am here with you and that we're having this conversation means that you have come a long way since. I am proud of you, I am proud of your individuality, although I may not agree to the extent you take it, and I know you'll do well in life."

Mehran was speechless. He thought about how, in less than 24 hours, his father would get on an airplane and they might, for the foreseeable future, not see each other. He leaned toward Barbod and hugged him. "I will miss you."

"I know. And your mother and I will miss you, but she'll see you in a couple of months, and I'll see you when I can come back."

They spent the rest of the day talking and reminiscing times gone by. After a modest dinner, they went to sleep. Nader, Pari and Mehran accompanied Barbod to the airport the next day. Mehran hugged his father one more time at the gate and didn't let go for a while. He noticed tears in Pari's eyes before she buried her face in Nader's shoulder.

Barbod went through the doors of the gate and disappeared.

Chapter Fourteen

Kirsten's eyes watered and she managed to utter, "That's awful."

Mehran checked the coffee cups by lifting them in the air and looking inside to make sure the ground coffee had somewhat cemented. He announced that the cups were ready, picked up Kirsten's and examined it for a minute. "Hmm, I don't know about this. There's a lot going on."

"What do you see?" asked Kirsten excitedly.

"Well, there's a mountain and an airplane. You'll be traveling soon."

"That's right! I'm going to Switzerland in a few weeks for business."

"Yup! And, while you're there, you will meet someone with glasses."

"Glasses? I don't know anybody with glasses whom I'll be meeting. I mean, the president of the bank has got glasses, but I don't think I'll be meeting him. Unless, oh, there is one person."

"It looks like he's going to propose a lucrative deal to you."

"Wow! Yeah. One of my meetings is supposed to be with this contact who wants to invest in the U.S. He's older and wears glasses."

"Yup. That must be it. Sooo, I see some music in the near future. An opera, perhaps?"

"Hmm, I don't know about that."

"Maybe not an opera, but some sort of concert or musical gathering for sure. And – uh oh."

"What?" Kirsten's expression changed to worry.

"It looks like you'll be getting into an accident. Not with a car, but something else. Looks all white, so I would say it's on snow, or in the air."

"I was planning on going skiing in the Alps on my trip. This could be an omen."

"Well, it doesn't look like an omen. It seems more benign. There's also money. A lot of money is going to come your way."

"True. The same person I'm supposed to meet is supposed to close a large deal with our bank, and my bonus this year could increase significantly."

"Yup. Lots of money."

"Good! I like easy money!"

"I don't see much else. Now, you're supposed to stick your index finger on the bottom of the cup to make your imprint on the coffee, and I can tell you one more thing that is to come in the near future."

He held the cup up to her, and she obediently stuck her finger in the cup, took a chunk of coffee from the bottom and wiped it on her napkin.

"Hmm," said Mehran. "This looks pretty good. It looks like in your future, or perhaps right now, there is a handsome man. He looks as tall as you and to be Middle Eastern. He is good-looking and is going to, or has, taken you on many dates and will continue to do so."

Kirsten broke out in laughter and punched Mehran in the shoulder. "You ass! None of this is real!"

Mehran laughed. "Of course it's not real! Did you really expect that your fortune would be left to the chance of coffee drippings at the bottom of your cup and an Iranian you just met who happens to know how to read your fortune?"

"Okay. Fine. Let me read your fortune."

"No problem." He pushed his coffee cup in front of her.

Kirsten picked up the coffee cup and spoke. "You will die!"

They both laughed. Mehran said, "I hope it's in your arms."

"No! It looks like it's in the hands of a stranger. He's going to set you on fire."

"Okay. Now *that's* an omen."

"Right. In a building, surrounded by others." She put the coffee cup down. "How about I just kill you now and get it over with?" she said as she reached with both hands toward his neck.

Mehran extended his neck, offered it to Kirsten's long fingers. "Kinky! I'd do anything to die in the hands of a beautiful blonde."

Kirsten retreated. "Yeah, you wish. Finger the cup." She offered him the cup.

Mehran stroked the bottom of the cup and put the coffee in his mouth.

"Okay, this is serious now. I foresee you cooking for a woman in the near future. Cooking jambalaya, it looks like."

"Kirsten, you're a good fortune teller. That's definitely going to happen."

They laughed and enjoyed the last few minutes of dinner. On their walk back to Kirsten's car, Kirsten grabbed Mehran's arm and ran her hand through his elbow.

"Mehran, I had a lovely evening and would love to repeat it with you," Kirsten said as she pulled the car in front of Mehran's apartment. "What do we do next?"

Mehran was puzzled. *What do we do next?* "I thought you were coming over to my place to eat jambalaya."

"I am. But I can't get together until Saturday night. I have a couple of business dinners on Thursday and Friday."

"We should talk before then."

"That's exactly what I'm thinking. Let me give you my phone number. Then we can talk at night."

They exchanged phone numbers and emails. When Mehran was about to get out of the car, Kirsten grabbed his arm to pull him back in. She grabbed his neck and brought him closer to her face to plant a light kiss on his lips. It wasn't a passionate kiss, nor was it a quick peck. It lasted for a few seconds. After they separated, Mehran looked at Kirsten, held her cheeks with both hands, and planted a soft kiss on her lips as well. He said goodnight and got out of the car.

Cloud nine? Is that what they call it? Mehran thought. *Why nine?* He was on 15. Fifty. Fifty thousand. He wanted to believe that he had played his cards right with Kirsten, but that wasn't it. He hadn't pretended to be anyone he wasn't. He was himself with Kirsten, and from the looks of things, Kirsten approved. He already had a feeling that their relationship would be long term, based on the cat and mouse games they had played and how things were moving slowly. He went upstairs to his apartment and promptly played Ink Spots' *If I didn't care.*

Chapter Fifteen

After his father's departure, Mehran took time to explore his new world, and a couple months seemed to pass quickly. Then again, he would find himself holding his head in his hands over his knees, looking at his tears falling on the wood floor. Overwhelmed with sadness bordering on depression, all he could think of were his parents and Bahar. He wondered what Bahar was up to. He had written her many letters, at least two every week, but he had received only three from Bahar so far. When he confronted her in a letter, she responded that she didn't have the will power to write letters. Mehran explained that, barring the letters he might receive from her, he had no way of knowing what she was going through. Communication through the mail was a slow process. Nevertheless, he continued to write, letting Bahar know what was going on in his new life in the United States.

Most days Nader seemed busy with his business. Mehran got along pretty well with Peyman, and Pari was nearly as sweet as Mahtab. Parisa stayed at UC Irvine for the summer to take additional classes for her double major in pre-law and business. Naghmeh was rarely home.

Though Peyman was in school during the day, he and Mehran played games on Peyman's Atari 2600 video game console in the afternoon and evening. Peyman had over two dozen games, including Mehran's favorite, Pitfall. They played hours and hours of video games. Mehran also played while Peyman was at school, but even that got boring.

On occasion Pari would take Mehran shopping. Pari had taken a liking to Mehran, feeling an attachment as if he were her own son. Mehran liked hanging out with Pari, even though he wasn't into shopping at all. What he liked to do was price items at different stores to get a sense of what the average price for an item was and determined which stores were over-priced and which were reasonable.

One thing Mehran noticed in the Iranian culture in Los Angeles was that people liked to get together, much like the affluent people in Iran would. They hosted or attended a party nearly every weekend. Mehran learned to blend in at the parties. Being new to the U.S., he didn't have any difficulty getting conversations started, but he noticed that those conversations ran shallow and deteriorated quickly. Conversations with physicians would succumb to medicine, especially if they were plastic surgeons. They would grab his chin and inspect the scar from a bicycle accident and make recommendations. Conversations with car salesmen inevitably led to cars.

He found that most talked about their professions and the rest talked about shopping, finding sales or other light subjects.

In Iran, however, most men were passionate about politics and made that the center of their conversations, or they'd argue about a single subject for tens of minutes. They were abreast of everything not only with their own government, but also what was happening in the world.

Mehran stereotyped most teenage conversations as well. Boys usually tended to talk about sports, which Mehran knew nothing about. American football, baseball and golf hardly existed outside of the United States, yet those sports were all boys talked about, with the exception of basketball and maybe tennis. Nobody talked about soccer, which rightly was the worldly sport. Mehran had played plenty of soccer in Iran, but nobody in the United States was interested in soccer. Teenage girls, on the other hand, talked mostly about boys, fashion, popular music, and, of course, shopping and sales.

Having watched the Iranian society abroad, Mehran wondered what caused these people to change so dramatically, with no regard for what was happening in Iran, their native land.

Mahtab arrived for a visit in late May. On the day before Memorial Day, they went to the airport to welcome her. Mehran stood anxiously at the customs exit doors, eyeing passengers every time the door opened. About 45 minutes after the flight landed, the doors opened and Mahtab walked out. Mehran ran toward her. When she saw Mehran, she dropped her luggage and opened her arms. The mother and son held onto each other tightly. True, it had been less than 3 months since they had seen each other, but they had never been apart for such a time, even when Mehran was exiled from his home. Happy tears rolled down Mahtab's face. Peyman walked behind them to take the luggage, and Pari approached them.

"Pari!" said Mahtab as she let go of Mehran.

"I know. I've aged," Pari said as she opened her arms.

"Oh my God! You don't look a day older than when I saw you last," Mahtab replied.

Mehran appreciated the sincerity between the two friends and wished for a day when he would see a friend after such a long time and pick things up where they left off many years ago. Bahar came to mind. *How nice would it be to see Bahar after many years? Or even sooner,* he wondered.

Mehran took a piece of luggage from Peyman in one hand and locked fingers with his mother with the other hand as they walked toward the exit. They looked at each other, smiling, neither feeling the need to say anything.

During Mahtab's stay, she, Pari and Mehran spent time together, drinking tea and catching up. Of course, they also went shopping. Mehran wondered how Mahtab would fit all the clothes and knickknacks she bought into her luggage when she returned.

Mahtab liked being able to go out without her manteau and headscarf. One day she and Mehran walked to the beach and sat on the same rocks Barbod and Mehran had sat on.

"You know, it has gotten worse in Iran since you left," said Mahtab. "Girls are constantly harassed for not covering their hair, or having nail polish or open-toed shoes. It's a good thing you got out when you did, Mehran."

"Probably." He paused and then abruptly asked, "Have you seen Bahar at all?"

"No, sweetheart. I know she lives only a few blocks from us, but I haven't seen her," said Mahtab. "Are you two still talking?"

"Well, not talking. We exchange letters. It's very hard. I miss her."

Mahtab saw Mehran's eyes tear up and grabbed his head, pressing it against her chest and wrapping her arms around him.

Mehran cried for a bit in his mother's arms. It felt good, better than it did crying alone. It was as if his mother had magical powers to soothe his feelings.

"Did you ever love someone before Baba?" asked Mehran.

Mahtab paused for a few seconds. "Not real love. I had crushes on a couple of boys before I met your father, but I don't think I loved anyone like I love your dad."

"How do you know if it's true love?"

"It's different for everyone. I can tell you what it feels like for me, but it might not be the same for you."

"How do *you* feel it?"

Mahtab paused again. "At first, when I met your dad, our love felt more like a crush. I wanted to be with him every waking moment, and every moment I wasn't with him I felt like I had a knot in my stomach."

"I have that for Bahar. It hurts. I've had a different feeling at times, like when she came to my birthday party – "

"Butterflies."

"Yes. It was a completely different feeling. I felt giddy seeing her at the party. But ever since, I've had the knot in my stomach."

"That's what a crush makes you feel like when you're not near your loved one."

"It hurts. It hurts so much."

"I know."

"When does it end?"

Mahtab paused again. "It doesn't. At least not as long as you keep in touch with each other."

"So, this is what I have to deal with? Either cut myself off from Bahar, or live with this knot?"

Mahtab remained silent.

"When did your crush for Baba change? What does the change feel like?"

"How love feels depends on the person."

"You love Baba. How does it feel? How do you know it's love?"

Mahtab remained silent.

"Tell me," said Mehran.

"To me, real love is when you're willing to forgo your own life for someone else."

Mehran appeared confused.

"It means that you don't want anything bad to happen to them. You don't want them to get sick. You don't want them to go through any hardships." She paused a bit.

Mehran picked her thoughts up. "You would sacrifice your own life for them no matter what the circumstance."

"Yes. In my opinion, that's true love. And when something goes wrong with true love, the knot that was in your stomach during a crush escalates to a knot in your whole torso and your whole body aches."

"How do you know that? Has something ever gone wrong with your love with Baba?"

Mahtab paused again to gather her thoughts. "When you truly love someone, all that it takes for you to get that knot is just the thought of something bad happening to the person you love. When you're truly in love with someone, that knot never goes away. It sits there, dormant, but it'll flare up when it wants to."

Mahtab told Mehran that Barbod wasn't doing too well, consumed even more so by alcohol than he had been before, though he was a lot more calm. Mehran hesitated and then told Mahtab that Barbod must be depressed. She didn't disagree. She mentioned that she herself seemed to often dwell on the trivial, until she realized what she was doing. Then she'd spend her days sewing and painting, two gifts that came to her naturally.

They walked back to the house.

Mahtab stayed for a month. Mehran knew that all good things came to an end. That was his experience in life, even though he had been spoiled. He knew that one could not hang on to what he wanted for a long time. He was trying to imagine what kind of person would be happy all the time, and he couldn't think of anybody who would meet the criteria. He would have loved for Mahtab to stay with him indefinitely, but that just wasn't possible. Mehran was glad for the time they had spent together. He knew that she'd visit often.

On the day she was leaving, Mahtab gave Mehran a watch. A 1930s Omega, it had belonged to her father when he was in the military. The band's quality had diminished with time, but the watch still worked. Mehran kissed Mahtab and watched her go through the departure gate at the airport, just as his father had done a couple of months earlier.

Not long after Mahtab left the United States, Mehran was overcome by sadness. His proximity to the beach allowed for him to walk there often. He always returned home before sunset, but one day he watched the sun set before walking back up the beach. A group of people had a small fire while one of them played a guitar and sang. Mehran was curious and strayed toward them as he passed them. He noticed the guitar player stop and the people start to talk in low voices to one another, but he couldn't hear what they were saying. Mehran had already passed them when he heard his name being called.

"Mehran!"

He turned around and tried to make out who was calling him. A girl ran toward him. It was Naghmeh.

"Hey, you want to hang around with us?"

Mehran thought a moment. "What about home? They will be worried about me."

"No, they won't! Come and sit with us for a bit. Not too long."

Mehran considered that he had told Pari that he'd be out until after sunset and agreed.

Naghmeh lead Mehran back.

"Everyone, this is Mehran, the guy I have been talking about."

"Hello," said Mehran. *She's been talking about me?* he thought.

"Hey, dude!" piped up the guitar player.

Others followed suit and said hello.

The guitar player continued. "Naghmeh told us you just came from Iran. That's totally bitchin'!"

"Bitchin'?"

Everyone laughed. The guitarist continued, "That means it's awesome. It's great!"

"Oh, thank you!"

"So, what are you gonna be doing?"

"I am going to study chemical engineering at the university."

"Fuck yeah! We need people like you, man! I like smart people."

Mehran's puzzled face must have been obvious, so the boy continued, "We need cool people in the industry, man."

"Okay," said Mehran, although he wasn't sure what he was saying okay to.

Naghmeh sat back down and made room between her and the girl next to her for Mehran. "Come and sit down."

Mehran sat between them.

"So, is this where you spend time?" Mehran asked Naghmeh.

"Here, there. I hang around anywhere," Naghmeh said in a lyrical tone while her friends laughed at her Dr. Seuss joke. "These are my friends," she opened both arms encompassing the group. "This is Sara," as she pointed to a blonde girl sitting next to her, "and these are Josh, Freddie, Carrie, Anna, Ben, Jacob, and Sera, S-E-R-A, to your left."

"Good to meet you everyone."

"So, dude, we were just smoking some pot and playing tunes. You wanna hear anything special?"

"No, I do not know what you play."

"Right on!" said Jacob, as he faced Naghmeh, "I like this dude! He's righteous and straight up!"

Mehran thought *Wow, so many words! Dude? Righteous? Pot? What the hell is that? It must be marijuana.*

With that, Jacob plucked the strings and sang *A Hard Rain's A-Gonna Fall* by Bob Dylan. Jacob knew the lyrics for the song until the first chorus ended, and he started to stumble on the rest. Laughter erupted and then everyone tried to fill in the blanks. The group enjoyed the music, bopping their bodies left and right with the rhythm.

Mehran thought about the song, the group, the guitar, the fire, and he had a warm feeling in his heart, as if he had found a group of new friends. After the song, everyone clapped. Ben lit a cigarette, took a hit, and told Jacob to play some more Dylan, as he passed the cigarette around.

"Dude, chill! Let me take a hit first," Jacob said, as he grabbed the cigarette, smoked a bit, and gave the cigarette to the next person.

Mehran quietly asked Naghmeh, "Is that marijuana?"

Naghmeh nodded. "Yeah, it's called a joint, but you don't have to smoke it if you don't want to."

When Sera had taken a hit, she offered the joint to Mehran. Mehran looked at Naghmeh, and Naghmeh took the joint from Sera, took a hit and passed it on to Sara sitting next to her.

Mehran was relieved. He had tried cigarettes before but wasn't too fond of them. He didn't think he'd like the joint either.

By the time the joint got back to Ben, it was nearly finished, and he threw it in the fire. For the next hour, they sat there, talking, singing, listening and enjoying the fire. Mehran enjoyed himself, but he thought that Pari might get worried; he told Naghmeh he'd head home. Walking back to the house, Mehran admitted to himself that his first impression of Naghmeh may have been incorrect.

He wondered again about Bahar. By now, letters from Bahar were rare and very far in between. While Mehran had written four or five letters in June to Bahar, he had received only a one-page letter back. He tried to rationalize reasons for her reluctance to write and the lack of feelings in her letters. He thought maybe she was depressed with their relationship in limbo. A part of him knew that there was almost no hope for the two of them to reunite, but just as large a part was willing to consider the possibility that someday they would be together. The thought of them not being in love was not an option for him. He was a romantic at heart and reminisced every occasion he had spent with her, whether it was separated by a wall, a door, a street, the telephone wire or the papers they had shared their thoughts on. The idea of moving on didn't even occur to him.

A couple weeks after seeing Naghmeh on the beach, Mehran was playing video games with Peyman when Naghmeh strolled into the family room. She was wearing her casual hippie outfit of a light blue tank-top, a loose paisley-patterned skirt that fell to her ankles, open-top sandals, thin leather wristbands, a string of yellow beads over her head and across her forehead, and the round, purple sunglasses that sat at the tip of her nose so she could see over the top while indoors. "Mehran, you wanna go grab some lunch?"

Peyman stopped playing and his eyes widened as he turned to look at Naghmeh.

Naghmeh saw his look, threw her hands up in exasperation and gave Peyman a snotty look. "What? I'm going to lunch!"

Mehran looked at Peyman, shrugged his shoulders and said, "Okay."

Naghmeh knew of a good fast food joint about a mile away, and they started walking. Mehran felt awkward at first, since they weren't talking, but Naghmeh soon broke the silence.

"So, I understand you'll be leaving in another month to go to UC Irvine. You excited?"

"I do not know. I think so. It is going to be tough not knowing anybody."

Naghmeh snapped, "Stop!"

They stopped.

"First things first. You need to learn contractions."

"I know those things, but I do not remember to use them."

"See, there you did it again."

"Why do I need to use them?"

"Because it makes you sound better. People will spot you a mile away when you talk like you're reading from a book. Well, people will spot you a mile away because of your accent, but you gotta start somewhere."

"Okay."

They continued walking. "So, it's no big deal if you don't know anyone. You make friends. Most people are nice here. As long as you're nice to them, they'll like you."

"Hmm, I do not have – "

Naghmeh frowned.

"I don't have any reason to not like people."

"Yeah, I know, but many people, even if they're nice, will give you trouble. Going through middle school and high school has been hell over here because people know my parents are Iranian and the whole hostage crisis in Iran turned everybody anti-Iranian over here."

"But do they not – or sorry. Don't they realize that the few students who took the hostages don't represent the Iranian people?"

"You could tell them all that until you're blue in the face, but it won't matter. So, I'm gonna give you this advice. If someone bothers you about the hostage situation, go to the school authorities."

"Will they understand?"

"It is their job to understand. You're here legally and your rights are protected."

"Yes, I have read the Constitution of the United States. It is a very elegant piece of history."

"It's, not it is. And that is an awesome thing that you have done. Most Americans haven't even read our own Constitution."

"So, why do you tell me to use contractions, but you didn't yourself?"

"Because I was emphasizing something in that sentence. You'll learn over time."

"I'll," said Mehran. Naghmeh laughed as she realized that using contractions wouldn't always work.

"What college are you going to?" asked Mehran.

"I'm going to be a senior in high school."

"You look older than that."

Naghmeh stopped and looked Mehran in the eyes over her glasses. "Never tell a woman she looks old."

"I'm sorry. I just thought you would be going to college at the same time as me."

"No, not quite yet," said Naghmeh as she started to walk again. "I'm 17, but because of my birthday, I won't graduate until I'm 18 plus."

"That's nice."

"Nice? Dude, you gotta learn the other jargon of teen talk as well."

"Jargon?"

"The way we talk. Every group talks differently. But I'll get you up to speed by the time you leave for college."

"How come now, after almost 3 months of me being here, you're suddenly interested in becoming friends?"

Naghmeh shrugged her shoulders. "I don't know. I figured you could use a few friends, so we'll hang around my friends until you leave for college."

"Okay. I love friends! I miss my friends from back home."

"What were your friends like?"

"Most of them I had gone to school with for many years, and we lived within blocks of each other, so we spent all of our time after school with each other, playing soccer in the street and going to popular teenage hangouts."

"What kind of hangouts?"

"There was this one ice cream shop called Baloot that all the teenage girls and boys hung around. Baloot was raided often by Komiteh."

"What is Komiteh?"

"The religious police. They enforce religious laws."

"Like what?"

"Like segregation of men and women, women's hijab, ban of Western music – "

"Women's what?"

"Hijab. It's like a manteau and a scarf. Women can't show their hair, legs, arms or any of their midsection in public. Only hands and below the knee. No nail polish or heavy makeup. Plus, no alcohol or parties. Lots of rules."

"So how did boys and girls meet?"

"They met on the street and exchanged phone numbers without anybody noticing."

"Did you have a girlfriend?"

Mehran paused and thought about the question. *Do I? Is Bahar a real girlfriend?* He stopped and looked up at the palm tree they were under; the noon sun shone in between the leaves while a slight wind shook them. He wondered what Bahar was doing right then. *Probably watching television,* he thought, *since it's 10:30 at night in Iran.* He looked down at Naghmeh, who was patiently awaiting an answer.

"I suppose I can call her a girlfriend," he said.

"Is she nice?"

Mehran thought for a second. "Yes, and no."

"Why? She either is, or she isn't."

"I only spent time with her once for a prolonged period."

"How long?"

"One hour."

Naghmeh chuckled, "You only met with her for an hour?"

"It was not lik – it wasn't like that. We knew each other for nearly 2 years and had been in love with each other for all of that. We wrote to each other and talked on the phone when we could, and saw each other on the street, but we never had a chance to be near each other except for the one hour a couple of weeks before I left Iran."

"So, why isn't she nice? And what's her name?"

"Her name is Bahar. It means spring."

"That's free-spirited."

"Free-spirited?"

"That means someone who doesn't let things bother them. Someone who is always herself."

"Well, the name may sound free-spirited, but she definitely is not."

"Why do you say she isn't nice?"

"I don't know what is going on between us. I hardly receive letters from her anymore, even though I send her letters all the time."

"And that's why she isn't nice? In what ways is she nice?"

"She loves me."

They paused for a moment and then continued walking.

"Maybe she is having a hard time with you not being there."

"I would be there if I could. It is not in my hands."

"Have you called her?"

"Calling Iran costs a lot. I don't want to impose on your family."

"That's nonsense. We will call her tomorrow. You can talk with her for a few minutes."

"Do you think we'll get in trouble?"

"Dude! My dad owns a car dealership. I'm pretty sure we can afford a phone call to Iran."

"'Dude'? What does that mean?"

"It's a cool way of calling a person."

"Cool?"

Naghmeh chuckled again. "Dude, we got a lot of work ahead of us," she smiled at Mehran. Mehran was starting to like their friendship.

That night Mehran could not sleep. The thought of hearing Bahar's voice and being able to talk with her, even for 5 minutes, was thrilling. He thought they'd be able to exchange much in that short time. Naghmeh asked him what time would be best to call her, and he had figured that calling her around 4 in the afternoon, Iran time, would be the best. That meant they had to make the call at 5:30 in the morning. Mehran tossed and turned until two in the morning before he fell asleep.

He felt a hand shake his shoulder.

"Mehran," Naghmeh whispered. "It's time."

Mehran woke right up, even though he had only slept a couple of hours. They tiptoed downstairs to the kitchen.

"How do we dial Iran?"

Mehran remembered the country code for Iran, 98, and city code for Tehran, 21. Nader had asked him to dial it a few times to talk with his family.

"I can dial it," he said.

His hands were shaking with excitement to talk to Bahar after three long months. He dialed the number and held the phone to his ear.

The phone beeped once. Then again. And then again. "Maybe they're not home," said Naghmeh. And then, there was a click and Mehran heard Bahar's voice.

"Alo?" Bahar asked.

Mehran was speechless.

"Alo?" Bahar asked again.

"Dude, talk!" Naghmeh whispered.

"Bahar," Mehran uttered.

There was a long pause. Mehran was sure that Bahar knew it was him calling, hence the long pause.

"Bahar, how are you?"

A voice on the other side asked Bahar, "Who is it?"

Bahar paused for a second, and then responded, "It's a wrong number." She whispered into the phone, "I can't talk right now," and hung up.

Mehran hung the phone back on the wall and looked at Naghmeh.

Naghmeh could see the look of disappointment on his face. "What happened?"

"She couldn't talk. Her mom was around."

Mehran felt defeated. He had waited for this moment for a long time, knowing that at some point he would talk with Bahar. The thought had never occurred to him that she wouldn't talk and that she would hang up the phone, knowing that it took 3 months for an opportunity for him to call her. Why couldn't Bahar make an excuse and tell her mother that it was one of her friends, then run to her room, pick up her phone while her sister hung up the phone in the family room, like she had done so many times before?

"I'm so sorry," Naghmeh said. "I know how much you wanted to talk with her."

"Why wouldn't she talk?"

Naghmeh laid her hand on his shoulder. "We'll try again."

They sat at the breakfast table for a while before Naghmeh said, "Let's go back to bed."

Mehran lifted his head and nodded. They went upstairs to their own bedrooms. Mehran closed the door. He was sad, but more than anything, he was frustrated. He wanted to punch the walls. He remembered having the same feeling when Bahar's mother had yanked her from the pizzeria, and how he had cried in the alley. This time, however, in addition to having the feelings of frustration, he had feelings of resentment toward Bahar. He grabbed a notebook and started to write an angry letter to her. He wrote two pages before he decided to stop. He turned off the light, laid in bed, and stared at the ceiling, now lit with the sunrise, and shortly fell asleep.

"Wake up!" Naghmeh jumped on the guest bed. She saw the notebook with the letter and grabbed it.

"Wow! You wrote this last night?"

"Yes," said a groggy Mehran.

"I wish I could read Farsi."

"What makes you think I would let you read it anyway?"

"Aren't we friends?"

"Yes. But I think I'm going to burn this letter. I was angry."

Naghmeh understood. "Let's go meet Sera and Ben."

"What time is it?"

"It's 2:30 in the afternoon. Let's go get some sun."

"Okay."

They put their swimsuits on, grabbed a snack from the fridge and headed to the beach.

Ben and Sera were already tanning under the hot sun when Naghmeh and Mehran arrived. They placed their towels on the sand and sat down.

"Here, rub some of this on my back," Naghmeh said to Mehran as she handed him the bottle of suntan lotion.

Mehran took the lotion, put some on the palm of his hand, and rubbed it on Naghmeh's back and shoulders. Her skin was smooth. He realized that this was the first time he had touched another girl in this way. Well, he wasn't counting the times he had done it on his cousin's back, when she had come over to their backyard pool, but this wasn't his cousin. Then again, Naghmeh was like a sister, a friend, a sounding board.

When he was done, she reciprocated and rubbed lotion on his back and shoulders, and they laid down.

"How long have you guys been here?" Naghmeh asked Sera.

"Oh, since before lunch. We're roasted *and* toasted."

Mehran was starting to catch the lingo. *Guys,* when Naghmeh was referring to both Ben and Sera. *Roasted,* as in roasted in an oven under the sun, and toasted. *Toasted?*

"Toasted?" he asked.

"That means they got high. They smoked pot," Naghmeh said.

"Hey, I never thanked you for helping me call Bahar this morning."

"Don't mention it. You're my new-found friend, and it makes me happy to see you happy."

Mehran laughed. "I wasn't happy this morning."

"You know what I mean. We will try again tomorrow morning. Maybe now that she knows you can call her, she'll make herself available."

They basked in the sun for a couple of hours, talking the whole time. Naghmeh was inquisitive about Iran, the customs, relationships between boys and girls, the weather, the streets and more. By late that afternoon, Mehran had gathered an immense amount of teen behavior and lingo, while Naghmeh had heard first-hand from someone what urban life was like in Iran. By then, Ben and Sera had left. After taking a quick dip in the ocean, Mehran and Naghmeh washed the sand and salt from their bodies under the open showers at the end of the walkway leading from public parking to the beach and headed home.

That night, Mehran couldn't sleep again. He kept thinking about what he would tell Bahar when they talked. He wanted to bring up the fact that she had hardly written him a letter, but he decided against it and thought that he should enjoy the few minutes they would have with each other.

Again the next morning, Naghmeh woke up Mehran. They headed downstairs, and Mehran made the call.

"Alo?" asked Bahar.

"Bahar."

"Hi."

"Can you talk?"

"For a little bit."

"Oh my God! How are you? I miss you so much."

"I miss you, too."

"How come you never write me any letters? I don't even know what's going on in your life nowadays. What have you been up to?" The moment he asked about the letters, Mehran was sorry he said it.

"Nothing much. Just trying to pass the summer so that I can busy myself with my studies."

"I miss you so much. I wrote such an angry letter after yesterday's call, but I'm so happy we're talking."

"I couldn't talk."

"I know. I figured, but I thought that you'd make an excuse and talk with me. I can't talk long, because it costs a lot of money to call Iran."

After a long pause, Bahar mumbled, "I can't."

"You can't what?"

There was another pause.

"Tell me. You can't what?" asked Mehran.

"I can't continue this."

Naghmeh was catching Farsi words here and there, but the troubled look on Mehran's face didn't need words for her to understand what was happening.

"What do you mean you can't continue this? You can't continue what?" Mehran asked.

"I mean us. I can't do this. It's tearing me apart. I can't continue to love you, knowing that we will never see each other again."

Mehran's eyes began to water and his stomach turned into a knot. "But I'm in the same shoes as you are."

"I don't know how you do it, but I'm sick to my stomach all the time. I can't eat. I haven't been getting together with my friends. My mom thinks I'm moody. She is having me see a therapist."

"But Bahar, I love you. I can't just turn off my love for you."

"My therapist thinks we should just cut everything clean and not have any contact with each other anymore."

"Your therapist is messed up in the head! How can she tell you such a thing? Has she ever been in love?"

"I don't know, but I think that's a good idea. I can't go on like this."

"Bahar, have you fallen in love with someone else?"

"How can you ask me that?"

"I don't know. If you ever truly loved me, how could you want to break us apart like this?"

"Because our love is doomed."

For the first time, Mehran heard words that he had known for a long time but had never admitted to himself to be true. Tears rolled freely down his face.

He tried to rationalize the inevitable. "Doomed as it may be, it's still there. I still love you." Bahar didn't say anything, but Mehran could hear her crying.

"I have to go."

"No! Please! Don't go. I can't let you go like this," Mehran cried.

"Please don't call back or write anymore," Bahar said.

"Bahar, no, these aren't your words. Your therapist has planted these thoughts in you."

"Mehran –" There was a long pause. "Goodbye."

"No!"

Mehran heard the click on the phone. He pulled the handset from his ear and stared at it until the phone started making a loud tone to denote that it was off the hook. Naghmeh walked over to him, took the phone from his hand and placed it back in the cradle on the kitchen wall. Mehran's head fell forward, and he began to cry rather loudly. Naghmeh approached him, grabbed his head and pushed it into her shoulder and held him.

Soon she heard footsteps on the stairs and saw her mother walk into the breakfast area with a puzzled look. "What's going on?" Pari quietly asked. Mehran's back was toward Pari, but Naghmeh had a clear view of her mother, so she raised her index finger to her lips and then waived her mom to go back upstairs.

Mehran cried on Naghmeh's shoulder for what seemed like an eternity. He pushed away when he realized he needed a tissue. When he did, he saw tears rolling down Naghmeh's face. Naghmeh grabbed tissues for both of them and handed one to Mehran.

"I'm so sorry, Mehran."

Mehran was dazed.

"Let's go to the beach," Naghmeh said.

They left the house, barefoot, Naghmeh in her pajamas and Mehran in shorts and a tee. They walked to the beach and sat down just far enough from the ocean so that the waves could not reach them. They sat in silence, until Mehran said, "I love her so much."

"She's a lucky girl." Naghmeh paused for a couple of minutes, and then asked, "What happened?"

Mehran told her everything Bahar had told him. They sat on the beach until the sun came up behind them. Mehran looked at Naghmeh and laughed. "You're still in your pajamas."

Naghmeh laughed. "Well, I didn't think we'd be coming to the beach."

"You're free-spirited, right?"

"Not completely."

"We should go back."

They walked back home and went to their own rooms.

Mehran's eyes were puffy from crying. He thought about how much he had poured into his relationship with Bahar, all the letters he had written, all the times he had cried when he missed her. He wondered about the knot in his stomach he had had since the phone call the day before.

Mehran woke up at 11. After brushing his teeth, he headed downstairs. He heard voices talking. When he reached the breakfast area, he saw Naghmeh and Pari sitting at the table with tea, bread, butter and feta cheese. He said hello and sat down. Pari looked at his sorrowed face. He figured that Naghmeh had told Pari what happened. He had heard Pari in the morning and figured that an explanation was due, so he didn't mind that Naghmeh had told her mother everything.

"Mehran joon, do you want sugar in your tea?"

"No thank you."

Pari talked while she poured Mehran's tea. "Mehran, Naghmeh told me everything. I'm so sorry azizam," *dear.*

Tears collected in Mehran's eyes. Naghmeh noticed. "Mom! Let's not talk about that."

"I know. I just want him to know that we're here for him," she said as she handed Mehran his tea.

"Thank you," said Mehran.

Pari tried to interject a few more times, until Naghmeh said, "Enough, mom!" After that Pari remained silent.

Mehran passed the next 2 months mostly with Naghmeh and her friends. They often hung around on the beach late into the night. Mehran tried a bit of everything with the group, from pot to playing games like spin the bottle. He learned that the traditional spin the bottle game involved kissing one another, while the version they played at the beach involved giving foot and back rubs to each other, or coming up with a haiku in praise of the person who was spinning the bottle. He learned such lingo as gnarly, awesome, bummer, mondo, dweeb, dork and hairy, in addition to saying, "I gotta take a piss," instead of "I have to pee." He also learned plenty of swear words and their proper use in the English language. He learned the versatility of words like shit and fuck, and the taboo in using the "C" word.

A month after his phone call with Bahar, Mehran sat down and wrote a letter, neither brief, nor lengthy, to Bahar. He realized that while he had busied himself with new friends and learning the youth culture in the U.S., Bahar may not have had any opportunities to take her mind off of their relationship. In reality, he hadn't either. He still dwelled on Bahar, wondering what she was doing or how she was feeling. In the letter, he tried to rationalize the decision Bahar had made, how he respected her for speaking her mind, and apologized for accusing her that the decision was her therapist talking. He left the letter open-ended, telling her that should she ever come to the U.S., they should definitely remain friends and keep in touch.

A week before his departure for college, Mehran's new friends jokingly got him a cap and gown to mark his graduation and readiness to enter college life. While some of his friends were going to college, none was going to UC Irvine. Back at Pari's home, they also had a going away party for him, although he thought the party his friends had given him was a thousand times more fun.

On the weekend before Mehran was to start college, Nader brought a pickup truck from the dealership to carry Mehran's belongings to the dorm. Mehran was both excited and sad. Over the past couple of months he had developed a deep relationship with Naghmeh and didn't want to let that go, but at the same time he was looking forward to being on his own and acclimating to a new environment. They all helped pack the truck on Friday and the next day took Mehran to the UC Irvine campus.

Chapter Sixteen

Mehran and Kirsten kept in touch during the next week, mostly via emails with a couple of phone calls. He let her know how excited he was about cooking for her on Saturday. She, in turn, told him how excited she was to see his apartment and eat a home-cooked meal, since she wasn't much of a cook and usually settled for cereal or fast food.

Mehran had a poker game at work on Friday night. He told his co-workers about Kirsten.

"Ooh, Swiss? Is she hot?" asked Joe, a fellow engineer and a good friend of Mehran's.

"Dude! She's Swiss. How can you be Swiss and not be hot?" another guy answered.

"So, you're gonna tap her, right?" Joe asked.

Tap her. Rude? Probably. Inappropriate? Yes. Right on? "I would like to," he said, and then he thought *tap her?* He continued, "Well, not tap her. I want to take things slow with her. I like her a lot."

"Good for you," said the second friend. "The slower, the more pressure you build and the better the release will be. It's laws of physics, man!"

On Saturday, Mehran went to the grocery store to buy ingredients for jambalaya. He had a small rack of wine already in his kitchen, but he bought two bottles so that he could replenish the holes in the rack after tonight's dinner.

Kirsten called Mehran at 6 p.m., asking if there was anything she could bring.

"Nada," he said.

"Okay! I'll be there in a jiffy."

He was excited. He hadn't started cooking since he wanted to cook while Kirsten was there. When Mehran opened the door, Kirsten smiled, gave him a bottle of Cabernet and briefly kissed him on the lips.

He opened the bottle of wine Kirsten had brought and poured a couple of glasses. They enjoyed the wine and talked while he prepared the jambalaya ingredients. Kirsten was very curious and impressed by Mehran's cooking. She stood next to him by the counter.

"You seem to know your way around food and the kitchen pretty well. What gives?"

"I took culinary classes at Northwestern."

"Wait! You went to Northwestern, of all universities, and took culinary classes?"

He pretended to use sign language, faking some movements with his hands. "Yes, I took culinary classes at Northwestern."

"What year were you there?"

"From 1986 to 1989."

"No way! I was there from 1984 to 1988. We never saw each other?"

"It's a big school. Besides, I think I saw you once and ignored you."

Kirsten punched him. "You couldn't ignore me if you wanted to."

He smiled. "You got me there, Kirsten!"

They talked about Northwestern and education in general while he finished preparing the meal. He put the mixture in the pot to cook for the next hour. They took their wine glasses and sat at the table.

The smell of the jambalaya began to waft through the apartment.

"My God! This smells so good. I'm dying to taste it."

"Patience! Only another hour while it cooks. I'll get some cheese and crackers."

Once Mehran brought the cheese and crackers, Kirsten wasted no time and asked him what happened after his father left. Mehran filled Kirsten in on the time he had spent acclimating to life in the U.S., Mahtab's visit, Mehran's finding new friends, his painful separation from Bahar and continued to his departure for college.

Chapter Seventeen

UC Irvine was just a 25-minute drive from the Shahab home on Huntington Beach during average traffic. Mehran was sure he would see Naghmeh often. Upon their arrival on campus, they checked in with the registration desk for new students and drove to the dorm. Everyone helped take Mehran's belongings to his room. Even Parisa came to help them.

Mehran did not get his first housing choice, The Shire, since he had not filed the housing paperwork until he had come to the United States in April. He was given the choice of Rivendell or Hobbiton, and he chose the latter since it was closer to the student commons and activity centers.

After they had moved everything, Peyman said, "Mehran, I have a surprise for you." He handed a box to Mehran.

Mehran looked in the box and found the Atari 2600 console they had played games on during the past few months.

"Peyman. Wow! I can't take this! This is your gaming machine."

"Don't worry," said Peyman. "Baba has promised me a Commodore 64!"

Mehran smiled. They had both played a bit on a Commodore 64, and Mehran knew that Peyman had wanted one for a long time. "Peyman, this is awesome!"

Nader and Pari looked at each other, and Nader said, "Awesome?"

"That means grand, cool, amazing!" said Mehran.

Naghmeh chuckled.

They wrote down the number to the phone in the commons area outside Mehran's room so that Mehran's parents could call him. Then they drove to Parisa's dorm, Camino, to drop off an old television for Parisa. Nader had recently replaced the old television at home with a newer model. By the time they were done, it was nearly 5 p.m. Naghmeh wanted to stay with Mehran on the campus while the others went to eat.

"Honey, we didn't get to say a proper farewell to Mehran," Pari said.

"Mom, geez. He's only a half-hour from home," Naghmeh said.

"Nevertheless, let's eat dinner together as a family," Nader said.

Mehran was touched that Nader considered him part of his own family. They settled on a Mexican canteen called *Los Pollos Primas* not far from the campus. Mehran had never had Mexican food before, but he thought it tasted delicious.

After dinner, they went out to the parking lot. "We should say our goodbyes here," Parisa said. I'll walk back to the campus with Mehran."

"Honey, are you sure? It's a couple of miles," Pari said.

"Mom, the campus is two miles wide. We'll be okay," Parisa said.

Naghmeh started to say something, but she stopped herself.

"Are you sure?" Nader asked.

Parisa looked at Mehran. "Yeah, why not? He's gotta learn his way around the campus, right?"

"Yes, of course," Nader said.

They hugged, kissed and said their farewells. When hugging Mehran, Naghmeh whispered in his ear, "I'll see you soon. Okay?"

Mehran felt blessed. The family he had been placed with seemed genuinely interested in his wellbeing, much like his own family. He could see tears in Pari's eyes, although she was smiling.

As the family left with the truck, Parisa looked at Mehran. "Are you okay?"

Mehran wiped away a tear. "I'm sorry. I didn't mean to cry. Yes, I am. Your family is so nice to me."

Parisa smiled. "I'm glad you're happy."

Over the next hour, Parisa acquainted Mehran with the surroundings of the campus, showing him many unknown places. She was starting her sophomore year. Mehran would have been a sophomore at 19 as well, but the accommodations he made for the changes in his life pushed him back a year.

Parisa's dorm was on the way to Mehran's. After he left Parisa, Mehran continued to walk toward his dorm, his new home for the next 4 years, the place he'd adorn with his pictures and posters. He noticed many boys and girls holding hands or walking arm in arm, and he instantly thought of Bahar. Even though a couple of months had passed, he still often wondered what she was doing. *Probably asleep right now.*

Mehran started organizing his dorm room and placed a few pictures on his desk and by his bed. Among the pictures was one of Bahar. *I must still be in love with her if I'm putting this by my bed,* he thought.

Mehran hadn't met his roommate yet. *Perhaps tomorrow.* Soon, there was a knock on the door. He opened to a guy about his own age, maybe a couple of years older. "Hi, Mehran? Did I say that right?"

"Yes, you did."

"Cool! I'm Ron, your resident assistant, or RA as we call it."

"Hi."

Mehran took a good glance at Ron. He was by most standards a very good-looking guy. Built, and he wore a tank top to show off his arms. His face was clean-shaven, with short, black curly hair, maybe styled to be a little higher in the front top. His eyes matched his hair, flanked by two thick eyebrows. *You don't need to know his name to know he's Italian,* Mehran thought.

"So, how are you settling down?" Ron asked.

"Okay. I like the room. Do you know who my roommate is going to be?"

"Hmm, let me see," Ron looked on the paper he was holding. "His name is Royce. He's a sophomore. That's all it says."

"Royce, as in Rolls Royce?"

Ron chuckled. "Yeah! Just like that. So, settle down and then all the students on this floor are going to meet in the common area on the first floor for a mandatory meeting at 9:00 tonight."

"Okay."

"And I just want to let you know that I'm your first contact should you have any problems with anything. The dorm, your roommate, the classes. You let me know first, and we'll take it from there."

"Okay, Ron. It's nice to meet you."

"And you, too, Mehran."

Mehran was already feeling welcome at his new home. That evening he attended the mandatory meeting and learned about the rules of the dorm, along with some other useful information, like the cafeteria hours, emergency numbers, and again how the RAs were there to help with any problems the students encountered.

He met his roommate, Royce, the next day. Royce was not what Mehran had expected. For one, he was short. Not comically short, but maybe 5' 3". His face and hairstyle reminded Mehran of Luke Skywalker in Star Wars. Royce seemed friendly enough and easy-going, but somewhat distracted and inattentive. He was a sophomore majoring in communication and had lived in the same building the previous year. Luckily he brought a television with him, and Mehran was able to make use of the Atari console Peyman had given him.

Mehran learned that orientation was a week of parties and getting to know each other. He made many friends in the dorm that first week. He became friends with a Jordanian boy named Khaled who lived across the hall. Khaled may have been born to Jordanian parents, but he was no Middle Eastern boy. He was born in the United States, spoke perfect English and was probably Mehran's nicest friend in the dorm, not to mention that he had a girlfriend who Mehran would consider one of the most gorgeous girls he had laid eyes on. Mehran also made friends with other kids whose parents were immigrants; a couple were Persian and Armenian. There was, however, a boy named Charlie who lived in the same wing as Mehran and seemed to despise him for no apparent reason. Charlie was probably a spitting image of Roger Moore, tall, handsome, minus the suit and tie, and an arrogant asshole. Mehran tried to think of how he may have offended Charlie but couldn't come up with anything.

Mehran received a few phone calls from Naghmeh that week on the commons phone. Usually someone else picked up the phone and knocked on Mehran's door to alert him of the call. On a couple of occasions during the week, he heard Charlie pick up the phone and rudely answer. "Who the fuck are you looking for?" and "Learn to speak fucking English." Mehran wondered whether those calls may have been from his parents. The next day when Naghmeh called him, he told her to get a message via Pari to Mehran's parents that, should they want to call, they should do so at a designated time, perhaps on Sunday nights. That way he'd be sure to hang around the phone and not miss their calls.

During the first week of classes, Mehran discovered the immense wealth of media, particularly music, available at the school library. After his discovery, he spent countless hours listening via tapes and phonographs to classical music, pieces he had never heard before and composers he had only read about.

Reading at the library about modern composers like Shostakovich and about Gershwin pieces like his Rhapsody in Blue, Mehran accidentally stumbled on jazz music and fell in love. He listened to the giants of jazz, such as Sonny Rollins, Dizzy Gillespie and John Coltrane. In the first few months at UC Irvine, Mehran listened to or skimmed through the library's entire jazz collection. He could not put his finger on what style of jazz he liked the most. One thing was for sure. He liked songs with a fast beat. While researching jazz, he determined it was the rhythm section that fascinated him the most, particularly the beat and tone of the upright bass instrument. Bass quickly became his favorite instrument to listen to in recordings.

After a few months, Mehran realized that the media catalogs for other UC libraries were on a computer he could search; he could request for them to be sent to the UC Irvine library. Suddenly the collection of music he had access to quadrupled. He also learned that the library had a tape deck with a phonograph player so that he could take blank tapes and record his favorite music. His personal library of cassettes expanded rapidly with quality jazz music.

Mehran quickly learned about the Greek life on campus. Through his new friends and Royce, Mehran quickly became a weekend regular at parties on and off-campus. Obtaining alcohol for consumption on the weekend without parties was a little more problematic. At first he had to ask others to purchase beer for him. Eventually he realized that by growing a beard he could easily purchase alcohol himself. Royce's fridge was always stocked. While Mehran enjoyed getting a buzz, he was afraid that he'd become like Barbod, relying on his "fix" every night. He remembered the nights he had suffered from Barbod's drinking and thought moderating his intake would avert his becoming like his dad.

Mehran intended to spend the winter break converting many albums onto tape, but instead he spent time with Naghmeh and her family. That year he witnessed the hustle of Christmas shopping in the U.S., and it reminded him of Iran and the hustle before Nowruz.

In January 1985, Mehran returned to college for the winter quarter. He spoke to Naghmeh more often, connecting with her a couple of times a week. Studies went well for him and he excelled in his classes. In the blink of an eye, summer arrived and Mehran returned to Nader's house. Mahtab came for a visit and they enjoyed extended time with each other. Mahtab told Mehran that she and Barbod planned to see Mehran in Spain during the winter break. Mehran was excited to know he would see his father by year's end. Even with his mom visiting, Mehran spent plenty of time on the beach, partying with Naghmeh and their friends. He thought of Bahar only occasionally; more often, he thought about several girls he had met on campus. The summer passed quickly, and he returned to school for fall.

Chapter Eighteen

Dinner was ready at 9 o'clock and Mehran served the food right out of the pot onto Kirsten's plate.

"So, this is Persian-style jambalaya," said Mehran.

Kirsten laughed. "You mean it's a dish from south Iran by the Persian Gulf?"

"Ha ha! No. I cooked it for an hour so that the rice would get a burnt crust at the bottom of the pan, the crust we call tahdeeg, meaning the bottom of the pot."

"Interesting. I want to try some of that."

Mehran fixed himself a plate and then dug to the bottom of the pan to break some tahdeeg. He put a bottle of hot sauce on the table and invited her to sit down.

Kirsten really liked the jambalaya. He enjoyed the food as well, although he added hot sauce to his. The wine intensified their feelings, both for the food and the good conversation they were having.

"What's the seafood in this?" asked Kirsten.

"Crawfish bits. I hope you're not allergic to shellfish."

"Me allergic to something? Not in my lifetime. I'm an ox!" said Kirsten.

"More like an oxen."

"Well, you can be the oxen, but I'll be the ox in this relationship."

Relationship? thought Mehran. *Is that what they had?* He liked Kirsten a lot and would let her take the lead in the relationship if she really wanted to. "If you want to be the ox and work harder than the oxen, then I'll be the oxen," he said.

She smiled. "Mule boy!"

"Bovine!"

They both laughed.

After dinner, Mehran made Kirsten an Iranian dessert, Khagineh, a sweet egg omelet with saffron. Kirsten enjoyed that as well. She wanted to help wash the dishes, but Mehran insisted that they leave everything in the kitchen and said he'd take care of them later. He had a habit of washing most of his dishes as he cooked anyway, so in the end there was only a handful that needed to be washed. The only thing he did was scoop the leftovers into small containers and put them in the refrigerator.

While he was busy in the kitchen, Kirsten roamed his apartment. When he finished putting the food away, he came out for Kirsten and found her in his bedroom. There was not much to look at in his bedroom, except the bed, an alarm clock, a dirty clothes hamper, a stereo with a CD player, and a framed piece of art on the wall. Kirsten was looking at the glass; inside was a patterned knot made out of what looked like a shoelace. The hard backing of the frame was pressing the knot against the front glass, holding it in place. It wasn't so much art as a memento, a cherished one, Kirsten thought.

"This is interesting. Tell me about it."

Mehran thought for a second. "Maybe some other time Kirsten."

"Ooh, that sounds enigmatic."

"You're absolutely right," he said without a smile. She understood the meaning in his tone and walked out of the bedroom. "Will you tell me more about the rest of college?" she asked.

Chapter Nineteen

By 1985, the war with Iraq was going well for Iran. Iran had gained all the land lost in the first year of the war and was on the offensive. As a result, the Iraqi government was receiving substantial financial support from the Arab states of the area, including Saudi Arabia. Saddam Hussein's regime in Iraq was, in turn, using the money to buy more advanced military equipment from the Soviets and Mirage F-1 Fighters from France. With the help of German engineers, the Iraqis also modified the Soviet Scud missiles for longer range since their air force was not able to penetrate the Iranian killing fields set up to take down Iraqi bombers and fighters.

It wasn't too long after Mehran had returned to college when, on a late Saturday afternoon, the phone rang at Nader's house. Naghmeh answered the phone and quickly called her mother. "Mom, someone wants to speak with you. It's in Farsi."

Pari took the phone and conversed with the man on the other side. Naghmeh could tell from her Mom's expression that the conversation wasn't going well. Pari was biting her fist between talking and listening, and her voice was shaking. The call lasted a few minutes, perhaps five, Naghmeh thought. When Pari hung up, she plopped herself in the chair with a dead stare into space.

"What's up, mom?"

Pari didn't answer at first.

"Mom?"

"Naghmeh joon. Give me some water."

Naghmeh filled a glass with water and set it in front of her. Tears were rolling down Pari's face.

"Mom, what's wrong? What?"

"Azizam," *my dear*, "Mehran's parents were killed in an accident."

Naghmeh felt her knees give and grabbed the table to balance herself.

"Their house was hit with an Iraqi missile."

Naghmeh thought about Mehran; he would be devastated.

"I can't believe this stupid war. How it simply has wiped off hundreds of thousands of Iranians off the face of the planet," Pari said. "How are we going to tell him of this? We can't tell him over the phone."

Naghmeh thought for a second. "I'll go see him."

"No. Nader needs to be the one who tells him. You're too young to break this kind of news to him."

"Mom, Mehran and I are very good friends. I think the last thing he needs is to be told of the news by Dad. I need to go see him."

"I don't think that's a good idea. Perhaps we should all go there together."

"Mom! I'm the one who's been hanging around with him. It's Saturday, I'll go tell him and I'll bring him home."

Pari seemed so devastated that she reluctantly agreed.

Naghmeh cried the whole way while driving to the campus, parking and walking to Mehran's dorm. His door was open and the sound of jazz music was coming through to the hallway. Naghmeh stood for a moment to compose herself, wiped her tears with her sleeve and approached the door. Mehran was sitting at his desk, writing in a notebook. He noticed someone standing in the doorway, lifted his head and then smiled.

"Naghmeh! What the hell are *you* doing here?"

Naghmeh closed the door behind her. Mehran got up from behind the desk and approached her.

"Have you been crying?"

"Mehran, sit down."

"Why? What's wrong? Why have you been crying?"

Naghmeh calmly grabbed his hand and sat him at his desk. She pulled his roommate's chair over and sat across from Mehran.

"Mehran, I have some bad news for you."

"What? What's happened?"

"I love you so much." She broke into tears.

Mehran was confused. "I love you, too. Tell me what happened? Why are you crying?"

Naghmeh hadn't thought about how she was going to share the news with Mehran. In a way, she felt she had done a hatchet job already. Maybe this task would have been better for Nader. He would have been way more composed and would've been able to deliver the sad news without buckling. It was too late to go back. She had to get through this.

"They called from Iran. There was an accident, and something has happened to your mom and dad."

Mehran felt a rush of adrenaline through his body; his breathing fastened and so did his heart rate.

"No!"

"I'm so sorry, Mehran. Their house was hit by an Iraqi missile."

"No!!!"

"Mehran," she grabbed his hands, "forgive me for giving you this news."

"No!!!"

He didn't need to hear her words that they were dead; her face was indication enough. Yet, the smallest hope in him wondered.

"It was just an accident. They're all right. No?"

Naghmeh shook her head.

Mehran's eyes filled with tears, but he didn't burst at first. It was as if he couldn't breathe. He closed his eyes and then started crying. Suddenly he let go of his breath. "Noooooo ..." and he began to wail. There was a knock on the door. Naghmeh exited and closed the door behind her. A minute later, she came back into the room. Mehran had collapsed on the floor.

Naghmeh sat with him on the floor and held his head in her lap. A few dorm friends came and stood in the doorway. Mehran's roommate managed to get through the boys and got into the room. "What's going on?"

Khaled pulled him back out.

Mehran came about and buried his face in Naghmeh's lap, crying loudly.

Royce came into the room, quickly grabbed a bag and a couple of clothes and left. Khaled pulled the door closed.

Mehran laid on the floor and cried, for how long he wasn't sure. He could hear Naghmeh crying with him. He moved to grab a tissue, and then he thought how futile it was to try and wipe his face with a tissue. He reluctantly grabbed his towel instead. He stood up, dazed, in the middle of his dorm room, looking at Naghmeh, his pictures on the wall and his bed. Neither of them spoke. Mehran stumbled toward the mattress and laid on it, facing the window, still crying. Naghmeh got on the bed behind him and wrapped her arm around his shoulder and her face against his back. He laid there, motionless, for a long, long time. But in his mind, time had stopped. A series of slides played through his mind: images of vacations, his father encouraging him to play the violin, his mother cooking dinner, the fight he had with his father that had gotten him kicked out of the house, birthdays, their home, and thousands of other images from the far reaches of his brain. Then he began to imagine what their house must look like after being struck by the missile. He wondered about how his parents had actually died and questioned the circumstances. *Was it fast? Were they eating dinner? Was Baba listening to music while mom was watching television? Was she sewing? Was she painting? Was she thinking of me? Did they live at all after the missile hit? When did it happen? What was I doing when it happened? Was I in class? Was I eating food in the cafeteria? Was I laughing with my dorm buddies? Did they suffer? What were the last thoughts that went through their minds? Would things have been different had I insisted on not leaving Iran alone? Would they have decided to come here as a family? How long was it before anyone got to them? Did they make it to a hospital? Could I go back for the funeral? No, I can't. Damn it.*

His thoughts shifted to bargaining with his past. *What if I had refused to leave the country? What if I had insisted that they meet me in the summer in Spain instead of Christmas? What if they had decided to leave the country right after the revolution, like they had considered? What if they had taken the weekend to travel to their villa by the Caspian Sea? What if they happened to be in a different part of the house?*

Suddenly his mind went blank, as if the slide reel had finished and a white screen had projected on the wall in front of him. No images. No thoughts. Just a blank, white emptiness was all he could see. And, he fell asleep.

A couple of hours later, Naghmeh woke up to a knock on the door. It was Khaled.

"There's a phone call for Mehran. He says his name is Nader."

"I'll talk to him. He's my dad."

Naghmeh walked over to the phone. "Dad?"

"Naghmeh. We were so worried about you two. What's going on."

"He's sleeping."

"Is he all right?"

"He will be. He needs to sleep this off."

"I'm going to come and get you both."

"No, dad. Let him stay here tonight. I'll stay with him and we'll drive home tomorrow morning."

"He needs us. He should come home."

"He will, but I don't want to bring him right now. Let him sleep tonight, and we'll come home tomorrow morning."

Nader sighed. "How did he take it?"

"He is devastated, like anybody who has just lost his parents."

"Poor boy."

"He'll be okay. He will just need some time."

"I really think you should both come home."

"Dad! When he's up, he's crying. What do you want him to do? Come home so he can sit in front of all of us and cry?"

"But we're all worried about him. He probably feels very alone. I don't want him to do something stupid that we'll all regret later.

"Dad. I'm here with him. His roommate is gone. I'll sleep on his roommate's bed tonight."

"I don't like this. How about we come up and see you both."

"Dad, he's been crying non-stop."

"Okay. Is he in the shape to talk so we can give him our condolences?"

"No, dad. He's in the room crying."

"Okay. Give him our condolences. We will see you tomorrow."

"Okay. Bye, dad."

Naghmeh went back to the dark room and closed the door behind her. She got in bed again behind Mehran and pulled a cover over both of them.

"We were supposed to see each other in Spain in a few months."

"I know."

"Why? Why *my* parents? Why *me*?"

Naghmeh didn't have an answer.

Mehran grabbed her hand and squeezed it into his chest. "Thanks for coming here. I don't know what I'm supposed to do."

Naghmeh squeezed him against her. "You would have done the same for me."

"What am I supposed to do now?"

"We'll figure it out." She kissed the back of his head.

He squeezed her hand again for a few seconds before relaxing. "My dad had a talk with me before he left. He talked just about something like this happening. I cut him off. I didn't want to hear him, to talk about it."

"Go back to sleep."

They remained silent after that. Mehran's thoughts continued to race. He couldn't focus on a single thing. He looked outside his window and saw the moon starting to rise in the sky. It was just the beginning of the lunar month and the moon was a bright sliver. He paid attention to the moon, its shape, and before he knew it, his eyes had adapted and he was able to make out the shape of the whole moon despite its lit crescent. He understood something he had never actually thought about before. The Earth and the sun existed on an axis. The moon was off-axis. But the moon orbited Earth. Half of the moon would always be lit, because it had its own axis with the sun, except when it was a lunar eclipse. But in other positions, the view from Earth would see only a fraction of the lit surface of the moon. That's why it looked like a crescent at first, the crescent grew to a full moon, and it dwindled on the other side until it became a crescent and then a black moon. He had been told the same thing many times before, but it wasn't until he had stared at the moon a little longer that he realized how the different shapes of the moon came to be. Then he slept.

When Mehran opened his eyes and lifted his head to look at the clock by his bed, it was 2:03 in the morning. He had turned around while sleeping and was now facing Naghmeh. He looked at her face, lightly lit. The moon was just the sliver, but the streetlights had peered into his room to shed some of their life. Her eyes were closed. He continued to look at her face, their breaths twirling and dancing between them and the heat dissipating as it traveled over their faces.

"Kiss me," said Naghmeh with her eyes still closed.

He laid there, motionless and stunned. A thousand thoughts crossed his mind. She was very dear to him. She was nice, despite what he had thought of her for his first few months in the U.S. What did she mean?

Naghmeh opened her eyes and looked at him in the dark. She was not a supermodel, he thought, but she was definitely an attractive

Persian girl: thick black hair, full brows, dark almond eyes, a smooth face.

They looked at each other for a bit until their breathing was in unison. Their chests expanded and contracted at the same time. Their eyes were locked into each other's. Naghmeh put her hand on his waist, pulled him closer and planted her lips on his. He twitched, as if a jolt of electricity had been shot through his body. She pulled him closer.

Thoughts began racing through Mehran's head. He loved her at a different level, in a different way. He loved her as a friend, even if he would have only dreamt of having a girlfriend as beautiful and nice as her. What will this do to their relationship?

With their eyes still locked onto one another, she continued to kiss him, biting his lips one at a time, her tongue occasionally tasting his lips before retracting back into her mouth. He closed his eyes and reciprocated by doing the same, trying to mimic her movements; he had never kissed a girl like this before.

She was squeezing him tighter now. Her other hand made its way between his neck and the pillow and grabbed his head from behind, so that she could press her lips harder against his or perhaps to make sure that he wouldn't pull back. He liked the feeling, both the physicality of the movements, the feeling of what was happening to his body and the force by which the thought of what the two of them were doing was occupying his mind and making him forget about all else.

He put his hand on her hip and drew her into him. Their lips were locked together, fervently enjoying each other's softness. She broke their kiss and tilted her head back and to the side, exposing her neck. He continued his kissing, planting pecks by her ear and moving down to her neck. As he moved down, he felt the pulse of her aorta and he stopped. His lips could feel her heart beat – *thump thump, thump thump*. He paused and enjoyed feeling the rhythm of life that went through her.

Their hips had found a rhythm of their own. He didn't remember having commanded the movement, yet nature seemed to have taken control of what he was doing, and he felt powerless to stop it. As his lips moved lower, he opened his eyes and the sight of her exposed neck and his proximity to her caught him off-guard. He took his hand off of her hip, placed it on her shoulder, and pushed her away.

"Stop!" he said.

She looked at him for a few moments, then gently pushed his shoulder so that he was on his back, and, in a swift move, she straddled him. His body tensed up. They continued to look at each other, eyes still locked together. She sat up on him, took her hands off his shoulders and started unbuttoning her shirt. When she had finished with the last button, the shirt parted a bit. Mehran could see her curves but not her entire breasts. She took Mehran's hands in hers and proceeded to move them toward her body. Mehran stopped at her shirt. She let go of his hands.

As much as Mehran thought what they were doing was wrong, he wanted to see Naghmeh – all of her. He wanted to be close to her and hold her. He parted the shirt and she moved her shoulders so that the shirt fell away, exposing her naked torso. She pulled her arms from her sleeves, one at a time, and threw the shirt on the floor. The streetlights coming from the window lit only half of her body, casting a shadow on the other half. Mehran looked at the beauty in her, the light splitting her into two halves, one enticing him, the other, unknown. She grabbed Mehran's hands in hers and moved them up to her breasts.

Mehran instinctively cupped her breasts and relished her softness. Naghmeh leaned over and started to kiss him again, but this time more gently, as if she was handling a porcelain doll and not wanting to break it. She, too, wanted to relish the moment. After all, he was very fragile. He relaxed his body and let her take over.

The next morning, Mehran was the first to get up. He slid out of the bed, put his pants back on, and sat on the chair next to the bed, looking at Naghmeh. The sun had lit the room. She was beautiful. And then he remembered his parents and tears started to form in his eyes. He was alone. He was the only person left of his family. No brothers. No sisters. No mother or father. It was only him. And then he realized what Naghmeh had done. With their act last night, she had explained very silently and eloquently to him that he was not alone. This morning, he realized that last night they had become one. As long as Naghmeh lived, he would never be alone. What they had shared last night was beautiful and far from meaningless sex. She had shared her love with him. She had sacrificed herself for him in a tender act.

Naghmeh opened her eyes and saw him staring at her. She slowly sat up in the bed cross-legged, one knee up and one knee down, still naked. Mehran wondered for a moment why she hadn't tried to cover or wrap herself with the blanket. She set her chin on her knee and hugged her shin with her arms. Mehran smiled, still teary-eyed. He picked up her shirt from the ground and put it over her shoulders. Neither felt an apology was needed. They both understood the meaning of what they had done.

Mehran broke the silence. "Life is going to be very different for me now."

"How so?"

Mehran didn't answer. He wasn't sure how, but he knew it would.

They left the dorm and rode back in Pari's car that Naghmeh had driven. Neither talked during the short Sunday morning drive. When they pulled in to Nader's driveway, everybody in the house came out. Pari broke into tears as she saw Mehran and grabbed him.

"Mehran, I am so sorry for your loss."

"Thank you, Pari."

Nader and Peyman each gave Mehran hugs, telling him how sorry they were.

Once inside, they sat at the kitchen table. Calls had started pouring in from aunts and uncles, cousins and far family, all from Iran.

Mehran ended up talking with each of them, often tearing up as he received their condolences. Nader wanted to have the ceremonious seventh-day gathering and the fortieth day remembrance for Mehran's mother and father, but Mehran said that wasn't necessary and that he'd have to go back to school in a couple of days so as to not fall behind.

Mehran spent the next couple of days at Pari's house. Naghmeh and Peyman had school, so only Pari and Mehran were home during the day. Mehran slept much of both days. On Tuesday night, the whole family took him back to college as he requested.

Mehran walked upstairs to his dorm room. His friends offered their condolences and assured him they'd be there for him. The mood at the dorm was somber, with everyone trying to respect Mehran and his mourning. Even Charlie was there to shake Mehran's hand and offer his sympathies.

Despite what Naghmeh and Mehran had shared on the very bed in his room, Mehran felt alone. Finally alone and with the door closed, he laid his head on his desk and sobbed. Alone. What an ugly word, he thought.

Chapter Twenty

"Mehran?" asked Kirsten.

"Yeah?"

"Are you okay?"

"I'm sorry. These memories are very strong, and I sometimes lose myself to them," said Mehran. He had left out the part about him and Naghmeh sharing their souls with each other; he didn't want to muddy the waters with Kirsten now that they had just started dating.

Kirsten felt awful for Mehran. Not only had his parents died while he was in school, but he had continued with school without missing a beat, or so she thought. "I don't know how you managed that. I am so sorry."

"I didn't manage it well."

"Do you want to tell me that?"

"Nah. Let's have a good time right now and listen to some music," he said.

"So, with all these records, do you have something you can play that's appropriate for the moment?" she asked.

Mehran thought for a second and then asked, "Would you like to dance?"

Kirsten smiled, tilted her head down a bit, but kept her gaze on Mehran and mumbled, "Sure."

Mehran smiled, walked over to his boxes of records, searched for a minute, pulled out a record, put it on the player, and walked over to Kirsten.

The music started playing.

"What is this?"

"It's called *Cheek to Cheek* by Fred Astaire."

He extended his arm and took Kirsten's hand in his and pulled her close to him. Dancing through the song, their faces were only inches apart. They both remained silent and listened to the song while they danced. At the end of the song, Mehran moved quickly to the player to stop it from advancing to the next song.

"Why did you stop it?"

"Ah, I don't care much for the next song."

"What you played was lovely. I hadn't heard that before. I take it there's much I can learn from this collection of yours."

"I hope so," said Mehran.

"Your apartment is sparse. How come you don't have a TV?"

"With all these records, what do I need a TV for?"

"There's a lot on the TV, especially in a city like Chicago. Have you heard of WTTW?"

"I have, and I donate on a regular basis. I used to have a TV, but I donated it as well; it was distracting me from the music."

Kirsten was intrigued. "You donate to WTTW, but you don't watch it?"

"There's so much I can already spend my time doing that I don't need to be watching any TV."

"Sure, music is great, books are great. But what about when you just want to be mindless?"

"A mind is a terrible thing to waste," said Mehran. "Haven't you ever heard that before?"

"Who says watching TV is a waste of the mind?"

Mehran couldn't argue that point. That argument would run into the morning.

"How about another song to dance to?" Mehran asked.

"How about we just sit and listen to some songs?" Kirsten filled up her wine glass.

They moved Mehran's listening chair out of the way and pushed the couch in front of the speakers.

"What would you like to listen to?"

"How about Beethoven's only violin concerto?"

"All right, but it's on two sides of the LP, so I'll have to flip it in the middle."

"I can deal with that."

Mehran put on Beethoven's *Violin Concerto No. 1* by Jascha Heifetz and sat down. They listened in silence as the music poured from the speakers. Mehran looked at Kirsten several times throughout the first movement. She looked beautiful; her eyes were closed and she was moving her head to the music. Mehran could tell that she was enjoying the concerto. For his part, Mehran's thoughts went back to the dim period after his parents died.

Chapter Twenty-One

After his parents' deaths, Mehran went through the motions of regular school activity, attending his classes and going to the cafeteria for food. But he really didn't eat anything. He didn't even visit the library once that first week back.

A week after he had returned to school, Khaled asked Mehran to go to a party with him at one of the Greek houses. Mehran agreed reluctantly. Once at the party, he grabbed a beer and drank a bit. He remembered how high a pedestal his father had placed alcohol on, and he chugged the beer down his throat.

"Another one," he asked. He downed that one quickly as well. "Give me another one."

The frat guy running the bar said, "Dude, if you want to get fucked up, why don't you do a beer bong?"

Mehran had seen beer bongs before. Usually, the receiver at the end of the tube ended up spilling beer all over his shirt since he couldn't handle the volume of the golden liquid pouring down his throat.

"Let's do it," said Mehran.

"Have you ever done this before?"

"I've seen it done."

"Hey, everybody! We got a virgin bonger here!"

The crowd cheered. In a minute, Mehran was on his knees, holding the end of a tube in his hand. The six-foot long hose tube had a funnel attached at the other end.

"The secret to a good beer bong is to make sure you get all the air out," the frat guy said. He lowered the funnel to the same level as the end Mehran was holding and slowly poured beer through a pitcher into the funnel. The tube quickly filled up until beer was about to spill from the end Mehran was holding. "Put your thumb on it now."

Mehran did as he was told. The frat guy continued to fill the funnel with beer, then got up on a chair to lift the tube.

"Chug! Chug! Chug! Chug!" the crowd cheered.

"Okay, put the tube in your mouth, straighten your neck, and on 'chug' move your thumb."

The crowd was pumped. "Chug! Chug! Chug!"

The frat guy counted down. "Three – two – one – chug!"

Mehran removed his thumb. Beer forced its way into Mehran's mouth and down his throat. Mehran couldn't stand the pressure. The beer had filled his mouth and his esophagus and was making its way to his stomach. The pressure had caused some beer to spill onto his chin and down his shirt. He continued to struggle to capture as much of the beer as possible. When he felt it had stopped, he let go of the tube and fell backward. The crowd cheered.

Mehran thought his stomach was going to explode. A couple of guys helped him up.

"You're no longer a virgin!" said the frat guy.

Mehran continued to dance and drink, his sobriety progressively deteriorating as the night progressed. After he visited the bathroom and took a group piss into a bathtub, Mehran stumbled on the threshold of the door frame and fell forward, laughing non-stop. A guy helped him up and told him that he had probably had enough. Mehran left the party and started walking toward what he believed was his dorm. Less than a few hundred feet from the party, he threw up on the sidewalk. There was nothing but liquid. He hadn't had anything to eat.

The next morning he woke up in his bed with a massive headache. He made his way to the bathroom, chose a stall and sat down. Within seconds, he got up, turned and puked in the toilet. After cleaning his face with toilet paper, Mehran through about last night, but he could not remember anything after throwing up on the sidewalk. He walked out of the bathroom, made his way to his room and passed out on the bed.

He woke up later to someone calling his name.

"Mehran. Dude."

It was Khaled.

"Hey!" he sat up on the bed.

"Man. How are you feeling?"

"Like shit. I threw up again this morning."

"Dude! You were fucking wasted!"

"You were there?"

"I was. Don't you remember talking to me?"

"Shit no. I don't remember walking home."

"You serious?"

"Yeah, I don't remember anything after throwing up outside the house."

"Obviously not from before either! Man, you were crazy. Don't you remember chasing those girls?"

"I chased girls?"

"You kept telling them they were beautiful and that they should fuck you."

"Jesus."

"Yeah! They passed by when you were done puking and we were trying to get you home."

"You tried to get me home? Damn dude. Were they cute?"

Khaled laughed. "Yeah, they were."

"Shit. I need an aspirin."

Mehran got dressed and walked to the drugstore. On his way back, he stopped by the liquor store and picked up a bottle of Smirnoff.

For the next few days, Mehran continued to go through the motions of being in college. He talked with Naghmeh on the telephone several times and filled her in on his adventures at the frat party. Their conversations were very emotional at times. Naghmeh wanted to come and stay with Mehran for the weekend, but she didn't want to raise Nader and Pari's suspicion.

The following weekend, Khaled went home to visit his family. Mehran sat in his room on Saturday afternoon, staring at the bottle of vodka sitting on his desk, still unopened. Naghmeh had asked if he wanted to come home, but he had refused, making an excuse that he had a paper to write. He cracked open the bottle and poured some of the vodka in a dirty glass. He held the glass up high, reminiscing about his father and how proud he would be of his son. "Salamati," *cheers*, Mehran said aloud and downed the glass.

The next morning he got up, again with a headache, but not as much as the previous weekend. He looked at the half-eaten fries and the

2/3 empty bottle of vodka on his desk. He remembered walking over to the fast-food joint nearby and getting the gyros and fries, but didn't remember walking back to the dorm. Is this what his father would have wanted? He wasn't sure. He decided that he'd make the best he could of his Sunday by visiting the library.

Week after week, his routine became the same. Drink on Friday and Saturday nights, and go through the motions during the week. Mehran wasn't interested in going home any longer. He dodged calls from Naghmeh on the weekends, knowing that, should she find out, he'd get an earful about his binge drinking.

Then on the long Thanksgiving weekend, he lied to Naghmeh and her family that he was going on a road trip with some guys to San Francisco. He had no intention of going on a trip, but he also had no intention of spending the weekend at home. The dorms were empty. Everyone had left to spend the holiday with their families. Mehran, on the other hand, had prepared for the five-day holiday by stocking up on vodka.

On Wednesday night, he drank and played games on the Atari and passed out in his bed. On Thursday, he started drinking earlier in the day in smaller doses to pace himself to make the feelings last longer. Mehran left his dorm room door open, in the hope that someone would come and talk with him, but the dorm was empty, except for a couple of students whose families lived far and had no means of flying home.

By late night, the loneliness overcame him and he took his bottle inside his jacket and started to scour the streets in the hope of seeing a friend, a stranger, anybody. As he continued to take swigs from his bottle, a girl in high heels approached him from the opposite direction.

"Feel like having some company, baby?" the girl asked.

"Company?" he slurred.

"Sure, honey. You want some company?"

"Okay!"

"What's your name?"

"Mehran"

"Oh, you're Persian."

"That I am!"

"I love your accent! What are you doing here on Thanksgiving?"

"Looking for you!"

"Awwww, that's sweet." The girl looked around and scanned the area. "You wanna have some fun?"

"I don't know. I want to talk."

"Walk with me so that we're not standing still."

Mehran looked at her. She was quite attractive, wearing a tight, short dress, high heels, lots of makeup and she had long, wavy blonde hair.

"Sure, babe, what's *your* name?"

"Candy," said the girl as she started to walk.

Mehran followed.

"Candy? As in sweet?"

"Yeah, I taste lovely."

"I bet!"

"So, where do you live?"

"I live in one of the dorms."

Candy hesitated. "You're a student?"

"Yeah. I'm studying chemical engineering."

Candy started to walk back the other way.

"Hey! What's wrong?"

"Get lost."

Mehran ran after her. "But why?"

"You're a student. You don't have any money. Talking to me costs money."

Mehran reached into his wallet and pulled out a couple hundred dollars. "I have money. See?"

Candy stopped. "So, what do you want to do?"

"I want to talk, and then I want to fuck you."

"A blowjob is $25 and a fuck is $100. If you want to fuck me in the ass, that's another $50."

"Fuck you in the ass? Seriously? People do that?"

"What will it be?"

"Let's go for the $100. How much to talk to me, too?"

"I'll charge you $25 for a half-hour of talking."

"Does talking while walking back to the dorm cost me, too?"

"No, but I want the money upfront."

Mehran counted $125 and gave it to her. "There. That's good for a half-hour of talking and a fuck."

"Okay, baby. Let's go."

They started to walk back to the dorm. Candy was walking at a fast pace and Mehran began to fall behind. He wondered how she could walk that fast with the high heels she was wearing.

"I just want you to know that I don't do this in dorms. I could get into a lot of trouble."

"Nobody's around. Everyone's gone home for Thanksgiving."

"Yeah, but still."

"Well, if you don't do it in the dorms, I got no other place. Give me back my money."

Candy stopped, and then softened up a little.

"Okay, let's go," she said.

They reached the dorm and made it into Mehran's room.

They sat down and Mehran took his jacket off.

"Hey, you gonna share that bottle?"

Mehran handed her the vodka. She took a swig, looked at her watch, and said, "Okay, your clock is ticking."

Mehran literally wasted his half-hour allotment talking about Iran and telling Candy the story of his life. Candy seemed to soften up more. She had taken a few swigs from the bottle they were sharing. About 45 minutes into their talk, Candy slid her chair closer to him and laid her hand on his thigh while the other hand rubbed his ear lobe, caressed his cheek and grazed his arm and shoulder. She spread her legs and Mehran could see that she wasn't wearing any panties. She had also pushed up her breasts so that they were, actually, falling out of her dress. Eventually, Candy told Mehran to lay on the bed. Mehran did as he was told.

"Don't worry about a thing. Candy will take care of you."

Mehran was somewhat nervous. Candy sensed this, got on her knees beside the bed and thrust her hand inside his pants.

"Oh, feels like you're ready!" she said, smiling.

She unzipped his pants and slid them off. She slid a condom on Mehran and straddled him on the bed.

The next few minutes went by quickly. Candy rode him hard. She moaned, groaned and talked dirty to Mehran. "Yeah, give it to me."

Mehran grabbed Candy's breasts and squeezed.

When Candy could tell that Mehran was close to climax, she increased her moaning. "Yes! Yes! Cum inside me. Yes! Yes!"

The whole event lasted about 6 or 7 minutes. After, Candy got up and gave Mehran a kiss on the cheek. "Thank you, baby! You were awesome."

She left her card on the desk and walked out the door. Mehran passed out.

Chapter Twenty-Two

The needle on the record started to make its tick-tick sound; it had reached the end of the first side. Mehran got up, flipped the record and started the B side, the Larghetto. He moved back to the couch next to Kirsten and got lost in his thoughts again.

Chapter Twenty-Three

On Friday after Thanksgiving, Mehran woke up still naked, and the first thing that he remembered was his evening with Candy, the prostitute. An immense feeling of guilt overtook him. How stupid. How shallow. This very bed in which he had shared an incredible night with Naghmeh had been tainted. A night when he was most in need, when Naghmeh had given herself to him, to show him that he wasn't alone, that he had an everlasting love with her. He had ruined the best memory he had of how a friend had tried to help him through a horrific time. He curled up in bed and started to ball. How he wished Naghmeh were there to comfort him. He had thrown away an opportunity to be with Naghmeh and her family on this holiday. Instead, he had wasted it on booze and the filth roaming the streets. He felt lonelier than ever.

He remained in bed the rest of the day, crying at times or simply staring into space.

Sometime in the afternoon, he moved his eyes around his room, looking for a picture of Naghmeh he had. Laying on the bed, his eyes scanned the bookshelf above his desk. Rather than a picture, a book caught his attention: *Satyagraha in South Africa*. Mehran crawled out of bed, picked up the book from the shelf and crawled back into bed. He opened the inside cover, "*To My Dearest Roshan on his 21st Birthday. With Love, Solmaz.*" He began to read.

Mehran finished reading at 3:15 in the morning. He lay in bed and couldn't get the contents of the book out of his head. He now understood why Roshan had given him the book, and how timely it was that he had read the book that night. Mehran thought about Gandhi's references to Gita and the ideas of inner renunciation, acts a person can do, disregarding one's own well-being or personal rewards. Mehran needed to change his life. He fell asleep with Gandhi's principles of self-purification on his mind.

The next morning, Mehran woke up much more clear-headed and hungry. He lay in bed for a minute, thinking about the events of the past few nights and saw the book still on his bed. He got up and headed to the shower. With warm water, he soaped himself, washing away the filth from the prostitute. He was determined to make the best out of this Saturday. Standing in the shower, he felt thirsty. He turned the handle to cool the water. He continued to turn the handle until the water was frigid. The water splashed off his body and drained below his feet. He opened his mouth and drank the droplets of water smashing his face until he felt full. The cold shower awakened him, he thought, but perhaps not as much as the book he had read the previous night. After a few minutes, he turned the faucet and toweled off.

It was 11:45, and he knew the library would be open from noon until 5. He put on his clothes and left the dorm.

At the library, he grabbed a sandwich from the vending machine and started searching the card catalog for books by Gandhi along with interpretations of his books. He picked up the "Bhagavad Gita" referenced in Satyagraha, and skimmed through it. Figuring that in his hungover state the previous day he may not have gotten the full depth of the book, he picked up the English copy of "Satyagraha" along with a few other books and checked out just before the library closed. Mehran returned to his dorm and started a load of laundry; he washed his bedsheets while he read one of the books.

For the next few weeks, Mehran focused his attention on a selection of books about revolution and the revolutionary life. He read books on the injustices done to people by the Roman Catholic Church throughout the ages, by oppressive regimes and by the rich. He missed many classes while he was reading, either in his dorm room or at the library. He started adding foreign news to his daily reading list. Not a day went by when he wasn't aware of what was happening in the Middle East.

The night with the prostitute was the last night Mehran had a drink. He still had the bottles of vodka on his desk, but he had no interest in drinking them any more. His life had found a new purpose.

That December, in 1985, Mehran made the decision to move from California. When he had applied to colleges in the United States, he had been accepted by several prestigious schools, including Northwestern University in Chicago. He contacted Northwestern and explained his situation, again he applied for a major in chemical engineering, this time with a minor in political science. Northwestern University seemed hesitant to enroll a student mid-semester. Mehran called the admissions office and pleaded with them.

The assistant dean of admissions in a phone interview asked him the reason he wanted to leave California.

Mehran thought much about the reasons behind his decision. A shallow justification was the weather; it was too sunny. Mehran liked cloudy days more than sunny ones. The assistant dean chuckled at that, suggesting that living in California was the holy grail for most people living in the Midwest. Another reason Mehran cited was the lack of culture: since living as an Iranian in Los Angeles was nothing out of the ordinary, and massive sections of the city were devoted to Iranian stores and purposes. The last reason, Mehran said, was that he needed a new start on life.

In the end, the ability to pay tuition without any financial aid was the deciding factor. Northwestern accepted Mehran for the winter quarter.

Mehran completed all of these negotiations without Nader, Pari or Naghmeh knowing of his plan. It was time he leveled with them.

Christmas holidays could not come fast enough. Mehran finished the first half of his sophomore year at UC Irvine, achieving mediocre grades, not bad considering all that had happened to him that semester. He packed his dorm room in preparation for the move to Chicago.

Mehran spent the Christmas holidays at home, with Nader, Pari, Parisa, Naghmeh and Peyman. He and Naghmeh spent countless hours walking on the beach, talking about his feelings about his parents being gone. Mehran had a deep love for Naghmeh, not only because they had made love, but also because she seemed genuinely concerned with his wellbeing. They understood each other. He felt like they had become one.

Mehran told Naghmeh about Northwestern first. He had to convince her of his reasons for moving out of California. She begged him not to leave, telling him that she would miss him immensely. He assured her that he would miss her just as much, but starting fresh would be the best thing for him. She understood. Having lost his parents just after being separated from them had taken a toll on Mehran. She finally gave him a hug and kissed him on his cheek in approval of his plan.

Mehran broke the news to Pari, who adamantly refused to accept his decision, though ultimately she agreed it was his to make. Nader wasn't any happier, but he also felt that Mehran was his own master and commander and that his destiny was in his own hands.

The one other person he had to talk to about his move was his uncle Roozbeh, who was supposed to liquidate everything and make money available to him. It wasn't so much that Mehran needed all the money accessible to him, but he still needed to make arrangements and let his uncle know what his plans were.

Uncle Roozbeh told Mehran that his family house was under repair; after the repairs were done, it would be sold. Barbod's partners had purchased his share of the company, and the cash was available to transfer to Mehran. Given the falling value of the Iranian currency, Mehran thought it would be best to transfer the money into dollars as soon as possible. He told his uncle he would contact him with a bank account in Chicago to transfer the money into.

Mehran shipped his packed boxes via freight to Chicago. On January 4, 1986, Mehran and Nader's family went to the airport. Mehran's departure had everyone except Nader in tears. Mehran assured them that he would visit as often as he could, and he invited them to come to Chicago as well.

January in Chicago was very cold that year – even more so than Mehran had expected. He checked into a hotel for a few days while he looked for a place to rent. Eventually, he settled on an apartment in the Lakeview neighborhood, not too far north of downtown, and accessible via the 'L' and buses to Northwestern campuses in both north suburban Evanston and downtown. He hired a moving van to collect his belongings from Union Station to take to his apartment, since he wasn't old enough to rent a truck and haul them himself.

The first items Mehran bought for his apartment were a Linn LP12 turntable, a Macintosh Mac 1900 receiver and a pair of Energy 22 Reference Connoisseur speakers. He frequented the stores selling LP records, scouring them for any jazz records he could find.

As the weather warmed with spring, Mehran discovered a fascinating thing: garage sales. He spent much of his Saturday mornings hunting sales for old records, classical and jazz in particular.

Attending Northwestern proved a challenge, especially minoring in political science. The number of classes and credits Mehran had to take meant he would spend an extra two quarters beyond the first 4 years finishing his degree. He took Spanish as a foreign language every quarter to expand his knowledge of the language. He didn't make many friends since he was very busy with schoolwork and didn't live on campus, but he did become friends with two girls who lived downstairs from him. Shortly thereafter, though, the girls moved out, and a married couple, Pavel and Olga, moved in.

Mehran also took time to learn how to cook. Eating cafeteria food in California, he had become accustomed to fast food. Cooking hadn't been possible then, but after reading Gandhi's view on self-sufficiency, Mehran began to practice skills that would apply to every aspect of his life, from cooking to fixing a broken lamp or fixing a leaky faucet to doing his own taxes. The one thing that made all of this possible – and something simply not available in Iran – was the sheer amount of information he could find in the library.

His ability to fix anything, he felt, was only limited by the tools and educational materials he had available to him.

Yet, even Mehran learned that there is a limit to what a person can do. Watching PBS's Bob Ross create a mountainous painting in less than 30 minutes lead Mehran to believe he could as well. But after just one session in front of the canvas, he set that effort aside.

Naghmeh visited often. She came in March and then again in June. In July, Mehran visited everyone in California for a week. He told them about his apartment and about all the skills he had tried. Pari was happy for him, for it seemed Mehran had overcome the death of his parents. He played a few games with Peyman on the new Compaq computer the family had purchased. Peyman's favorite game was "Starflight," a space exploration game. Mehran was pleasantly surprised with new computer games, which had become more immersive and required more thought to play.

The week went by quickly. Mehran promised to return often. They took Mehran to the airport to return to Chicago.

Chapter Twenty-Four

"Wow!" said Kirsten. "I had never heard this performance before. Heifetz was truly amazing."

"He died just a few years ago. All these great performers who just passed recently. Don't you wish you could have seen them live?"

"Absolutely." Then, "I think we should go to the Chicago Symphony Orchestra sometime."

Mehran smiled. He was sure now that he had found the right girl.

Mehran grabbed the bottle of wine and moved to fill Kirsten's glass.

"I don't think I'll be able to drive if I drink any more," Kirsten said. She pondered the idea of staying for more and then taking a cab home. Instead, she asked, "Would it be okay if I spent the night here?"

"Of course. You can have my bed, and I'll sleep on the couch."

"No, I can't do that to you. I can sleep on the couch."

Mehran thought for a second. *Is she tarofing? Does she not want to sleep in my bed? Or is she just modest?*

"Kirsten, whatever you like. This couch turns into a bed, and you can sleep here if you want."

"That sounds good. In that case, pour me another," and she handed her glass to Mehran. He opened another bottle of Cabernet.

"What do we listen to now?" asked Kirsten.

"Whatever you'd like."

"I chose the last piece, how about you choose this time?"

Mehran put on a few jazz pieces, one after another. He explained in between each about what they would hear next. After he put on the fourth piece, he turned around and realized that Kirsten had closed her eyes. He turned the music down, then turned the stereo off. He took a blanket from the closet, put it on Kirsten and dimmed the lights. He went into his bedroom and silently closed the door. As Mehran passed the frame on the wall, he looked at it and paused. His eyes watered with tears, and he said softly, "I'm sorry." He wasn't sure why he said he was sorry. Perhaps it was the wine. He turned off the lights and fell asleep.

Mehran woke up in the middle of the night to the sound of his door opening. Kirsten stood at the door.

"Hey," Kirsten whispered.

"Hey. Are you okay? I didn't want to wake you up."

"That was nice of you. But it got cold out here."

Mehran was about to get out of bed when Kirsten walked over and slid in under the covers.

"You think you can keep your hands to yourself?" she asked.

"I'm offended you asked. I'm a gentleman."

"Good, because it's a lot warmer under this blanket than it is on your couch."

With Kirsten in his bed, Mehran couldn't sleep. He tossed and turned until Kirsten asked, "For the love of God, would you please stop moving?" He laid still then and let his memories settle him.

Chapter Twenty-Five

Mehran could have graduated in December 1988, but Pari insisted that she wanted to come to his graduation ceremony and see him with his cap and gown. He decided to wait until June for Northwestern's annual graduation ceremony. So Mehran took an extra two quarters of courses that he was interested in, but which had nothing to do with his major or minor. In the winter quarter he took two culinary classes and an advanced Spanish class; in the spring quarter he took a photography class, the continuation of advanced Spanish, and another culinary class. With a light schedule during the last two quarters, Mehran had time to look for a job in chemical engineering. After searching for a month and interviewing at several companies, he landed a job as a paper materials engineer. He would be responsible for quality improvement made to the array of paper products the company produced, from paper for newspapers to cardboard for frozen dinner packaging. He didn't think the position had a future, at least none that he was interested in, but it would be a good start for a resume that was lacking quite a bit in volume and details, since Mehran had never held a job in his life. The job paid $65,000 annually and came with an array of benefits; the only caveat would be that he could not start until he had graduated. That was fine with Mehran.

In June 1989, Pari, Nader, Peyman and Naghmeh flew to Chicago to see Mehran graduate. Pari looked upon Mehran as her own son and was as proud of Mehran as her other children. Peyman was now 14 and growing up fast. Naghmeh was studying at The Art Institute of California. Parisa had just finished her second year at law school and was doing an internship at the county courthouse. Nader had purchased another dealership, and Pari was taking real estate classes in the hope of becoming a broker.

The family stayed in Chicago for a couple of days. Peyman and Naghmeh stayed at Mehran's apartment, while Pari and Nader stayed at a hotel downtown. Peyman hadn't been to Mehran's place before, so he was amazed when he saw the collection of records Mehran had amassed.

"Dude! Do you have anything besides classical and jazz?"

Mehran laughed. "No, not really. What are you looking for?"

"I don't know. You got any Tom Petty? Elvis Costello? The Cure?"

Mehran didn't have any of those. "No, but I have a New Order LP."

"Cool! *Bizarre Love Triangle*?"

"That I've got!"

Mehran put the record on. Peyman nodded his head in approval and smiled and then continued to look through the records. Mehran and Naghmeh went to the kitchen to open a bottle of wine. In the kitchen, Naghmeh unexpectedly grabbed Mehran by the waist and wrapped her arms around him.

"I'm really proud of you. Your graduation would have made your parents proud. I know it does mine."

Mehran reciprocated, wrapping his arms around her. She gave him a quick kiss on the lips.

"How's school going?" Mehran asked.

Disappointed, Naghmeh withdrew her arms. "It's going good. I'm learning a lot. The more I learn, the more I understand that there's more out there than I can learn."

"Absolutely true. The more we read, the more we realize how minuscule our knowledge really is."

"So, do you have a girlfriend?"

"I wish! I don't have time for a girlfriend."

"You have to *make* time."

"Well, now that my studies are done, I'll be on the prowl," he grinned. "How about you?"

"Do I have a girlfriend?"

Mehran laughed. "No dummy! Do you have a boyfriend?"

"What if I like girls?"

Mehran hadn't thought about that. "Do you?"

"No. Not in that way. I think a woman's body is way more beautiful than a man's, but I'm not sexually attracted to girls."

"So, do you have a boyfriend?"

"I have had many, but none right now." She started, "I –" and then stopped.

"You what?"

"I – I always tried to recreate what you and I had that one night, but I couldn't. It just wasn't the same with anybody else."

Mehran knew precisely what she meant. He had hooked up with a few girls in the years since that night with Naghmeh. He even dated one of them for a couple of months. Ultimately, he convinced himself that he could never again have what he and Naghmeh shared that night. "I don't think we can ever recreate that."

Tears collected in Naghmeh's eyes. Mehran thought about what he had said. "I'm sorry."

Naghmeh shook her head, dismissing his words. Tears were rolling down her face.

Mehran went to hug her, and she pushed him away. "You never know. We may feel at some point the need to give ourselves to each other again," said Mehran.

She continued to shake her head and said, "No, that's not it. Believe me, I would love to make love to you right now."

Mehran remained in place, puzzled, waiting for her to compose herself.

She grabbed a paper towel from the kitchen counter and wiped her face. "Mehran. I have AIDS," Naghmeh said as she broke into tears again.

Mehran felt the walls close in on them. *AIDS? Why? Why Naghmeh?* His thoughts fast-forwarded to a few years ahead, thinking about a life without Naghmeh. *Why? Why must all good things in my life be complicated and come to an end?*

"I have had symptoms for the past year. I went to the clinic at the school and they ran some tests."

Mehran was stunned. He managed to ask, "Do Nader and Pari know?"

"No. Parisa knows. I told her after I found out a few weeks ago."

Thoughts again raced through Mehran's mind. "How do they know? Did they repeat the tests?" he asked.

"Yes," she continued crying.

He couldn't take it any longer. He lunged at her, grabbed her face, and pulled her into his chest. He held her there and let her cry on him. Peyman walked into the kitchen. "Hey, what's up?"

"Nothing. Can you give us a few minutes, bud?"

Peyman looked at Naghmeh crying and then at Mehran. "Sure," and he walked back out.

Naghmeh made space between her and Mehran. "You should get tested. I don't know when I contracted the virus."

Mehran thought of himself. *What if I contracted the virus that night? Will I die, too? What about the few girls I have been with in the meantime?* Mehran had practiced safe sex with all, but there was his girlfriend of 2 months. He decided that there was no point in worrying about it until he had had his own test results. "Naghmeh, you've got to tell your parents."

"I know. I know."

After some silence, Mehran tried to question Naghmeh about her condition and the doctors' plans to care for her, but she didn't want to talk about her condition. She promised him that she'd tell her parents when they returned to California.

After they composed themselves, they went to the living room, carrying their wine. Peyman was playing *How Does It Feel*. Mehran and Naghmeh sat on the opposite ends of the sofa, while Peyman looked through the record collection, bopping his head to the rhythm.

Mehran looked at Naghmeh. He was worried about her future. But she had been pretty clear in the kitchen that she didn't want to discuss her situation. He extended his arm on top of the sofa back to the middle and so did Naghmeh. Their fingers met and played a dance while they stared into each other's eyes. Eventually, Mehran leaned over enough so that they could lock their fingers for the remainder of the song.

When the Shahab family left on Sunday, Mehran went to the Northwestern library to research HIV and AIDS. Literature was extremely limited; the disease was only discovered a few years prior. The only known treatment was an antiretroviral medication called azidothymidine, or AZT for short, but it wasn't an actual treatment. It was meant to slow the progress of HIV into AIDS. Naghmeh had already been diagnosed with AIDS. There didn't appear to be any treatment for her condition. Mehran thought the outcome looked dim. The more he read, the more he developed a knot in his stomach. After hours of reading, he laid his head on the table and sobbed.

That summer, Mehran qualified to apply for U.S. citizenship. He had lived in the United States for 5 years. He went through the process and received his citizenship a few months later.

Though Mehran couldn't yet take time off from his new job, he still flew to California at least one weekend a month to spend time with Naghmeh. She was on a regimen of drugs to slow the symptoms, though the doctors indicated there was no hope of survival. The medications only prolonged the inevitable.

In summer 1991, Mehran took two weeks vacation. He flew to Los Angeles, rented a white Ford Mustang convertible and took Naghmeh away with him. Their plan was to go to Northern California's Redwood National Park, swing over the Sierra Nevada mountains and see Tahoe, Reno and Yosemite before going back to Los Angeles.

Driving up the coastal highway was picturesque. They stopped often to admire the beauty of the Pacific Ocean and the California coast. One stop happened to be at an old, abandoned cemetery. They walked through it to reach the cliffs overlooking the ocean.

Naghmeh was reading the headstones and calculating the ages of the dead. She wondered what may have killed Abigail Williams in 1933 at the age of 27, and how 24-year-old Gertrude "Gertie" Schloss managed to die in 1873. Thoughts of death ran through her head. *Childbirth? Falling from a carriage? How nice it would be to know what had happened to these women.*

"I don't want to be buried. As beautiful as this is, there's no point. Once you're dead, you're dead," she said to Mehran.

"If not buried, then what?"

"I want to be cremated."

"Your parents will argue. Iranian custom is pretty strict about this."

"I don't care."

Mehran stayed silent. He enjoyed the feel of the breeze coming from the ocean on his face. He walked over to Naghmeh and put his arm around her.

"I will let your parents know."

She put her arm around his waist and leaned her head into him.

They stayed the night in Monterey and went to the aquarium the next morning before heading further north into San Francisco. The drive from Monterey to San Francisco was breathtaking. They passed through Santa Cruz and stopped in Half Moon Bay to buy sandwiches and go to the beach to eat a late lunch and watch surfers catch waves.

They drove through South San Francisco, fighting some traffic before crossing the Golden Gate Bridge into Sausalito and their hotel. That night they ate at a hole-in-the-wall Italian restaurant in San Francisco. The wine flowed easily from the hand of the one and only waiter at the restaurant and the food was delicious, although Naghmeh had little appetite nowadays. She had lost some weight, visible on her already slender body. Mehran had a bit too much wine to drive, though, so after dinner they headed down the street and walked along the bay. They could see the lights from Alcatraz and Sausalito. They walked hand in hand, mostly in silence. Mehran wondered what she was thinking and thought she may be thinking about the nearness of her impending mortality. That was all he could think about, how he would lose her in the near future, about their relationship and everything she had done for him. Curiosity got the best of him.

"What are you thinking?" asked Mehran.

"Nothing."

"Nothing?"

"Yeah, really nothing. I am just enjoying walking with you."

Mehran thought if she was able to ignore her future, then so would he. "And I, too."

They walked all the way to Fisherman's Wharf, before deciding that Mehran was okay to drive. They took a cab to their rental car and drove back to the hotel.

San Francisco was under clouds the next day. They parked their car on the north side of the bay and started to walk across the bridge. Mehran had brought his camera and took many photos, some of the bridge, whose red color against the white clouds and the fog had created an unearthly scene. He also took many pictures of Naghmeh, some with her posing and some while she looked out over the bay. They reached the middle of the bridge, a spot that was clearly marked; it was a very popular spot among tourists by the count of them taking pictures.

"What do you want to do? Do you want to cross the bridge, or do you want to go back?" Mehran asked.

"I don't care. Let's just walk."

Mehran took her hand in his and continued walking. They walked silently, until Naghmeh said, "You know, I really loved you."

Mehran paused. "I know."

"No, I mean I *really* loved you."

"You mean?"

"Yes. I mean I wanted to be with you."

Mehran didn't know what to say. He played along. "We *were* together."

"No, we weren't. We were together for just one night. I loved you. I wanted to be with you all the time."

Mehran remained silent.

"Say something."

"Why? Why me?"

Naghmeh took her time to answer. "You were simple. I could read you. I don't mean that in a bad way. What I mean is that when I looked at you, when I interacted with you, how you behaved was who you were. I didn't have to guess or be suspicious whether you were genuine or not. And the way you loved Bahar, the way she broke your heart, it broke my heart, too. I felt your heart break, deep within me," she said as she pounded her chest.

Mehran remembered a lecture in his psychology class when the professor had talked about the difference between sympathy and empathy. Mehran had mixed feelings about empathy. When he heard about someone else's pain, he literally felt that pain in his guts. He didn't try to make someone feel better by pointing out how their situation could be worst, but rather he put himself in their shoes and felt what it must feel like to be the other person in the situation. He thought empathy could be considered a gift or a curse. A gift because it helped connect two individuals. A curse because it caused pain for the individual who wasn't in the dire situation. He had decided during that lecture that he was given a gift and not a curse. It didn't matter that he suffered because of the current situation of another person.

He realized then that all these years he had not read Naghmeh's emotions correctly. He hadn't realized that she was, just like him, empathetic in nature.

"You never gave me any cues."

"Cues? I even told you I loved you," Naghmeh yelled as tears started to roll down her cheeks.

"Right before you told me that my parents died?"

"I suppose so," Naghmeh managed to say between her tears. She paused for a minute. "Did you ever love me?"

Naghmeh's yelling and crying had touched Mehran, and he was feeling deep empathy for her. To have loved someone as she had, only for it to not be reciprocated. How awful she must have felt. How Mehran's life may have changed had they actually made a solid connection. How it may have even prevented her ailment. He wanted to cry, but he couldn't. He was simply bewildered and numb.

He finally managed to say, "Of course I did, and I still do. But it's probably not the kind of love you were hoping for. I love you as a human being, as someone who cares for me a lot. I would have loved for the two of us to be together, but the circumstances never happened. After that night, it took a lot of soul searching for me to find my way back to the path I'm on now. I did some things I'm ashamed of and didn't even feel that you'd want to hear from me." Then he told Naghmeh about his ordeal with alcohol and the prostitute, about how he felt that he had betrayed Naghmeh and what she had done for him that night. Naghmeh's empathetic nature tore her apart at that moment. She wished she would have seen Mehran more during that time. *Missed connections,* Naghmeh thought. How things may have turned out differently with a little communication.

"Naghmeh. What you did for me that night was immense. It made me feel not lonely, right after my last connections to this world were severed. You have no idea how much respect and love I developed for you after that night." Finally, Mehran said, "I wish I could turn back time and do things differently."

"Me, too."

"I do love you. You know that."

"I do."

As they embraced near the center of Golden Gate Bridge they cried on one another's shoulders.

"I love you Naghmeh. I'm here now. I don't want the inevitable to happen." Mehran realized he started every sentence with "I." How he had centered everything upon himself. But there was no point in explaining things he was sure she knew.

He held her at arms' length and looked into her eyes, "What do you want me to do? Tell me."

Naghmeh knew of nothing. There was nothing he could do. She had this unknown disease ravaging her body, and based on everything she had read, she was doomed to die. But, death notwithstanding, she felt if there was a chance for them to be with each other for the rest of her life, she'd want that.

Reluctantly, she asked, "You love me now. Can you love me until I die?" She felt selfish asking for this, but her feelings for Mehran were so strong that she didn't even think about the consequences of what she was asking.

Mehran closed the space between them. He laid his lips on hers and kissed her deeply. "Let me make up for the opportunity we missed. I'll love you as I do right now, this moment. As it was meant to be," Mehran said.

Naghmeh put her head down and cried. She felt ashamed of asking him to love her, and said so through her tears. Mehran stopped her. "It's not like that. I have loved you since that very night. We belong to each other. We just didn't realize it back then. We do now. I am yours. I'm here now. And I love you."

Naghmeh hugged him, buried her face in his chest and sobbed.

For the rest of the vacation, Mehran felt closer to Naghmeh that he had ever before. They enjoyed taking hikes through the national parks and seeing the amazing scenery nature had created, although even these short excursions took a toll on Naghmeh. She often stopped to catch her breath. In Tahoe, they circled the crystal-clear lake in the car and took the gondola to the top of the mountain. From there, they could see the shape of the lake. *It almost looks like Illinois*, Mehran thought.

That night, they stayed at the Silver Legacy Resort Casino in Reno, taking their free drinks in exchange for their contribution to the casino's funds. They played a bit of everything and lost at most. Neither had ever been to a casino before, so the whole experience was new and entertaining, especially because they were sharing it. That night, and for the rest of the trip, they slept in the same bed and held each other.

After Mehran returned to Chicago, he continued to visit Naghmeh often. They considered the idea of her moving to Chicago, but Naghmeh thought it better to stay with her parents. Her condition was deteriorating rapidly. He could tell during his last few visits to California that the medications she was on were no longer working. Lesions had developed over her body, and she was losing her strength. Her parents wanted to keep her at home, which increased her immobility and contributed to her muscle fatigue.

Mehran noticed Naghmeh's deterioration and wanted to be with her. He asked his employer for a leave of absence, but the request was denied since there would be nobody to perform his functions. Mehran chose to quit his job in fall 1992. He flew to California to spend an extended time with Naghmeh. She scolded him for quitting his job, but they both knew that she was thankful.

By this time, Naghmeh was in a wheelchair. Mehran often pushed Naghmeh to the beach where they would sit for hours. One night, he arranged for all their beach friends, at least those who were still living in the area, to get together. They made a fire, played songs and danced. Naghmeh smiled throughout the night.

Two months after Mehran arrived, Naghmeh contracted pneumonia and was admitted to the hospital. Between her family and Mehran, Naghmeh's bedside was never unattended. Her condition worsened.

One evening, a few nights after Naghmeh was admitted, Mehran stayed behind after everyone went home. He turned the lights down to make her more comfortable. He was asleep on the chair by her bed when he heard her call his name.

"Mehran."

"Yes?"

"I'm dying," said Naghmeh. Her speaking was quiet and slow.

"Stop it. You're gonna get better and leave this hospital on your own."

"No, I'm not." She stared at Mehran. "Can I have some water please?"

Mehran poured a bit of water and held it up to her lips.

"Open the drawer over there. I have something for you," she said.

Mehran opened the drawer. "Your purse and your clothes are here."

"Open my purse. There's a knotted shoelace in there."

Mehran opened the purse and searched for the shoelace. It was buried in a corner. "Here it is."

"I want you to keep this as a reminder of my love for you. The knot is called the 'True Lovers' Knot.' I learned it in art class and made it out of my own shoelace. I was thinking of you when I tied it."

Mehran wrapped his fingers around the shoelace and squeezed it, leaned over her and kissed her on her forehead.

"I want to go."

"Honey, they will not release you in this condition."

"No. I am done. I am ready."

Her subtle tone was purposeful, and Mehran understood. But he remained in denial. His feelings betrayed him, as tears started to collect in his eyes. "No! You are not done!"

"Mehran. I want you to remember my love for you."

"I will. I will never forget you."

"Tell me that you love me."

Mehran cried, "I love you. I love you." He laid his head on her chest and continued to cry.

She moved her arm and put it on his back, "You will be fine. I will miss you."

"No. Please don't go. I love you. I promise to always love you. Please. Stay with me. Naghmeh –"

"I want to, but –"

She stopped talking.

He lifted his head and, just like that, she was gone. Her arm fell to the side of the bed.

Mehran fell to his knees, held her arm and continued to cry. A minute later, a nurse walked into the room, turned up the lights, checked the monitors hooked up to Naghmeh, and called for the doctor. She then walked over to Mehran and put her hand on his shoulder.

Mehran sat on the ground until the doctor came in.

"Time of death, 2:34 a.m., December 4," the doctor pronounced after a few minutes. He turned to Mehran. "I am so sorry for your loss."

Mehran walked out of the room like a zombie. He walked over to the nurses' station, asked if he could borrow the phone, and called home. "I think you should come back to the hospital."

"Is she okay?" Pari asked.

"Come to the hospital, Pari."

Nader and Pari arrived in tears. Mehran had never seen Nader cry. Mehran's tears continued until he saw Peyman crying. Mehran took hold of him and headed outside.

"When did you know?" Peyman asked.

"That night when you caught her crying in my kitchen," Mehran answered.

Peyman remained silent for a long time. "I can't believe she's gone."

"You will miss her greatly, Peyman. But we must go on living."

Naghmeh was cremated a couple of days later and her ashes were given to Nader. Nader brought them home in the cardboard box they came in. He placed it on the table, and they all sat down around it. Pari was crying while they all looked at what Naghmeh had been reduced to. They decided that they would scatter her ashes in the Pacific Ocean, as tribute to the free soul she had been for much of her life. They had purchased five cremation lockets so that each could keep a portion of her remains with them. The lockets were already filled and sealed at the crematorium. Nader handed out the lockets.

They hired a boat for the five of them and rode offshore until they couldn't see the beach any longer. Nader opened the cardboard box, unsnapped the inner box and took out the plastic bag containing Naghmeh's ashes. He unsealed the bag and asked the captain to drive the boat while he slowly and steadily emptied the contents of the bag into the ocean.

Mehran's locket was in his pocket. He felt the urge to listen to one of his favorite blues songs, *St. James Infirmary Blues*. He would have to wait until he returned to Chicago, so he played the song in his head:

> *I went down to the St. James Infirmary,*
> *Saw my baby there,*
> *Stretched out on a long, white table,*
> *So cold, so sweet, so fair.*

Let her go, let her go, may God bless her,
Wherever she may be,
She can look this wide world over,
But she'll never find a sweet man like me

Mehran thought the song was a little self-absorbed at the end of the chorus, but it was the combination of the tune and the lyrics that made the song what it was.

Back at the house, they had a small gathering, mostly Naghmeh's friends and close family friends. There was a table set up with pictures of Naghmeh from various times of her life. Many photos were of her on the beach with her friends, but Mehran also found a picture of Naghmeh's first time on her bicycle without her training wheels, a photo of her driving for the first time, birthday pictures, and a family picture Nader had hired a professional photographer to take of the whole family, including Mehran. The photo was taken just about the time Naghmeh and Mehran were becoming friends. The setup on the table, with a framed studio photo of Naghmeh with a ribbon triangulating a corner of the frame was too much to bear. Mehran walked away.

He walked over to Nader and for the first time, gave him his condolences. He then walked over to Pari, gave her a hug, and gave his condolences to her, and then to Parisa and Peyman. He grabbed a beer and walked out to the back yard.

Soon after, Nader came out, holding a beer as well, and stood by Mehran.

"I never asked her how she contracted HIV," said Nader.

"Does it matter?"

"I suppose not. On the other hand, I feel like I could walk up to the person responsible and just kill him."

"He's probably either suffered the same or is suffering right now."

"Good! Because if he's not dead, I want him to continue suffering."

Mehran thought about what Nader was saying. *That is one way of looking at things. The other way, and the way Naghmeh would have looked at things, is that it's not good for anyone to suffer.* "Everyone should be afforded the dignity to die well," Naghmeh had said to him once. Mehran believed that Naghmeh did die without much suffering, compared to some other AIDS patients he had read about. *Everyone should be afforded the dignity to die well,* he agreed in his head.

He stayed a few more days before heading back to Chicago.

Chapter Twenty-Six

Searching for a job in January in Chicago was not easy. The balance in his bank account stood a bit over $500,000, and he had another $7 million invested in various bonds, mutual funds, real estate funds and more. Mehran didn't need to find a job right away, but he felt that he needed to busy himself. It was by luck when one of his co-workers from the paper mill called him. He said that after Mehran quit, management hired a consulting firm to oversee a re-haul of the engineering team. The consulting firm recommended that they restructure the teams and ended up promoting a dweeb to head the engineering team. Mehran's friend had taken a better job at a competing paper company. The competitor was expanding its reach into Chicago and the Midwest and was opening a new mill. They needed someone to oversee their team of engineers. Mehran's former co-worker thought he would be a perfect fit for the job.

Mehran's interview with the company went well. He and the interviewer clicked instantly. Initially, Mehran had concerns about the amount of work that would be required for the job. He wanted to make sure he'd have time available outside of the office, but the interviewer assured him that the hours would be manageable after the new mill was up and running. Mehran took the job, which paid $87,000 a year.

Mehran worked very hard for the next year. The mill became operational shortly after Mehran started. Overseeing the team of engineers, while challenging, was enjoyable and fun. He made a few friends at work; they occasionally hung around late on Fridays to drink a few beers and play poker. Just as the company had said, work hours slowed down after the first year and the job was quite manageable.

Mehran's life outside of work revolved around his music collection, his favorite music stores and his favorite jazz bars. He would often zero in on a tune and continue listening to it until he knew every note. He frequented his local music stores, especially resale ones, in search of rare LP records. By now he had added a Rotel RCD-955AX compact disc player to his setup, since newer recordings were only available on CDs.

Mehran had a bicycle so that he could travel the city easier and exercise as well. On weekends, he biked the path in front of Lake Michigan. On his way home, he would stop for groceries and carry them home on his bicycle. He reserved the use of taxis for those times when he needed to purchase more than he could handle on the bike.

His apartment was relatively bare with only a few necessities, such as a table and chairs. He had a sleeper couch, along with a listening chair positioned the perfect distance and height from his speakers so that his ears would line up with the tweeters when he sank in the chair. Milk crates holding LP records covered the floor. A large number of book-filled shelves were scattered through the apartment. His bed was queen-sized with a simple antique headboard he had picked up at a garage sale and refinished. Across from his bed, hanging on the wall, was a special frame containing the shoelace Naghmeh had given to him on her deathbed. He used to carry the locket containing her ashes in his pocket at all times, but he was extremely worried that he would lose the locket. So he visited a crematorium and had the ashes split into a second locket. Then he made a unique frame to hold the knotted shoelace up against the front glass, with a compartment beneath it to store the locket behind the glass as well. He often stood in front of the frame and thought of Naghmeh. Not a day went by, though, when he didn't think of the other loved ones he had lost, his parents.

The only exception to his sparse setup was his well-stocked kitchen. Mehran cooked often and always took leftovers to the office, where his friends would devour the food he brought. He was told that he was a good cook, although he believed he still needed more practice.

Eventually, Mehran made it a practice to take two vacations a year, each for two weeks. He traveled much of Europe and Central and South Americas. Of course, he could not return to Iran because of his illegal departure.

Visiting central American countries was an eye-opener for Mehran. He saw first-hand what poverty looked like, something he had barely gotten a glimpse of in Iran. Traveling by car in the countries, he spent countless hours with the people in their villages and huts, often preferring to stay in huts with the locals as opposed to hotels and motels. He carried his own sleeping bag throughout these trips so as not to burden the families he stayed with. He broke bread and ate with them, usually sitting on the ground as they did. Upon departure, he compensated the families handsomely. Mehran compiled an immense collection of quality photos of the indigenous people on most of his trips. He captured many images of everyday life on his trips to Mexico, Guatemala, Belize and other countries.

One thing that always amazed him was the prevalence of satellite television in poor, rural areas. No matter how poor people were in the countries he visited, they always managed to have a television. He thought that was interesting, since he didn't own a television back in his apartment in Chicago, and so he questioned his hosts on this choice. The single common answer among them all was that television was their only source of entertainment and that life without entertainment was no fun. Much of the entertainment from the television revolved around seeing how the people of the world lived. The satellite dishes and the televisions were always hand-me-downs since these people couldn't afford to buy new televisions.

He continued to visit the doctor and getting tested for the HIV virus every 6 months since Naghmeh had told him in 1989. His results were always negative. By 1996 11 years had passed since his only sexual encounter with Naghmeh. He decided that he was in the clear.

It was at this point that he decided to liquidate some of his bond holdings and convert them to bank CDs to have them more available. He chose to open an account with a non-American bank in case he would decide to invest his money abroad, and chose the Swiss Bank Corp. specifically because it was headquartered in Switzerland and would allow him the most flexibility to access his money and invest it. One Friday morning, he got up and decided to visit the bank to inquire about their services. He was directed to the offices of an international personal banker named Marie.

Chapter Twenty-Seven

The next morning, Kirsten woke up before Mehran and prepared to go home. Mehran was a bit disappointed. He wasn't sure what he was hoping for, but he knew that he didn't want her to leave like that in the morning. They made plans to talk in the afternoon.

Mehran cleaned the dishes from the previous night. It was too early to head to the record store, so he rode his bike to the lake and enjoyed the breezy May weather. When he came back, he noticed a note stuck to his doorbell. "Meet me at the Art Institute – Kirsten." A big smile filled his face. Kirsten seemed to surprise him all the time, starting with when she had called back to confirm that they could date, and now her return to his home in just under 4 hours after she left that morning. He showered and took a cab to the Art Institute. He wasn't sure where to wait for her, so he decided that he'd stand outside near one of the lion statues.

After waiting a bit, he felt a pair of hands close over his eyes from behind.

"Kirsten," he said as he turned around.

Kirsten's smile was beautiful. "The Art Institute is a good place to be on a Sunday, yes?"

He leaned forward and whispered in her ear, "I would have met you at the bottom of hell if you told me to."

Kirsten laughed. "Well, let's hope we have plenty of better places than that to meet before we run out." They looked into each other's eyes for a brief moment before Mehran took her hand and headed to the ticket booth.

"We don't need tickets. I'm a member and have a guest pass for you," said Kirsten.

Kirsten told Mehran that the Art Institute of Chicago was founded in 1879 and moved into its current home, initially just the building fronting Michigan Avenue, in 1893. Throughout the years additional buildings were added to accommodate the ever-expanding collection of fine arts and educational facilities.

Mehran had visited the museum on a few occasions, but decided to lay his cards down. "I want you to know that when it comes to fine arts outside of music, I'm somewhat of an illiterate."

She laughed. "Somehow I doubt that."

"No, seriously! I don't understand most of the art in this building."

"Well, that's genuine. But I don't think you're alone. Most people don't fully understand art, to begin with."

They walked into the museum, still holding hands.

"What do you want to concentrate on today?" Kirsten asked.

"Like I said, I's got the dumbs."

Kirsten chuckled.

Mehran continued, "I assume they follow some of the eras of history, like Renaissance, Baroque, Classical, Romantic, Modern, right?"

"Yes, but with some differences. For instance, the Romantic era is broken down into Romanticism, Realism and Impressionism. The Modern era is broken down into even more subcategories."

"Okay, so which one do we concentrate on?"

"Do you like modern art?"

"Not really. Some I can relate to, like the surrealist works of Dali, but most modern art is too abstract for my taste."

"Aha. I knew you weren't the idiot you made yourself out to be."

"Well, thanks. I think I'm gonna leave the decision to you."

Kirsten wondered if she wanted to bore him today with modern art or stick with older stuff. On the other hand, he did say he liked Surrealism.

"Let's go to the second floor," she said.

They went up the grand staircase to the second floor.

"They have an exhibition of René Magritte's works. Let's spend today looking at only those," she said.

"Didn't he paint *Black Magic*?" asked Mehran.

Kirsten thought for a second that Mehran must be pulling her leg. Magritte, indeed, had a painting he had called that. She gave him an evil look.

"What? I think he did. Didn't he?" Mehran asked.

"He sure did. What did you do? Look in painting books for porn?" asked Kirsten.

Mehran laughed. "Maybe."

When they reached the special exhibit hall, Kirsten stopped. "What do you know about Magritte?"

"I've seen some of his works in books. Namely *Black Magic*. I also remember *Time Transfixed*."

"I bet you've seen other works by him as well. Let's go in."

Once inside the room, Kirsten motioned for Mehran to follow her. She proceeded through the gallery toward a book on a podium on the other side. "Here, let's look at the chronology of his works."

They started looking through the book. His earliest work on record was *Nude* from 1919, followed by several exercises in Cubism, and then a series of paintings titled *Advertisement for Norine*. It looked like he had not forayed into Surrealism until *Nocturne* in 1925. For the next few years, he was very productive, creating an array of surreal paintings. On a couple of occasions, he changed his stroke techniques and created paintings such as *The First Day* or *The Harvest*. He also created paintings that could be considered variations on themes, perhaps meant to be shown with each other. Later on in life, his affinity was for men in overcoats and bowler hats.

Skimming through the book alone took the better of 15 minutes. Mehran recognized a couple of other works he had seen before, namely *The Anger of Gods* and *Golconda*. He went back to that page and pointed to *Golconda*. "I've seen this before."

"Well, not in person, but that's about to change today." She put her arm through his and led him to the north wall in the gallery.

"Wow." Mehran stepped back.

"Here, let's sit down," said Kirsten.

They sat at the bench facing *Golconda* and immersed themselves in the painting. A couple of young girls passed by them. When one of the girls saw the painting, she exclaimed, "Oh my God!" and sang, "It's raining men, Hallelujah, it's raining men."

Kirsten was not pleased and grumbled under her breath, "Teenagers."

"Oh, come on. It is literally raining men," said Mehran.

"Sure. But what else do you see?" Kirsten asked in a serious tone.

"Well, the men look exactly the same."

"Go on."

"I love his choice of colors. The red roof, the color of the building, along with the men's black coats against the sky add to the Surrealism."

"Are they all the same?"

Mehran paid more attention to the painting. "Well, no. Some have their hands in their pockets, some don't."

"Look at the detail in each window, look at the detail of the distant men and the shadows of each on the building."

"It's extremely detailed."

"What about the men?"

Mehran thought for a minute. "I don't know. What?"

"All the same? Like droplets of rain?"

"I suppose."

"Let's assume that he means that they're all the same. Or does he? Could those each be their own individual, even though they're dressed the same way and look the same, or does each have his own personality?"

"I would like to think they do. Everyone is a unique individual."

"Yes, but at the same time he forces you to believe that everyone's the same."

They continued to study the painting. Mehran didn't want to get up before Kirsten, since he didn't want his actions interpreted as boredom. He wasn't bored. He was enjoying their connection. While he was thinking this, Kirsten got up and offered her hand to him. They walked to the next painting.

"This, my friend, is *The Lovers* from 1928," Kirsten said.

Mehran stepped back and noticed another painting also titled *The Lovers*. "These must be meant to be shown as a pair. Which is a really interesting point. It takes two to be lovers, and there are two paintings."

"Do you think that's a coincidence, or did he mean it to be interpreted that way?"

"I think he meant it. There's gotta be so much meaning to any and all of these paintings that this cannot simply be a coincidence."

"I think so, too," said Kirsten as she slid her arm into his and pulled him to the one where the lovers were kissing. "What do you think of their pose?"

"Suggestive."

She turned to look at him while he continued to look at the painting. She turned back toward the painting. "Why the veils?"

"It looks like he wanted to hide something."

"Or perhaps add to the suspense. Had the veil not been there, it might have turned out to be a completely ordinary painting."

"My turn to ask. What do *you* think he meant to portray?"

"Look at the bold colors of the room, and the bold colors in their clothes," Kirsten said. "He is wearing black, she is wearing red. I think the white veil represents innocence. I have read somewhere that the black the man is wearing represents death, the red the woman is wearing represents love, while the white veil represents purity, and the painting brings all of them together. I'd agree."

She turned toward Mehran and pushed his arm to twist him toward her. They were facing each other. Mehran looked in Kirsten's eyes and tried to read her expression. Before he had a chance to engage her, she leaned forward and kissed him on the lips. He grasped her wrist to keep her from moving away and to ensure that the kiss would last a couple of moments longer. It did. Kirsten felt his firm grasp on her wrist and understood. They kissed for a few seconds and then pulled back in respect for other art spectators.

"I like the way you think, Kirsten," said Mehran.

Kirsten gave an approving smile, not only because of the kiss, but also because of the engaging conversation they were having.

They spent the next hour admiring other paintings in the gallery. With every painting, with every discussion, with every touch, and with every gaze into each other's eyes, their passion and wanting grew. By the time they were in front of Magritte's "Discovery," they didn't need to say anything to each other to appreciate the painting and its beauty, its hidden meanings, its suggestiveness or its complex simplicity. Kirsten took Mehran's hand and pulled him toward the exit. They dashed down the staircase, through the doors and toward the sidewalk on Michigan Avenue, where they kissed again. It was more than a gentle kiss; Mehran held Kirsten's lower lip between his lips while Kirsten did the same with his upper lip, both relishing the taste of each other's lips without being intrusive. The kiss lasted for about 30 seconds. The crowd parted around them to cross the street when the pedestrian signal changed. When they separated, Kirsten took a step back and closed her eyes to catch a deep breath. "You're a good kisser."

"A good kisser is only as good as his partner."

"Let's walk to my place," she responded.

Mehran knew the address to her place but in the moment lost his bearings. "Where is your place?"

They ran across the street before the light turned and walked at a brisk pace, continually jaywalking and running through intersections. By the time they got inside Kirsten's high-rise, they were hot from the pace they set to her apartment. They called the elevator while still holding hands. Sweat beads were starting to form on Mehran's forehead. The elevator doors opened. They dashed inside the elevator and waited for the doors to close. By the time the doors did, they had already lunged at each other, continuing to kiss with fervor. The elevator ride wasn't long. The doors opened, Kirsten pulled Mehran by the hand to her door and fumbled with her keys. Mehran turned her around and pushed her back against the door. They continued to kiss until Kirsten managed to unlock the door with a free hand. Her weight pushed the door open and they moved inside. She slammed the door shut behind them as they continued to kiss. They began to undress each other right behind the door. She pushed Mehran to the ground, straddled him and lowered her face to his. The physics of life took over and their bodies connected to become one for a few minutes of intense, pleasureful sex.

Kirsten collapsed on top of Mehran; they both were breathing heavily. After a minute, she rolled off and languished next to him on the floor while trying to catch her breath.

"Oh my God," she said.

"Too bad I'm an atheist," Mehran managed to say between breaths.

Kirsten chuckled. "I never thought talking about paintings could be so arousing."

Mehran tilted his head to the side and looked at Kirsten, her breasts rising in unison with her heavy breathing. He propped himself up enough to be able to look her in the eyes. His eyes moved down to her breasts and he cupped one with his free hand, not squeezing, but gently laying his hand there. Kirsten had just the smallest hint of a smile on her lips and closed her eyes. Mehran took a moment to move his hand up to her chin and lower his lips on hers.

They showered together, holding each other under the lukewarm water at first, and then washing each other's hair and body. When Mehran was rinsing his hair, Kirsten moved behind him, wrapped her arms around his belly and laid her ear against his back. She felt lucky to be with him. He was engaging, smart, passionate, had a sense of humor and she knew that he was genuinely interested in her. She was happy to be with him.

They dried off and moved to Kirsten's bedroom to lay on the bed. Kirsten wanted to know everything about Mehran, and the one piece of information he had withheld from her had been nagging at her: the frame in his bedroom. But she wasn't sure how to bring up the subject. She decided to ask him point-blank. "Will you tell me what the frame in your bedroom is all about?"

Mehran sighed. "A girl I once loved made that knot and gave it to me. It's called 'True Lovers' Knot.' The locket in the frame holds her ashes."

Kirsten paused for a while before she said, "She must have meant a lot to you."

"She did, and she does."

"She does? You just said the frame held her ashes."

"She does. There's still a place in my heart for her, hence the frame."

"How did she die?"

"She contracted HIV and died of AIDS in 1992."

Kirsten propped herself on her elbow and looked at Mehran. "Did you have sex with her?"

Mehran tilted his head and looked at Kirsten. "Yes. Once in 1985. I've tested for HIV every 6 months since 1989 and I'm clean. I wouldn't have had sex with you if I wasn't. After what she went through, I wouldn't want to see anybody else go through that."

Kirsten distanced herself. "You should have told me before."

"I'm sorry. I just figured that I am in the clear after 11 years."

Kirsten's stance relaxed a bit. "Why does she mean so much to you?" Kirsten asked, although she already had a suspicion that the girl who had made the knot and whose ashes rested in the locket in the frame was Naghmeh. She was the one who broke the news of his parents' death.

Mehran paused, and then continued, "She was there for me when my parents couldn't be."

Kirsten understood now, but still, she didn't say anything. Instead, she said, "We never talked about what happened after your parents died."

"What would you like to know?"

"You left California for Chicago in the middle of your college years. Why?"

Mehran told her the rest of his story after the death of his parents, including Naghmeh's death and his changing jobs, up until meeting Kirsten for the first time. He left out the details about the prostitute; he had regretted the incident ever since.

When Mehran was done, Kirsten instinctively asked, "Naghmeh made love to you on the night she told you your parents died. And she made the knot, and those are her ashes in the locket. Right?"

Mehran remained silent. Kirsten knew then that she was right but decided that there was no point in getting upset about something that had happened a long time ago. After all, she had had boyfriends in the past and it wouldn't be fair to judge Mehran on his past relationships.

Mehran wasn't sure how all this affected Kirsten or their new relationship. He turned his head and looked her way. She turned her face away from him for a few seconds, but couldn't bring herself to hold something like this against him and turned her face back to meet his gaze. She then leaned toward him and put her head on his chest and her arm across his belly.

"I just realized that I don't know anything about your past either, except that you're Swiss," said Mehran.

Kirsten shared her life story as they laid in bed for the next couple of hours. They made love again before realizing that it was 8 at night, and they were hungry. They dressed and headed to the garage. Kirsten drove them to a restaurant for a bite to eat and then dropped off Mehran at his place.

Mehran stuck his head through the passenger window. "So, when am I going to see you again?"

"I don't know. How about a couple of weekends from now?"

He looked into her serious face, shrugged his shoulders and said, "Okay. See you," and started to walk away. She honked her horn, and he turned around. She had her arm out the window and was motioning her index finger for him to come back. He stuck his head through the passenger side.

She playfully grabbed his ear and pulled him inward while she leaned forward. "You'd be okay with not seeing me for two weeks?" and she planted a kiss on his lips.

"Not really, but I'm catching on to your games."

"No games. How about a movie tomorrow night?"

"Sounds good!"

Chapter Twenty-Eight

On Monday night, Mehran left work and took a cab to Water Tower Place. He looked through the list of movies and was disappointed. *Twister* had just come out on Friday. As he continued to look, a set of arms wrapped around him from behind. He smiled and turned around.

"Hey!" he said.

She kissed him deeply, which he appreciated. He enjoyed kissing Kirsten. Her lips were soft and knew when to offer themselves to be nibbled on, and when to open up for more intense kisses. Kirsten broke the kiss but still held her arms around his waist. "What are we watching?"

"If you want to watch something now, we'd have to watch *Twister* or *Sgt. Bilko*. If you're willing to wait until 9, we can watch *Fargo* or *The Birdcage*."

"I don't care. We can walk around until 9."

"Then *Fargo* it is."

Mehran purchased tickets for *Fargo* and they started to roam around the mall. Within a few minutes, a guy excitedly called Kirsten's name and approached her.

"Hey," said Kirsten.

The guy tried to hug Kirsten, but she hesitated and gave him a half twisted, shoulders only hug and pulled back quickly. "What are you doing here?" Kirsten asked.

"I was just finishing off a bad date," he said. "How've you been?"

"Great! Great! Sam, this is Mehran, my boyfriend. Mehran, this is Sam. He used to work at the bank."

"Nice to meet you," Mehran extended his right hand for a shake. He could tell that Sam didn't like what Kirsten said, because Sam's face stayed completely indifferent. He reluctantly shook Mehran's hand. "You, too."

"So, what are you doing here?" Sam asked.

"We're going to see a movie later and are killing time in the mall," said Kirsten.

"Oh, what movie?"

"*Fargo*," Mehran said.

"I hear that's supposed to be pretty good. Can I hang with you guys?"

Kirsten looked at Mehran, and then said, "Sam, we're on a date."

"A date? Really?" he said as he laughed.

Kirsten tried to change the subject. "So, what have you been up to?"

"Well, after they let me go, I took off a couple of weeks and did nothing. Then I started looking for another job and eventually found a position at another bank."

"Nice. Where?"

"I'm a teller at IBC."

"That's great. I hear those Canadians take care of their employees."

"I don't know. It feels just like another job. Can I walk with you guys and catch up until you go into the theater?"

Kirsten looked at Mehran for help, but Mehran just shrugged his shoulders and raised his eyebrows with a look of "Whatever. I don't care if he hangs around." Instead, Kirsten said, "Maybe we can hang out some other time, Sam."

Sam smiled and shrugged his shoulders, "Well, I figured I'd ask. Anyway. It was good to see you, Kirsten."

"Yeah, you, too. Stop by the bank to say hi. Marie would love to catch up with you."

"Oh, yeah. Okay. I'll call you sometime. Bye!" and he walked away from them.

Mehran and Kirsten walked in silence for a minute.

"Aren't you going to ask me who that was?"

"Well, I believe his name was Sam, and he used to work at the bank."

"That's it? You're not jealous?"

He laughed. "Jealous of what? It's clear that you didn't want him around."

"Yeah, but –" She turned back to see how far Sam had gone. He was nowhere in sight. "You're right. I don't want him around. He asked me out for a couple of dates when I was dating another guy. It's like there's something wrong with him. He doesn't catch social cues. Like wanting to hang around with us on our date."

"That's hardly a fault, especially when beautiful Kirsten is the subject. Some people are just quirky. I really wouldn't have minded if you were okay with him hanging around."

Beautiful Kirsten? Ooh, he's smooth, Kirsten thought. "You don't mind sharing me with someone else?"

"I don't own you. But you did say something interesting. You just told him that I was your boyfriend. So, by the same right, I can call you my girlfriend now, right?"

Kirsten was intrigued. Everything she had heard about Middle Eastern guys was that they were the jealous kind, yet Mehran had played the situation as if he were Yo-Yo Ma playing at a concert hall. It was just like Kirsten would have wanted him to.

She nodded. "Yes, I am your girlfriend."

"There, that settles it. Besides, if I was jealous, I'd never act on it."

That made her feel even better. A man who *does* get jealous but won't act on it.

They continued walking in and out of stores. As some stores started to close, they made their way to the theater, bought some popcorn and drinks and headed into the movie. After they sat down, Kirsten told Mehran that she was going away on business to Switzerland on Saturday; she would return on Wednesday.

"Would you drive me to the airport on Saturday and pick me back up?"

Mehran hesitated. "I would, but I don't know how to drive stick."

Kirsten had a puzzled look on her face. "You grew up in a country that has nothing but manual transmission cars and you don't know how to drive one?"

"Well, I never drove in Iran, and I never had the opportunity to learn to drive a stick over here," he explained. "I wouldn't mind dropping you off and picking you up in a cab."

"No way! Now you *have to* learn to drive a stick."

"Okay. But can we watch the movie first?" he jokingly asked.

"How about tomorrow after work? There aren't too many places in the city that don't have traffic, but there's a cemetery by Irving Park Road we can go to. You won't kill anybody over there."

Mehran laughed. "Do I say 'It's a date' if we're now boyfriend-girlfriend?"

Kirsten hit him in the arm. "Yes! It's always going to be a date when we go out."

The movie came on and immediately caught their attention. It was quirky, peculiar and compelling. They talked about it until they were outside Water Tower Place.

"I'm going to catch a cab home, if that's okay with you. It's late, and it's a work night," Kirsten said.

"Of course," he said as he took her by the waist and pulled her close. "Remember, I want to learn how to drive a stick tomorrow."

"You will. I promise."

They kissed, and Mehran hailed a cab for Kirsten. He grabbed the next cab home.

Chapter Twenty-Nine

Mehran was excited on Tuesday. He'd finally be able to trap Kirsten in her own cat and mouse game. He knew perfectly well how to drive a stick shift. He was amused all day and left work early so he could meet her on time. It wasn't that far from his apartment, so he rode his bicycle, not thinking about what they would do with it later. He arrived at the cemetery around 7:30 p.m. The sky was still lit.

Kirsten showed up shortly after. She got out of the car and they kissed. Kirsten gave him the keys.

"Okay. The big test is here. You do have an idea how stick shift cars drive, right?"

"Well, I think any time you're changing gears you have to push the clutch in."

"Good! That's one-third of the whole thing. The other thing is that any time you're stopping, you either have to be in neutral or have your foot on the clutch."

"You know I've taken physics and I understand the mechanics behind a clutch, a gearbox and an engine. Let's get on with it."

He got in the driver's seat. Kirsten put her seat belt on and reminded him to do the same.

"Okay, so in order to start the car, you always, *always*, push the clutch in and hold it there until you're ready to move."

"Okay." He pushed the clutch in and started the car.

"Great! You're doing good. Now, let's study the gears. Here's the pattern." She showed him the pattern imprinted on the stick shift, 1 2 3 4 5 and R. "Go ahead and practice them. You shouldn't skip gears unless you know what you're doing."

He pretended to go through the gears. "How do I know which one's the first gear, which one's the third, and which one's the fifth?"

"Well, that comes with practice. Just try to feel their positions and where they're supposed to be. The good thing is this car makes it really hard to go into the first gear if you're going too fast. That way you don't blow the engine."

Mehran went through the motions.

"Okay. I think you're ready to move," Kirsten said as she put her hand over the handbrake. "Put it in 1st and slowly let up the clutch as you're pushing in the gas, so that you can take off."

Mehran purposefully lifted his foot off the clutch faster than he should have, the tires screeched, the car jumped, and then it stalled.

"That's okay. Start the car again. This time lift your foot off the clutch more slowly while applying some gas."

"Okay."

Mehran started the car and revved the engine.

"Okay, easy now. Don't rev the engine so much. Let's try it again."

Mehran looked at her and pushed the DSC button on the M3 to disengage the dynamic stability control on the tires.

"What are you doing? Don't push that."

Mehran floored the gas pedal and popped the clutch. The tires squealed and the car took off, sending their heads against the headrests. He quickly pushed the clutch, moved into second gear, and popped the clutch again, causing the tires to squeal a second time.

Kirsten started to hit him with both hands, "You ass! Stop the car!"

Mehran started to laugh uncontrollably and stopped the car short of a turn.

"Why?" asked Kirsten.

She seemed serious but not enough to warrant an apology.

"How do you think I drove through all those third-world countries in Central America if I didn't know stick? They don't have any automatics down there."

Kirsten thought for a second, and then said, "Well played. You had me going."

"I got you back."

"Yes, but I'll come back bigger," she said as she leaned over the center console to kiss him.

She then looked through the car windows like a spy. "It's almost dark and there's nobody here."

"I like the darkness."

Kirsten unbuckled her seat belt and climbed over Mehran, using the controls on the side of the seat to push his seat back. She sat on top of him and began to kiss him. After a minute or two, she took another look around and, not seeing anybody, lifted her skirt and unzipped his pants.

"Right here?" Mehran said, panicked.

"Yes, right here. With all the dead watching," she said with a mischievous smile.

She used the seat controls to tilt his seat back all the way down. Space was cramped, but they managed to have sex in the car at a cemetery.

When they were done, Mehran brought the seat back up.

"What now?" asked Mehran.

"I've got a couple of hours before I have to turn in," she said.

Mehran got out of the car and told her to follow him in the car while he rode his bicycle. He rode to one of his favorite jazz clubs about a mile away while Kirsten followed. She found a parking space a couple of blocks away and walked back to the club.

"Let's have a drink and listen to some music," said Mehran.

They sat through the second half of a set and another full one at the jazz club. Mehran ordered two rounds of martinis. The band happened to be a trio that night. Just piano, drums and an upright bass. The drummer was the singer for the group, which seemed odd. Mehran knew that usually the piano player was the singer in a trio. Nevertheless, the band played a few good tunes, some of which surprised Mehran.

At one point, Mehran walked over to the band's tip jar and slipped a bill in it.

"How much did you put in there?"

"Uh, not much."

Kirsten looked at him inquisitively and reached in her purse to grab a $10 bill. She got up and walked over to the tip jar. While dropping her bill in, she noticed the bill on top. She came back and sat down.

"A hundred dollars?" asked Kirsten.

"So?"

"A hundred dollars? Nobody slips hundred-dollar bills into a musician's collection jar."

"I'm sure I'm not the first and also sure they need it more than I do."

"But $100?"

"What did you put in their jar?"

"$10."

"Did it bring a smile to your face?"

"Yes, until I saw what you put in there."

"Well, it does for me, too, when I put whatever I put in there. It brings a smile to my face."

Kirsten looked at him. Who *was* this guy? He definitely wasn't just some guy she was dating. She started to add to the list of adjectives she had first constructed for him in the shower: compassionate, affectionate, Iranian. Was he? He went so much against the grain and the stereotype.

"I'd like to bring a smile to your face, too," she said.

He smiled, "You've succeeded." She hugged him.

They met again on Wednesday night, this time at a bowling alley, where Kirsten blew him away. They could not meet on Thursday, but they decided to go to a dance club with several of Kirsten's friends and co-workers on Friday night.

Chapter Thirty

Mehran took a cab to Baja Beach Club to meet Kirsten. He wasn't sure if this would be awkward, in a way, the "showing" of the boyfriend. He thought that he'd be judged like a model on a New York runway. On the other hand, it could be something completely benign and just a way for him to meet some of Kirsten's other friends. She did, after all, have other friends. He usually dressed casually for work. That Friday, however, he dressed up in suit and tie, knowing that Kirsten would be coming from work to the club and that she'd be dressed up. He arrived at the club after Kirsten and her friends were already there.

Kirsten introduced Mehran to a few of her friends and coworkers at the bank, including Marie. It didn't seem that any of Kirsten's acquaintances knew she was dating Mehran. Soon enough, though, Marie, already clearly buzzed, pulled Mehran aside and said, "I'm so glad the two of you are dating. She really needed this."

"Needed this?"

"She'd kill me if she knew I told you this. She dated this Aussie guy and he broke her heart."

"He broke up with her?"

"No, she broke up with him."

Mehran looked at Marie with her glazed eyes and decided to be more inquisitive. "Was he an asshole?"

"Completely. He was really good-looking, and he had that Mick Dundee accent, but he cheated on her."

"Wow. She hasn't told me."

"Yeah, she'll never tell you."

Mehran didn't agree that Kirsten would never tell him. Marie cut into his thoughts. "Yeah, I like you. I know you'll be nice to her."

"I really appreciate your winking at me that day. If not for that wink, I wouldn't have felt welcome to pursue Kirsten."

Marie winked at him and smiled as she took another sip of her drink.

Mehran spent a good deal of time on the dance floor that night.

"He's such a good dancer," said Lorena, one of Kirsten's co-workers.

"Yeah! He keeps surprising me," said Kirsten, looking at Mehran dancing with her friend, Amanda, and added yet another adjective to her list of Mehran's qualities; good dancer.

She approached the dance floor and danced her way toward Amanda and Mehran. The song playing was a remix of *Missing* by Everything But the Girl. Mehran let her in and started to dance with both of them, but to him it looked like Kirsten was trying to monopolize the dance triangle. After a little bit, Amanda left the dance floor, and it was only Mehran and Kirsten.

As they danced, she leaned over and said in a loud voice so as to overpower the speakers, "You're mine."

He looked at her and talked into her ear the same way. "If I'm yours, then you're mine."

Kirsten looked into his eyes, still dancing, then leaned forward and said in a lower voice, directly into his ear, "That's all well and good. Just remember, I'm the jealous type."

Mehran felt good. He read into her statement that she cared about him, most likely a lot. That she didn't want to share him with anybody. The comment boosted his ego. He kissed Kirsten on the dance floor, making sure all of her friends saw them kissing. Kirsten enjoyed being part of the show. Every time they kissed, she got turned on. As they danced, Mehran noticed that Sam had shown up to the party.

"Hey, it's your boyfriend wannabe," Mehran jested.

"Stop it!" Kirsten said and she pulled him close to her and said in his ear, "I am all yours."

Mehran was satisfied. Their relationship had blossomed and he was at the stage he wanted to be with Kirsten. His only point of judgment when they had first met was Kirsten's looks and the basic knowledge they shared in that one-minute encounter. *Am I shallow for allowing looks to dictate whether I am interested in a girl?* He dismissed the thought; he was initially intrigued by her knowledge of foreign languages and her recognition that his name was Persian. Besides, had he known Kirsten before seeing her in person, maybe as a pen pal, he would have liked to go out with her regardless of her looks.

Kirsten leaned her head on his shoulder while dancing, causing him to slow down against the beat of the music.

When the song finished, they headed back to the group. Sam came toward Kirsten to hug her. Kirsten reluctantly hugged him.

"Jamie told me you guys were getting together and that I should show up."

"Oh, really," said Kirsten. "That's awesome."

Sam leaned toward Kirsten and said in crescendo, "I see you're still dating that dweeb."

Mehran heard the last part. Kirsten thought about responding, but decided to give Sam a dead stare.

Sam felt Kirsten's cold gaze and was caught off guard, but bounced back. "Eh, your loss."

Mehran saw the interaction and took Kirsten's hand in his and pulled her away from the crowd toward the bathroom. They stopped in the hallway leading to the bathrooms.

"What was that all about?" Mehran asked.

"There was this thing at the bank. He didn't just ask me out on a couple of dates. He had a crush on me, but I had no interest in him. He wouldn't take no for an answer. He went on a date with Marie, and she seemed to like him. After a while, he quit the bank and didn't tell anyone where he was going."

Mehran looked into Kirsten's eyes.

Kirsten looked back at him. "You've got nothing to worry about. I am *yours*."

"Good, because I am very protective of what's mine."

Kirsten felt like she had sold her soul to Mehran. She had just told him that she was his. She thought for a second about exactly what she had said. *Am I yours so you can take me out to dinner? Am I yours so that you can summon me on a Sunday? Am I yours for you to do with as you please?* She wondered. Alcohol had loosened her mind and tongue.

"I am yours," she repeated.

He pressed her against the wall of the hallway, pushing his whole body against hers. He raised her hands above her head against the wall. The sides of his suit jacket covered the two of them like a pair of bat wings. A couple of young boys, barely legal drinking age, passed them by on their way to the bathroom. "Yeah! Do her against the wall right here, man!"

Mehran looked into Kirsten's eyes. "I *would* like to do you right here."

"Nobody's looking," Kirsten replied.

"I know you're not serious. Why do you say that?"

"I mean that I'm willing to let you take me anywhere and anytime. I am yours."

Mehran thought before he answered, smiling, "I'm sorry, but I don't have balls of brass. We'll have to postpone this for later." He let her arms down. The sentiment and what she had said stuck in his brain: 'I'm willing to let you take me anywhere and anytime.'

He swung his arm around her shoulder and pulled her back toward the party, planting a kiss on her temple.

Mehran avoided Sam for the rest of the night. He wanted to play all the cards right. He seemed to have struck the right chord with Kirsten and nothing was worth losing her. Sam danced a couple of songs with some of the girls from the office before he left.

"I'm going to miss you," Mehran said, thinking of Kirsten's trip.

"It's only for a few days. I have to go see my boyfriend in Switzerland," she joked.

"You shouldn't make him wait this long," he responded.

"Mehran, you're so understanding. Why?"

"You don't want to know."

"Yes, I do."

Mehran thought for a few moments. He felt like saying he loved her. But love wasn't a simple proposition. He had loved Naghmeh, and that had come after several different incidents, including one when he felt Naghmeh had given all of herself to him. Did he have the same love for Kirsten? No. He didn't have the same love for Kirsten as Naghmeh; however he did love Kirsten in a certain way. She had become a part of his life and he was in no way ready to do without her.

"Because I love you," he said.

Déjà vu, that feeling that something happening at a specific moment has happened before happened to Mehran just then. One of the explanations for Déjà vu is that the pathways to the memory in a person, at a particular moment in time, are so fast that committing the present situation to memory happens before the person is able to access the memory location, and thus it appears that the accessed memory has been there for a while. Mehran's uttering of the words "I love you" seemed to happen due to possibly similar circumstances. Before he had a chance to analyze whether he loved Kirsten or not, the feelings of love were committed to memory and replayed, bypassing his frontal cortex.

Nobody could hear him say it, except for Kirsten. Right there, in the middle of the bar, with her friends not 10 feet away, Mehran said that he loved her.

"No, you don't," said Kirsten, shaking her head.

"Don't tell me whether I do or do not."

"You cannot possibly love me," said Kirsten, perhaps a bit louder than she should have.

Marie heard it and turned slightly. Mehran noticed and took Kirsten by the hand to the dance floor. It happened to be a slow song, so they embraced and Kirsten leaned her head against his shoulder.

"Why not?" asked Mehran.

"Because we've just met."

Mehran took a deep breath. Saying all he wanted to say to Kirsten was going to require extra oxygen. "I want to be honest with you. Do I love you as deep as a husband of 25 years loves his wife? Probably not, although I have never been married. Do I love you as deep as a mother loves her newborn son? No, I wouldn't know. But I love being with you and the way you make me feel."

Kirsten heard the words. She heard the longing. She knew exactly what he was talking about. How could she love him as her mother loved her dad? She couldn't. But there was a feeling that she was willing and wanted to explore. "Mehran. That's the sweetest thing anybody's said to me. In the past 30 minutes."

Mehran smiled. "Yeah, more like 30 years."

She lifted her head from his shoulder and piped up, "Hey, I'm only 29! July will make 30."

"Okay! That's the sweetest thing anybody's said to you in the past 29 years."

"Yes, it is." She put her head back on his shoulder.

Mehran was puzzled. "Well, that's it?"

Kirsten thought about messing with him, but thought the stakes were too high. She decided to be serious. She wasn't sure if she loved him yet, but she wasn't willing to relinquish the conversation yet.

"I love you," her lips spoke.

Had her feelings betrayed her? She didn't mean to tell Mehran that she loved him, but she wasn't willing to lose the momentum of their conversation on a technicality. He had said that he loved her. He had qualified it as neither the love of a mother for her son, nor the love of a long-married couple, but he had said the magic words. He loved her. Did she love him? She searched inside herself for her feelings. She did love him. She had yet to find something wrong with him. And what if she did? Would finding something wrong with him preclude her from loving him?

Mehran was enthused. "Really?" He felt like a 12-year-old boy. *Really? Is that all I could come up with,* he wondered. Before he had a chance to rephrase his thoughts, she said, "Yes, really."

The song had changed to *Be My Lover* by La Bouche. They disconnected and started dancing to the song while keeping their eyes locked on one another. *Such a simple song, yet such straightforward lyrics,* Mehran thought.

They took a cab to Kirsten's apartment and stayed there for the night. The next morning he drove her to the airport for her trip to Europe.

Chapter Thirty-One

On Monday, Mehran called Pari to chat.

"Azizam. How are you?"

"I'm doing well, Pari. How's everyone over there?"

Pari told him that Peyman started a job at a computer gaming company in L.A., utilizing his computer science degree, and that Parisa's daughter was now walking and talking, and Nader had four dealerships.

"Yes, but how are *you*?" asked Mehran.

Pari paused. "I still miss her. You know. The love of a mother for her child does not diminish over time. It's as if she's still upstairs and is going to wake up, come down and grab something from the fridge."

"Pari, no parent should have to go through the pain you have gone through and are doing so still."

"Merci, azizam. Enough about me. What's going on in your life?"

Mehran filled Pari in on his dating Kirsten.

"When can we see this lucky girl?"

"It might be a little too early for that."

Pari laughed. "You know, you're getting older."

"I am. And I really like Kirsten. I'll let you know when's a good time to meet."

They said their goodbyes and hung up.

Wednesday couldn't come soon enough for Mehran. The weekend was the hardest part of their separation; on weekdays he busied himself with work. He even stayed late on Monday and Tuesday. Kirsten sent him a couple of brief emails, letting him know how her days had gone. He emailed that he missed her and that he wanted her back home.

Kirsten's plane was to land at O'Hare Airport at 3:30 in the afternoon. Mehran was at the airport at 3. He roamed the terminal, busying himself by watching all the foreigners arriving. Watching family members wait for their guests to arrive reminded him of how far removed from his culture he had become while living in the United States. He noticed how, upon sighting their loved ones coming through the exit doors of the customs area, people would run up and greet the newcomers. Sometimes they had flowers, a tradition he remembered from Iran when friends and family came from abroad.

The screens updated information that the Swissair flight from Zurich landed at 3:10. Just before 4, he saw Kirsten walking behind a family through the exit doors. She saw him, smiled and walked toward him. Once they met, she let go of her luggage, grabbed Mehran and gave him a quick kiss before hugging him.

"Ohhh, I missed you so much," she said.

"Me, too! I'm so glad you're back."

They kissed again for a few moments before they broke their embrace. Mehran reached for her suitcase and they walked to the escalator.

"Did you enjoy the trip?"

"It was mostly work, but I did. It's always good to go back and see old friends."

"And old boyfriends?"

They walked to Kirsten's car. Before Mehran had a chance to put the luggage in the trunk, Kirsten leaned against the car and drew him near. They kissed for some time before getting in the car.

"Are you tired?"

"Not really. I slept on the plane. I was sitting next to this woman traveling from Saudi. She didn't speak much English, or any of the languages I spoke for that matter, so I just read and slept."

"She was alone? That is odd."

"That's what I thought, too. I thought they were supposed to be accompanied by a male family member at all times when not at home."

"I guess, but surely there are some who are modern and don't believe in that. Why don't you investigate *that* a little like you investigated me?"

Kirsten laughed. "Maybe I will."

"What would you like to do?"

"I'd like to go to my place, take a shower, and make passionate love to you."

Mehran looked at her. "Getting right down to business, eh?"

She leaned over and started playfully rubbing her finger up and down against his crotch and said in a voice resembling a mother talking to a newborn, "Yes, I missed you, too, my little friend."

Mehran started laughing uncontrollably.

She smiled. "It wasn't *that* funny."

Mehran managed to get out a "Yes, it was," in between breaths.

Kirsten thought about it and started laughing herself.

Mehran parked the car in Kirsten's building garage and they headed upstairs. Mehran stayed in the bathroom while Kirsten took a shower.

"When's the next time you're going to Europe?"

"My next trip is going to be Poland," Kirsten said through the shower door. "It's in three weeks. After that, the only one I'm sure of right now is Lucerne in July."

"Do you have vacation time coming up?"

Kirsten opened the shower door and stuck her head through the crack. "Why?"

"I just had an idea that after your business was finished, I could join you in Lucerne and we could roam the land for a few days."

Kirsten smiled and motioned Mehran to come closer.

She whispered into his ear, "Why don't you take those clothes off, come in here with me and we can talk about it."

Mehran didn't need to be asked twice. He was in the shower in less than a minute. Their planned lovemaking session didn't make it to the bedroom.

Chapter Thirty-Two

The next three weeks passed quickly. Mehran and Kirsten spent a good deal of time together and were outdoors much of that time. Mehran despised being in the sun. Kirsten wasn't a sun lover by any means, either. The sun always gave her light skin a sunburn, but she enjoyed being outdoors nonetheless. They started biking along the lake together on Saturdays and playing golf on Sundays. Kirsten was decent at golf, but Mehran needed major work, so on some weeknights, they went to a driving range. By the time Kirsten was ready to leave three weeks later, Mehran had caught the gist of golf and was excited to have picked up a new hobby.

Mehran kept his thoughts positive. *She'll be back in 4 days*, he told himself.

Kirsten, too, was unhappy about leaving. Boring plane rides, boring meetings, when she could be with Mehran instead. On the other hand, they had planned the next trip to Lucerne, just like Mehran had suggested. Kirsten would leave on July 7, Mehran would join her on July 10 and they'd travel together until July 17.

After seeing Kirsten off, Mehran felt mildly depressed. He had become very attached to Kirsten. It was more than the sex. The sex was great, but they did things together. They talked about their feelings for each other and the things that happened around them. They also had similar taste in music and the arts.

He went home and decided to play some records. *Ah, I know the one*, he thought. He carefully took out an LP from its sleeve and looked at it: *Blues My Naughty Sweetie Gives to Me* by Blue Barron Orchestra, a big band from the 40s. He carefully placed the record on his player.

The song was extremely short at just over 2 minutes with a very upbeat tempo. The lyrics lasted only 45 seconds:

> *There are blues that you get from worrying*
> *There are blues that you get from pain*
> *And there are blues when you're lonely*
> *For your one and only*
> *The blues you can never explain*
>
> *There are blues that you get from longing*
> *But the bluest blues that be*
> *Are the sort of blues that's on my mind*
> *They're the very meanest kind*
> *The blues my naughty sweetie gives to me*

Mehran played the song three times. He missed Kirsten a lot already and figured he should get out of the house and do something. He had not yet bought a computer for home and thought that it was about time he should get one. He headed out to Elek-Tek, a computer store in Pulaski Park neighborhood, looked over their laptops and eventually settled on a 14" IBM Thinkpad. He took a free AOL floppy disk, so he could hook up to the Internet via the built-in modem in the laptop.

He began to get excited. One of the things he had meant to do for the longest time was cataloging his massive collection of records. His new computer, running Windows 95, would be able to run a spreadsheet and allow him to create the catalog.

At home, he set the laptop on the table, ran the cable to the phone jack and turned on the computer. He inserted the AOL disk and ran the installation program. In a short time, the software was installed and he was directed to call AOL on the phone to set up an account. He did so and fired up the software. He heard the familiar sound of the modem handshake, two long beeps followed by white noise. He was in! He fired up NCSA Mosaic and shortly thereafter he was on Hotmail, composing a new email to Kirsten:

> Hey! Guess where I'm typing this to you from? My shiny brand new laptop at home! I figured this will keep me busy

until you get back. I miss you already and can't wait for you to get home. Be safe. I want you back in one piece!

Love,
Mehran.

He started a spreadsheet to track his record collection and began to pound in the information.

The next morning, his phone rang at 6:30 just before he was to get up.

"Hello?"

"Hi, sweetie!"

"Kirsten, hi!" he said as he wiped the corner of his mouth. "How's it going?"

"I'm fine. The flight was fine. I got here and checked my emails and saw yours, but it would've been the middle of the night if I called you then."

"You know you can wake me up anytime."

Kirsten started whispering, "Yeah, but if it was the middle of night over there, I might have wanted to talk dirty to you."

"Nice! Be sure to call me tonight then!"

"Okay. I just wanted to hear your voice. I love you."

"I love you, too. Don't do anything I would do."

"Does that mean I can't visit the red-light district?"

"Visit, you can. But no touching!"

Kirsten laughed. "You're funny. I'll talk to you later."

"Okay. Have a good time."

They hung up. Mehran lay in bed, thinking of Kirsten and how it was already past noon for her. He thought of her throughout the day at work, wondering what she was doing. *She must be finishing her day right now. She must be eating dinner right now with some business associates. She must be getting ready for bed.*

Back at home, he continued to work on his record catalog. On Friday evening, he was at the airport early. He people-watched again, travelers coming in, families waiting for them. He noticed a family who spoke in Arabic, all dressed in black. The family included a woman, most likely in her late 40s, a boy about 19, and a girl about 17. It was clear from their eyes that they had all been crying.

Perhaps a mourning family, Mehran thought. He was trying to figure out where they were from, when it occurred to him that he may be able to find the answer from the arrival monitor, listing plane arrivals and their origination. He looked for cities in the Middle East, but he couldn't find any flights that would fit the bill.

He noticed that the woman was not wearing a hijab but wearing only a black scarf over her head. Eventually they waived their hands to a young woman who exited customs with her child sleeping on her shoulder, dragging her luggage behind her. The boy ran toward her and took the luggage from her. It appeared that he talked with her, but he didn't shake her hand or give her a hug. When the woman came closer to the older woman and the young girl, they all broke into tears, wailing.

Definitely mourning, thought Mehran. A lot of people around them were looking at them. The crying got louder. Mehran noticed a few other Arabic-speaking families listening in on the private conversation of the family, and a couple of men even went over to the boy, shook his hand and put their hands on his shoulder as a sign of solidarity. Mehran continued to watch the spectacle for a couple of minutes until he heard his name.

"Mehran."

He turned and there she was, wearing a short skirt and high heels, dragging her luggage behind her. "Oooh, babe," Mehran said.

Kirsten held Mehran's face in her hands. "You have no idea how much I've missed you."

Mehran felt her chilly hands on his face. He liked being able to warm her hands with the heat from his face. He reached for her waist and pulled her close. "Wow! Look at you! Dressed so well for a flight!"

She whispered in his ear, "I changed in the bathroom in the last hour just for you," as she bit his ear between her lips.

This is what I've been missing, Mehran thought, *her biting my ear, her thinking of me on her flight and trying to surprise me, her being here.*

They quickly kissed and left the airport.

Mehran drove back to her apartment as quickly as he could. They pulled into a parking space in the building garage and kissed passionately in the car. Mehran broke their kiss. "Let's get out. I want to eat you right here."

Kirsten had a surprised look on her face. She wasn't sure if that was a literal or figurative sentiment. Mehran exited the car, walked over to the passenger door and opened it. Kirsten turned to get out and spread her legs so that Mehran could see up her skirt. He offered his hand and pulled her up. He closed the door and moved her to the front of the car; it was only a couple of feet from the garage wall, where it was darker. They started kissing and he propped her up on the car, pushing her flat against the warm surface of the hood as he moved his kisses lower, until his face was under her skirt. Kirsten didn't ask him to stop. As a matter of fact, she didn't utter any words at all. She ran her fingers through his hair. She let out a few soft moans, none in rhythm, but random. Her hips were gyrating between the hood of the car and Mehran, and then she grabbed the sides of his head and pulled him against her, writhing, her legs raised. He felt Kirsten's orgasm and the small convulsions that followed. Then she let go of his head.

Kirsten sat up but continued to catch her breath while still sitting on the hood. After a couple of minutes, she asked, "So, short skirts and high heels are what do it for you, huh?"

"Actually, it was seeing you in them that did me in."

"Well, let's head upstairs. I want you in bed."

Chapter Thirty-Three

In the 4 weeks before Kirsten's trip to Lucerne, she and Mehran continued to explore each other, both physically and intellectually. They got together with Kirsten's friends on a couple of occasions, and then Mehran's company threw a party, which they went to. The company rented a restaurant for an evening, and everyone at the mill was invited.

Mehran always looked forward to seeing his co-workers' families and enjoyed being with his co-workers outside of work. The company had done similar parties on a couple of other occasions since they started the new mill in Chicago. The parties worked to keep employees engaged while they promoted more friendships at the workplace. Mehran, his team of engineers and most of the workers at the mill were a close bunch. Besides their occasional Friday poker games, they had competitions during lunch hours. They would vote on a game, and they'd have a tournament for a month, pitting worker against worker to find the champion among them. The games they voted on could be any game that was playable between two players. In the past, they had held a chess championship, which was well received. The favorite championship series was the rock-paper-scissor tournament. Workers passing each other in the mill and office hallways would stop for a quick 20-second match to psych each other or get reads on each other, so that they could carry their knowledge to the "official" championship games. Mehran had never won any of the competitions. This month the competition was to be a Battleship tournament. One of the programmers at the mill even wrote the game in his spare time and installed it on the server, so that workers could play against each other over the computer network.

None of Mehran's friends had met Kirsten before, so he spent a lot of time introducing her to his friends. Kirsten wasn't the only new guest at the party. Mehran's friend Amy had a new Australian boyfriend, and Mehran's friend Joe was dating an Iranian girl.

"Mehran, I would like to introduce my girlfriend, Niloofar," Joe said.

"You SOB! You never told me you were dating a Persian girl!" said Mehran.

He extended his hand for a shake, "Salam! Khoshbakhtam. In Joe-e ma kheili pesare khoobiye."

"Kheili mamnoon. Man ham hamintor," said Niloofar.

"Okay! That is the weirdest language I have ever heard. All I recognized was my name," said Joe.

"And I recognized the hello at the beginning," said Kirsten.

"Joe, Niloofar, this is my girlfriend, Kirsten."

They all shook hands. As the party got underway, Mehran and Kirsten went in different directions. Mehran noticed Kirsten and Niloofar talking. He excused himself and joined them. As he approached, he threw up his hands and said, "Guilty as charged! She's telling you all the bad things about me, right?"

The girls broke into laughter and Niloofar said, "You have nothing to worry about. This is just casual girl gossip. If it was nefarious, Kirsten would be giving you the evil eye right now."

Mehran took Kirsten by the waist and said, "I've never given her any reason to give me the evil eye. Have I?" he asked Kirsten.

"No, he's a good boy."

"This is so great that you're dating. My mother is always telling me that intercultural relationships never work," said Niloofar.

Mehran thought there was some truth to that. "Well, she's probably right, to a point."

Kirsten propped her hands on her hips, turned her upper body toward him, and exclaimed, "Dear sir, would you mind clarifying yourself a bit?"

"Well, there are just some cultural things that won't ever jive right in an intercultural relationship," said Mehran. "For instance, take the respect and duty most Middle-Eastern kids feel toward their parents. For someone who is not from that culture, that notion seems completely out of whack."

"I'd like to think that anything can be taught and learned in a relationship," said Kirsten.

"I don't know. Some of these things are ingrained into the fabric of a person. The other way is also true. Take someone who has grown up in Saudi Arabia and all he's seen are women in niqabs and hijabs. He'd probably lose his mind if he saw you standing here, as beautiful as you are, in your short skirt and high heels. He would never understand, or I should say he'd have a hard time understanding, that your right to wear what you want trumps his right to be offended by what you're wearing."

"If you think I'm offensive, wait until I get my hands on you later," smiled Kirsten.

Niloofar laughed, held her hands over her ears in a joking manner. "T.M.I! T.M.I!"

Mehran left Kirsten with Niloofar and walked over to some friends who were standing nearby.

"Wow, Mehran! You don't deserve that!" said Joe, looking toward Kirsten.

Mehran laughed and thought about it for a second. He looked at Kirsten and remembered his love for this woman who he had just met not long ago. Did he not deserve her? Damn right he did! After everything that had happened to him, having to leave his country, his parents and Naghmeh dying, he sure did deserve a "Kirsten" in his life. He raised his glass to her while she had her back to him and he told his friends, "I do. I sure do deserve her."

His friends all raised their glasses with him and drank.

Soon after dinner, the dancing started. Mehran and Kirsten danced until the party ended at midnight.

Chapter Thirty-Four

On July 7, Mehran drove Kirsten to the airport; this time, he was excited that she was leaving. He flew to Zurich a few days later. There he rented a Cabriolet and drove to Lucerne. Kirsten had given him the name and address of the hotel she was staying in. He had a hard time finding it on the map, but eventually he saw a cross street and followed it until he was in front of Hotel des Balances. He found a garage near the hotel, parked the car and went in, but didn't see Kirsten in the lobby. After talking to the front desk clerk, he was given a note Kirsten had left for him. He took the folded note and a key from the clerk and headed to the elevator. Inside, he unfolded the note and read, "Working late tonight. It's the last night I have to work. I'll meet you in the room later. Love, Kirsten."

What a bummer, he thought. Their first night together and he wouldn't see her until late. It was only 3 in the afternoon; he took a nap for a couple of hours to adjust for jet lag and then headed outside to walk.

Mehran had never been to Lucerne. He took a short walk across the bridge to the shopping district, where he spent a couple of hours browsing. He stopped at a cafe with outdoor seating and spent a couple of hours drinking beer and people-watching before he realized he was tired. He went back to the hotel to sleep.

He woke up from the blow of warm air over his ears. He rolled on his back, and Kirsten straddled him. "Who is this girl on top of me, disturbing my slumber?" he asked.

She lowered her head to his. "I missed you, too."

The next morning they woke up and had breakfast at the hotel.

"So, what's the plan?" Mehran asked.

"What do you want to do? What do you want to see?"

"I don't like big cities much. We should get out in the country and enjoy the Alps."

"Okay. We'll do whatever you want to do," she said.

"I want to travel the Alps and stay in bed and breakfasts, making love to you every night."

"Then that's what we'll do."

They checked out of the hotel, loaded their luggage in the car and set out. Kirsten directed him to take Highway 2 toward Italy, but Mehran, having looked at the map, decided that he didn't want to take the short route. To the south of Lucerne were a gorgeous series of lakes, which the local road hugged. They took Highway 4 around the lakes to Highway 2. Doing so, he missed the 6-mile Seelisberg tunnel, but he figured they'd catch it on the way back to Lucerne. Driving on Highway 2, they were about to reach the Gotthard Tunnel, an even longer tunnel of 10 miles underneath the Alps. Mehran asked how he could circumvent the tunnel, the rationale being that going over the Alps as opposed to going underneath them would be a much more scenic drive. Kirsten knew that he was right and didn't argue. She looked on the map and directed him to the old road, which climbed the mountain and descended on the other side. It was the road everyone who wanted to cross the Alps at that spot took before the Gotthard Tunnel was opened in the 80s.

The view over the Alps was breathtaking. They stopped often and took most of the day to cross the Alps; on the other side they arrived at Lugano. Mehran had noticed that most of the names on the south side of the Alps sounded more Italian than German, and it all made sense when they started looking for a bed-and-breakfast around 4 in the afternoon. Everyone spoke Italian, even though they were still in Switzerland. They happened to get addresses for two bed and breakfast locations just outside the city. The first one was booked, but the second one had a room available. They unloaded their luggage before they went into town to eat.

That evening, Mehran noticed that Kirsten seemed preoccupied.

"Are you okay?" asked Mehran.

"I'm fine. Why?"

"You just don't seem to be yourself at all. Starting with last night."

"What did I do – or not do – last night?"

"Don't get defensive," said Mehran.

"I'm sorry. I didn't mean it to come out that way. Why do you ask?"

"I felt like you didn't have a lot to say today. Our conversations have been short, mostly to do with the road, the map, finding a place to stay and other trivial subjects. And this morning, you just submitted to my whim to do anything I wanted."

"Submitted? That's rather chauvinistic."

"Okay, let me take that back. You didn't offer any input into what we were going to do for the vacation. Most of the day, your conversations have been short."

"Let's get some wine first."

They ordered a bottle of Cabernet and stared at each other for the longest time.

"Well?" asked Mehran.

"I don't know where to start."

"Kirsten! It's me here. You can start anywhere you want. I don't judge."

"These past few days, I am starting to realize that things aren't the same as they were before, for me."

Mehran didn't like the sound of that. *Has she met with an old fling? Have her friends talked sense into her, a sense that doesn't match where I want our relationship to go to?*

"Like what?" he asked.

"Well, I was thinking of my last boyfriend."

The Aussie? I'm fucked! In the middle of the Alps of all places, he thought. He blurted out, without thinking, "The Aussie?"

"How do you know about him?"

This was going to be tough to get out of. He decided he'd level with her and tell her that Marie had told him about the ex. "Marie kind of mentioned him."

"Really?" Kirsten had a hint of a smile on her face. "What did she say?"

"She didn't have much good to say about him."

"Did she tell you that I thought I loved him?"

"No."

"Did she tell you that he cheated on me?"

"Yes."

Kirsten paused. "I don't know. I have been thinking for the past few days. I just got out of that relationship a couple of months before you and I met."

The waiter arrived with wine and poured both of their glasses and left.

"Go on," Mehran said as he took a big gulp. He needed it. She did the same.

"I am questioning myself whether I have gotten in our relationship too quickly."

"What bothers you about the relationship?"

"Well, it's just that I feel like I'm falling head-over-heels in love with you, and I was so hurt in my last relationship that I don't want to go through that again if I can avoid it."

Mehran thought a bit about what she had said. Not everything had progressed that fast, he thought. For instance, they hadn't had sex on their first, second or even third date. But he, too, felt that the speed in which they were falling in love with each other was pretty fast-paced. On the other hand, he had a few points of knowledge in his head that she, in her current position as a recovering, broken-hearted woman, did not have. He knew that he loved her. He knew that he wasn't going to cheat on her. He knew that he'd stick by her. It wasn't in his nature to "use" women, like the Aussie had done to Kirsten. He was sure Kirsten was the woman he wanted to be with. She was intelligent and caring, had a sense of humor, and was attractive and sexy. He thought for a minute whether he was a good match for her, but that was up to her to decide. Besides, it wasn't his qualifications that she had questioned, but more the speed with which they were getting involved with each other and potentially his commitment. He had no control over that speed, though. To try to tame the stallion that had already jumped over the fence would be futile at this point.

What I need to do, he thought, *is to try and explain to her that this isn't necessarily a one-way street she is entering*. There would be no guarantee that she wouldn't treat Mehran in an unfair manner, like the Aussie had treated her. He thought that he may want to approach the problem by coming to terms together and promising a "guarantee" of a sort to each other.

He got up and went around the table to sit on the small bench beside Kirsten. He put his arm around her waist, looked her in the eye, and said, "Kirsten. I love you, and I have no intention of hurting you. I will take this relationship as far as you want to go, and I'll go as slow as you want to take it, and I'll be with you every step of the way."

He paused to gauge her response. The expression on her face didn't change much. He continued, "I understand what you may be feeling, although I have never gone through it myself. But I have this lucky, uncanny ability to put myself in other people's situations, and believe me when I say that I feel your ache." He did, at the bottom of his heart. He felt the worry Kirsten had. He felt the uncertainty of the future Kirsten was feeling. "I really don't have any proof to offer you, since there's no telling what each of us may decide to do tomorrow. Tomorrow we may decide to jump off of a cliff. Tomorrow you may decide that the Italian man sitting at the bar," he nodded his head toward a good-looking guy in his 20s, "is who you want to be with. But I can assure you of one thing, and I ask you to do the same."

"What is that?"

"That if we do feel the need to go against the grain of our relationship, the love we have professed for each other, the feelings we have shared with each other, that we have the courage to let each other know before acting upon our decisions."

What a thoughtful way of looking at the relationship, thought Kirsten. *There is neither the promise that Mehran would never leave me nor the promise that I wouldn't leave him, either. Instead, a simple gesture of truth, of being honest. Something we could both share and, as human beings, trust each other on. What he is offering is the opportunity that, should one of us decide on something that might hurt the other, we would have a chance to face things together.*

She felt bold. She felt empowered. Was this the man of her dreams? She smiled. "That means we need to tell the truth to each other, no matter what, if I understand it correctly."

"Absolutely!" said Mehran. "That is the one promise we can make to each other, that, no matter what, we will always tell each other the truth."

"I can live with that," she said. She paused for a few seconds. "And I certainly appreciate that."

"So, let me say this," he said. "I am giving myself to you. I am yours and nobody else's. You have added much to my life in the short time we've been with each other and you fulfill it."

She smiled.

He chuckled and decided to lighten the mood by throwing some cheesy sentences in there. "You are the cherry to my cake. You are the North star of my sky. You are the electron to my proton. I am the Oreo and you're the creme inside it."

Kirsten had tears rolling down her cheeks. She managed to say, "It's called 'You are the cherry to my sundae,' not 'to my cake.'"

"What if I don't like sundaes?"

She laughed, "Everybody likes sundaes!"

That night, Kirsten let herself go. She started shedding doubts about their relationship and started trusting Mehran implicitly. He was the man in her life, now and for the foreseeable future.

The next day they explored Lake Lugano and St. Lawrence Cathedral, after which they celebrated Kirsten's 30th birthday with dinner and dancing around Lugano.

Chapter Thirty-Five

Kirsten hung up the phone.

"How are your parents?"

"They're well. I was talking to my sister. She's going to be coming to Chicago."

"I hate that you speak German and French to them. I never know if you're talking about me, and if so, I don't know whether you're telling them anything good or bad."

"Is there anything bad to tell them about you?"

"You could be telling them about the wart on my elbow."

"Stop it! I love your wart!" Kirsten said, touching it with the tip of her finger as she embraced Mehran.

"I hate it. It gets in the way of making love to you."

"Yeah? I don't think so. Back to my sister. She is coming from Denver for a visit."

"Uh oh. So, time to meet the family?" Mehran asked with reluctance.

"Come on! We've been dating for 4 months. They want to see you. I've told them so much about you."

"I suppose the time was going to come. You are so lucky that there's nobody on my side to approve of you, but me."

Kirsten separated from Mehran and lifted her T-shirt to her neck. She wasn't wearing a bra. "Do you approve?"

Mehran's eyes widened, "Oh, yes!"

"Stop it. I'm serious."

"Hey! You're the one who lifted your shirt up, and you're asking *me* to be serious?"

"Seriously, though," she let her shirt down. "My sister will be flying in on Friday night."

"That soon? We're supposed to go to Ravinia on Saturday."

"Can't we take her with? She loves classical music."

"Sure. That'll be fine. We'll show her a good time in Chicago."

"She's not here to see Chicago. She's been here before. She's here to see you."

"What am I? A shrine?"

"Come on! My family wants to meet you. She's a segue into bigger things, you know."

Mehran thought about the junction they had come to. Meeting her family was a big step. He was not afraid of it. On the contrary, he was excited. This showed a significant commitment on Kirsten's part.

"I'm just kidding. I'd love to meet your sister. Is she as cute as you?"

"Listen, buster! I will kick you in your gonads if you so much as look at her the wrong way," she said as she punched him hard on the arm.

"Oh my god! Chill. I'm just kidding!" he laughed.

On Friday night, they went to the airport to pick up Kirsten's sister, Anja. They were waiting at the gate when Kirsten yelled, "Anja!" seeing her sister through the elephant trunk that connected the gate to the airplane, and ran toward a slim blonde girl exiting the gate.

Mehran looked at Anja. *Wow!* he thought. She looked like a supermodel. Kirsten was quite the looker, but her younger sister seemed completely flawless. Mehran stood back while Kirsten and Anja approached him, Kirsten's arm over Anja's shoulder.

"Anja, this is the man in my life. Mehran."

Anja came forward to hug Mehran. "I have heard so much about you."

"Hi. I hope all good things!"

"Yes! Kirsten doesn't have anything bad to say about you," she smiled.

Mehran grabbed Anja's carry-on and let the two of them walk ahead of him and talk. They walked to the garage; Kirsten sat in the back of the coupe, allowing Anja to sit in front with Mehran.

"So, Kirsten tells me that you're into the fine arts like your mother," Mehran said.

"I am. My mother helped me get a job at the Denver Art Museum after I graduated. I'm working at the museum and on my master's degree."

"That's great. Kirsten and I have been to the Art Institute of Chicago several times in the past few months. She's taught me a lot about the arts."

Anja smiled. "Yes, the fine arts run deep in our family, and we're all very passionate about them."

Anja and Kirsten continued to talk together while Mehran drove. Once he was near Kirsten's apartment, Mehran asked, "So, what's the plan tonight?"

"Tapas!" said Anja. "I've been dying for some good tapas since there aren't any good places in Denver."

"We can do that, but we'll have to wait a bit to be seated on a Friday night," Kirsten said,

"I'm ready to go now," said Anja. "I'm already dressed and don't need to drop off my luggage."

Mehran turned the car around and headed toward his apartment, where there was a great tapas bar around.

After dinner, they walked over to Mehran's since they had had a bit too much sangria over the course of dinner. They thought they'd all crash there.

Soon after Anja had settled down, she started looking through Mehran's records and quickly became obsessed with the collection. They opened a bottle of wine and listened to a selection Mehran chose. At times they spoke during the pieces, and at times they simply listened.

Mehran excused himself to go to bed around midnight.

The next morning Mehran woke up before Kirsten and went to the bathroom to brush his teeth. When he came out, Anja was ready to head into the bathroom.

"Would you like tea or coffee?" Mehran asked as they passed each other.

"Either will do," said Anja as she headed into the bathroom.

Mehran brewed a kettle of tea and prepared a small breakfast of bread, butter, cheese and walnuts and set the table.

Anja came out and sat down at the table.

"Like I said last night, Kirsten has said so many good things about you," said Anja.

"And I can say a million good things about Kirsten."

"She says you're very nice."

Is this an interview? Mehran thought. *It sure seems like it.* "Well, she hasn't seen my bad side yet."

Anja gave a frown.

"I'm just kidding! I'm really one of those wysiwig guys."

"Wysiwyg?"

"What you see is what you get."

"Ah. Somehow I doubt that."

"Why?"

"Well, there's more to charming a woman than being honest."

"Like what?"

"You have to do the right things, and more importantly, you have to do the right things at the right times."

She may have been young, Mehran thought, but she was right on. "So, does she tell you that I'm doing the right things at the right time?"

"I don't know. I can't read her correctly. She says you do the right things all the time, which is scary. No guy should be able to do the right thing all the time. You sure you're not gay?"

Gay? Mehran thought. *What does that have to do with anything?* "Why? Do gay men do the right things all the time?"

"They certainly know how to be true friends with girls better than guys can."

"I'm not sure I believe that," said Mehran as he took a sip of his tea.

She picked up her tea and took a sip as well. "It's true. I have met many gay men, and many of them are among my best friends. That's more than I can say about any hetero guy I've ever met."

"I think you're stereotyping the gay community. I live three blocks away from Belmont and Sheffield, the heart of the gay community in Chicago, and I can assure you some gay guys are just as much assholes and snobs as any hetero guy."

"Ooh, colorful words."

"Could it be that the particular population of gays you've been around, those studying art, are the nicer guys?"

"I suppose. Maybe I'm saying this because I've been burnt by so many guys who seemed interested in me, just to find out they really weren't."

What a double-edged sword! Mehran thought. *They were most likely interested in Anja because she looked like a supermodel, but any guy who is shallow enough to be interested in someone else because of their looks surely won't be looking for anything else.* Then he thought about the circumstances under which he himself had met Kirsten and thought of the hypocrisy. "I hope that doesn't mean you've given up on men," said Mehran.

Anja smiled and took a sip of her tea.

Kirsten came out of the bedroom and looked at the table. "Yum! I'll take some tea, please," she said as she went to brush her teeth.

Later in the afternoon, they headed up to Ravinia, an indoor/outdoor concert arena in a northern suburb of Chicago. The featured event that day was a concert version of Mozart's *Cosi Fan Tutte*. Mehran had packed a picnic basket full of sandwiches, sweets, cheese, bread and wine, and they spread a blanket over the grass to enjoy the music from the lawn seating. During the next few hours, they had many conversations, ranging from the fine arts to picking one's nose in public. At the end of the evening, they had enjoyed a fine concert as well as their time together.

On Sunday, they drove Anja back to the airport. As they walked to the gate, Mehran laid his arm over Anja's shoulder and asked, "So, what will you be reporting back to your mother and father about me?"

Anja smiled, put her hand on his cheek, and said, "You've got nothing to worry about." That made Mehran feel good.

Kirsten and Mehran bid Anja farewell and headed back to the car.

On the way back to the city, Kirsten started to ask a question a couple of times, but she wasn't sure how to start it. Eventually, Mehran told her to just spit it out.

"My lease for my apartment is going to be over at the end of August. I need to know whether I should renew it or not."

"Why wouldn't you renew it?"

Kirsten seemed bewildered and stunned. *Why? Because I want to come and live with you,* she thought of saying, but instead said, "Well, I don't know. We never seem to be spending any time at my place."

"Kirsten, I'm fucking with you. What would you like to do?"

"What do *you* think we should do?"

"I think you should not renew your lease and move into my apartment. We can buy some shelves for my records so that they're not scattered in milk crates all over the floor. My apartment is bare anyway. That'll open up room for your things. I would love for you to move in with me."

Kirsten's eyes lit up. "Really?"

"Kirsten, you are so silly. From the bottom of my heart, I want to spend every waking moment of my life with you, and if I'm not awake, I want to be lying next to you."

Kirsten grabbed his right arm between her hands and laid her head on his arm while he continued to drive. She then raised her head up and said, "How much is your lease? I'll pay for half of it and all the utilities."

Mehran smiled. "There's no need. I'm already paying for them. No reason to muddy the bills."

"No, that wouldn't be fair. I know you probably make good money as a chemist, but that's no reason to take advantage of you."

"Fine. In that case, I think we should share your payments for your car, since I'm the one who seems to be driving it all the time."

Kirsten smiled. "That's fair."

At the end of the month, they hired a couple of movers to move Kirsten's belongings into Mehran's apartment. Space was tight, especially closet space, but they made do. The next day Mehran ordered deep bookshelves over the phone from Ikea, and they arrived a week later. Soon the apartment was organized and much livelier than it had ever been. They donated most of Kirsten's kitchen accessories, since Mehran's kitchen was already well-stocked. They also threw away Mehran's old mattress in favor of Kirsten's newer and more firm one.

Mehran wasn't used to living with anybody. Even though he was in love with Kirsten, it took a bit to get used to having someone around all the time. They now had a television and a VCR, so they could watch movies at home. Mehran also cooked more often than he had before.

Chapter Thirty-Six

A few weeks after Kirsten had moved in, she was asked to go to Switzerland on short notice. Mehran dropped her off on a Tuesday and headed home. Their home actually seemed empty without Kirsten, so Mehran went out to one of the local music stores he frequented. He was browsing the collection of CDs and enjoying the music they were playing on the overhead speakers. Two other patrons were browsing as well. Mehran thought one of them looked familiar. *Where have I seen him before?* he thought. *At the airport,* he remembered. The boy browsing the store was the same boy he had seen at the airport dressed in all black along with the older woman and the younger girl. *What a coincidence,* he thought.

He kept an eye on the boy, curious about what music he was browsing. Mehran walked by and saw that he was looking through Ella Fitzgerald CDs. *Interesting,* thought Mehran. Mehran continued walking toward the cashier, Thomas. As a frequent music buyer, Mehran knew all the clerks, including Thomas, well. They were talking when they both noticed the boy take a CD from the shelf, put it inside his jacket and start to head out the door. Thomas moved to intercept the boy and was about to yell out when Mehran grabbed his arm.

"I'll pay for it," said Mehran.

By now the boy was at the door, exiting the store.

"Why? He's a thief," said Thomas.

"Let me take care of this. Here! Take this. I'll talk to him." Mehran tossed a $20 bill on the counter and hurried to the door. He followed the boy. The boy looked behind to make sure Thomas wasn't following him and noticed Mehran. They continued to walk for several blocks until the boy turned onto a side street. Mehran also turned the corner and found that the boy had stopped to tie his shoe, so Mehran slowed down. When the boy got up, he started walking faster; Mehran kept pace. The boy looked back and saw Mehran still there, so he took off running. Mehran started to run as well. When the boy checked behind him while still running, he tripped over the uneven sidewalk and face planted on the ground. Mehran caught up to him. The boy started to get up to try and run, when Mehran yelled, "Wait! I'm not a cop."

The boy stopped and turned to Mehran. "Then why are you following me?"

Mehran tried to catch his breath from the sprint he had just done. "You don't have to worry. I paid for the CD. Which one did you take anyway?"

The boy cautiously took out the CD and handed it to Mehran.

Mehran looked at the CD and the list of songs. "Ah, I don't have this one, but I have many of the songs on an LP."

"What's an LP?"

"Long Play. They were called that because before they came to the market, the 78 only had a capacity of 5 minutes, compared to over 20 minutes on the LP. Why did you take the CD?"

"Because I wanted to listen to it."

Mehran handed the CD back to the boy.

"Why? Why did you pay for it?" asked the boy.

"Because I had the money and wanted you to have the CD."

"I can't take the CD."

"You can't take the CD now that you know I paid for it, but you could take the CD from the store without paying for it?"

Mehran specifically didn't use the word "steal" because he didn't want to alarm the boy. It was then that Mehran noticed the boy bleeding from his chin.

"Hey, you're bleeding. You must have banged your face pretty hard. Where do you live?"

"About 10 blocks from here, west of Clark. I came this way just to make sure nobody was following me."

"Here, come with me. I live just a couple of blocks away."

The boy looked conflicted and wasn't sure whether he should follow Mehran, but he figured he'd be able to fend off Mehran should anything happen.

They went upstairs to Mehran's apartment. By now the boy had blood all over his T-shirt. Mehran grabbed a plastic bag and filled it with ice and wrapped a towel around it. "Here, hold this up to your chin."

The boy did so.

"You're an Arab, aren't you?"

"I'm Palestinian."

"Aha, that'd explain why you spoke Arabic."

"When did you hear me speak Arabic?"

"At the airport. I was picking up my girlfriend a while back when I noticed you and your family greeting someone coming from abroad. Then I recognized you in the music store."

Girlfriend? thought the boy. *Good! At least he's not gay and is not going to make a move on me.*

"I'm Mehran." Mehran extended his hand for a shake.

"I'm Fallah."

They shook hands. "At the airport I saw that you were all wearing black in mourning."

"Yes, my brother was killed in Palestine."

"Oh. I'm so sorry to hear that."

"We all were. Him and his wife, the one you saw coming to the airport, were going to be coming here in 2 months."

"How did he die? Car accident?"

"No. He was shot by an Israeli soldier at a border crossing."

Mehran didn't know what to say.

"He was going to be here, and then he was dead," said Fallah.

"That is very unfortunate."

"Yes. My mother and his wife will wear black for the next year."

"I'm originally from Iran, so I know about the customs and wearing of black garments."

"You're from Iran? But you don't have an accent."

"Some people can still detect an accent when I speak, but for the most part it's gone. I've been here for 12 years now."

"I have been here only for 4 years."

"How's your chin? Let me look."

Fallah removed the ice pack. "It stopped bleeding, but you should go wash the dirt away and continue to ice it, because it'll bleed after you wash it. There's the bathroom."

Fallah went to the bathroom to wash his face, and Mehran went to the kitchen to brew some tea. When he came out of the kitchen, he noticed Fallah looking at his CD collection.

"Ella Fitzgerald is an odd thing for – what are you, 18, 19?"

"I'm 19."

"Why jazz? That's an odd thing for a 19-year-old Palestinian to be interested in."

"I went to high school over here for 3 years and was part of the jazz band."

"Oh, nice. What did you play?"

"I had played a melodica when I was younger. They asked what I wanted to learn when I got here. I always wanted to play the piano, but they said piano was too hard to learn. They put me on drums."

Mehran remembered his own melodica and how it was his primary instrument for most of his childhood. "So, did you play drums in the jazz band?"

"I was never good enough to play as the primary drummer, but I liked the music they played, so I continued to take it. In my senior year, I was getting to be pretty good at drums, so I played every once in a while."

"That's nice. Have you ever heard of Max Roach?"

"No."

"Here. Let me play a tune for you."

Mehran headed over to the LP collection, pulled out a Sonny Rolling LP and put it on.

When the tune was over, Fallah said, "Wow! What was that?"

"That was *Strode Rode*. The drummer is Max Roach."

"That was amazing! Can we listen to it again?"

Mehran played the track one more time.

"I love the conversation between the sax and the drums," said Fallah.

"I tell you what. I'll put in a tape and record the whole album for you."

"Thank you!"

Mehran started taping the first side of the LP and then headed into the kitchen to get the tea ready. They sat and drank their tea until Mehran finished taping both sides of the LP.

"Here you go," Mehran gave the tape to Fallah.

"I will listen to this tonight. I should get going, though. My mom will worry."

"You can't go like that, not with all the blood on your shirt."

"I'll be fine."

"You will be fine, but your mom won't."

Mehran headed into the bedroom and grabbed a T-shirt. "Here, you can change in the bathroom."

Fallah changed his shirt and came out.

"Amsterdam? Is this T-shirt from Amsterdam?" asked Fallah.

"Yes, it is."

"Have you been there?"

"Yes. They have good jazz music over there, too."

"I hope to travel someday."

"Insha'Allah," *God willing,* said Mehran.

Fallah started to head out the door. "I will bring back your shirt."

"It's no big deal."

After Fallah left, Mehran thought about how fortunate he was to be able to enjoy music without having to steal it. *Music should be free. Music wants to be free. Everyone should be able to listen to whatever music they want, just like everyone should be able to view a piece of art if they desire.* That said, the logistics of delivering music to the masses would be much easier than some other forms of art because of the easiness of duplicating music, just like he had given Fallah a copy of his jazz LP. *Of course, how would artists make money then?* His thoughts went back to his conversation with Roshan. *Cut out the middleman. I wish there was a way for musicians to receive the full monetary benefit of their creations.* Mehran listened to more music before he called it a night and went to bed without eating.

The next morning, the phone rang. He picked up the phone, knowing it would be Kirsten.

"Hello?" he asked.

"Hi, honey!"

"Hi! How are you?"

"I'm fine. I just wanted to hear your voice before you left for work."

"I miss you, and so does our bed."

"And I miss our bed, too. I'll be home in a couple of days."

"When? Let me know, and I'll come and pick you up."

"Don't worry. I'll take a cab."

"I don't mind."

"I know you don't. Don't worry. I love you, and I miss you."

"I love you, too."

Mehran laid in bed, thinking about how his life had changed since he met Kirsten. He looked forward to being with her, talking with her. He enjoyed what they had. Then his eyes fell on the frame on the wall, holding the knot and the locket. He remembered Naghmeh and all they had been through. He missed her as well. How would Naghmeh react if she was alive and knew that Mehran was living with Kirsten? Naghmeh had loved him without telling him, so she probably would have kept her feelings to herself about this as well. But she wasn't alive.

Mehran thought about Naghmeh a few minutes more. Then he got up, walked to the frame, took it off the wall and kissed it before putting it in a dresser drawer under his shirts.

Chapter Thirty-Seven

Mehran came home from work 2 days later and headed straight to the bedroom to change. Once there, he almost dropped the keys still in his hand. Kirsten was dressed in high heels, thigh-highs and a corset and seductively lay on the bed, smiling at Mehran.

Mehran's eyes widened as he uttered, "Hubba hubba." Kirsten smiled and watched him undress before he jumped into bed with her.

"So, did you pick these up in Zurich?" Mehran asked later, while they were still in bed.

Kirsten nodded her head seductively. "Uh-huh."

"Did you miss me?"

"Uh-huh."

"Do you love me?"

"Uh-huh."

"Do you want me to cook you dinner?"

"Uh-huh."

"Can you respond with anything besides uh-huh?"

"Uh-huh," as she moved on top of him.

"Do you need more satisfaction?"

"Uh-huh."

"Is this the position you want?"

"Uh-huh."

Mehran laughed and said, "Uh-huh," as they embraced.

While Mehran made dinner for them later, he told Kirsten about Fallah.

"It's a good thing you helped him. I'm proud of you," she said.

"Thank you! I always strive for your approval."

They both laughed.

"When I was waiting in bed for you, I noticed that the frame on the wall was gone," Kirsten said quietly.

"Yes. I took it down."

"Why?"

"I was looking at it the other day when you called me. I figured it had no place on the wall of the bedroom we make love in."

"You did that for me?"

"I'm not sure if I would say I did it for you, but I just didn't think it should be there anymore. I put it in a dresser drawer."

"I know how much she means to you."

"Thank you for understanding. She will always have a place in my heart. I just don't think either of us should be reminded of it with the frame hanging in a prominent place in our bedroom."

Kirsten laid her hand on his for a while as they ate. Suddenly, she snapped her fingers and said, "Oh, I forgot. You have a letter from Guatemala."

"Really, where is it?"

Kirsten got up, retrieved the letter and gave it to Mehran. Mehran opened the letter and read it while Kirsten ate a few bites more.

Mehran had tears in his eyes, but they didn't seem like sad tears. He was smiling.

"What is it?" Kirsten asked.

Mehran finished the letter and handed it to Kirsten.

Kirsten looked over the letter. It was in Spanish. She recognized words similar to English and Italian, but couldn't understand the whole thing. At the bottom, there was a heart drawn on the paper and a signature. The signature read "Isabel." "What is this?" she asked.

Mehran wiped his tears. "There's something I haven't told you."

Kirsten's heart dropped. What could this be? Had he not told her everything? Obviously he hadn't, or he wouldn't be warning her about withholding information from her. After the conversation they had in Switzerland about not lying to each other and giving themselves to each other, she wanted to believe that this would most likely be nothing, but deep down in her stomach she feared the worst. She put her fork down and managed to utter, "What haven't you told me?"

"This is my first child who has just graduated from college in Guatemala."

"Your child?"

"Remember how I said that on every trip that I took to Mexico and Central America, I always backpacked and stayed with the poor?"

"Go on."

"My trips were more than vacations for me. At many small towns that I stayed at, I always met with a local high school teacher. After learning about the school, I always asked the teacher one question, 'Which child, in your opinion, has the greatest potential to make an impact on your society if he or she were to attend college but won't get a chance to make that impact because he or she can't afford college?' The teacher would usually point me to a couple of kids. I sat with the kids in their huts and ate dinner with their families. At the end of my stay in their town, I assured them that I would be paying for their college fees should they decide to attend college. I started doing this more than 5 years ago. This is the first one of those kids who graduated from college a couple of months ago. She has just received a scholarship to medical school."

Kirsten looked down at the letter and then stared at Mehran, shocked. "How many kids have you done this for?"

"Twenty-three, so far." He got up and went into the bedroom and returned shortly with a shoebox. He put the box next to Kirsten and sat back down at the table. Kirsten opened the shoe box. It was filled with letters. She picked up a few.

"Please keep them in order for me," said Mehran.

She combed through the letters. They were from all over North and Central America. Guatemala, Mexico, Belize, El Salvador, Honduras, Nicaragua. The list even included the United States. "United States?" she asked.

"Believe it or not, there are people here who deserve the same."

"How much has this cost you?"

"Nothing. This has all been paid with proceeds from my investments."

"Your investments?" And then she understood. That's why Mehran was at their bank. He was funding an account in Switzerland so that he could transfer the money at will to banks in all these countries without scrutiny from the taxman. "How did you get all this money?"

"It was left to me by my parents."

"Why wouldn't you tell me about what you did in these countries?"

"I didn't want to look like I was boasting. That's the last impression I would have wanted to leave on you."

"I love you more now than I did 5 minutes ago." She added generous and benevolent to her list of adjectives to describe Mehran.

Mehran laughed. "Why? Because I have money?"

"Shut up. Don't ruin my moment," she said as she closed her eyes.

Mehran remained silent. Eventually, Kirsten got up and walked over to him. She straddled him on the chair and kissed him, romantically first and then with lust.

Chapter Thirty-Eight

A couple of nights later, Fallah showed up at their door. He brought Mehran's shirt back. Mehran buzzed him in and asked him to come up. Once inside, Mehran introduced Fallah to Kirsten.

"It's nice to meet you, Miss Kirsten."

Kirsten laughed. "You can just call me Kirsten. It's nice to meet you as well. I hope you don't mind, but Mehran told me how you two met."

Fallah put his head down. He felt ashamed of what he had done. Then he looked up and said, "It was very nice of Mehran to pay for the CD."

"Well, that's Mehran for you!"

"Mehran, when I went home, my mother asked me what happened to my chin and where I'd gotten the shirt from, so I told her I fell in the street and that I met you. I didn't tell her about the music store. But because you took me in and gave me your shirt, and you're Middle Eastern yourself, she wants you to come over for dinner."

"Ah, that's very nice of her. She doesn't have to cook for us," said Mehran. He knew he was tarofing, because he really wanted to learn more about this family, just like he had about countless families he had met with before during his trips.

"She insisted. It is our custom."

"Well, Kirsten, when will you be out of town again?"

Kirsten gave Mehran a dirty look and said, "What if I want to go, too?"

"Of course, you're invited as well," said Fallah.

"There! Now you don't have to wait for me to be out of town, Mister," Kirsten said to Mehran.

"Well, in that case, I suppose any night is good," said Mehran.

"I'll tell her Friday night. That's okay, isn't it?" asked Fallah.

"That's perfect!" said Kirsten. "What should we bring?"

"Oh, nothing. My mom will have everything."

"How about we bring dessert?"

"That sounds good." Fallah gave them his address and left.

That week, Mehran and Kirsten discussed going to Fallah's apartment and decided they should not go empty handed. They ended up going to a local shop and picked up a vase to take over.

On Friday night, they walked over to Fallah's, figuring they could take a cab back. On their way, they stopped by a Middle Eastern bakery to pick up fresh baklava. When they arrived, Fallah was looking out the window and came downstairs to greet them. They went to the second-floor apartment and were greeted by Fallah's mother and his sister-in-law. Fallah told Mehran and Kirsten that his mother didn't speak English, so he would translate, and that his sister-in-law spoke broken English.

Mehran said, "Hello," while Kirsten said, "As-salam alaykom." Fallah's mother smiled and said something and he spoke back to her, then turned to Kirsten and laughed. "She says hello and thinks it's great that you know how to say hello in Arabic." Mehran was again in awe of Kirsten. She never ceased to amaze him.

The women nodded to Mehran, but they came forward to hug Kirsten. Kirsten, surprisingly, seemed very comfortable acting out the foreign customs.

"Please give her my condolences for the death of her son, and then my condolences to your sister-in-law for the death of her husband," said Mehran.

Fallah translated and then said, "and they thank you. Come in. Come in and sit."

Mehran extended the vase to Fallah's mother and said, as was customary in the Middle East, "It's unworthy of your home."

Fallah's mother took the gift and nodded her head in thanks.

They went and sat at the table. On the mantle above the fireplace, a few pictures of a young man rested. One of them had a ribbon running across one corner.

"Is that your brother, Fallah?" asked Kirsten.

"Yes."

A few seconds later, a child came out of one of the bedrooms. She was wearing a pink dress and ran toward and wrapped her hands around Fallah's sister-in-law's leg.

"This is my niece, Malak. She likes to be tickled," said Fallah and he started wiggling his fingers while looking at the little girl. The girl broke into laughter.

"She's adorable," said Kirsten. She got up from the table and sat on the ground and motioned the girl to come over. At first, the girl was hesitant, but her mother told her something in Arabic and she walked toward Kirsten.

"Is that a little doll in your hand?"

Fallah translated and the girl nodded.

"What's her name?"

Fallah again translated and the girl said, "Mina."

"Oh, she's almost as cute as you! You want to sit here and we play with the doll?"

Fallah translated and in a second, the girl sat in front of Kirsten, speaking to her in Arabic while Kirsten spoke to Mina in English. Mehran watched the whole conversation. *Amazing. Who knew dolls could be such natural translators.*

Fallah's mother came out of the kitchen with a tray full of tea glasses. Everyone took one. When she finally sat, she said something to Fallah.

"She says you've come from a great country. How she wishes that Palestine would turn like Iran someday."

Mehran wasn't sure how to answer, so he just said, "Thank you." He wasn't sure because he didn't know if she was referring to Iran, or Persia as it was known throughout history, with its Persian empire spanning continents, or if she was referring to the post-revolution Iran as an Islamic Republic. Perhaps she was just referring to Iran because it was a country that ruled its own internal affairs, as opposed to Palestine that was basically an occupied country and an apartheid state.

Fallah translated and then asked, "What kind of work do you do?"

"I'm a chemical engineer."

Fallah spoke to his mother and they exchanged a couple of sentences. From her tone, Mehran could tell that she was chiding him. "What's wrong?"

"Nothing, she keeps saying that I should go to college and become an engineer, too."

"What *are* you doing now that you've graduated from high school?"

"I work at a restaurant around the corner a few days a week. I'm ashamed to say it, but I'm a dishwasher. We don't have any money for me to go to college."

"If I may ask, where is your dad?"

"He'll be home late. He is a taxi driver. Since he had to go to Palestine to arrange everything for my brother's funeral, he missed a couple of weeks of work and is pulling double shifts."

"He is hard work," Fallah's sister-in-law said.

Mehran faced the sister-in-law. "What kind of business was your husband in?"

She turned to Fallah and asked, "Business?"

Fallah responded in Arabic. She nodded and said, "Electricity."

"Oh, he was an electrician?"

"Yes."

Mehran looked at the two on the floor playing together with the doll.

Fallah's mother spoke in Arabic to Fallah and he said, "She says dinner will be ready in half an hour."

She continued to speak and Fallah translated. "She wants to again thank you for taking care of me the day I tripped on the sidewalk. I am now her only son, and she doesn't want anything to happen to me. It was very nice of you to give me your shirt."

"Tell her I didn't do anything that she wouldn't have done for me had it been me who fell on the street in front of your home."

Fallah translated and his mother looked at Mehran, smiled and nodded.

"When I saw you at the airport, I also saw a young girl with you."

"That is my sister. She's in the bedroom studying."

Fallah's mother yelled, "Nawal." Mehran realized that the mother actually understood a bit of English.

A door opened, and the girl came out and stood by her mother. The mother told her something in Arabic and the girl said, "Hello."

Mehran and Kirsten both said hello.

"Nawal, that's your name?" Kirsten asked.

"Yes."

"That's a lovely name. What does it mean?" asked Mehran.

"It means 'gift.'"

"Very interesting. Could that be because your mother always wanted a daughter and after two sons, she had you, her last child?" Mehran asked.

"Yes, that's what she tells me."

"That's great. What are you studying?"

"Chemistry. I hate it."

Mehran laughed. "Hate it? Chemistry is really cool!"

"I don't understand why I have to learn about the atoms if I can't see them."

"You believe in God, don't you?"

"Yes. I am a Muslim."

"Do you see God?"

"No."

"Yet, you believe in him and know he's there."

Nawal felt like she was caught in a bind. "Yes, but I see his creations."

"What about everything that's around us? What about ourselves? Aren't we made up of atoms as well?"

Nawal, defeated, said, "I suppose so."

Fallah was trying to keep up with the conversation, translating for his mother as Mehran and Nawal spoke.

"What are you specifically having a problem with anyway?"

"With electron configuration."

"I'm a chemical engineer; I could explain that to you. Do you want to bring your homework over here and we'll go over it?"

She looked at her mother for approval, and the mother said something to her in Arabic. "I don't want to take your time. You're our guest here."

"Nonsense. I would be happy to help."

She ran to the bedroom to get her homework.

"Your mother must understand some English," said Mehran to Fallah.

"A little."

Kirsten asked Malak, "Do you have any other dolls?"

Fallah translated and Malak ran into the same room Nawal had gone into and came back with a handful of dolls. Kirsten looked at Mehran and smiled.

Nawal also came back out with her homework and sat at the table near Mehran. They spent the next 20 minutes going over the basics leading into and including electron configuration. It was Kirsten's turn to be amazed at how easily Mehran was able to talk to the teen girl and keep her attention, explaining chemistry like it was nothing extraordinary. While Nawal was working on one of the problems, Mehran was browsing the book. Inside, between the pages, he found several drawings.

"Nawal, did you draw these?" asked Mehran.

"Yes. In chemistry class."

Mehran handed the drawings to Kirsten. Kirsten looked at the drawings. They were quite good.

"Nawal, do you have any other drawings?" asked Kirsten.

"Yes, in my room."

After Mehran had helped Nawal finish her homework, Nawal smiled at Mehran. "Thank you! I wish they explained this at school the way you did. I understand it now."

"You're welcome. Any time you get stuck, just have Fallah bring you over, and I'll tutor you."

While Mehran and Kirsten were busy with the kids, Fallah's mother and sister-in-law had started setting the table. When they began bringing the food, there was no end to it. There was a little bit of everything on the table, including condiments like olives and pickles.

After they sat down, Mehran asked Fallah to tell them what everything was.

"This is maqluba. It's rice and eggplant, with other vegetables, and then chicken and nuts on top. This other one is mansaf. It's yellow rice with a thick yogurt over it, with nuts, then poured over a piece of bread and lamb. The bread at the bottom is the best part, since all the lamb juices go in it."

"Wow! This is a lot of food," said Kirsten.

"Please, please," said Fallah's mother as she pointed to the food.

They all dug into the homemade meal. There was plenty of food, and Mehran and Kirsten didn't hold back. They continued to converse throughout dinner and learned much about what was happening in Palestine.

After dinner, they sat back at the table and enjoyed tea and the baklava Mehran and Kirsten had brought.

"Do you want to show us your drawings, Nawal?" asked Kirsten.

"There are many of them."

"Are they on your walls? Can you show them to us?" Kirsten continued.

"Sure."

They got up and went to the bedroom. The walls were covered with drawings, mostly in pencil, some in pen. There was one oil painting on the wall.

"Are all these yours?" asked Mehran.

Nawal nodded.

"Nawal, you have a great talent. Have you taken any art classes?" asked Kirsten.

"I have in high school. I really want to study art."

"Have you done any oil besides this one?" asked Mehran.

"We couldn't afford the supplies. I begged Fallah to buy me this canvas, and I borrowed the supplies from a friend in order to paint this. It was required for the class."

Mehran and Kirsten looked at each other. They looked at the oil painting more closely. The painting was the face and hair of a girl against a red background. The girl seemed to be falling, facing upwards with her hair and pendant being dragged upwards, defying gravity. Upside down tears were falling upward from her face toward the top of the painting.

After a minute or two of intensely looking at the painting, Kirsten put her hand on Nawal's shoulder. "Nawal, this is great work for your first oil piece. So much depth and meaning. You have the potential to become a great artist."

Nawal smiled. "Thank you."

As Mehran and Kirsten prepared to leave, Mehran thanked Fallah's mother for a lovely meal. Malak ran toward Kirsten and offered her one of her dolls.

"Ah, that is your doll. I can't take that from you!"

Nawal translated to Malak and then responded, "She says if you take the doll, then you can play with the doll, too, just like she plays with her dolls."

Kirsten bent down, picked up Malak in her arms, and gave her a kiss. When she put Malak back down, she took the doll from Malak's hands and smiled, "Shukraan." *Thank You.*

Fallah walked them downstairs. Before they left, Mehran asked, "Do you have any means of transportation?"

"We have only the taxi. I have a bicycle, too. Why?"

"The paper mill I work for is a straight shot down the road, about three miles, on the west side of Chicago. There's a bus that goes down North Avenue and passes right in front of the mill. Give me a call on Monday. I'm sure we can find you something better to do than washing dishes," Mehran said as he handed one of his business cards to Fallah.

Fallah's eyes widened. "Really? I would do anything to not wash dishes anymore."

"Call me on Monday."

"Bye, Fallah," said Kirsten.

"Bye, Kirsten. Thank you, Mehran."

Kirsten and Mehran decided to enjoy the September night and walk home. Kirsten's arms were wrapped around Mehran's, but they realized it would make for a slow walk home. They held hands instead.

"You were pretty good with Malak tonight," Mehran said.

"My sister and I used to play with dolls all the time. Don't you think she's cute?" She held up the doll.

"Not as cute as you!"

"You weren't too bad with Nawal yourself."

"Chemistry is not that hard. It just needs to be explained well."

Secretly, they each adored the fact that the other was great with kids.

They continued their fast-paced walk toward their place. By now they were zigzagging the blocks and going through some dark streets. They were a few blocks from their apartment on Clifton Avenue when they noticed a dark shadow approaching them. Mehran and Kirsten got closer to each other to make room on the sidewalk, but the closer they got to the shadow it became apparent that the shadow had no intention of switching sides, so Mehran pushed Kirsten to the left of the sidewalk to give the shadow space on the right to pass. When they were about eight feet from the man, the man stopped.

"Give me your wallet," said the man.

"I don't think so," Mehran said and continued to walk.

The man took a couple of steps back to keep his distance from them, quickly pulled out a gun and said, "Give me your fucking wallet now. Your watch, too."

Mehran instinctively pulled Kirsten behind himself and said, "Fine," while taking off his watch.

"Throw it to me."

"What if while you're trying to catch the fucking watch, you miss and pull the trigger?" Mehran threw the watch on the grass by the sidewalk.

"Your wallet, too."

Mehran was holding Kirsten back with one hand as she tried to come around to the front until Mehran said, "Stop Kirsten!" She stopped with one hand over his shoulder, and the hand with the doll over his arm. "Mehran!" she said in a panicky voice.

Mehran took out his wallet. "Credit cards, too? Or do you just want the cash?"

"Give me the fucking wallet before I gut you both."

Mehran threw the wallet on the grass as well. "There! Now move aside so we can pass."

The man was eyeing Kirsten. "Give me the fucking doll."

Kirsten was about to extend her hand, when Mehran said, "Fuck you! No!"

"You wanna fuckin' die?" he asked as he raised the gun up to Mehran's face. "Give me the fucking doll now!"

Kirsten threw the doll on the grass as well. The man moved over, and Mehran and Kirsten started to pass. Just then, they heard the chirp of a siren and the blue lights from a squad car turned on. Police were coming down the street, not 50 feet from where they were.

The robber didn't have time to pick up anything from the ground before he took off running. The police car revved and quickly caught up to the man. The officer in the passenger seat jumped out of the car and took off running after the robber. Mehran yelled, "He's armed." The car sped past the robber, slammed on its brakes, and the driving officer got out. They had the robber cornered at about 150 feet from Mehran and Kirsten when they both pulled their guns on him. The robber threw his hands up.

"Get down on the ground. Now!"

Mehran suddenly felt he had no muscle control over his legs. He had heard the phrase "giving out at the knees," and he had always dismissed it as bullshit, but he actually felt that he could not continue to stand. He sat on the sidewalk, his heart beating so fast and so hard that he thought it would jump out of his chest. Kirsten sat down next to him and hugged his arm, in shock herself.

"I didn't do nothin' officers," said the robber.

"Get down on the ground. This is your last warning."

The robber got down on the ground, and the officers quickly hand-cuffed him and put him in the back of the squad car. It was clear that the officers had seen the interaction between the man, Mehran and Kirsten and got suspicious. By now two other squad cars were pulling up. The officers from the first car walked back to Mehran.

"Are you two okay?"

Mehran looked up, but couldn't open his mouth.

"Dillon, grab a couple bottles of water for these guys."

One of the arriving officers opened his trunk and came back with two bottles of water. Mehran took them and opened one. His hands visibly shaking. He took a gulp and handed it to Kirsten. Kirsten just shook her head.

"It's okay. He's in the back of the squad car. He can't see you, hear you or hurt you."

Mehran's nerves gave out and he broke into tears as did Kirsten.

It took Mehran several minutes to regain his composure and try to get up.

"He – he had a gun," uttered Mehran.

"Jones, did you see any gun on him?"

"No."

"Are you sure he had a gun?"

"Yes! He had it pointed right at me!" said Mehran.

"Jones, Dillon, start looking for a gun."

The other officers started to scour the street between where Mehran was and the location where the robber was apprehended. Meanwhile, the officer said, "My name is Officer Sklodowski. I'm sorry, but I'm gonna have to make a report and take down some information."

Mehran and Kirsten nodded their heads. The officer pointed his flashlight to the watch, the wallet and the doll. "Did he touch any of these?"

"No. He wanted me to throw them at him, but I was afraid he might miss and fire the gun, so I threw them on the ground."

"Good thinking." He bent down and picked up the items and gave them back to Mehran. "Cute doll!"

Cute doll? Mehran thought. He and Kirsten had just had a gun pointed at their faces. Mehran decided the officer was just trying to make them comfortable.

The officer started to make a report. Meanwhile, Officer Dillon came back and said, "We can't find the gun. He must have thrown it over one of the fences into one of the yards."

"Well, start knocking on some doors, starting from this house here," he pointed to the house they were standing in front of. Knocking wasn't necessary, though, since the siren, the lights and the yelling had everybody either out or looking out from behind their windows.

"We've been looking for this asshole for the past 2 hours. He robbed some other guy earlier tonight at knife-point, and the other guy reported it. We had no idea he had a gun on him, too."

He started to write the report and then interviewed Mehran and Kirsten separately to get each of their versions of the story.

"Bingo!" said Officer Dillon. "Bring me an evidence bag," as he walked out of the yard three houses down, holding the gun with his pen.

"All right! Now we're gonna get him for armed robbery!" said Officer Sklodowski.

"Are we through here?" asked Mehran.

"Yes. I have your phone numbers. Should we need you to testify, the prosecutor's office will be in touch with you."

"I hate to do this to you, but would you mind calling a cab for us?" Mehran asked.

"How far do you live?" he looked at the report for Mehran's address.

"Just a few blocks, but I don't think we're up to walking after all this."

"Yo, Dillon. Can you give these nice folks a ride to their place?"

They got in the back of the squad car, and Mehran gave him the address.

Officer Dillon continued to talk about thieves like this guy roaming the streets every night and how it's best to carry a cell phone to report suspicious activity and such, but Mehran and Kirsten weren't listening. They were squeezing each other's hands in the back seat. When the squad car pulled up in front of their home, Mehran reached for the door handle, and for the first time, realized that they were sitting in the back of a squad car with no access to get out. Officer Dillon opened the door for them. They got out, thanked him and walked upstairs.

That night, Mehran and Kirsten laid in bed with the night light on, holding each other and looking into each other's eyes.

"You threw me behind you," said Kirsten.

Mehran remained silent.

"And you wouldn't let me get on your side."

Mehran continued to look into Kirsten's eyes and remained silent.

"I love you," she said.

Mehran was still silent.

"Say something."

Mehran broke his silence, "All I could think of was losing you."

"And I wouldn't have wanted you to face him alone. You didn't let us face him together."

"I know. But the decision was mine to make."

"It wasn't. I care about you just as much as you care about me."

"It's over and done. It would've been just a wallet and a watch."

"What about the doll?" asked Kirsten.

"The doll was yours. I couldn't make that decision for you. I wanted you to have that doll."

"I love you."

"I love you. I couldn't think of anything happening to you. I wanted to grab his gun and shoot him in the face with it, the same way he had pointed it at my face. If I wasn't with you, I would have done that and probably died right there on the concrete."

They fell asleep, hugging each other.

Chapter Thirty-Nine

On Saturday morning, they woke up and stayed in bed talking.

"Would you like to go to Orchestra Hall tonight?" Kirsten asked.

"Isn't tonight the opening night of the season?"

"Why, yes. It is!" smiled Kirsten. "Yo-Yo Ma is playing Elgar and Dvorak concertos with Barenboim conducting. It's a benefit concert."

"How do you know that, and how are we going to get tickets on such short notice?"

Kirsten stepped out of bed, picked up her briefcase and set it on the bed. She opened it, reached in and waved two tickets at Mehran. "It was supposed to be a surprise for tonight, but I figured you could use some cheering up this morning."

"Thank you," he managed to say.

They spent the day walking by the lake and returned home with plenty of time to dress for the event. They were early to the concert and were looking over the season schedule when they noticed that Solti was to conduct Shostakovich's *Symphony No. 15* later in the season.

"I have never seen Solti in person. We need to go to this concert," Mehran said.

Kirsten made a mental note of the March 29-31, 1997, performance and planned to buy tickets.

The opening night was phenomenal if the applause was any indication. It was just what Mehran and Kirsten needed after the previous night's incident. For most of the performance, they held hands, fingers locked, inseparable after facing the threat of death together.

After the concert, they took a cab to a diner on the North Side. They were a bit overdressed for the diner, with Mehran in his tux and Kirsten in a long black dress, but that wasn't unheard of in the late hours of the night in Chicago.

At the diner, they sat across from each other and played with each other's hands.

"What was your favorite part of the concert?" Kirsten asked.

"That I was sitting next to you."

"No, seriously."

"The concert was great. I'm not a huge fan of Elgar, and pretty picky of Dvorak's works as well. The *Cello Concerto* by Elgar, though, is an amazing piece. First things first. It's in E minor, and you know my fondness for pieces in minor."

"Yes, and you have to tell me why after this."

"Okay. The first movement is calm by most standards. Compare this to, say, Saint-Saens' *Cello Concerto*, where the first movement is fast and ferocious. Elgar doesn't do that until his second movement. It's like he teased us with the first movement. The third movement was probably my least favorite, until toward the end. The melody just didn't do it for me at the beginning of the movement. Of course, he sets the stage for the final movement without the pause between the two. Then the passion of this piece came out. Barenboim does a great job. Ma made the movement bold and ferocious. I have to say, I don't know what to think of the end of the concerto, slowing to the pace of the first movement, but it still had the explosive ending I was looking for. Barenboim and Ma can't do wrong. Consider this: Barenboim conducted his newlywed wife, Jacqueline du Pre, back in

1967, playing this same piece. I wonder how he feels conducting it with Ma this time." Mehran paused. "You know who I'd like to see?"

"Who?"

"Rostropovich. His technique on the cello is amazing."

"So, why do you like the minor scale so much?"

Mehran thought for a bit. "I feel I can relate to the piece better."

"That's it? You're gonna have to do better than that."

"You're testing my ability to put my feelings into words."

"You're a grown-up man. Try!"

Mehran thought a bit more. "The minor scale is dear to me because it always reminds me of the pains in my life. I cherish the pains. I would never want to do without those memories. If someone walked up to me and said I had to lose either all the happy memories in my head, or the sad ones, I would gladly throw away the happy ones. Even in happy memories I find sadness, and in sad memories I find happiness."

"Tell me a happy memory of yours."

Mehran thought for a few seconds. "Remember Bahar, my girlfriend in Iran?"

"Yes."

"One day, when passing her on a crowded sidewalk, we were forced to stop right by each other."

"Or perhaps you *decided* to stop by each other."

"Maybe. Anyway, I grabbed her hand for a total of 5 seconds."

"Must have been a thrill!"

"Oh, it was. So much so, that I ran to the nearest drugstore and bought gauze so that I could wrap my hand in it. I didn't want the few molecules from her hand to be washed away from mine. I didn't wash my hand for a week, and I wrapped it in plastic when I took showers."

"Wow, that's sweet! That's a good memory."

"Yeah, except every time I think of it, I recognize how I would never again be able to recapture that moment."

"I think it's called time."

"I know, I know."

"You just don't like getting old."

"I wouldn't mind growing old with *you*."

Kirsten smiled as the waitress brought their dinner.

Chapter Forty

Monday morning, Fallah called Mehran. Mehran had already talked with Human Resources about hiring Fallah. They had decided that he could work in the stock room, but that he needed to come in for an interview anyway.

"Fallah."

"Hi, Mehran."

"I think I may have a job here for you, but you will need to come in for an interview."

"I have never been to an interview, except for my dishwashing job."

"It's nothing. Tell me you took chemistry in high school."

"I did. I actually took AP chemistry."

"That's really good, because the job is for a stockroom man. Our stockroom clerk is retiring in the next few months, and we need to find a replacement. You'll need to keep track of chemicals coming in and going out. You'll also need to maintain the stock ledgers."

"Are you sure I can do that job? It sounds like I'll need to be good with papers as well as chemicals."

"You are going to need some accounting skills, but some basic accounting will do. You can take those courses after you're hired."

"That sounds great! When should I come in?"

"Come in tomorrow. You don't need to dress up or anything. We all dress casually over here. Just come in jeans and a buttoned shirt. That's what you'll have to wear everyday anyway."

"Okay! Thank you so much, Mehran!"

"No problem. Be here at 10; ask for me."

"Are you the only Mehran there?"

Mehran laughed. "I hope so." He gave Fallah the address to the mill.

"Great. See you tomorrow."

"Yup. See you."

Mehran hung up the phone. He thought Fallah would do fine.

The next day, Fallah came to the mill. "Hello. I am here to see Mr. Mehran Noori."

"Hi! And who may I say is here to see him?"

"I'm Fallah."

The receptionist picked up the phone. "Mehran, there's a Mr. Fallah here to see you."

"I'll be right up."

Fallah had never heard his name preceded by "Mr." He felt good.

Mehran came up front a couple of minutes later.

"You're early!"

"I didn't want to take a chance and miss the bus or anything. You know, I hate washing dishes."

Mehran laughed. "I know. Come! I'll show you the mill before your interview."

Mehran took Fallah to one end of the mill and began a tour. "We don't actually produce the paper you can buy in the store. We take wood that has already been pulped and that's the start of our process. We chemically treat the wood and filter it according to the specifications for the type of paper we're trying to make. A lot of water goes into treating the wood, and we reuse that water as much as we can."

Mehran moved to the next section. "The pulp moves onto this machine, and we remove as much of the water as possible before the pulp goes into the press. The press here produces 1,500 pounds per square inch of pressure to get as much of the water out of the pulp as possible."

"Then we pass the pressed pulp through a dryer section. We have experimented with different drying techniques, and our favorite is cylinder drying, which is the machine you see right here with the big rollers."

They went through a closed double door and into a giant room with deafening fans running. Mehran had to yell over the sound of the fans. "The fans you hear take all the moisture out of the air and the paper. We don't let people stand in this room without ear protection for more than a few minutes, since you could sustain permanent damage to your ears."

They passed through another double door into a more quiet room. "This is the coating room. Some of the chemicals you'll be tracking are used in this room. They change the color and coating of the paper. After the paper is coated, depending on what type of paper we're trying to make, it goes through the reels. The reels determine the thickness of the paper as well as the texture."

"Finally, we take the paper and roll it onto these huge drums. The winder cuts the huge rolls into manageable chunks so that we can ship them to places that can cut them at different sizes and package them."

"Wow! This is an amazing process," said Fallah.

"Yes. Not many chemicals are used in this process. Probably two dozen or so. However, a part of our process is research and development, so we have a well-stocked inventory of chemicals. Our stock man is going to be retiring soon, so this is a good opportunity for him to train his replacement."

"I am excited!"

"Good. Let me take you to Human Resources."

They walked down a hallway and into an office.

"Eileen, this is Fallah."

Eileen got up from her chair and approached them.

"Fallah, it's very nice to meet you." She extended her hand.

Fallah thought twice about shaking her hand, but he didn't hesitate since he wanted to give a good first impression. "It's nice to meet you, too."

"Mehran tells me you have taken chemistry. How was your math in high school?"

"I got good grades. As and Bs."

"Great. Do you have any college classes?"

Before Fallah could get a chance to respond, Mehran said, "He plans to take additional chemistry and an accounting class at a city college near his home."

Fallah looked at Mehran. "Yes, I am going to take accounting."

"That's great! Because that will help you immensely in this job." She looked at Mehran. "Okay?"

"Okay. I'll leave you two be."

Mehran walked out of the room.

About a half hour later, Eileen brought Fallah to Mehran's office, "We're done here." She turned to Fallah. "Fallah, I will be in contact with you."

"Thank you," said Fallah.

"So, how did it go?" Mehran asked once Eileen had left.

"I don't think I did well. She asked a lot of questions."

"Don't worry. It's her job."

"She wanted to know if I would have any trouble getting to work."

"And what did you say?"

"I said I wouldn't, since I have a bicycle and live only a few miles away."

"Good! I'll talk to her to get a feel. She'll call you. Don't worry!"

"Okay."

Mehran walked Fallah to the front of the building, and they shook hands before Fallah left. The company hired him a couple of days later. Fallah called Mehran to give him the good news.

"That's great, Fallah!"

"Yes, and I owe it all to you."

"Why don't you come over for dinner tonight and we'll celebrate."

That night, Fallah arrived with a Middle Eastern pastry box.

"Fallah, you shouldn't have gotten us anything," Kirsten said.

"My mother told me I should, and I wanted to thank Mehran for getting me that job."

"Come on in. Mehran's in the kitchen cooking."

Fallah went into the kitchen and saw that Mehran was busy at work. "Come in and sit down Fallah," said Mehran. Fallah sat down at the small table in the kitchen and so did Kirsten.

"So, are you excited about the job?" Kirsten asked.

"Very much so. I am so glad to not be washing dishes anymore."

"Yes! I know the feeling. Mehran makes me wash the dishes because he cooks."

Fallah laughed.

"Fallah, you need to enroll in college for the accounting and the chemistry courses," said Mehran.

"I am going to. It's –" Fallah paused.

"It's what?" Mehran asked.

"Nothing."

"No, what is it? You have to start the courses."

"It's just that I don't have the money for the courses right now."

"Don't worry about that. I'll pay up front, and as you make money, you'll pay me back."

"That's nice of you, but I can't take that offer."

"Sure you can! How much did you settle for salary, anyway?"

"$24,000."

"Good! You'll be able to pay me back in less than a year and catch up so that you can pay for the rest of your college."

"That is very nice of you, but I can't."

"Fallah! Don't be so stubborn that you won't see a good thing coming. I have the means to help you, and you should take the help."

"I'll think about it."

"That's fine. Think about it as much as you want, as long as tomorrow you register for the classes."

"What if the classes have started?"

"They have; they started in August. You'll sign up for November classes."

"The classes will be really good for you," Kirsten added.

That night Mehran and Kirsten enjoyed good food and music with their new friend.

Chapter Forty-One

Mehran and Kirsten spent the fall getting used to living together. They enjoyed going to jazz clubs and to the movies. Sometimes they stayed home to watch television. They had some small arguments on a couple of occasions. Perhaps they weren't even arguments, but disagreements, over non-issue subjects like the flavor of wine, or a movie they had just watched. But none had lasted more than a few minutes.

One night in early November, when they were lounging on the couch reading books, Kirsten seemed a bit occupied. She kept staring at Mehran. Mehran looked up and caught her staring.

"What?"

"Have you ever skied before?" Kirsten asked.

"I used to ski in Iran. Some of the best pistes in the Middle East are in Iran in Dizin and Shemshak."

Kirsten laughed. "Pistes? That what the slopes are called in French. Is that what they call them in Farsi, too?"

"Yes. Foreign words have a way of wiggling their way into Farsi. Why do you ask?"

"You know, my parents want me to go home for Thanksgiving. How would you like to come with me, and we hit the slopes?"

Mehran thought about what Kirsten just said. *She called her parents' home in Colorado "home." What about the home we live in? Kirsten has living parents and considers their home as hers, and I call this apartment my home.*

What if my parents were alive? Would I call their place "home"? "Is this meet-the-parents time?"

Kirsten laughed. "Do you think it is?"

"Are you forcing me to go?"

"No, but I will miss you during Thanksgiving and would like to be with you. If you weren't with me on Thanksgiving, I would keep wondering about you being alone."

"So you're feeling sorry for me and want me not to be alone?"

"Don't put words in my mouth. I love you and want you with me."

"Of course I would love to go with you."

"Good! Because I've already bought the tickets."

Mehran picked up a couch pillow and threw it at her. "Dork!"

Kirsten threw the pillow back, and Mehran lunged at her and laid on top of her on the couch. "Making decisions for me now?" he asked.

"You need decisions made for you."

"You're not the boss of me."

"I think I am."

"I'm not sure if I like the sound of that. You know, I'm not submissive."

"Yes, you are."

Mehran looked into her eyes. "When it comes to you, I will be anything you want me to be."

"Good! Because right now I want you to be my lover."

Chapter Forty-Two

Mehran was excited to meet Kirsten's parents. Meeting them would take his relationship with Kirsten to the next level. He and Kirsten flew from a busy O'Hare Airport to Denver on the day before Thanksgiving. Anja picked them up at the airport.

"Mehran, welcome to Denver!" Anja said.

"Anja! It's good to see you again." Mehran gave her a hug and a kiss on the cheek.

Kirsten and Anja hugged.

"How was your flight?" Anja asked.

"The flight was short, but the airport was a mess to get through," Kirsten said.

"You're here now. Let's get out of this place."

Anja drove them to Kirsten's parents'. It was snowing, though none was sticking to the ground.

Kirsten's parents lived in a high-rise in downtown Denver. Anja parked the car in the garage, and with the use of a special key, they took the elevator to the penthouse. The elevator door opened to the inside of the apartment. Anja stepped in first, followed by Kirsten and then Mehran.

A man who Mehran presumed to be Kirsten's father waved his wine glass at Kirsten. "Ah, Kirsten." He put the glass down and opened his arms. Kirsten walked toward him and said in an excited voice,

"Papa!" They embraced and exchanged some words in German. They broke their hug and Kirsten's father said, "So, show me this young man you've been dating."

"Papa, this is Mehran. Mehran, this is my dad, Walter."

"Walter, it is great to meet you," Mehran extended his hand.

Walter pushed his hand aside. "In this house, we hug!"

Mehran was pleasantly surprised. He believed in hugs much more than handshakes anyway, and it was nice that Kirsten's father didn't have a phobia of hugging another male, like most Americans he had known. But then, Kirsten's father wasn't born in the United States.

Walter gave Mehran a hug and then put his hands on Mehran's shoulders and pushed him back. "Let me look at you."

Mehran felt a bit scrutinized. Would his looks pass muster with Walter?

Walter was a bit taller than Mehran, probably two or three inches. He inspected Mehran for a bit. "Mehran, Kirsten has told us a lot about you. Now that I'm seeing you in person, I tend to agree with her." He turned to Kirsten without letting go of Mehran and smiled at her.

Kirsten smiled as well.

"What about me? Have I done well?" Mehran joked.

Walter laughed. "You will not find a girl better in this world than Kirsten. Come! Come let's drink some wine."

"Where's mama?" Kirsten asked.

"She's not back from work yet. They had a shipment arrive earlier today, and they have to secure it in the vault before closing the museum for the holiday," Walter said.

They walked toward the bar.

Walter looked at Mehran inquisitively. "Let me guess. You are a –"

"I'll drink anything."

"You are a Shiraz man."

"Definitely," said Kirsten. She looked Mehran in the eyes and said, "He loves it because his parents met in Shiraz."

"Shiraz it is." Walter grabbed a bottle and opened it.
"Kirsten? Anja?"

"Yes, please!" exclaimed Kirsten.

"I'm fine. I'll make a drink in a bit," said Anja.

Walter poured two glasses of wine and handed them to Kirsten and Mehran. "So, Kirsten tells me you're a chemical engineer."

"I am. I work at a paper mill."

"And what do you do there?"

"I oversee a team of engineers in charge of production, research and development."

"And you're also a musician?"

Mehran laughed and looked at Kirsten. "I wouldn't go that far. I have played an instrument or two."

"Kirsten is an accomplished pianist," said Walter.

"Why haven't I ever heard you play?" Mehran asked Kirsten.

"We don't have a piano."

"Then we shall get one when we get back to Chicago."

"We don't have room in the apartment."

"There's *always* room for musical instruments in one's home. Bach owned five harpsichords at the time of his death, as well as numerous other instruments."

Walter nodded. "He is right."

They sat down as they continued talking. Shortly the elevator opened and Kirsten's mother entered the apartment.

"Dieu! Je meme pas imaginé je pourrais me debarasser de là bas."

"Mama!" said Kirsten, excited.

They greeted each other in French, hugged and kissed. Kirsten's mother looked at Mehran and continued to speak French to Kirsten for a bit.

"Mama!" Kirsten said in an annoyed voice and then said something in French. Kirsten walked over to Mehran. "Mama, this is Mehran. Mehran, this is my mother, Amandine."

"Amandine, it is a pleasure to finally meet you," said Mehran.

Amandine said something in French.

"Now I really wish I would have learned French instead of Spanish," said Mehran.

"It's never too late," said Amandine, switching to English.

"Maybe Kirsten will teach me."

"Her French is, how do you say, rusty."

"It is not!" exclaimed Kirsten.

"How was your day, dear?" asked Walter.

"I really have to find someone else I trust with the vault. It's ridiculous that I have to stay just so we can close it."

"You're here now. Go freshen up. I'll have a glass of wine ready when you return," Walter said.

Amandine said something in French as she exited the room.

"You'll have to forgive her. She's very proud of her heritage and language," said Walter.

"There's nothing to forgive. I understand," said Mehran, although he wasn't being sincere. He understood the part about Amandine being proud of her language, but when faced with someone who doesn't speak your language and you do theirs, it would be polite to speak that language. He decided not to pay attention to that any longer and instead concentrated his senses on the smell of food throughout the condo. "Is there someone in the kitchen cooking? I am smelling something good."

"You must be hungry," said Walter.

"Not yet, but it smells delicious."

"That's our chef for the night who is cooking."

"Wow! That's great. Can't wait to meet … him? Her?" said Mehran.

"Mehran loves to cook, Papa," Kirsten offered.

"I'll take you," said Walter. They all moved toward the kitchen.

"Boris! You've got company."

The chef turned away from the stove and looked at Walter and his entourage. "Great!"

"What kind of wine would you like?" Walter asked.

"Something red. If you have a Cabernet open, that would work."

Walter left the kitchen to get a glass of wine for Boris.

"It smells delicious!" Mehran said.

"Tonight we're having a wine-braised leg of lamb. That's most likely what you're smelling. To accompany the lamb, I'm cooking saffron rice with slivered almonds over here. Another dish for non-lamb lovers is the tas-kabob there, which is a stew of potato and beef with a turmeric tomato sauce and a hint of cumin. For sides, I have shallot yogurt, Shirazi salad, Olivier salad and steamed vegetables. And last but not least, for dessert, we have my favorite, khagineh."

Mehran looked at Boris in amazement and asked, "Somehow I didn't think you were Persian with a name like Boris."

Boris laughed. "No! I'm Russian."

"Yet everything you're making is Persian."

Walter walked in and interrupted. "We have never had Persian food, so we asked our friend who is a master chef for advice on a chef familiar with Persian cooking, and he introduced us to Boris. We wanted to share authentic Persian dishes with you."

"That was very thoughtful of you," Mehran said. To Boris, he asked, "How did you come to learn Persian cooking?"

"I happened to get my start cooking in a Persian restaurant in New York. I have branched out much since and now share a restaurant here in Denver with another chef, but I am always glad to be cooking Persian food."

"That's great!" Mehran said.

They sat at the kitchen island and watched Boris cook, while Walter and Mehran got acquainted.

After a few minutes, Amandine walked into the kitchen, speaking in French.

Kirsten translated. "She says why is everyone here in the kitchen?"

Walter said in English, "Dear, we're here to keep both of our guests company," as he nodded at Boris.

Amandine said something in French, and Kirsten whispered to Mehran, "She says 'But it is so hot in here.'"

It was a bit hot in the kitchen, with the oven on and several items cooking over the stove. Boris said, "I wanted the flavor of the lamb to fill up the place before I turned on the hood," and he turned on the vent above the stove.

Amandine said something in French again. Kirsten, frowning, said to her mother, "Because we have friends here who don't speak French. That's why I am translating."

"Fine, fine!" said Amandine in English. "I need some wine," she said as she turned to leave the kitchen.

Mehran thought about the impression he was getting of Amandine. He would really have to impress her if he wanted her to accept him as Kirsten's boyfriend. He asked Kirsten, "Can we go to the other room for a second? I wanted to look at a painting."

"Be careful with my Chagall!" Amandine said as she was walking.

"You mean 'Les Maries dans le ciel de Paris'?" Mehran asked Amandine.

She seemed surprised and stopped at the door to turn toward Mehran. "Your French is awful, but you recognized the piece. How did you know the name of the painting?"

Mehran smiled. "Kirsten has been a good art teacher."

Amandine headed to the bar. Kirsten grasped Mehran's wrist to keep him by the door and whispered, "I'm really sorry about my mom."

"Ah, not to worry. Before the night's over I'll have her adoring me. She is just as you said she would be. Likes to be the center of attention."

The whole condo was decorated rather tastefully, with mostly European modern art. They had a couple of paintings by Chagall and some other ones that Mehran had never seen before.

"I don't recognize most of these paintings," he said to Kirsten.

"That's because they're from newer artists," Amandine said. "My home is kind of a gallery for up and coming artists to show their work at the parties I throw."

"That's fascinating," Mehran responded as he moved in front of the first Chagall. He stood still, but then started to shift his distance and position from the painting.

"What is he doing?" Amandine asked Kirsten.

"Mehran believes that he can understand a piece better if he varies his viewing perspective. He sees new things depending on where he's standing."

"Interesting," said Amandine.

"I remember seeing a picture of this painting. I never thought I would see it in person, since it's in a private collection," Mehran said.

"It is – how do you say in English? A double-edged sword?"

"Double-edged sword?"

"Yes. For art lovers, such as myself, this is a most prized possession. One that I can enjoy every day. But as a museum director, I believe that everyone should have the opportunity to see it. I loan it often, as long as I get something else to replace it while it's gone. In a way, I have my own museum in this home."

"That's a beautiful way of splitting art," Mehran said as he continued to look at the painting. "I wonder why Chagall has so many paintings with the subjects in the sky."

"Why do you think that is?" Amandine asked as she winked at Kirsten.

Mehran turned to Amandine. "I'm not sure. If I were to guess, I would think that he liked to dream, or that he liked to capture his dreams. It could also mean a broken heart, the one that got away," he pointed to the painting on the wall.

Amandine seemed intrigued. "But *what do you feel?*"

Mehran paused, looked at Amandine, and said, "I believe it was the death of his one and only true love, his first wife, the same girl who he had to convince her parents that he was worthy of marrying their daughter. He certainly made many paintings of her, usually as a bride and accompanied by the groom; it's clear that he adored her. By painting the ghostly married couple in the sky over and over, he essentially resurrects her and practically ensures that his love for his wife would live forever, not only in his mind but also on canvas."

Amandine was quiet. Kirsten didn't know where Mehran had gotten everything he had just said, because it certainly wasn't something they had talked about before. Amandine seemed surprised.

Mehran continued. "This specific piece is even more melancholy than some of his other pieces. The rooster pecking at the balloon-like structure lifting the couple into the sky could be interpreted as the disease that killed his wife, or the war that had caused them to be displaced from Europe and in a way lead to the death of his wife. I do believe it's the latter in this case. If you notice, there's a hen trapped in the balloon. The rooster is the feeling of resentment his wife had because of being displaced, and the hen is the dream of Europe.

Mehran stopped talking, engrossed in his own thoughts on the painting. The painting clearly showed the sadness Chagall must have felt when his first wife died, a grief fully visible through his repeated attempts to connect with his dead wife by painting the bride and groom in numerous paintings. Even in this painting, by his signature, there was a drawing of a couple holding each other.

His thoughts were broken when Kirsten laid her hand on his shoulder. Amandine turned to Kirsten, smiled, and said, "I like him." She extended her arm to Mehran and said, "Come, dear. Let's go back to the kitchen and drink wine. We can look at paintings later when the wine has set in." She slid her arm through Mehran's and pulled him into the kitchen.

Kirsten was shocked. She turned around, looked at the painting, and loudly asked, "It says all that?" Her heart was pumping hard, excited that Mehran had followed through with what he promised her only minutes ago.

By the end of the night, they had gone through seven bottles of wine. Boris left for home, while Mehran and Kirsten slept in the guest bedroom, and Anja slept on the couch in the family room.

Kirsten was the first one up the next morning. She made her way to the kitchen to put on a pot of coffee and left to take a quick shower before returning to the kitchen. The smell of coffee woke Anja. They each filled a cup and sat down at the island.

"He is quite an amazing person," said Anja.

"You have no idea."

"How's sex?"

"Sex is great. I have never felt closer to anyone than I have with him, physically and emotionally."

"Is he the one?"

"If he asked me, I'd say 'yes' in a heartbeat."

"Why don't you ask him?"

"We've only been dating for 8 months. I'm pretty sure he feels the same way about me that I do about him. I want to give him some room. It'll happen. We're both getting older. He's almost 32 and I just turned 30. It'll happen soon."

That day, Anja and Kirsten prepared a Thanksgiving meal that they all enjoyed together. Amandine had warmed up quite well to Mehran, and Mehran got along with Walter very nicely. The following day, they all drove west for 3 days of skiing. Mehran and Kirsten headed back home on Monday.

Chapter Forty-Three

Mehran had never celebrated Christmas since being on his own after coming to the United States. Kirsten, on the other hand, always celebrated Christmas. They purchased a tree and decorated it together with the ornaments and lights Kirsten had brought when she moved in. They spent many hours listening to music while admiring their tree.

For Mehran, setting up the Christmas tree was more than just going through the motions of Christmas. It made him feel like he had a family with Kirsten. He thought that he had met his one and only. Kirsten was the best thing in his life, and he didn't want to let her go. He sat down one day and made a list of things he liked the most in life: music, helping others, cooking and being in love with Kirsten. He thought he would love having children and so added that to the list. Then he created two additional columns titled "Alone" and "Kirsten." On each square he put a checkmark where it applied. The "Alone" column was full, except for the "Being in Love with Kirsten" and "Children." Every box under "Kirsten" had a checkmark.

He looked at the sheet and wondered if he was putting too much thought into it. *I'm in love with her; she is the only person in my life. Do I really need a bunch of checkmarks to tell me that we are meant for each other?*

He got up and threw the paper away. He knew the perfect gift for Kirsten.

Mehran and Kirsten went shopping on several occasions in December and made a point to separate so that they could purchase presents for one another. They would meet later in the mall to either eat or see a movie, or both. On their first visit to the mall, Mehran visited some of the jewelers and decided that he would come back alone during the day to find the perfect engagement ring.

At work the next day, he checked on Fallah to see how he was doing at his job.

"Good morning, Mehran."

"Good morning, Victor. How are things working out with Fallah?"

"He's coming along nicely. His accounting is a bit weak, but the class he's taking should help. It's just a matter of paper and tracking. He'll be fine."

"That's good news. Any problems?"

"Not really. He's a nice guy. Pleasant to work with. He's eager to make this work."

"I appreciate your working with him."

Mehran saw Fallah in the back taking inventory of the chemicals.

"Fallah!"

Fallah walked to the counter. "Mehran!"

"How are things?"

"I have much to learn, but Victor is a master at this and he's teaching me."

"Good. I'm glad. How about you come over for dinner sometime?"

"That would be nice. I'd love to see you and Kirsten."

"Good. Come over tonight if you're available."

"That will work."

Mehran left the office in the afternoon and went to several jewelers; he took his time looking at rings. One of the jewelers happened to be Iranian. Once he heard Mehran's name, he started talking with him in Farsi. He asked Mehran about Kirsten and asked what rings Mehran had seen and what he liked.

"I want a ring that signifies our devoted love for one another," said Mehran.

The jeweler showed him a couple of rings that contained birthstones to better understand what Mehran liked. He drew several designs on paper that Mehran studied. Finally, Mehran settled on a simple style. The metal would come from the bottom of the ring on both sides and be attached to a circle where a diamond would be nestled. Two pillars would continue to go to the top and expand in both directions each, and grab the diamond at four locations, pushing it on to the circle below. The two sides would never meet each other, but it would be the diamond that would connect them to each other. In a way, it looked as if two lovers stood on the two sides and cupped the sides of the diamond in their arms and hands to hold it in place. It was simple yet very elegant. The idea of a single diamond was that Kirsten was the only diamond in Mehran's life. He didn't want to adorn the ring with any other jewels. Mehran hand-picked a diamond from the jeweler's selection of loose diamonds and selected platinum as the ring material. As a chemist, Mehran knew that platinum would dull to a natural patina over time, thus enhancing the diamond and making it look more sparkly. The jeweler said that they'd have to forge and make the ring. It would take two weeks. Mehran walked out of the jeweler a happy man.

Kirsten walked in the apartment and knew immediately that Mehran was cooking. She walked behind him at the stove, wrapped her arms around his waist and laid her head on his back. "Have I told you how much I love you?"

"Never! How much?" He put the wooden spoon down and turned around to hug her.

She looked up into his eyes. "So much that if I were to die today, I'd die a happy woman."

Her words touched Mehran. He wanted to drop to his knees and propose to Kirsten right there, without a ring in hand, but he stopped himself. "I love you so much that I couldn't live without you in my life."

They stood in the kitchen, holding one another and savoring the moment. "How come you're home early?" Kirsten asked.

"I figured I'd come home and cook the Persian dish I had promised you a long time ago."

"It smells awfully good. What is it?" She peered around him on the stove.

"It's called fesenjoon."

"Fesenjoon? What's in it? It looks chocolaty."

"It's chicken, with onions, cinnamon, walnuts, sugar and pomegranate syrup. But you can call it 'chocolate chicken.'"

"Chocolate chicken it is," she laughed.

"Oh, and Fallah is coming over for dinner. I figured I'd catch up with him. I'm also going to offer to put his sister through college. They surely can't afford it."

"Mehran, oh Mehran. You're the least selfish person I have ever met."

"That's not true. I am selfish when it comes to wanting you all to myself."

"You have me. Can I get a taste of the chicken now?"

Mehran stirred the dish and took a half spoon out, blew on it to cool it and put it in Kirsten's mouth.

Kirsten's eyes widened and lit up. "Wow! So much flavor!"

"It's easily my favorite Persian dish."

"Yeah, I have a feeling it'll be mine, too, after tonight."

"Go change and come back. I'll open a bottle."

Later that night, Fallah came to their home directly from the mill. They listened to some jazz while the food finished simmering.

"Fallah, do you have a girlfriend?" Kirsten asked.

"No. I really feel like I don't have time to meet girls."

"You have to make time, Fallah. It's our God-given right to sweep them off the floor and lift them high," said Mehran as he swept Kirsten off the floor and held her in his arms.

"Put me down! I don't want you to hurt yourself."

Mehran laughed and put her down. "How about Chrissy at the mill? She's single and unattached."

"Which one is she?"

"She's the one with the freaky red hair."

"Telling him that she's got freaky hair is not all that enticing," said Kirsten.

"I know who you're talking about. She delivers the mail."

"Yup! That one. You get to see her when she's dropping off the mail, and also in the cafeteria, no?"

"Yes."

"You should make a move, man!"

Fallah laughed.

"Don't let him tell you what to do, Fallah. You do what you think is right," said Kirsten.

Fallah smiled at Kirsten. "If she's half as nice as you, I'd be a lucky man."

They sat down to eat. Both Kirsten and Fallah thoroughly enjoyed the fesenjoon.

"Fallah, I want to ask you something," said Mehran, as they finished eating. "How are your parents doing financially? I know you said your father had to pick up double shifts after he came back from Palestine."

"We do okay. My mother doesn't work, neither does my sister. Only my father and I are working. We bring enough to pay the rent and put food on the table."

Kirsten knew where Mehran was going with this line of questioning, but wasn't sure how Fallah would respond.

"The reason why I'm asking is because I know your sister wants to go to college, but I am wondering if you'll have the money to pay for her."

"She wants to study art," Fallah said.

"I know. She told me."

"There's no money in art."

Mehran looked at Kirsten. *Fallah was right,* thought Kirsten. It is an unfortunate fact of life that artists often struggle to make ends meet. But she was more concerned that Fallah and his family wouldn't appreciate or understand what Mehran was trying to do. It was one thing to do something like this for someone in Guatemala whom you'd most likely never see again, unless they made it a point to visit you. But doing this to a family whose son you'd see almost daily might strain the very relationship Mehran was seeking to strengthen.

Mehran thought of all the artists whose financial situations he knew. Picasso was one exception whose art actually brought him money. Most other artists failed financially during their lifetime, and then their works brought money to people who had literally stolen the works from them for peanuts and then profited after the artists died. He thought of what today's "artists" brought to the table compared to their counterparts throughout the centuries.

"That depends," said Mehran. "Some artists scrape by. Some don't. Most of the wealthy artists' works are marginal at best, and grotesque at worst."

"If you can't afford to eat, what's a life worth living?"

Mehran chuckled. "Fallah, look at Vincent van Gogh or Franz Schubert. They were poorer than dirt, yet their contributions to the fine arts were immense. There's even reason to believe that, had they not dealt with poverty so much, their art may not have had the impact it currently has on the world."

"Or Allan Poe, Cezanne, even Monet," added Kirsten.

"I don't know any of those artists, besides Schubert," said Fallah.

"Okay. You know the song *Ave Maria,* right?" asked Mehran.

"Yes."

"Schubert composed that song. It has been played countless times in churches, castles, concert halls, not to mention households of people who don't listen to *any* classical music. It has been rearranged and rendered for blues, jazz, rock, gospel, you name it. Schubert is now considered one of the greatest composers of the Romantic era."

"I don't understand what that has to do with Nawal. Whether she studies art or anything else, we don't have the money to send her to college."

"That's what I wanted to talk with you about," Mehran said as he glanced at Kirsten.

Kirsten got up and looked at Mehran. She shook her head side to side very minutely, ensuring that Fallah didn't see her motion, but Mehran did. She picked up a couple of plates and walked to the kitchen.

Mehran considered Kirsten's disapproval. *Why? This is what I do, help the needy, try to increase the role of the fine arts in the world, and give to those who deserved to better educate themselves, but didn't get a chance to, to make a difference.* He decided that he'd have to talk about this with Kirsten later. But right now, he needed to convince Fallah that letting him pay for Nawal's education was a good thing.

"What if I told you that I would pay for her college education?"

"Why? You've already been very helpful to my family. You even got me a good job at your mill."

"Listen. I am going to let you in on a secret. She wouldn't be the first one I've done this for. I have over 20 students like her throughout the world who I support to go to college."

Fallah was taken aback. "But you don't look like you have a lot of money."

"Well, actually I do have the means. I don't take loans for this."

"That is very generous of you, Mehran, but we cannot accept this."

"Yes, you can. I've seen your sister's artwork. She has talent. She needs to go to college and explore what she's good at."

Fallah remained silent.

"Fallah, I do this because I want the world to be a better place. I want to help those in need. I hope if you had the means, that you'd do the same. In this world, we need to help each other."

Fallah remained silent. The offer made him very uncomfortable, yet he believed he understood Mehran's intentions, and they were good.

But it also looked like Mehran was trying to make a charity case out of his family.

"I tell you what. Go back and discuss this with your parents. Make sure you tell Nawal as well, since she has the ultimate say in this."

Kirsten came back out of the kitchen. Fallah got up, as did Mehran.

"Talk to them and let me know. I will arrange the whole thing, but she'll need to start applying to colleges now."

"Mehran, I really, really appreciate the offer you have made. But I can almost positively tell you that my parents won't consider this at all."

"Why not?" asked Mehran.

Kirsten stepped in. "Mehran, let him discuss it with his parents and Nawal first."

By the look Mehran gave her, Kirsten knew he was saying don't get in the middle of this.

"Yes, let me talk this over with my parents."

Mehran's gaze returned to Fallah. "Fine. Let me know soon, because she needs to start the application process quickly."

"I will," Fallah said. "Thank you."

Usually, Fallah offered to do the dishes with them, an offer they had always refused, but this night he headed toward the door.

When Fallah was gone, Mehran turned to Kirsten. "What was that all about?"

"Hey! Don't take it out on me. He wasn't that fond of the idea either. You saw it yourself," she said as she approached him and put her hand on his arm.

Mehran shook her hand off. "Why not? It would be a waste if she didn't go to college and develop herself."

Kirsten frowned a bit. "Yes, but do you realize for every art student you meet who has the potential to become something bigger, there are thousands more who you don't meet? You can't help them all."

"Yes, but I wanted to help *this* one. It would be utter foolishness of them to refuse my offer."

"Hmm. I wonder if you've ever done something foolish in your life."

Mehran's thoughts went to all the stupid things he had done in his life. Hooking up with a prostitute would make the top of the list. He softened a bit but was still annoyed. He realized that his feelings weren't directed at Kirsten; he put his arm behind her and pulled her to him. "Yes. But it irks me that they would let pride get in the way of their daughter succeeding."

"Who's to say she'll succeed? You, of all people, should know how hard it is for artists to succeed and make ends meet. Even from your own examples earlier, Picasso was the only one who reaped the benefit of his art monetarily during his lifetime."

"Yes, but note how much richer our lives are because of the art that so many artists have sacrificed their lives for."

"And that's something her family, or even she, may not be willing to do. You cannot force something like this on a person or a family."

Mehran lowered his head. He knew Kirsten was right.

Chapter Forty-Four

A couple of weeks later, Kirsten and Mehran went to the mall to do some last-minute Christmas shopping. They separated, and Mehran went to the jeweler. The jeweler brought out the ring.

"Wow! I love it," said Mehran. He took the ring and inspected it under the bright lights of the jewelry store. He looked at the jeweler and smiled. "You did a beautiful job with this ring."

"It is for a fellow countryman. I had to."

Satisfied, Mehran purchased the ring and brought it home to hide it.

On Christmas morning, Mehran was the first to get up. He tip-toed around to Kirsten's side of the bed and kissed her on the cheek. She opened her eyes, yawned and stretched. "Is it time? Can you come under the covers and keep me warm?"

"Come on! I want to open the gifts!" Mehran said.

They took turns in the bathroom to brush their teeth and Mehran fixed morning tea. Then they sat down to open their gifts.

"Remember, we put a dollar limit on what we were to buy for each other," said Kirsten.

"I know. Let's do this!" said Mehran as he looked at his watch. It was 8:52 a.m.

They each took their stockings from the fireplace and opened the trinkets in them: lip gloss, beef jerky, lottery tickets and the like.

They were laughing and poking fun at the silly stocking fillers when the doorbell rang.

"This is the biggest gift I got you," Mehran said.

Kirsten seemed puzzled. "A gift that comes to you at the door?" she asked. Mehran pushed the intercom, said, "Come on up," and buzzed the visitor in.

"Don't you want to know who it is?"

Mehran smiled and opened the apartment door. A few seconds later a man was at their door with a paper pad in his hand.

"Merry Christmas," said the man.

"Merry Christmas to you as well. Thanks for making this delivery on Christmas morning," said Mehran.

"It's a pleasure."

Kirsten walked over and asked, "What are you delivering?"

Mehran looked at Kirsten while the man said, "Ma'am, you're getting your piano today."

Kirsten's eyes lit up and she looked at Mehran. "Really?"

"Really!"

Kirsten ran to the window to look down at the street. It had snowed some overnight, and it was still snowing. But, she could easily see the delivery truck parked on the street in front of the apartment. The truck had a picture of a piano on it.

She walked over to Mehran and punched him gently on the arm. "You cheated! That's way over what we agreed we'd spend."

"Lady, this Christmas day delivery alone is probably costing him more than you agreed to spend," the man said with a smile.

Kirsten hadn't thought about that. Mehran must have paid an arm and a leg to have the piano delivered on Christmas morning.

"Where do you want the piano?" the man asked.

"Kirsten, it's just a spinet, don't get too excited. Where do we want this?"

Kirsten looked around the place; she chose a spot by the dining table.

"Okay! We'll bring it up in a minute." The man headed back downstairs.

"Mehran. I wasn't expecting this."

"You should start to expect the unexpected from me. Let's clean that space."

They quickly moved some things out of the way and made room for the piano. The two movers brought the spinet up the narrow staircase and put it in its final place. "Okay. We're done here. We just need your signature," said the man.

Kirsten was already sitting at the piano and checking the sound and the action on the keys.

"I really do appreciate your bringing the piano on Christmas," Mehran said as he signed the paper and gave them each $100. "Merry Christmas!"

"That's very generous of you. Thank you! And Merry Christmas to you as well."

The men left and Mehran walked over to Kirsten; he put his hands on her shoulders. "It's probably out of tune. We'll have to have a piano tuner come this week."

Kirsten thought the piano sounded lovely despite being a spinet just delivered in the cold. "Mehran, this piano sounds good."

"I'm glad it's to your liking."

She turned around to look at him. "Why did you do this? We agreed on what we would spend."

"Let's say this is not a Christmas present. Let's even say that it's not just for you, because I'm going to enjoy listening to you play it as much as you'll enjoy playing it. It's for both of us."

Kirsten ran her fingers over the piano keys. "It's really lovely."

"Great! So, I know it's out of tune, but can you play something for me? I've never heard you play."

Knowing that Mehran liked Chopin and that he liked pieces in the minor scale, she started to play Chopin's *Nocturne in C-sharp minor*. Mehran pulled a chair diagonal from her and sat to listen. The beauty of Chopin's music was awe-inspiring, and Kirsten played the piece with feeling. She was making a few mistakes, but continued to play through most of the song until she stopped, threw her hands up and said, "Oh my God! I am so rusty and need so much practice." Mehran had no idea that Kirsten was such an accomplished player that she had the piece memorized. "Kirsten, that was beautiful. You choose such a beautiful piece to play for me first," he said as a tear rolled down his face.

She moved from the piano bench and stood by him, holding his head against her belly.

He looked up at her. She smiled and said, "Let's open our gifts."

They proceeded to open their gifts, one at a time and alternating between them. Mehran gave Kirsten a portable CD player, a Galileo thermometer for her desk and several clothing items. Mehran received a Kitchenaid mixer Kirsten had noticed him looking at while they were at the mall, a pair of Sennheiser headphones, and the entire first season of Star Trek: The Next Generation on VHS, a 13-volume behemoth.

"What is this?" asked Mehran.

"It's the next iteration of Star Trek. Don't you remember Kirk and Spock?"

"I think I saw a couple of episodes when I was a kid, but I don't really remember."

"Oh my God! Now I have to get the old stuff for you first."

"Or we can just watch these and see if I like them."

Kirsten looked at him, closed her eyes and shook her head in disbelief as she smiled.

After opening their gifts, they took turns to call their families. Kirsten called her mom and dad. Anja had spent the night at her parents' as well, and they caught up and wished all a merry Christmas.

Mehran called Nader and Pari. Peyman, Parisa, her husband and daughter had all stayed overnight there and Mehran wished them all a merry Christmas and told them they'd be seeing each other soon.

Later that day, Mehran suggested that they go for a long walk in the snow. The snow had continued to fall that day, and that was a rare occasion on Christmas in Chicago. Mehran loved snow. He always joked that he was born in the middle of snow, since his birthday was in January, although there was little chance of snow in Shiraz in January. He thought the falling snowflakes always made the landscape look surreal, especially if there was no wind and the flakes were small and dry. He loved watching individual flakes fall on top of all the other snowflakes already on the ground, each becoming indistinguishable from the crowd it was joining. When he was looking at a slow falling snowflake, he knew he was the only lucky person on the planet to witness this flake and become friends with it, only to lose the friendship in a matter of seconds.

On that day the snowflakes were quite big. The snow had accumulated; 7 or 8 inches were on the ground already.

They walked toward the lake, where there were usually open spaces of grass, but now it was snow. "What do you want in life?" Mehran asked Kirsten as they walked hand in hand.

"I just want you," said Kirsten.

"You have me. You've conquered me. So, now that you have me, what else do you want?"

Kirsten thought for a second. "Eternal love."

"I promise you, as long as we're together, I'll love you."

"That's not eternal love. What if we're not together anymore?"

"You mean you want someone who you're no longer with to continue to love you forever?"

Kirsten laughed. "No, silly! That's taking my words out of context." She paused for a few seconds and said, "Why don't you let me think about that?"

Mehran smiled and nodded. They continued to walk under the falling snow toward the lake. They slowed down at a park.

"This is so beautiful," Mehran began. "The snow on the ground is fresh and white. The snow falling from the sky is creating this surreal picture in my head. I am with you on Christmas, and we're all alone in this park. Everyone else is in their cozy little homes enjoying their Christmas, but I'm here with you, enjoying the beauty of winter. I couldn't be happier."

"Ohhh, I am happy, too, to be with you. Happy and in love. I can't believe these last 9 months have passed so quickly."

Mehran ran away from her a bit and started to make a snowball. Kirsten saw what was happening and ran a few yards the other way to make her own snowball. The snow was very powdery, though, and didn't pack very well. Nevertheless, they continued to hurl a few powder balls at each other, moving closer and closer to each other so that the powder balls wouldn't disintegrate before hitting the target. Kirsten bent down and grabbed snow, double the amount she previously had. She packed it as well as she could into a big ball and hurled it at Mehran. It hit him smack dab in the middle of the nose.

"Oooh!" screamed Kirsten as she held her hands to her mouth.

"My eyes!" yelled Mehran as he dropped to his knees and fell on to his back.

Kirsten panicked and rushed over to him. "I'm so sorry. Are you okay?"

She got on her knees and bent over him. "Open your eyes. Open your eyes."

He opened his eyes, smiled, and said, "I'm a lot better now," he said as he threw a handful of snow at her.

"You cheater!" She straddled him and started picking snow from the ground and throwing it on his face.

"I'm sorry! I'm sorry!" Mehran said until Kirsten stopped.

She was still sitting on his hip. He looked at her. The sky behind her had painted a gray canvas, against which was her beautiful face, holding the only colors he could see, since she was wearing a black jacket. She was truly beautiful, her face filling most of the canvas, her sapphire eyes, her fair skin and beautiful smile. Her blonde hair faded into the background. This is the woman he wanted to be with for the rest of his life. This is the woman he wanted to have children with. This is the woman he adored and wanted to make happy, and he thought what he was about to do next would achieve that. Mehran was ready. He was prepared to commit his life to this woman who had brought him so much joy. He twisted his shoulder and threw her on her back and got on top of her.

"Kirsten."

"Yes?" she said, laughing.

"I have thought much about this and believe this is where I want to be right now. I also know where I want to be tomorrow. You have brought so much joy to my life. You have added much meaning to my life. I love you more than I have anybody else, and I cannot fathom being separated from you. I want you for me for the rest of our lives."

"You have me."

"No. Not yet. But I will." He rolled off her and propped himself on his elbow to look at her as they lay side by side in the snow.

"Kirsten, I want to marry you. Will you marry me?"

Kirsten was shocked. She knew she wanted this. She had even told Anja that she did. But something inside her had kept telling her not to get her hopes up. And then, on this Christmas day, he proposed. Her eyes started to tear up. She had thought about this moment for years, even before she had met Mehran. Mehran was the one. The man who brought so much happiness to her life. He was gentle, kind, thoughtful of others and selfless, and best of all he loved her from the bottom of his heart. Of course she wanted to marry him. Of course.

While she was engrossed in these thoughts, he reached inside his coat, took out the box, opened it and held the ring in front of her.

She hadn't even had a chance to look at the ring yet, when she said, "I will. I will marry you, and we will live side by side like we are now, and we will love each other forever and nothing will separate us. I cannot imagine my life without you, either. I have given myself to you before. Now I give you myself for life."

Mehran got on his knees and pulled her up. They faced each other on their knees. "Kirsten, I don't think any ring will ever do justice for my love for you, but please accept this as a reminder of that love."

By now Kirsten's tears were rolling down her face. Mehran had proposed to her and she had accepted. He took her left glove off of her hand before taking his own off, took the ring and slid it on her ring finger. Kirsten was excited about the ring, but she couldn't take her eyes off of Mehran. He was smiling. He was happy. She was speechless. With the gray skies, the snow falling around them and Mehran's black coat, she felt as surreal as the ghostly couple in Chagall's painting in her parents' home. *The wedding in the sky,* she thought. *Eternal love.* Now she understood what Mehran had said to her mother a month ago. He had practically asked for her hand in marriage right there in their living room, and her mother had said, "Yes." *What is my life going to be like in 10 years? In 20 years? How many kids will we have? How many boys? How many girls?*

"Earth to Kirsten!" said Mehran.

"I'm sorry. What did you say?"

"Tell me what you're feeling."

She looked at him and, ever so gently, leaned forward to plant a kiss on his lips. Their lips danced over each other's. They locked the bare fingers of their left hands, and Mehran could feel the ring against his own fingers. He would have to get used to this minute difference in their handholding, feeling this metal against his own skin. But it was the ring he had wanted to give her. The perfect one.

They began to walk back to their apartment. Up to that point, Kirsten hadn't paid much attention to the ring. She stretched her hand in front of her to better view the ring and then she inspected it carefully. "Mehran, this is a stunning ring."

"I chose the design and the jeweler hand forged it."

She stopped and gave him a hug again on the sidewalk. Back at home, she called her sister and parents to give them the news. Mehran also called Nader and Pari to tell them. They were eager to meet Kirsten and made a plan to visit Chicago in a few weeks for an engagement party.

Chapter Forty-Five

"Absolutely not!" said Fallah's dad. "I will not take his money to put my daughter through school."

"Dad, you haven't met this guy. He's a nice guy. He doesn't mean anything by it. And he doesn't want anything back," said Fallah.

"Why did you have another man in this house anyway, without me being here? I am the head of this household. It is wrong for us to have guests here without me present."

"He had his girlfriend with. Plus I was here. Nothing was going to happen."

"Why does he want to pay for Nawal's education?"

"Apparently he has done this many times before. He said he has done this over 20 times."

"What is he? Mr. Benevolent? How does he think that makes me feel?"

"I don't think he thinks that way or has thought that far. He sees students who have potential and wants to help them."

"I do not even know if Nawal should go to school to study. Look at you! You graduated from high school, and you now have a good job."

Fallah chuckled and thought it was only because of Mehran that he had the job he did. "Yes, but what are you going to do? Let Nawal just marry right out of high school? She has a lot of talent."

Nawal yelled from behind the closed bedroom door, "I won't marry anyone until I've gone to school."

"See what you have done?" asked Fallah's dad. "What am I supposed to do with a kid that now thinks she is going to go to college?" He turned to the door and yelled, "We do not have money for you to go to college."

"But he's going to pay for college. You don't have – " Nawal uttered before being cut off.

"He is not going to be paying for you, because we do not need his money," said Fallah's dad.

Fallah's mom was quietly sitting in a chair with this commotion. Her daughter-in-law also was there listening.

Nawal started crying behind the closed door, as did Malak who was with her.

Fallah's father grabbed his temples between the thumb and middle finger of one hand. He wiped the sweat from his forehead, grabbed a chair and sat down at the table.

"Dad, she is not going to just marry someone the moment she graduates from high school. She needs to further her studies," Fallah explained.

The father was silent. Eventually he asked, "How much is college?"

Fallah shook his head. "I don't know. I'm taking courses at the junior college and that's about $750 each quarter. Maybe for her, going to a four-year university, it would be $10,000 a year, if she stayed home and commuted."

"We do not have that kind of money," said Fallah's mom.

"I don't know," said Fallah. "Maybe. I'm making $24,000 a year. Dad makes another $30 or $40K. Maybe we would be able to apply for financial aid for her. She can work, too."

"I can work, too," said Fallah's sister-in-law. "I have been here for too long without anything to do. As long as mom," she referred to Fallah's mom, "takes care of Malak, I want to work and contribute to this family as well."

Fallah's dad looked at his daughter-in-law, shook his head in disappointment and lowered his gaze to the ground. He felt like he couldn't provide for the needs of his family.

Fallah saw that and walked over to put his hand on his father's shoulder. "Life here is much different than in Palestine, but we'll make it."

His father raised his head. "We will see what happens, but we are not taking charity money from this guy."

Chapter Forty-Six

In early January, Mehran called his lawyer and asked to stop by. At his lawyer's office, he waited for a few minutes. Finally the door opened. "Mehran! Come on in."

Mehran stepped into the office. "Greg, how are you?"

"Couldn't be better. Starting the new year busier than ever. How've you been?"

"I'm doing well! I recently got engaged."

"That's great! Who's the lucky girl?"

"Kirsten Hostetler; she's a banker. International banking."

"Congratulations!"

"Thank you."

"How's everything else with you?"

"Still working at the mill. All is well, and the clock just keeps on ticking."

"Tell me about it. I feel like I'm getting older by the second." He paused and then continued, "So, what can I do for you today?"

"I'd like to change my will."

"Okay. Let me see what we have," Greg said as he opened Mehran's file on his desk.

"I want to change the beneficiaries."

"Right now it says that half of your assets should go to your uncle to be distributed as he sees fit, which I've warned you, may not be doable. Moving all that money to another country will be problematic."

"I've spoken with him. Should the need arise, he was to come here and manage the money from over here, although that'll be a moot point now."

"Then you have $100,000 going to each of the 23 kids you're supporting for college, and the rest is to be put into a trust for the purpose of betterment and integration of classical and jazz music into popular culture."

"Yes. I would like some changes. The half that is going to my uncle should now be going to my fiancée. In addition, I may have a 24th kid who should receive $100,000, but I'll have to let you know about that when I find out for sure."

Greg leaned back in his chair. He wanted to be tactful and yet respectful. "You trust your fiancée to do what you think should be done with the money?"

"Yes, I do. She's a very decent human being. My life is so much richer because of her."

"Not a problem. Write down her full name here and I'll make the changes into the computer right now and you can sign it. When you find out about the 24th, let me know and I'll make those changes. You'll have to come back and sign it again then."

Mehran wrote Kirsten's name down. Greg pulled up Word Perfect, made the edits and printed it. He called in his secretary, who was a notary public, to witness the signing, and seal and sign the will as well.

"Done!" Greg said.

"Thank you, Greg."

"Don't mention it."

Chapter Forty-Seven

Mehran asked Fallah to come for dinner one night. While he was cooking, Mehran shared the good news with Fallah.

"Fallah, Kirsten and I are engaged to be married."

"Mehran! That is great news!" He gave Mehran a hug.

"What about me? Don't I get a hug?" Kirsten said, walking into the kitchen.

Fallah shyly gave a hug to Kirsten.

"I am so happy for you both. You make an amazing couple. You share so many interests and are both very nice people."

"Thank you, Fallah. I wanted to ask you to stand up as my groomsman."

"Wow. I would be honored, although I have never stood up in a wedding. What do I do?"

"Nothing, you just get fitted for a tux and show up," said Kirsten.

"Hey! Don't forget about the bachelor party!" said Mehran.

Kirsten said, "What? So you can sow your wild oats?"

"Hey! A man's gotta have a bachelor party. Aren't you having a bachelorette party?"

"Of course I am, now!"

"Good. I hope you have fun at it, because I will at mine."

"What are you gonna do? Fallah is not 21 yet. He can't drink. He can't even go to bars if he's not 21."

"Who says we're gonna go to bars? How about strip clubs?" asked Mehran.

Fallah's eyes widened and he chuckled.

"See?" said Kirsten. "He doesn't want to do that."

"I guess we'll just sit home and watch porn on the VCR."

Fallah choked on the water he was drinking.

"I'm just kidding buddy. I wouldn't do that to you," said Mehran while smacking Fallah on his back.

Fallah cleared his throat and took a sip of water. "I would be honored to stand up in your wedding. It'll be beautiful. I appreciate everything you've done for me and if there was any way I could ever repay you, please let me know."

"Just don't steal CDs anymore!" said Mehran. "Although, if it wasn't because of that, we wouldn't have ever met."

Fallah silently nodded. They sat down to eat dinner.

"How is your sister-in-law coping with being here?" asked Kirsten.

"She is sad most of the time. But I think she's going to start to look for a job. She's here on a visitor's visa, so she can't legally work, but there are plenty of jobs she can do under the radar."

"I know we briefly talked about this before, but what did happen with your brother?" asked Mehran.

"He was shot by an Israeli soldier at the border."

"That's awful," Kirsten said.

"But there was more to the story, no?" asked Mehran.

"It was just after his birthday," said Fallah. "For his birthday, his wife had given him a hand-carved pocketknife. He was crossing the border for his daily work and when searched, they found the knife on him. They told him to surrender the knife, but he insisted that it was just a pocketknife. From what I've heard, he started shouting at the Israeli soldiers, how they were occupiers, and he wouldn't give up his knife. Things escalated and a fight broke out. They subdued him and dragged him away from the crowd, but he wouldn't stop resisting. When they raised him on his feet, the argument continued and a soldier shot him in the heart point-blank with a handgun."

Kirsten was horrified. Fallah had tears in his eyes.

"Wasn't there an investigation?" asked Kirsten.

"There was. In the end, the army said they investigated the incident and cleared the soldier of any wrongdoing. They got away with murder."

There was a long pause. "It seems that they did," Kirsten finally said.

"Was this documented at all?" Mehran asked.

"Witnesses were ready to testify, but the Israeli army didn't consider their testimony. They trusted only the soldiers' testimonies."

"Man, I'm so sorry," said Mehran.

"I know. It's like these people were given all this power because of what happened to them in World War II, but now they're abusing the very power they were given and behaving like the very people they were tortured by."

"That seems to be the Israeli government's stance," Mehran said.

"It's like we are ants to them."

Everyone was quiet and digesting the pain Fallah was going through. Mehran changed the subject.

"Fallah, did you get a chance to talk with your parents about Nawal's education?" Mehran asked.

Kirsten looked at Mehran and then back at her plate, disappointed, but Mehran didn't see her face.

Fallah was silent. Mehran considered for a few seconds if Fallah had heard him, but he waited.

After an uncomfortable silence, Fallah spoke. "We did talk about it and decided that we would pay for her college on our own."

Mehran was baffled. Why would they put themselves through that hardship when his helping hand was right there?

"Why not? Let me pay for her college. It'll be so much easier on her and everyone in your family."

"I tried, but my dad was very adamant that we had to do this our way."

Mehran gave Kirsten a puzzled look. Kirsten looked into his eyes, put her hand on his and shook her head again.

"Hey! What happened with Chrissy? Did you ever ask her out?" asked Kirsten, trying to change the subject.

Mehran sat stunned but didn't say anything.

"I did. A couple of days ago she stopped to drop off the mail and we started talking. She's taking classes at the college, too. We decided to get coffee and tea one night next week."

Mehran tried to dismiss the previous conversation and get into this one. "That's great! Now, don't stare at her freaky hair; don't say anything about it."

"I have to see this girl and her freaky hair. How bad can it be?" asked Kirsten.

Mehran and Fallah looked at each other. Mehran wanted to laugh but couldn't bring himself to. Fallah laughed.

"Well, let's put it this way," Mehran said. "She's a punk rocker."

"Ah. I've got it. I take it you weren't talking about Irish red, and it's not her natural color?" Kirsten asked.

"Probably not. At least, not that shade of red," said Mehran.

"I could probably never take her home to show my parents," said Fallah.

Mehran thought Fallah was probably right. Chrissy wouldn't last 2 minutes in their home. The conversation continued through dinner with no further mention of the tuition.

Kirsten knew what was on Mehran's mind when they were washing the dishes after Fallah left. "Let it go," she said.

Mehran shook his head. "All these stupid customs."

"I think this is more than just customs. Sometimes people are proud. Sometimes people are arrogant. Sometimes they're jealous. And sometimes just ignorant. Let it go."

And then it occurred to Mehran. He had failed to put himself in Fallah's dad's shoes. Of the four adjectives Kirsten had used, "proud" stood out. He thought about how Fallah's dad's would feel about this offer. Immediately, Mehran understood why Fallah's dad refused his money. Mehran wondered how many of the other 23 families had gone through the same issues.

Chapter Forty-Eight

The engagement party was at a local Persian restaurant in Chicago on a Saturday in February. Nader, Pari and Peyman flew in for the party on the Friday before, as did Walter, Amandine and Anja. Kirsten invited some of her friends from the bank while Mehran invited some of his from the mill, including Fallah and his family.

On Friday night, both families gathered in Kirsten and Mehran's apartment for dinner. The table at the apartment was a bit small, but they pushed the small table from the kitchen against the table in the dining room to fit as many as they could and sat down. Mehran had cooked a mixture of Persian foods. This was the first time Nader and Pari had seen Mehran cook.

"Oh, he's a great cook!" said Kirsten.

"Obviously! When did you learn to cook like this, dear?" asked Pari.

"You know I always enjoyed cooking; I watched my mother cook. I took some culinary classes at the university here and then just practiced."

"God rest her soul," said Nader. "I remember one time when I came to your house in Iran. You were 4 years old, and I came over for dinner. Your mother cooked the best ghormeh sabzi I have ever had to this date."

"Ghormeh sabzi? What's that?" asked Kirsten.

Pari answered. "It's a Persian dish with lots of vegetables, some meat and beans, and flavored with dried limes. It's quite good."

"How come you've never made it for me, Mehran?"

"The vegetables are usually hard to come by. I'll make an attempt for you, though," said Mehran. He looked around the table at the families gathered together. "I want to thank everyone for being here. This means a lot to Kirsten and me." He held Kirsten's hand in his. "We've set June 14 as our wedding date. It'll be a small wedding, but we can't wait."

Pari smiled. "That is so wonderful. Where will you be getting married?"

Kirsten answered, "Mehran didn't care, but I wanted a church wedding. We are getting married at the Divine Savior Church near downtown Chicago. We will have two bridesmaids and two groomsmen." She turned her head to Anja. "Anja, I would very much like you to be my maid of honor."

The table erupted with delight. Through a smile and teary eyes, Anja looked at Kirsten, and they both got up to embrace. Mehran took the opportunity and said, "And Peyman, I hope you'll be here a few days before the wedding, because I would like to ask you to be my best man."

"Me? Wow! Of course! It'd be an honor to stand up with you both," Peyman replied.

Nader and Pari smiled. Mehran may not have physically been with them, but they understood that he must have considered them to be his family all along.

"We plan to have a rehearsal dinner on the Friday night before the wedding," Kirsten said, "and then the wedding in church on Saturday, followed by the reception."

"Where are you holding the reception?" asked Amandine.

Kirsten gazed at her mom. "We will be holding it at the Art Institute of Chicago. Their main hall was already reserved, but because of the small size of our reception, we can use their small hall, which had availability."

"Art Institute? That's so exciting!" said Amandine.

"There's no reason to give the money to anyone else. They deserve and need it," said Mehran. "Please eat! The food is getting cold."

After dinner, Kirsten and Anja said that they'd take care of the dishes and asked everyone else to stay out of the kitchen. Pari pulled Mehran aside.

"Mehran joon, I am so happy for you. Kirsten seems like a very nice girl. Where's she from?"

"She's from Switzerland."

"What a fine country that is. I want to let you know that, had Naghmeh been here, she would have approved of Kirsten as well."

Mehran was puzzled. Pari couldn't have known about them. "What do you mean?"

"When Naghmeh was sick, we often talked. She told me how she had been in love with you, but that she had never felt – " Pari hesitated. She had tears in her eyes.

Mehran knew how she was going to finish that sentence and said, "... had never felt that I loved her the same way."

"Yes. I would have liked for the two of you to be together. You would have made a great couple."

"I miss her much and think about her often," said Mehran.

"Me, too," said Pari. "Anyway, Kirsten is perfect. She's educated, she's gorgeous and smart, and she plays the piano." She then yelled at the kitchen door, "Kirsten, we want you to play some piano for us."

Pari looked at Mehran's teary eyes, wiped them with her thumbs, pulled his head down and kissed him on his forehead. After that, she couldn't hold her own tears and ran to the bathroom.

That Saturday, Anja, Kirsten, Pari and Amandine went shopping for a wedding gown. Kirsten was very particular about the gown she wanted to find. It was to be made of a heavy, white fabric with Victorian pattern brocade. It was to be corseted with a white ribbon in the back and the fabric in the front would stop just above the bust and instead continued with a piece of beaded silk fabric to cover her shoulders and go down her arms a few inches. The silk would also be embroidered throughout with leaf patterns. She did not want to wear gloves, as she wanted her ring to stand out.

The four women took the whole morning and the better part of the afternoon to look at dresses. At one point in the afternoon, Kirsten tried on a particular corseted gown which matched some of her criteria. The gown took almost 10 minutes to be put on her. Kirsten looked at herself in the mirror and smiled. "Mehran would have a lot of fun taking this gown off." Anja chuckled. Kirsten examined her looks in the mirror further and decided she liked the shape of the gown. It was not overly wide at the bottom, yet it wasn't form-fitting below the waist at all. It didn't have the silk top, and the loops for the corset needed to be altered to accommodate a ribbon instead of lace, but the fabric, its liner and the overall shape of the gown was perfect. She decided on that gown and discussed the needed alterations with the salesperson. By the time they got out of the store, they had to rush to the apartment and their hotels to get ready for the engagement party.

At the restaurant, Mehran and Kirsten stood by the door to greet their guests.

When Mehran saw Fallah hold the door for his mother, he saw Fallah's dad for the first time. Mehran and Kirsten walked over to greet them.

"Mr. Mehran. It is nice to meet you," said Fallah's father.

"It's a pleasure to meet you as well. I'm sorry, I don't even know your name."

"Latif."

"It means gentle, right?"

"You speak Arabic?"

"No, but the word is the same in Farsi."

"Yes, it means gentle."

"Thank you for coming to the party."

"Mr. Mehran —"

"Just Mehran, please."

"Mehran, I want to thank you for everything you have done for Fallah, and for offering to pay for Nawal's college. It is very generous of you."

Mehran grasped Latif's arm and looked him in the eyes. "I apologize if I overstepped my bounds. I want you to know that I only meant well."

Latif nodded his head in agreement.

"Welcome to the party," said Mehran.

Mehran greeted Fallah's mother, as well as Nawal. Fallah's sister-in-law and Malak hadn't come. Nawal gave Mehran a hug and thanked him for what he had tried to do for her.

"Nawal, you have a gift. It should not go to waste," said Mehran.

Kirsten was standing right by him and said, "I could feel your meaning in your oil work in your room. You need to continue your good work."

"I am. I have applied to a couple of colleges and am planning on going part-time to one in the fall."

Mehran and Kirsten looked at each other. Kirsten gave a small jab to Mehran and said to Nawal, "I'm glad you're pursuing your talent. Just remember us when you get famous!"

Nawal laughed. "I will!"

Mehran went to talk with Walter and Amandine, who were standing by Nader and Pari. They were all happy to be in Chicago, despite the cold weather that had moved in that week.

"Everyone thinks Denver gets cold, but we rarely go below 20 degrees. What is it here now? In the single digits?" Walter asked.

"Yes, it is. This is quite cold according to our average for February. Of course, the coldest it has ever been here in Chicago was in January or February of 1985, but I missed it since I came here after. The temperatures then got down to -27 Fahrenheit, and about -76 if you include windchill."

"My God! What do people do in that temperature?" asked Nader.

"Well, they try not to go out but cars still seem to run okay. You'd be surprised to find that life still goes on," said Mehran.

"I'm glad I live in California," said Pari.

"California was nice," said Amandine, "but Denver is perfect for us."

The restaurant did a superb job of keeping up with the guests' requests. At the end of the night, Mehran left a generous tip for the staff. The owner of the restaurant, a Persian woman, pulled him aside. "I have a son your age. I am so happy for you to have found such a lovely woman to spend your life with. May God accompany you both on your journey through your lives."

Chapter Forty-Nine

During the next few months, Mehran and Kirsten prepared for their wedding. They chose the designs on the invitations and hand wrote the addresses themselves. Kirsten worked with Mehran on his cursive for a week before she felt comfortable with him writing on the envelopes. She had taken care of the church and the flowers. Together, they chose dinner for the reception: lobster bisque and salad; then a choice of filet mignon or salmon, both served with saffron rice. The saffron rice was as close an option they had to Persian food, although they did manage to get the Institute to serve hot Persian style tea with bamiye along with coffee and the wedding cake. The couple also paid for an open bar for the whole evening.

They registered only for 16 settings of china from Carson Pirie Scott; Kirsten liked a pattern she had found there. Guests would be asked to donate to the Art Institute of Chicago in lieu of gifts. The Chicago Hilton and Tower on Michigan Avenue was reserved for brunch the next day, and that's where they booked a block of rooms for out-of-town guests.

Kirsten chose a very simple black dress with a red cloth belt around the waist for her attendants. The men all wore black tuxes, white shirts and black bow ties and cummerbunds. Kirsten thought that her white dress would stand out against the rest of the wedding party wearing black.

The cake was also ordered from a Danish bakery in Burr Ridge. It was a three-layer cake with a smiling bride and groom depicted as kids on top. The top layer was a chocolate cake, the middle a yellow cake, and the bottom a white cake. They interviewed a few photographers before settling on the one they thought offered the best pictures, while still being conscious of the value for the money since their guests might want to buy pictures as well.

Their choice of music was both classical and jazz. For the first 3 hours of the reception, they scheduled a classical piano trio, and they had hired a jazz quintet with a singer for the 3 hours after dinner. Mehran and Kirsten had a specific list of music they wanted played, along with anything else the bands felt comfortable playing, but their list was absolutely to be played with no exceptions. The classical musicians were familiar with most of the items on their list, although Mehran had thrown Schubert's *Piano Trio No. 2* at them, which they had never played before. The jazz band had a harder time with their list, since Mehran's collection of jazz was extensive and he was particular about what rendition of what song he wanted played.

While all the wedding planning was going on, Kirsten also started teaching Mehran to play the piano. Mehran already was familiar with the keyboard, since he used to play a melodica when he was a kid. For the piano, though, he needed to learn to play with both hands.

The next couple of months passed quickly. Mehran busied himself with learning to play the piano. Kirsten did her own piano studying; she planned on playing the Chopin *Nocturne in E minor* at their wedding in honor of Mehran's love for Chopin nocturnes. She did business in Switzerland a couple of times. During those trips, Mehran spent a lot of time with Fallah, visiting jazz clubs and listening to music at his apartment. Fallah passed his accounting course and enrolled in advanced accounting. He also dated Chrissy a few times and then broke up because he could not reconcile her looks and behavior with his upbringing. How had he put it to Mehran? "If I wasn't bound by my culture, I would really be digging her."

By April, everything for the wedding was in motion. The tuxes had been measured and ordered, the bridesmaids had their dresses ordered as well. Kirsten's gown had been fitted perfectly. Mehran and Kirsten sighed with relief that most of their work was done. The only thing left to plan was their honeymoon.

"I am going to leave it up to you to plan our honeymoon. I'm done with planning things," Kirsten said one morning.

"Seriously? You don't want any input into it?"

"Actually, I do. I want to lay on the beach somewhere. And I mean a vacation spot, not somewhere secluded. I want to make love to you every day and night of our honeymoon. If you do this for me, I promise to go with you on one of your Third World country trips later. For our honeymoon, I want to be your priority."

Mehran smiled. "You are always my priority." He thought for a bit and asked, "How about Jamaica?"

"That sounds fabulous."

Chapter Fifty

With less than two months until their wedding, Mehran told Kirsten he had a surprise for her.

"Ooh, is it going to be kinky? Because I'm in the mood," Kirsten said.

Mehran raised his eyebrows. "Good to know." He directed her toward their bedroom while he walked behind her with his hands over her eyes. Once in the bedroom, he took his hands off.

"What is this?"

"It's a box," replied Mehran.

Kirsten looked at the box. It was a plain, white box about the size of a pillow. "Is it for me?"

"I think you should open it."

Kirsten smiled. "A gift for me?" She walked toward the bed and ran her fingers along the crease between the box top and bottom. She lifted the box top to find a flowery dress, neatly folded and displayed in the box.

"Really? You got me a dress?"

"Yes. Please try it on."

Kirsten lifted the dress out of the box and looked at the tag and the measurements. "Laura Ashley?" she asked.

"Yes. I hope you like the dress as much as I liked seeing it on the mannequin."

"Was she pretty? Did you get a hard-on?" Kirsten joked.

Mehran just smiled and didn't say anything.

Kirsten dropped her clothes to the floor and put on the dress.

Mehran looked at the woman he loved so much and adored her even more standing there, in front of him, posing almost seductively, wearing this new dress he had bought for her. He reached into his pocket and pulled out two tickets.

"Tickets? To what?"

"It's a concert. We're going to see a fado singer tonight."

"You got this dress for me, for tonight?"

"Well, I got the dress for you, but I think you should wear it for more than just one night."

Kirsten walked over to the full-length mirror on the inside of the closet door and admired herself. She put her hand on her hip. "You know, I'm fucking sexy."

Mehran laughed. "Seriously? Make sure you don't go into the closet because I'm not sure you'll ever get out with a head that big."

She turned around and gave him an evil eye. "Do you disagree?"

"Hell no! But I think you should leave that decision to me and concentrate on being a good person."

Kirsten took her hand off her hip, put on a pouty face. "Or do you like them innocent? In a Laura Ashley dress, all prim and proper?"

Mehran was getting turned on by all of Kirsten's poses, but he looked at his watch. "If we want to catch the concert, we need to leave now."

"Fine! Be that way!" She chose a pair of shoes that would match the dress, walked out of the bedroom with Mehran following close behind her. "What kind of concert did you say?"

"Fado. It's traditional Portuguese music.

They took a cab down to a club on Randolph Street that featured a new and upcoming fado singer. Mehran had a few LPs of the most famous and influential fadista, Amália Rodrigues. Rodrigues was no longer giving concerts, but the art she had perfected over her 50-year career had been picked up by several newcomers.

Kirsten had never listened to fado, which shocked Mehran.

"Fado is the most romantic kind of music, after classical," said Mehran.

"Even more romantic than jazz?"

"Oh, yeah."

"Wow! Home come you've never played any of the music for me?"

Mehran shrugged his shoulders. "It never occurred to me that you hadn't heard fado before."

They sat down and ordered a bottle of Cabernet to start the night. Their location was about 10 feet from the stage with a great view. Their proximity to the stage was an advantage since fado wasn't blaring music.

They had almost finished their bottle of wine when the performer came on the stage with her two guitar players, one classical and the other Portuguese. The guitarists sat while the singer stood in front of the crowd. The crowd was on their feet and clapping until the music started. The fadista started with a ferocious version of *Los*

Aceituneros, followed by *Confesso* and *As Penas,* before she spoke to the audience in broken English. With only the first three songs played, Kirsten knew exactly why Mehran liked Fado. The pieces were all in minor scale, and their melancholy toll on the emotions of the listeners was immense. Even the toll they took on the singer was hard to miss, both emotional and physical. The intonations and feeling she put into the performance was exceptional. Kirsten could see the veins in the singer's neck swell every time she took a breath and sang a verse, as if all her muscles were trying to push the air through a constricted windpipe, and then again after she pushed the last bit of air out of her lungs she still tried to push more out of them.

Mehran could see that Kirsten was enjoying the music. She turned her chair toward the stage and leaned back on Mehran and let him wrap his arms around her. They ordered another bottle of Cabernet.

During the show's brief break, Mehran put his chin on her shoulder so they could hear one another.

"I can see why you like this music. It is beautiful and sad at the same time," Kirsten said.

"I agree."

"Mehran, I can't wait until we get married. I love you and everything new you have brought to my life."

"Do you know why we're here?"

"Because the music is good?"

"Yes. What else?"

"Because you love me."

"Yes. What else?"

"Because you bought me this dress?"

Mehran poked her arm. "Be serious!"

Kirsten thought before answering. "I don't know, what?"

"Tomorrow is April 27th. It's the anniversary of our first date at that restaurant and the ice cream shop."

Kirsten thought for a moment. "Oh my God! You're right!"

"Did you think that night we'd be sitting here a year later, engaged, at a fado concert?" Mehran asked.

"I didn't know what to think that night. I knew I liked you, because you were so concerned for the poor waiter."

"I knew I liked you from the moment I saw you by Marie's desk."

"Just based on my looks?"

"Yes."

"You really went just based on my looks?"

"Well, not totally. I had some additional information about you already. Like your speaking multiple romance languages, and that you were Swiss. Plus Marie did that wink thing."

"True. And then you brought me chocolate, not only chocolate, but a box from one of Chicago's finest, to ask for a date."

"Well, I wanted to catch your attention."

"You did. I'm so glad we're here together now."

"Me, too. I love you, Kirsten."

Kirsten turned her face back toward Mehran and they kissed. She turned back to face the stage. Mehran kissed the back of her head and took a deep breath of Opium, the perfume she had splashed behind her ear lobes earlier.

The concert ended just before 10:30. They paid their tab and walked out. Mehran hailed a cab. The cab driver took the address to the apartment and drove.

"I want to make love to you like I never have before," Kirsten whispered in Mehran's ear.

"Why?"

"It's the music. It turned me on and I feel like we need to channel our emotions."

Mehran understood exactly. The depth of sadness that the music had evoked was almost unbearable for him. They played with each other's fingers throughout the ride back. A few blocks away from the apartment, Kirsten told the taxi driver to stop on the corner of Seminary and Belmont by a pantry.

"What's up?" asked Mehran.

"We need milk."

"Now?"

"It'll take 2 seconds."

The cab turned onto Seminary and stopped at the corner. Kirsten took a $5 from her purse, hopped out and crossed the street to the pantry. Mehran moved to the middle of the back seat and looked at the cab driver in the rearview mirror and they struck up a conversation about the oddest cab rides the cab driver had had. In a couple of minute, Kirsten exited the pantry with a half-gallon of milk in her hand. Underneath the rearview mirror, Mehran saw lights of a car approaching.

Chapter Fifty-One

"Daniel, come down from your room right now."

"Arrgh. Here we go again," said Daniel as he left his friend, Kevin, playing video games in his room.

"What dad?"

"I just got off the phone with your high school counselor. Get over here."

Ariel held up the paper he had written Daniel's grades on. "These are your grades?"

"Dad, I'm the only kid in this house. If you were on the phone with *my* counselor, they *must* be my grades."

"Do these look like A's to you?"

"No."

"Do they look like B's to you?"

Daniel looked at the paper and said, "They look like an A, 2 Bs, 3 Cs and a D."

"A D in calculus?"

"Dad, the class is hard."

"And a C in gym? How do you get a C in gym?"

"I don't know. You should ask the gym teacher."

"You're grounded tonight."

"Dad! No! I'm supposed to go to a party in the city."

"Just because we pulled some strings and got you accepted into Northwestern doesn't mean that you can slack off on your grades. What about when you go to college and I'm not there to keep you on track? What kind of grades are you going to get then?"

That'll be a fucking relief, Daniel thought, but said, "Dad, I can pull my grades back up."

"Give me the keys to the Hanzo."

"No, dad! I have to go to this party."

"Where are the keys?"

"Dad, please. Ground me tomorrow night instead."

"Ariel, he's been really excited about this party. Let him go and ground him tomorrow," Daniel's mother, Talia, said as she walked into the room.

"Please, dad. Let me go tonight."

"Give me the keys."

Daniel reached into his jeans and pulled out the keys and gave them to his dad.

"Let that be a lesson to you. For every week that you don't pull up your grades to a B average, and you only have 4 weeks, you'll lose your car privileges on Saturday nights."

"Whatever," said Daniel as he turned around to walk back upstairs to his room.

"That kid is spoiled rotten," said Ariel angrily.

"We created this situation," said Talia.

"I swear he will fail miserably in life if he continues to behave this way."

"And that's why we're here. We're here to make sure he doesn't fail."

Ariel walked over to the fireplace and rested his arm on the mantle. He then turned to Talia. "I just hope he doesn't bring us down and that he grows up to be a respectful son."

"He will."

Upstairs, Daniel walked into his room and slammed the door. "What was that about?" Kevin asked.

"He took the keys to the fucking car."

"What? How are we supposed to get to that party tonight?"

"There's a spare set of keys in the kitchen. We'll be fine."

"The moment you turn on the car everyone in the neighborhood, including your parents, will hear the exhaust."

"No, dummy! We put the car in neutral while we roll it down the driveway and down the block, and then we can turn it on. They won't even know we're gone."

"Cool!"

Daniel picked up his game controller and jumped back in the game with Kevin. They played for a few hours. A little after 8 p.m., Daniel took a shower, blow-dried and gelled his hair and came out of the bathroom.

"Ready?" he asked Kevin.

"Yeah. What now?"

"They're either in the office or the TV room in the basement. Leave the game in demo mode, so that it makes noise. They'll think we're still here. I just gotta stop by the kitchen to grab the spare keys."

They tiptoed downstairs, Daniel retrieved the spare keys and they exited through the kitchen door. The Hanzo was parked in the driveway circle in front of the garage; it couldn't be seen from the house windows. Daniel got in the driver's seat and put the key in. He turned the ignition to the accessory position, pushed a button for the window to go down and closed the door. He put the car in neutral and told Kevin to push the car. Kevin started pushing. It was a bit hard to push at first, but it was easier once the car was rolling. Kevin continued to push until the car cleared the driveway and was rolling down the block. They waited until the car stopped a couple of houses down.

"Get in," said Daniel as he turned the car on. The exhaust was loud as the engine turned over. Kevin got in on the passenger side and Daniel hit the accelerator. The ride from Northbrook to Chicago was not too long at just under 30 minutes. Once in Chicago, Daniel navigated Lake Shore Drive to Wrigleyville. They had a hard time finding parking, but eventually found a spot and walked to the party. They walked in a little before 9:30; the party was well underway with music blaring.

"Let's grab some beer, dude," Kevin said to Daniel. They made their way to the two kegs on the back porch and poured a couple of beers before heading inside to find Becky, Daniel's girlfriend. "Becks!" said Daniel.

"Hey, you! So glad you guys came. I wasn't sure you'd show up, since it's so late."

"Yeah, I had some parent trouble. Looks like I'm behind," Daniel said as he chugged back his beer and went back to the porch to fill another cupful.

"How did you land this place?" Kevin asked Becky.

"This is my brother's place, and this is my graduation present. He said since I was graduating from high school next month, I deserved a proper party, which my parents would never throw."

"Yeah, this party is bitchin'!"

Becky smiled. Daniel returned; he had already drunk half of his second beer.

Becky pulled Daniel toward her and said in his ear, "Don't drink so much that you'd get whiskey dick. I need you alive tonight."

"Ha ha! Don't worry about me," Daniel said as he took another chug of his beer.

They started walking around the party and talked with some of their high school classmates. Becky's brother had a DJ friend who was playing a mixture of rap, disco and popular pop music. About 50 to 60 people, mostly teenagers, were dancing in all the rooms of the apartment. The kegs were flowing.

Daniel had just gotten another beer when the DJ put on *Can't Nobody Hold Me Down*. The teens started jumping up and down in unison with the rhythm. Daniel found Becky and they started dancing together. He put his right leg forwards while she straddled it and let herself brush his thighs while they danced. After the song was over, Becky left to talk with other friends, while Daniel and Kevin talked to some other friends.

"Did you drive the Hanzo tonight?" one friend asked Daniel.

"Yeah. My dad doesn't know. He grounded me, but who gives a shit? They probably don't even know I'm gone."

"Dude, you've got some balls."

"What is he gonna do? I'm his only kid."

"That car is so sweet. It sounds so nice when you rev the engine."

"Yeah, I had that thing redlining on the way here."

"Fuck yeah. Now *that's* a sports car."

"Hell yeah. I love driving that car. My dad's gonna let me take it to Northwestern in August."

"I wish I had a dad like yours, man. My dad's got a nice car, but he never lets me drive it."

"Dude, my dad is constantly giving me lectures about things that are important in life. I'm like, what's the point of the important things if you can't enjoy life?"

"Right on."

Daniel finished his beer and went for another one. When he came back, the DJ put on a slow song, and Daniel looked for Becky. They started dancing, head to head, arms wrapped around each other.

"Hey, let's go to one of the bedrooms," Daniel whispered loudly.

"I can't yet, babe! It's my party. I can't leave for a half hour to be with you."

"Sure you can. Nobody'll notice."

"Wait for an hour, and stop drinking! I'll show you the best time of your life later tonight."

"But I'm horny *now*."

Becky laughed. "You'll still be horny in an hour. A couple of more slow dances and I'll be horny, too," she said as she nibbled his ear.

"I can't stay that long. I'm supposed to be grounded. Let's go."

"You know, the longer you wait for it, the more it builds up. Just stay here tonight with me."

Daniel started to raise his voice. "Come on! Just one blowjob."

A couple of friends dancing close to them heard him and stared.

"Jesus Daniel," Becky said. "Can you shut up? I still have to walk among all these friends."

"What's the use of being a boyfriend-girlfriend if we can't have sex when we want?"

Becky separated from him and headed to the porch to get a beer.

"Fucking tease," Daniel said loudly as he headed for the door. Kevin saw him leave and followed.

As they walked out of the building, Kevin asked, "What happened?"

"Fuck her. I don't need her. Let's go find a couple of hookers and get blowjobs," Daniel said as he and Kevin continued down the sidewalk.

"No way man. I ain't putting my dick inside some hooker's mouth. Who knows what I'll get."

"Whatever. You can watch me get a blowjob then."

They made their way to the car.

"Are you okay to drive?" Kevin asked.

"Of course I am! I only had 5 cups of beer. Look at this parking space. I bet you I can pull out of this spot in one move."

"$10 says you can't."

Daniel gauged the distance to the front car and said, "You're on."

They got in the car. He started the car, revved the engine, turned the steering wheel all the way to the left and started to inch forward. He almost made it, but his bumper scratched the other car's bumper.

"See, you didn't make it!" said Kevin.

"Of course I made it. Did I go back and forth?"

"No, but you hit the other car."

"Well, I never said I was gonna make it without hitting the other car."

"Dude!"

"Hey, just shut up and let's have some fun. There's gotta be hookers around here."

Daniel started to drive the Hanzo hard between stop signs on the city blocks. After each stop sign, he'd floor the gas pedal and screech the tires before slamming the brakes just before the next stop sign. "This is a rush, man!" Kevin said above the roar of the engine.

Daniel made a left turn on a major street and prowled for prostitutes. Not finding any, he turned again on a side street.

"See, this is the cool thing about this car. It can roar like this," Daniel said as he floored the gas pedal and quickly reached 45 mph before putting the car in neutral, letting it coast to the next stop sign, and continued, "but then when you put it in neutral, it becomes completely silent."

Kevin closed his eyes and leaned back into the headrest.

By the time Daniel turned his attention back to the road, he was almost at the end of the block. He looked for the stop sign on the right hand side by the intersection and didn't see any, but instead noticed a woman entering the pedestrian walkway. He swerved to the left to avoid hitting her, but the Hanzo careened off a parked car and veered directly toward Kirsten.

Kirsten was looking through the cab window at Mehran and smiling as she started to cross the street. Mehran quickly glanced at the approaching car lights and back to Kirsten. "That car is coming the wrong way down Seminary," he told the cab driver as he turned his head and looked at Kirsten. By the time Mehran moved to bang on the window of the cab, he heard the screech of tires. Kirsten never looked to her left since Seminary was a one-way street in the direction the cab was parked and headed, nor did she have any time to step forward or backward. Mehran watched in horror as Kirsten's body and the Hanzo met. The car caught her just below the left knee. She hit the hood first and then the windshield before getting thrown up in the air like a rag doll.

Mehran felt like he watched the accident in slow motion. He saw Kirsten's face as she turned in the air, the force of the impact tearing the half-gallon of milk from her hand. She hit the asphalt head first before her body slammed down as well, followed shortly by the splatter of milk all over the street. By then, the Hanzo had already hit a car entering the intersection on Belmont.

Mehran screamed, "NOOOOOOOOOO!"

Chapter Fifty-Two

The cab driver was the first one to get out and go over to Kirsten.

"Someone call 911," the cab driver yelled. A pantry employee who had come out after the screech of the tires ran back inside to make the call.

Mehran managed to exit the passenger door, ran toward Kirsten and kneeled next to her. He wanted to hold her to him, but the cab driver stopped him. "Don't move her. Her neck or back may be broken."

Kirsten lay on her back with her legs somewhat spread apart, one bent at the knee and the other clearly broken below the knee; her arms lay at her sides. Mehran looked over Kirsten's lifeless body and felt his own life drain from his body.

"Baby, I'm sorry. I should've gone in to get the milk. It should be me on the ground right now. I'm sorry. I'm sorry. I'm sorry." He broke into tears.

A crowd gathered in the area. Most were looking at Kirsten, but some were tending to the driver of the other car that was hit in the intersection. The car was older and didn't have airbags. The force of the collision had pushed his car backward past the stop line while hurling his body forward; he had hit his head on the windshield. He was conscious but required medical attention.

A few bystanders walked to the Hanzo. Behind the airbags of the Hanzo, Daniel and Kevin felt like they had been punched in the face. Daniel looked at Kevin, who was looking at him, and then they looked out the side and saw the crowd in the middle of the intersection.

The cab driver pulled Kirsten's skirt down to cover her upper legs and knelt down by her to take her pulse.

"She's got a pulse," he told Mehran. "It's strong."

Mehran looked at him and then back at Kirsten. Blood had started to pool around her head, as she was bleeding through her mouth and nostrils.

Two police cars arrived within a few minutes of the 911 call. One officer ran toward Kirsten while the other three started to clear Kirsten's immediate area of bystanders. The officer near Kirsten asked, "Did anybody see the accident?" while he checked Kirsten's pulse.

The cab driver said, "I did. She was my fare along with this man," and he pointed to Mehran. A man and woman who were standing near also said that they had witnessed the two vehicles' collision.

The officer raised his two-way radio, "8442 here. 11-80, intersection of Belmont and Seminary. Also need 11-84s for traffic control." He then started asking questions of the cab driver; the cab driver explained the accident in a couple of sentences. Another policeman approached the officer in charge and said, "We need another ambulance for the other car and maybe a third one."

The officer contacted dispatch again. "8442 here. 11-41, two needed. Relay to EMS, pedestrian collision, condition is 10-45C, bleeding through mouth and nose, broken leg. She has a pulse."

Mehran could hear police sirens getting closer. A few other police cars arrived and blocked the four intersections leading to the site of the accident, and officers cleared the traffic from both streets leading to the accident, paving the way for the ambulance to drive in near Kirsten.

The medics hurried out and quickly got on the ground.

"Was she with anybody?" asked one medic.

"With me. I'm her fiancé."

"I am going to ask you some questions. Answer them the best you can."

The other medic contacted the emergency department at Northwestern Memorial Hospital to give an update, "Female patient in late 20s, blunt head trauma, possible TBI, bleeding through mouth and nose, pupils are equal and respond to light, looks like a broken left leg as well, possible spinal injury. Heart rate is strong at 60 bpm, BP 95 over 40, RR is 5." One medic bag-valve ventilated Kirsten and asked Mehran, "Does she have any medical conditions you are aware of?"

"None that I know."

"Is she allergic to anything?"

"Not that I know."

The second medic had already started an IV and said, "She's losing a lot of blood."

"What's her name?"

"Kirsten. K-I-R-S-T-E-N. Last name, Hostetler. H-O-S-T-E-T-L-E-R."

The medics started to put a neck brace around Kirsten's neck and slid a hardboard underneath her to keep her neck and spine from moving. They moved quickly, placing the board on the stretcher and Kirsten into the ambulance. Mehran tried to get in the back.

"No, you can't ride in the back. You can ride in front," said the medic as he closed the door.

Mehran got in the passenger door.

"Buckle up, please," said the driver.

Mehran buckled up and for the first time, looked at the Hanzo and its passengers.

The ambulance took off.

Chapter Fifty-Three

Daniel dug in his pocket for his cell phone and dialed a number.

"Hello?"

"Dad, it's me. I got into an accident."

"What are you talking about? Where are you? You're grounded. I thought you were in your room."

"Dad, I hit a woman."

"You what? Where are you?"

"Where are we?" Daniel asked Kevin.

Kevin looked at the street signs. "Seminary and Belmont."

"We're near the corner of Seminary and Belmont in Chicago," Daniel told his dad.

"What the fuck are you doing in Chicago?"

"Dad, I hit a woman and another car."

"Oh my God. Okay. Have you been drinking?"

Daniel paused before answering. "Yes."

"I am going to fucking kill you. Stay there, I'll be there soon. Do *not* talk to the police and do *not* take the breathalyzer if they ask you to."

"I'm sorry, dad."

Ariel hung up the phone, grabbed his wallet and keys and headed toward the city. While he was driving, he called his lawyer and told him to meet at the scene of the accident.

Chapter Fifty-Four

The ambulance arrived at the hospital in less than 10 minutes. The driver pulled into an emergency bay and the back doors were open before Mehran had a chance to open his own door.

By the time he made it around, they had already pulled the stretcher out of the ambulance and were wheeling Kirsten through the sliding doors. Mehran tried to follow them, but a security guard stopped him, "Sir, you cannot go that way. Please follow me. We'll take you to the front and someone will speak with you there."

Mehran looked on as the stretcher was pushed by doctors and nurses down the hallway until it disappeared around a corner. He followed the security guard to the registration desk. The registration person took him into a private room and took Kirsten's information, including their address and date of birth. She asked for Kirsten's insurance card.

"It's in her purse," said Mehran, and then realized that the purse was probably left in the cab. "I don't have it. You can bill me."

"Well, we can work that out later. Why don't you have a seat outside and someone will be with you shortly."

"When?"

"Probably in the next 10 to 15 minutes."

Mehran stepped back out into the emergency room sitting area. He was pacing the short hallway when someone called out "Kirsten Hostetler."

He ran toward the voice and was greeted by an ER doctor.

"Hi. I'm Dr. Frank. I'm an ER physician. And you are?"

"Mehran."

"Are you her husband?"

"fiancé."

"Good. You can make decisions for now, but we should let her parents know. Are they alive?"

"Yes, I'll call them as soon as I can. But what's her condition?"

"Follow me," Dr. Frank said and spoke as they walked. "We took a quick X-ray to check for spinal damage; that was clear. So that's good news. She has taken a hard hit to her head, so we're taking a CT scan to see the extent of the damage. My guess is that she has a fractured skull. She has good pulse, which means the brain is still sending signals to the heart, but her breathing is slow, so we have intubated her. She also has a broken right arm and a broken left leg, but they're both clean breaks, so there won't be any complications there. Her blood pressure is falling, though, and that's not a good thing. I'll know more as soon as the CT scan is done."

They had reached a waiting area in the back.

"Please have a seat here, and I'll be back in 5 minutes."

The next 5 minutes seemed like hours for Mehran. He thought that the news from the doctor so far had been good, with the exception of the blood pressure. He paced the small room for a bit before he noticed another family, most likely a husband and wife, sitting together in a corner.

Dr. Frank came back and motioned for Mehran to step into the hallway.

"The CT came back, and it doesn't look good. There's evidence of a clot that is causing pressure on the brain. The midline shift of the brain appears to be about four millimeters. That's an indication that there's ICP; we need to take her in for surgery."

"I'm sorry, what's ICP?"

"Intracranial pressure. That's when the pressure in the skull goes up."

"I understand pressure. I'm a chemist. What's the cause?"

"According to the CT scan, there's an epidural hematoma, which is basically bleeding in the brain. We have to perform a craniotomy on Kirsten to remove the excess blood and reduce the pressure. Then we'll have to repair the damage. We need to move fast on this."

"Whatever you need to do. She's in your hands."

"Good. We'll take her in for surgery now. It'll take a few hours, so don't get panicked if you don't hear from us for a while."

"Okay. Thank you, doctor."

"Someone will be here with the consent forms for the surgery. The surgeon's name is Dr. Keshavarz."

"Tell me he's good."

"He's the best we have," said Dr. Frank. "Someone will come and take you to the surgical area waiting room."

Mehran went back to the ER waiting room and sat down; he put his head between his knees. He wanted to cry, but tears just wouldn't flow.

Less than half an hour later, a clerk walked in. "Mr. Noori, there's someone up front to see you."

"Me?"

"Yes. Please follow me."

He followed the clerk to the front emergency waiting area. It was the taxi cab driver.

Mehran approached the man. "Here. I thought you may need this," the driver said as he raised his hand with Kirsten's purse in it.

Mehran reached for the purse and looked at him with some relief.

"How is she?"

"She's undergoing brain surgery. I don't know."

And that was when tears started to roll down his cheeks, as if he had been waiting for someone to offer a shoulder for him to cry on. The tall, black taxi driver grabbed Mehran and let him cry on his shoulders. To others waiting in the emergency room, the sight must have looked completely disheartening.

After a minute, Mehran removed himself from the taxi driver's arms. "Thank you for bringing me the purse." He reached for his wallet and took out a $100 bill to hand to the taxi driver when the driver put his hand on Mehran's. "No, man. I can't take your money." He then reached into his jacket and handed Mehran one of his business cards and said, "Let me know how she comes out. And the cops want to talk to you as well. They'll probably come here. I didn't tell the cops I had the purse. I hope you don't mind, but I had to open up her purse and get her ID to ask for her when I got here."

"Thank you," Mehran said again.

"Not a problem, man. I'm sorry." He turned around and left.

Mehran walked back to the registration desk where an aide was ready to take him to the surgical area waiting room.

Once he sat down, Mehran looked through Kirsten's purse for her phone book. She had a number written under "Mom and Dad." Mehran walked over to the payphone and dialed zero.

"This is the operator."

"Hi. I would like to make a collect call to Denver."

"What is the number?"

Mehran read the number.

"And what's your name?"

"Mehran."

The phone rang a few times before Walter picked up the line.

"Hello?"

"Yes, this is the operator making a collect call from Mehran in Chicago. Will you accept the charges?"

"Yes."

"Thank you. You may speak now." The operator disconnected herself.

"Mehran, is everything okay?"

Mehran tried to swallow his tears and managed to say, "Walter, there has been an accident."

"Is Kirsten okay?"

"I'm at the hospital. She was hit by a car while crossing the street. She's in surgery right now."

Mehran could hear him say something in German to Amandine. "When did this happen?"

"About an hour ago. They say she's got bleeding in the brain. They're doing a craniotomy right now to remove the excess blood and repair the vein."

"Which hospital?"

"Northwestern Memorial."

"We'll take the first flight we can get. Hang on son. We'll be there. Take my cell phone number, and call us if anything changes."

Mehran paced the surgical waiting area. A few other families were awaiting the outcome of surgeries on their loved ones. Every once in a while a surgeon walked in and talked with a family. The families didn't break down and cry after the conversations. They must have gotten good news, Mehran thought. How he longed to be in their shoes and receive good news as well.

About an hour later, a hospital clerk brought two policemen into the waiting area and asked for Mehran. The policemen came toward him. One introduced himself as Officer Lange and started to ask Mehran questions.

"How is she?"

"She's in surgery. I don't know what's going on yet."

"Okay. We'll talk to the doctors later, and we'll have to interview her as well."

"She was unconscious the whole time."

"Be that as it may, she may remember what happened when she wakes up."

"I can tell you exactly what happened."

"What's your relationship with her?" asked the second cop.

"I'm her fiancé."

"Go ahead," said Officer Lange.

"She went into the store to buy milk. I was sitting in the backseat of the driver and talking with the drive. I saw a set of lights approach the cab, coming the wrong way on the street. When Kirsten came out of the pantry, I turned to look at her. She must have heard the screech of the tires, because she looked to her left, but she couldn't get out of the way. The car hit her. She bounced off the hood into the windshield before getting thrown up in the air and hitting the ground," Mehran said with a tremble in his voice.

"That's just like the taxi cab driver described things. Did you hear the car coming?"

"I don't know. My window was rolled up. How is the driver of the other car that got hit?"

"He's got some bumps and bruises, but he's fine."

"And what about the car that hit Kirsten?"

"Not a scratch. The driver refused to take a breathalyzer. We ticketed him for a moving violation and arrested him. He's in jail until he appears before a judge on Monday morning."

"Was he drunk? He was going the wrong way down a one-way street."

The officers looked at each other. The second officer said, "We don't know," while Officer Lange looked down and nodded his head a couple of times. Officer Lange continued, "He's probably gonna post bail on Monday. For now, I need to fill in the blanks on this police report, starting with her address and your information."

Mehran told him enough information for the report. They waited together for word from the operating room.

Another hour passed before a surgeon came out.

"Mehran?"

"Yes?"

"I am Dr. Jamal Keshavarz. I've been operating on Kirsten. I understand you are her fiancé." Dr. Keshavarz looked to be in his 60s with a full head of white hair and round glasses. He was still wearing scrubs.

"How is she?"

"She's stable. We've removed the blood clot and are repairing the lacerated artery. The prognosis is good. Her pulse is strong and her blood pressure should stabilize after we're done. I believe she'll recover."

Mehran bent down and put his hands on his knees, taking deep breaths before coming back up. "Oh my God! That is the first good thing I've heard."

"You're Persian?"

"Yes," said Mehran. Then he realized that he had been so fixated on the news that he didn't realize Jamal Keshavarz was a Persian name.

"Salam pesaram," *hello son.*

"Salam aghaye doctor."

"I'm confident that she will recover. She got here right in time. With things like this, time dictates the outcome, and she had plenty of time left before things got really ugly."

"Thank you so much. Thank you."

"When do you think she may be able to talk to us?" Officer Lange asked.

"It's hard to say. You should call back in a couple of days. She'll be in no shape to talk to anybody until at least then." He turned to Mehran. "I'll see you again in a couple of hours."

The officers left, and Mehran called Walter to give him the news from the doctor.

"That's great news. We'll see you soon," Walter said.

Mehran hung around the room, his spirits somewhat lifted. Dr. Keshavarz returned to the waiting room a couple of hours later.

"The operation went well. We were able to remove the blood clot, repair the vessel and relieve the pressure. The next 24 hours will be crucial for her recovery. We have left a small opening for fluid build-up to drain. We have also left an ICP monitor in there. That will tell us if the pressure starts to build up again."

"I thought she was dead when she hit the pavement."

"And she may have been if she didn't get here in time. How do they say it, Americans? It's not over until the fat lady sings."

"Thank you so much."

"Of course. She will be in post-op for the next few hours. We will then move her to ICU, and you can visit her there."

Mehran was happy. He called Walter again.

"Ah, that's such a relief," said Walter. I got us booked on a flight. We're leaving here at 6 a.m., 7 your time. We'll be there by 10 o'clock your time."

"I'll be here at Northwestern somewhere. Maybe still in the surgical waiting room."

Mehran sat down. His heart was pumping and he was buoyed that Kirsten would survive this horrific crash. His mind raced with images of their life together this past year. How ironic that exactly a year after their first date, this should happen. He leaned his head back against the wall and within minutes fell asleep.

He was awakened by an announcement. "Code blue, code blue," said the voice on the speaker. Mehran panicked as he watched several doctors and nurses rush through the door to the recovery area. He walked down the hall to the nursing station and asked what was going on. They calmly responded that he should wait and if anything developed with his loved one, someone would notify him.

What if something has happened with Kirsten in the recovery room? What were all the doctors and nurses rushing for? he wondered. He tortured himself for the next few minutes, worrying and fearing the worst-case scenario. *What if Kirsten has died? How could I face Walter and Amandine in a few hours and tell them that their daughter had died after I had given them good news?*

It was nearly an hour before anyone came in, nearly an hour that tortured not only Mehran, but the three other families in the surgical waiting room. Two doctors came out of the double doors and approached the waiting area. Mehran glanced at the doctors and tried to follow their gaze. *Please, please, let it be one of them. Please let it be someone else's dear one,* he thought. The doctors approached one of the families in the waiting area and tried to convince the family to go into a private room. "No! Tell me what's going on with my son," yelled the woman. The doctors talked with her and her husband in a low voice. Mehran couldn't hear them, but he could tell from the family's expression that it wasn't good news. The woman nearly passed out in the chair she had stood up from. The man stood still while the doctor put his hand on the man's shoulder, trying to comfort him. The young teenage girl they were with started wailing. The doctors waited until someone wearing non-surgical clothes, perhaps a social worker or counselor, came to stay with the family before they left.

Mehran thought about what he had just witnessed and what he had wished for. He had wished that the bad news wouldn't be for him, but for someone else. He felt ashamed. *How selfish,* he thought. But the stakes were too high for him. He didn't want anything to happen to Kirsten under any circumstance. And then he remembered when Naghmeh had brought the news of his parents' death to him, and when Naghmeh had died. How awful it must feel to be in this family's situation, having lost a son, or a brother or boyfriend for the teenage girl. He put his elbows on his knees and clutched his head between his hands, letting tears roll down his face, watching them fall on the carpet beneath his feet, much like he had when he had first come to the United States. He felt the sword of empathy slice his heart into two pieces, torn between his desire for Kirsten to be safe and understanding the pain the other family was feeling. He managed to look up for a few seconds. The father was still dazed, standing still near the chair his wife was barely sitting in, since she had almost stooped to the ground; the social worker was on one knee in front of her. Mehran thought about the life of a surgical unit social worker. They had to be empathetic, otherwise how could they be effective in their job, helping family after family grieve over their loved ones? Or was it a skill they learned? Did they fake their empathy? He thought there was no way he could go home every day and lead a normal life had he been in their shoes. He would be a wreck before he left work. He looked for a tissue box and noticed that there was one at almost every table in the room, between the chairs, on the coffee table holding magazines. He grabbed a few from the nearest one and wiped at his face and stuffed them into his pocket afterward. He leaned back in his chair and closed his eyes, trying to switch his thoughts away from what was happening to the other family, but he couldn't. Even after the social worker had led the family to a grieving room off to the side of the waiting area and had closed the door behind them, Mehran's thoughts stayed with the family and the social worker.

He couldn't fall back asleep, nor did he want to. It was 7 a.m. A doctor came out of the double doors and approached him. His heart fell after seeing what had just happened to the other family.

"Hello. Are you the family of Miss Kirsten Hostetler?"

Mehran nodded.

"My name is Dr. Gomez. I just wanted to let you know that Kirsten is still in the recovery room. Her pulse is strong and everything looks good so far. She'll be in the recovery room until she comes out of anesthesia."

"Thank you, doctor."

He sat back down. His gaze fixed on the magazines on the coffee table in front of him. *Golf, Modern Living, Car and Driver, National Geographic* and *People*. He instinctively grabbed the copy of *National*

Geographic, but he couldn't bring himself to actually open the magazine. He wondered who in their right mind would leave magazines in such a room, let alone who would actually browse a magazine in this room. The thought pissed him off. He sprang from his seat and threw the magazine against the wall closest to him, followed immediately by him covering his face with his hands. The sound of the magazine hitting the wall and the pages flapping as they came down to the floor must have startled the other families in the room, because when he removed his hands from his face, everyone was staring at him. He wanted to apologize but couldn't bring himself to. All he could manage was to pick up the magazine from the floor and drop it back on the coffee table. He went back to his chair, leaned his head against the wall and closed his eyes. Eventually, he dozed off.

Chapter Fifty-Five

"Mehran!" Walter was shaking his shoulder.

Mehran opened his eyes. "Walter! Amandine!"

He got up. They both gave him a hug at the same time; it felt like a three-way solidarity hug.

"How is she?" Amandine asked as they sat down.

"Last they told me she was still in recovery. Her pulse was good, and they were waiting for her to come out of anesthesia before they would move her."

"What happened?" Walter asked.

Mehran put his head down and then lifted it. "It should've been me. She left the cab to get milk, and on her way back to the cab she was hit by a drunk driver."

"A drunk driver?" asked Walter.

"It should've been me. I should've gone in to get the milk."

"Don't say that. It doesn't make a difference. If it was you, we would have been here with Kirsten worrying about you," said Amandine.

Mehran thought about that for a second and wondered if Amandine was genuine in what she had just said. Had he been genuine in what he had just said, he thought. *I would have given my life so that Kirsten would be fine,* he thought.

He looked at Walter and Amandine. They looked worried.

"Is Anja coming?"

"She will be here in a few hours. We couldn't get a seat on our plane for her," said Walter.

"I am so sorry about this. I should've been taking more care of her," Mehran said.

Walter grabbed Mehran's shoulders and looked directly into his eyes. "Son, you are not responsible for this. It was an accident. You didn't do this."

Mehran looked at Walter. True, it had just been an accident. But what if he had noticed the car earlier and called out to Kirsten? What if he had asked the cab driver to honk his horn?

"There were so many things I could have done differently. I saw the car coming toward her, but I didn't have enough time to warn her. By the time I tried to bang on the window to warn her, the car was there. Maybe if I wasn't talking with the cab driver, I might have been able to warn her earlier."

"You cannot blame yourself for this. The drunk driver should be the one to take the blame for this," said Walter.

Mehran looked at Walter and Amandine with teary eyes and said, "I'm sorry."

Walter put his arm around Mehran and squeezed him.

A doctor approached them and asked for Mehran.

"That's me."

"And these folks?"

"They are Kirsten's father and mother."

"Great. I just want to let you all know that we're still waiting for Kirsten to come out of anesthesia. It has been about 6 hours since surgery finished, so it should be real soon now. We're going to move her out of recovery into ICU. Once she's in ICU, you will be able to see her one at a time."

"Thank you, doctor," said Walter.

Mehran, Walter and Amandine walked to the ICU waiting room. Mehran asked if Walter and Amandine wanted any coffee. "We're fine," said Amandine. "Maybe you want to get some fresh air for a little bit, Mehran?"

Mehran left the room and headed outside. It was Sunday morning and the weather was sunny and pleasant. He looked up at the skyscrapers and the sun reflecting off of the glass siding of the tall buildings. It provided the illusion that multiple suns were shining right through the skyscrapers. He stood outside for a few minutes before grabbing a cup of coffee and heading inside.

"Where is Amandine?" Mehran asked Walter when he returned to the waiting room.

"They asked if one of us wanted to see her and Amandine went."

"Walter."

"Don't worry. Everything will be fine."

They waited for a half hour before Amandine came back.

"How is she?" asked Mehran as he stood.

Amandine's eyes were red. "She's unconcious, intubated, her head is wrapped in a white band. It's awful."

"You go next," Walter said to Mehran.

"No, you're her father. You should go next."

"Son, she loves you and needs you more."

Did she really? Had she told them that? No child would tell her parents that she loves her fiancé more than them. Is that the impression that Walter had gotten from Kirsten?

Mehran nodded and headed into the ICU. He checked with a nurse who took him to Kirsten's room.

She was just as Amandine had described. Lifeless, eyes closed, head wrapped in white gauze, her right arm and lower leg in braces, a tube was in her mouth, and electrodes were attached to her head and body going into machines at her side. Mehran stood at the end of her bed, put his hand on her foot and wept. He really did wish that it had been him there in the hospital bed with all the electrodes and tubes. "Please wake up, Kirsten. Please. Please tell me you're okay."

A nurse entered the room and greeted Mehran.

"When will she come out of anesthesia?"

The nurse looked at Kirsten's chart. "Soon."

Mehran looked at Kirsten's beautiful face. She had a couple of scratches. Mehran thought through the accident and considered when she might have gotten the scratches. *The only time could have been when she was sliding across the hood; her face must have caught the windshield wipers.* He looked at her broken leg. *That must have happened when the car hit her.* His eyes moved to her left hand and noticed that her engagement ring was gone, *probably with the rest of her personal belongings they removed when she came into the emergency room.* He lifted her hand and kissed it ever so gently before putting it down.

For the next quarter-hour Mehran talked to Kirsten, begging her to awaken. Eventually, he decided that he didn't want to keep Walter away from Kirsten any longer. Walter had been kind to him, and he deserved to see his daughter. Mehran kissed Kirsten's hand one more time before leaving the room. He went back to the waiting area, and Walter made his way to his daughter.

Mehran sat next to Amandine.

She looked at Mehran and smiled through swollen eyes. "You know what I love about you and Kirsten?"

"No."

"It's the newness, the shininess, the adventurousness of your love for each other. You know she adores you, don't you?"

"I didn't know that."

"She'd never tell you, but she's put you on the highest pedestal she could find."

"And so have I. At times I feel that I want to preserve the love we have right now. I want to put it in a glass jar with a hammer on the side and a sign that says 'Break in Case of Emergency.' I don't ever want it to go away."

"It will, over time, you know."

"I don't think so."

"Yes, it will. Your love will eventually morph into a different kind of love. Love is like a tree, in that it grows roots. It's like a kitten who's cute at the beginning but eventually grows to be a big cat who will have problems from time to time, except you don't just throw it away, and you cannot fathom living without it. Love's the same way. It'll grow roots and become a part of you that you cannot separate yourself from."

"Is that your love for Walter?"

Amandine laughed. "No, we're still at the glass jar stage."

They sat in silence until Walter returned.

"She's strong. She'll make it through," said Walter.

"Is she awake yet?" asked Amandine.

"No, not yet."

The three of them rotated their visits to Kirsten's ICU room for the next few hours. Mehran napped on and off in the waiting room. He woke up when Walter brought him a soda and a sandwich.

"Mehran, here, take this."

"I can't eat."

Walter put the sandwich and the drink on the seat next to Mehran.

Shortly after 3 in the afternoon, two doctors walked in. "Mr. and Mrs. Hostetler," said one.

They all got up.

"Do I have your permission to discuss Kirsten's case with her fiancé as well?"

They looked at each other and then Mehran. Amandine's face changed from a look of bewilderment into a look of absurdity. "Of course!" she said in the snottiest voice and manner possible, thoroughly disgusted and repulsed by the question.

"My name is Dr. Chandrasekhar, but you can call me Chand. I'm a neurologist here. This is Dr. Chase, the anesthesiologist during Kirsten's surgery."

"Hello," Walter said.

"We are a little concerned that Kirsten is not lucid yet," said Dr. Chand.

Dr. Chase continued, "The anesthetics should have worn off hours ago. We have double checked the surgical logs, and in relation to anesthesia, everything went smoothly and proper doses were administered." Dr. Chand turned to Mehran. "Did Kirsten take any recreational drugs or alcohol before the accident happened?"

Mehran thought back to 24 hours earlier. "We shared a couple of bottles of wine at a concert. She probably had two thirds of a bottle over several hours."

Dr. Chand turned to Walter and Amandine. "How about previous medical history? Strokes, hypoxia, previous brain trauma? How about epilepsy or black-out spells?"

They shook their heads.

"Was she taking any over-the-counter drugs or prescription medications?" asked Dr. Chase.

"Not that I know," Mehran answered.

"Probably just birth-control pills," said Amandine.

"It is too early for me to diagnose why Kirsten has not yet regained consciousness. We will have to wait until tomorrow before we can consider other causes," said Dr. Chand.

"What could other causes be?" Mehran asked.

"The injury she suffered may have affected parts of the brain that are responsible for consciousness or helping her wake up," said Dr. Chand. "We need time to observe her."

"Yes, but what are those other parts?"

Dr. Chand hesitated at first to answer, but then said, "Obviously in such traumatic injuries to the head, there are always reasons to suspect damage to the cerebral cortex or the RAS, the reticular activating system, which is responsible for producing wakefulness from sleep. I have looked over the CT scan taken of Kirsten's skull when she was first brought here. The intracranial pressure had caused what we call a midline shift, where pressure on the left side of Kirsten's skull cavity had caused the brain to shift to the right. It was measured at four millimeters; I don't believe it has caused any damage to Kirsten's RAS. Damage to the cerebral cortex, however, is of bigger concern. But I have to repeat: It is too early to make any diagnosis. We will know by tomorrow whether she is comatose, and then we can weigh our options."

"Options?" blurted Mehran.

"Let's not get ahead of ourselves. There's no need to discuss contingencies right now. Things like this can change any minute, at the drop of a hat. Let's wait and see what happens," Dr. Chand said.

"Thank you, doctor," Walter said.

Not so good news, thought Mehran, but he said nothing.

They sat down after the doctors left. "Well, it looks like we're going to be here for a while," Walter said. "We need to do this in shifts. We can't all be here all the time."

"I can't leave," said Mehran.

"Son, you've been here for 16 hours straight; who knows how long you've been up. You need to get some rest."

"I'll be fine."

Walter looked at Amandine. Amandine got up and stood in front of Mehran. "Come on. Let's go. You need to eat something and get some rest."

He looked up at her. For the first time, he could see a little of Kirsten in her mother. Their noses and chins were very much alike.

He got up and followed Amandine. They took a cab to the apartment. When he reached his room, he saw the open box from Laura Ashley still on the bed. Kirsten's clothes that she had shed in favor of the dress he had bought her were still on the floor. Mehran picked up the clothes, brought them to his face and inhaled deeply. He could smell both Kirsten's deodorant and her perfume on her shirt. For a few seconds, his mind completely forgot about the accident that had happened, and he thought he was back home with Kirsten. The sense of smell holds power to take you back, fly your mind to the past. Mehran took another deep breath through his nose, still holding her shirt over his face, but the feelings weren't as strong as the first inhale. He opened his eyes and was back in reality. *Shame*, he thought. *Shame on the drunk asshole who caused this mess.* He stayed motionless for a minute, looking at the clothes in his hands. He put them in the box and put the box in their closet. He took a shower, laid on the bed and passed out.

A few hours later, he woke up to Amandine calling him.

"Mehran!"

"Yes?"

"I think we should go back now."

"Why? Did she wake up?"

"I don't know."

Mehran dressed and they walked out together. They took a cab to the hospital and headed to the ICU waiting room. Anja was there now, and when she saw Mehran, she walked toward him, wrapped her arms around him and held on. "Everything will be fine," she whispered. "It has to be."

"Any updates?" asked Amandine.

"Nothing. Anja just finished visiting her," said Walter.

"I'm going in to see her," Mehran said.

"They said she can have two visitors at a time now," Anja offered.

"I'll go in with Mehran, then," said Amandine.

They checked in with the nursing station before walking in. The nurse said they were checking Kirsten's drains and would be done in a few minutes.

Mehran looked around the ICU. The rooms were like spokes around the center nurses' station. Each room had glass windows. The mood was somber in the unit. A family was talking with a doctor outside one of the rooms. Mehran could see some family members visiting loved ones in others. A few minutes later, the nurse told them they could go in.

The lights were on, and they could see Kirsten better. The left side of her face to the middle of her cheek had turned purple. Mehran covered his face and squeezed his templates, as if he didn't want to see Kirsten in that condition. *How could this have happened to the love of my life?* he thought. Amandine reached over and hugged him. "We should talk about positive things. You never know if she can hear us."

It seemed unlikely that she'd be in a coma and still hear what they were saying. But on the other hand, the human brain is a complex machine with working mechanisms that nobody truly understands. There was no harm in positive talk, plus it might keep Amandine and Mehran in better spirits.

He pulled up a chair near Kirsten and held her hand.

"Hi, Kirsten. It's me. I'm holding your hand. Can you feel me?" He kissed her hand. "I just kissed your hand. Did you feel my lips?" He couldn't continue pretending that nothing was wrong. He got up and left the room.

Amandine sat in the chair Mehran left and started talking to Kirsten in French.

Mehran walked into the waiting room and saw Dr. Chand talking with Walter.

"... after which we'll know if everything is going okay," said Dr. Chand.

"What's going on?" asked Mehran.

"We are going to take Kirsten for another CT scan to make sure no more blood is pooling in her cranial cavity. The pressure sensor indicates that everything is fine, but I'd like a CT scan to be sure. After that we'll know what should happen next."

"Okay, doc. Thank you," said Walter.

Amandine rejoined them and the four sat together for a couple of hours before Dr. Chand returned.

"Come with me," he said. He led the family and Mehran into a room near the ICU waiting room. The room was full of X-ray lightboxes. He stuffed a few of the CT scans he had in his hand on to a lightbox, pointed to one, and said, "This is the CT scan we took of Kirsten last night." He pointed to a white area on the image and continued. "This is the pool of blood, and as you can see, the pressure shifted the brain. The surgery last night released the pressure." He pointed to the next image. "This is the CT scan of Kirsten's brain we just performed. As you can see, the brain is back to a nice center line and looks normal. So this is all good news."

Mehran and the family simultaneously sighed with relief and then looked to Dr. Chand for more answers.

"What about her not waking up?" Mehran asked.

Dr. Chand started to walk back to Kirsten's room while talking with the family. "I have performed a series of tests on Kirsten. Her oculocephalic reflex, in which her eyes follow a light source when her head is turned, is good. This indicates that there is most likely no damage to the brain stem. We've verified that there's no damage to the brain stem via another test, the caloric reflex test, where we inject a jet of cold water into her ear and monitor her eye movements. She responds nicely to this test as well. She also has responded to a noxious stimuli test, where she actually opens her eyes in response to pain." Once they entered Kirsten's room, Dr. Chand walked over to Kirsten and picked her hand up. He then grabbed a pen from his pocket and put the tip of the pen on

Kirsten's index finger's nail and pressed the pen hard against the nail. Kirsten's eyes popped open.

Mehran jumped forward. "Her eyes!"

"That's the noxious stimuli test," Dr. Chand continued. "It tells us that she can feel the pain and responds to it. We measure the responses in regard to eye opening, verbal response, and motor response and we combine them to come up with a number that we use to determine the depth of her coma. The scale is called Glascow. Kirsten scored a 5. The minimum on the scale is a 3, which is considered totally unresponsive, while the high is 15; you and I would score a 15, completely aware and functioning. By all definitions, at this point, she is in a coma. In a couple of days, if she can breathe on her own, we will move her out of ICU. If so, that'll be an excellent sign. We'll take another CT scan in a couple of days and see how she's doing. Until then, just keep your fingers crossed."

Chapter Fifty-Six

Mehran and Anja spent the night at the hospital, while Walter and Amandine went back to the apartment. They returned on Monday morning, and Mehran and Anja went to the apartment.

Mehran woke up at 1 p.m. and realized that he had not notified his company. He called his manager and let her know what happened and that he would not be in for the next few days, at least. He called the bank where Kirsten worked and spoke with Marie. He explained what happened and told her that for the foreseeable future, Kirsten would not be at work. Marie wanted to come and visit Kirsten, but Mehran told her that only family members were allowed in the ICU. He told Marie he'd check back with her in a couple of days.

Thinking about all that was happening, Mehran realized he needed a cell phone so that the hospital, Walter or his company could get in touch with him. He left a note for Anja, who was sleeping on the couch, and left the apartment. At the nearest Best Buy, he purchased the smallest phone they had, a Motorola StarTAC. They assigned him a phone number and said that it would be working in a few hours. Driving back to the apartment, Mehran passed the intersection where the accident happened on Saturday night. Life was going on as usual, it seemed. Nobody, perhaps other than the folks living in the apartments straddling the two streets near the intersection and the cashiers at the pantry, would have known of the grotesque collision that happened here less than 48 hours ago.

He parked the car and returned to the apartment. Anja was in the shower. He looked at the piano and the sheet music Kirsten was practicing for their wedding, the Chopin nocturne. How empty and void this place was without Kirsten. How he wished he had never taken her out to the fado concert that night and instead cooked her a home-made meal. So many things had contributed to the accident: getting the milk, crossing the street. *What if we had caught just one extra red light in the cab? Or even a green light? What if Kirsten had dropped some of her change when paying for the milk and had bent down to pick it up? Or maybe she did and dropping the change was the catalyst? What if she had thought about getting a gallon instead of a half-gallon? What if the store was out of her favorite brand of milk? What if she had bumped into someone coming out of the store, or going into the store? What if she had actually bumped into someone on her way in or out? What if someone had asked the cashier a question while Kirsten was checking out? What if someone did indeed ask the cashier a question while Kirsten was checking out?* Jesus. Why did the stars have to align for something as ominous as this to happen?

Or was it his luck? He was only 32 and so many bad things had happened to him already. Had the stars decided to align themselves to cause him more pain? He didn't believe in God, since he was an atheist, but if he did believe in God, why was God so merciless? *For this accident to have happened, the stars must have aligned precisely in the opposite position of where they would have had to align for something good to happen.*

Thoughts of what-if, what-if raced through his head. He felt doomed once again. The same feelings he had when he heard of his parents dying, or when Naghmeh died just after giving him the true lovers' knot. Was this the fate of his life? Constant death? Constant pain? Maybe it was him. Perhaps he wasn't meant to have anything good doled out to him of all the good things being allocated to people throughout the world.

Then he remembered the things he loved and how they had not failed him. The music he listened to. The children throughout the world he had helped. And what about Kirsten? He couldn't just give up on her. She's alive. She could snap out of her coma at any time.

Anja stepped out of the bathroom with a T-shirt and shorts, drying her head with a towel.

"Oh, Mehran, I wasn't expecting you."

"I'm sorry. I went out for a bit to purchase a cell phone."

"That's a good idea. Do you have anything to eat?"

"Yes. I'll warm something up."

He went into the kitchen, heated some leftovers and fixed two plates. They sat in the kitchen and ate together.

"She knew you were going to propose when you came to Denver."

"She did?"

"Yes. Her exact words were 'If he asked me, I would say yes in a heartbeat.'"

"I keep thinking what-ifs. What if I hadn't proposed to her? The timeline would have changed and she wouldn't have gotten into this accident."

"Mehran, you can't go through life wondering about what-ifs. There's no changing what happened."

"Yes, but what-if –"

He stopped himself, paused for a long time, trying to gather his thoughts together. "I know. I just wish a tiny thing leading to the accident would have deviated a little so that the crash wouldn't have happened. Maybe even a butterfly across the country."

"It's an accident. If there's one blaming factor, it is the driver who was drunk."

Mehran agreed with that. Why should he blame anybody or any particular minuscule event for the collision, when the real cause was the drunk driver? It was the driver who should have been more responsible, not time-shifts changing the order of things in Kirsten's life. Nor the sequence of events that had been set because of the timing of red and green streetlights.

"At this point," Anja continued, "it's only Kirsten we should be thinking of."

She was right, Mehran knew. They finished their food and left for the hospital.

Mehran gave his cell phone number to Walter and the ICU staff.

The next day the doctors took another CT scan of Kirsten's brain. Her vitals were strong and stable, and the doctors felt she could be moved to a regular hospital room. They had already extubated her and she was breathing on her own, which was the last sign that she was ready to move into a regular room.

Mehran and the family opted for a private room. When patient transport brought her in, she looked more normal, despite her bruised face. Maybe it was the tubes, maybe there was more light in the new room coming through the window. Either way, the family and Mehran were happy with the progress and the change in location.

The police officers from Saturday night arrived in the room soon after. They wanted to question Kirsten, but the nurse told them that she had been in a coma since she had arrived at the hospital and that the hospital would call them should her circumstances change. Mehran walked out with the officers. Once they were outside, he asked, "What happened with the driver?"

"His lawyer posted bail yesterday. There's an arraignment next month to determine what charges will be brought against him."

"Thank you," Mehran said. When the officers left, he called his lawyer.

"Greg."

"Mehran! Hey. How are you doing?"

"Not so well, Greg." He explained the situation, and then asked, "What will the prosecutor do?"

"Well, it depends if he can establish a DUI. If he can establish that, then it'll be considered an aggravating circumstance and the driver will face jail time. If he cannot establish a DUI, it'll be just a traffic ticket, unless the pedestrian dies, in which case it'll be involuntary manslaughter, granted if the prosecutor can prove that he was driving recklessly. It's unfortunate that the law doesn't often side with pedestrians in cases like this. Of course, all is fair game in a civil lawsuit, but that doesn't land the driver in jail. It'll just be for money."

"The arraignment is next month when the prosecutor is supposed to decide what to charge him with. Can you keep tabs on that and let me know?"

"Sure thing. I'm sorry, brother."

"As am I, Greg."

He hung up the phone and went back into the room.

Shortly after, Dr. Chand arrived. He performed a brief examination of Kirsten's motor reflexes and her eye movements. There didn't appear to be any motor reflexes, but her eyes were still responding to pain.

"We also performed an MRI to look for evidence of cerebellum injury we may have missed in the CT scans, but the MRI came out clean," said Dr. Chand. "She is still responding with respect to the eye movement reflexes, but what we're really hoping for is a motor reflex."

"What does that mean?" asked Walter.

"Sometimes patients take weeks, or even months, to awaken from a comatose state. The truth is, we do not know enough to declare whether she will awaken or not. There are a series of procedures we use to induce a wakeful state in comatose patients. Some of those I have performed already, such as a painful stimuli. In another method, we purposefully lower the body temperature by up to three degrees centigrade in the hope that the RAS will send an awake signal to the brain. We don't normally perform this on comatose patients, but I think it's worth a shot. We need to be sure that she is stable. If by tomorrow her state has not changed, we'll induce the temperature change."

"What about brain functions?" asked Mehran.

"I am hoping that she'll come out of her coma before we have to resort to functional neuroimaging, or testing for brain functions. There is a school of thought that has recently emerged in which doctors use PET, or positron emission tomography, to map brain activity, but those are in experimental stages and PET machines have not yet been built for production. In the past few years, doctors have used functional magnetic resonance imaging to map out activity in the brain. That is something we can do here. That will tell us if Kirsten's brain responds to outside stimuli by mapping her brain during the stimuli. But before we resort to that, we need to exhaust all other options."

"So what should we do meanwhile?" asked Amandine.

"You should try to stimulate her. Try to engage her with conversations. Hold her hand, hold her foot or leg. Those should all stimulate her."

The doctor didn't believe that any of those would stimulate Kirsten, but he knew better than to let the family know that.

Later that day, Marie and another co-worker of Kirsten's showed up. They sat with Kirsten for a while and talked to Mehran and Amandine before they left.

The next day, Dr. Chand came to the room while Walter and Mehran were there. The doctor explained that he was going to induce the drop in Kirsten's temperature.

"Usually we have a machine which can control temperature via intravascular cooling. When using that machine, we insert a catheter in the femoral artery and the machine can cool the blood in place. But in Kirsten's case, I do not believe we need to resort to intravascular cooling, since time is not of the essence. We will induce the temperature drop via water-cooled blankets. To monitor

Kirsten's core temperature, we will insert an esophageal probe into her mouth. We will have to move Kirsten back to ICU for this process so that she is under constant care. This procedure takes about 24 hours anyway, during which time you cannot visit her. I suggest you both go home and rest. We have your cell phone numbers and will alert you should anything change."

Walter faced Mehran. "Son, let's go home."

Before they left the hospital, Walter walked to the registration desk and signed a release, giving Mehran full decision-making for Kirsten's health care in Walter's and Amandine's absence. Mehran also updated Kirsten's records with information from her insurance card. They took a cab home. When they arrived, Anja was sleeping and Amandine was on the phone with a doctor friend of hers.

Amandine hung up the phone. "What are you doing here?"

Walter told his wife about this new procedure. Anja woke up from the talking and they all sat down at the table.

"I know we all want to be here for Kirsten, but there is no need," Walter began. "Anja, you should head back home. Amandine, there is no need for both of us to stay here. If you can take off from work, you can stay and I'll go," Amandine nodded. "Anja and I will fly to Colorado. I'll come back on Friday night," Walter concluded.

On Thursday morning, Mehran told Amandine that he was going to his office to check in on work before going to the hospital. He left home at 8. At the office, he talked with several of his coworkers who were eager to hear how Kirsten was. They wanted to make sure Mehran was okay as well. Mehran walked to the stock room and saw the manager, Victor.

"I heard what happened to your fiancée. That's a rotten thing."

"I know, Victor."

"You let me know if there's anything I can do. I know there's not much I can do for you, but if you ever need anything, just ask."

"Thanks, Victor. Is Fallah here?"

"He just got here." He called out, "Fallah?"

"How is he coming along? Will he be able to take over your job after you retire next week?"

"The boy's smart, and the classes he's taken have helped a lot. I think he'll be fine. I've given him my home phone number and told him he can call me at any time. It's not like I'm going to Florida or anything once I retire. All I'm gonna do is sit home, work on projects I need to finish and drink beer."

Mehran smiled. Fallah showed up shortly at the stockroom counter.

"Mehran! Oh my God! Where have you been? I called you many times. How is Kirsten?"

Mehran gave Fallah a synopsis of the past few days. Fallah seemed devastated, though Mehran couldn't understand why. He wasn't *that* close to Kirsten.

"How could something like this happen?" Fallah asked.

"It's an accident. It happens."

"But for it to happen to such a nice person?"

"Accidents don't distinguish between nice people and assholes."

"Mehran. I feel your sadness. I feel what you're feeling. My brother died also because of a stupid accident. At least that's what they called it."

"Fallah, I don't believe in God, but in your words, it's the will of God."

"There must be a reason why God decided for this to happen. I don't like it, but he's the almighty and knows best."

Mehran thought for a second how satisfying it might be to just dismiss an avoidable accident as the work of God. *If he's a forgiving God, why bestow something like this to a subject of his who has never harmed anyone?* Then Mehran realized that he didn't know everything Kirsten had done throughout her life; maybe, if there was a God, that God would have known and punished her accordingly.

"I will be in an out of the office for the next few weeks, Fallah. This is my cell phone number. Call if you need anything."

Fallah took the number and put it in his pocket. "Stay strong my friend. It will all work out."

Mehran took a cab to the hospital. When he got there, he decided to check to see if Kirsten was still in the ICU.

"Yes, she's still here under the cold blankets," the nurse said.

Mehran stepped back into the ICU waiting room and sat down.

Amandine showed up in an hour, and they sat there together for a couple of hours more before Dr. Chand came to meet with them.

"I'm sorry that I'm not a bearer of good news," said Dr. Chand. "The temperature jump-start did not work. We are bringing her temperature back up and will be transferring her to a hospital room again."

Mehran and Amandine looked at each other and could see the hopelessness in each other's eyes. They found out the room that Kirsten would be transferred to and went there to wait. Patient transport arrived with an unconscious Kirsten within the hour. Once Kirsten's bed was in place, a nurse came to hook Kirsten to all the monitors that reported back to the nurses' station: the oxygen sensor, heart rate, blood pressure and respiratory rate monitors.

Mehran and Amandine switched eight-hour shifts for the next day. When Mehran was there alone on Friday morning, Dr. Chand came to the room.

"I really hoped that she would have responded to lowering her body temperature."

"What else can we do, Dr. Chand?"

"I am going to arrange for the functional MRI later this morning. Let's hope for some activity during the test."

He started to walk out but turned around.

"There have been a lot of indications that music stimulates the brain. There has even been an instance or two when comatose patients have woken up to music that they're familiar with. I would like to try that. Is there a piece of music that she is familiar with or fond of?"

"Our wedding date is June 14. Kirsten had been practicing a Chopin nocturne, so that she could play it at our wedding. I believe that would be a good choice."

"Do you want to bring that in, or should I acquire a copy?"

"I'll go get it right now."

"Great. We'll get started in the afternoon."

Mehran took a cab back to the apartment. He hurriedly made a copy from the LP to a cassette. The sound woke Amandine.

"Mehran, what's going on?"

"They're going to perform the neural activity test, and they want a piece of music that could possibly stimulate her senses."

"Chopin? I didn't think she liked Chopin that much."

"I think she does. I'm also going to put the first song that she played on the piano here on the cassette and continue alternating between them until the cassette is full."

In a little over a half hour, one side of the cassette was filled with the two nocturnes. Amandine dressed quickly, and together they took a cab back to the hospital.

They waited in Kirsten's room until patient transport came to take her for the MRI.

"They said you had something that should go down with her," said the young woman transporting Kirsten.

"Here, this is it." Mehran gave her the cassette.

"Thank you."

The woman left the room with Kirsten.

Mehran played the nocturne over and over in his head. He wanted to be listening to it at the same time as Kirsten. It brought him closer to her, he thought. He sat down in a chair, closed his eyes and played the music in his mind. He first imagined Kirsten playing it in their apartment, practicing until she got all the kinks out. Once she got the kinks out of the piece in his head, he imagined himself and Kirsten on their wedding night, Kirsten in a beautiful white dress sitting behind a black grand piano, playing the piece that she had practiced over and over in their apartment. She played it flawlessly, with feeling and love. He imagined himself sitting next to the piano as Kirsten played the piece, ignoring everyone else in the room. It was just the two of them. It was he who she was performing this piece for. It was he who she was in love with, and no one else mattered. He looked at Kirsten, and she looked at him. She smiled, but then her nose started bleeding. She didn't mind, though. Blood was staining her white wedding dress and Kirsten was still smiling. Mehran panicked and looked for help, but the two of them were trapped in an abyss, at the bottom of a dark well with no place to go. Kirsten continued to play the piece, smiling. Blood had started to come out of her eyes, her ears, her mouth. He heard the screech of car tires from afar. Kirsten stopped playing and looked at him. Mehran was crying and asking for help. "Please help her. Please call emergency. She's dying." Kirsten said, "I love you. I always will. I live this life for you." Help! Help!

He woke up. Amandine had her hand on his shoulder. "Help with what?" she asked.

Mehran stuttered. "Nothing. It was a nightmare."

"You were crying in your sleep. Was it about Kirsten?"

"Yes."

Amandine walked to his side and pulled his head to her belly. She tried to say something but decided that words could not help or comfort him. She knew what he must be going through. She, too, had been in love before like that.

Patient transport brought Kirsten back in a couple of hours. Mehran and Amandine patiently waited for Dr. Chand. He came a few hours after that.

"How did the test go, Dr. Chand?" Mehran asked.

"I just received the results of the test. I think the results are excellent."

He showed them a couple of print-outs of Kirsten's brain.

"This one is when we first took her in. Surprisingly, it looks like a minimally conscious state of the brain. There's too much activity for us to consider this a completely vegetative state."

He showed them the next print-out. "Now this one is after we played the nocturne over loudspeakers and took measurements. What you're looking for is the increased activity around the same areas as the previous picture."

He held the two side-by-side. The one on the right was labeled "Nocturne" while the one on the left was labeled "Silence."

"Look at the difference between the two."

The picture on the right showed a far greater area of color, red with lots of yellow, while the image on the left showed a smaller area of red with smaller areas of yellow.

"Is the yellow color indicative of higher brain activity?" Mehran asked.

"Yes, it is. The readings from when the music was playing seem to indicate that her brain is functional and processing auditory input."

Mehran looked at Amandine, and they smiled at one another.

"So, what do we do now?" Amandine asked.

Dr. Chand's excitement seemed to fizzle a bit. "Now we just have to wait and hope that she comes out of her coma."

Mehran looked at Amandine again. "Is there nothing else we can do?"

"Obviously she is responding to stimulation, so I would keep that up. That means talk to her when you're here, touch her so that she can feel your hands. You may even want to open her eyelids and look into her eyes."

"What about smells? I can bring her perfume," said Mehran.

"Whatever can add to her sensory input cannot be bad for her."

Dr. Chand paused for a long time, as if he wanted to say something more. Amandine noticed and asked, "What is it, doctor?"

"I will have to get together with the neurosurgeon, but Kirsten's healing is on track. In a few days there is no reason for us to keep her in the hospital. My guess is that the neurosurgeon would like to keep her here until at least Monday to make sure everything is done and over with her surgery. Whatever facility she's at, a qualified physician or nurse practitioner would have to remove the staples in a couple of weeks. I am going to have someone come in and talk with you about your options. But let's hope she comes out of this in the next couple of days."

Amandine called Walter on his cell phone and gave him the update.

"That's great news. I'll see you tonight."

A representative from the hospital's placement office came to the room.

"My name is Corrien. I'm here to assist you in choosing a destination for Kirsten."

"A destination?" asked Amandine.

"A discharge location. She is comatose, and she will need to be cared for around the clock."

"We are hoping that she's going to come out of it by Monday or Tuesday when she'll be discharged," said Mehran.

"Yes! And we hope that will be the case as well. But we should plan for a contingency, should things not go the way we hope."

Mehran and Amandine looked at each other. They had not even considered a contingency. "What does that mean exactly?" asked Mehran.

"Well, as a comatose patient, Kirsten will require around-the-clock care. She will need her diaper changed often and the catheter replaced periodically. She will need to be moved every 2 or 3 hours to prevent bedsores. In cases of coma, pneumonia is always a big concern, since she cannot swallow, so her vitals will need to be monitored closely. She will need physical therapy to prevent long-term muscle damage. Finally, there's the matter of her diet. She will need a balanced diet to ensure that her organ functions continue."

"What are our options?" asked Amandine.

"There are three choices. I will go over the pros and cons of each with you. The first choice is, of course, for her to continue to stay in a hospital. That is the most expensive option but will provide the best care for Kirsten. Nurses would be checking on her every hour and handle all the care she needs."

She continued. "The second choice is hospice care, although their philosophy of care is palliative, which does not fit long-term care. They can be instructed to continue care and provide the nutritional diet needed to keep the patient alive, but in general they are geared toward preventing the suffering of the terminally ill."

"Lastly, there's the option of home care. Committing to home care is a big responsibility. I recommend that you do not take this lightly, should you choose to go this route. To be able to properly care for Kirsten at home, it requires either a dedicated around-the-clock nurse or a part-time nurse as well as a dedicated individual."

Mehran and Amandine looked at one another before Amandine told Corrien that they'd have to think through the options before making a decision.

"Take your time. We have at least until early next week to figure out what we are going to do."

Mehran excused himself and left the hospital building. He called the Chicago Tribune to place an advertisement for a caregiver.

The advertisement read, "Dedicated around-the-clock nurse wanted for care of individual with severe disability. Must have prior experience. Certification is preferred. Accommodation provided on-site. Weekends negotiable."

He added his phone number and was assured that the advertisement would be printed in the Sunday edition of the paper.

Walter arrived a few hours later and came to the hospital. Mehran and Amandine were both in the room when he arrived. They discussed the discharge options with Walter.

"What do you think, Mehran?"

"Well, I would like her to come back home with me. Actually, I thought I'd get started on that option, so I already placed an ad in the paper for a nurse, in case that's what we decide," said Mehran.

"Mehran, that's not going to work. You don't have any room in your apartment for a hospital bed, let alone an extra bedroom for a full-time nurse," said Amandine.

She was right. He didn't have the room.

"Well, I am not too fond of the hospice option, since I don't believe she'll receive the care she needs," Mehran said.

"That leaves only the option of her staying in a hospital, or live elsewhere," said Amandine.

"What if I get a bigger place?" asked Mehran.

Walter and Amandine remained silent.

"What if I get the apartment right below me? That way the nurse will have a room to stay at all times and the rest of the apartment can be dedicated to Kirsten, and I'll be with her every night."

"Is the apartment downstairs empty?" asked Walter.

"No, but I can try to convince the tenants to leave. I can offer them money and pay for their move."

"It might be best if she came to Denver with us," Amandine said.

Mehran stayed silent for a bit and then, as firmly as he could in an effort to convince Amandine, said, "I don't know how I'll ever be able to live without her."

Walter and Amandine looked at each other. Walter broke the silence. "If you can get the apartment on the first floor *and* get a full-time nurse, then this just might work for her to stay here with you."

"Walter," said Amandine.

"Amandine. You know how much she loved Mehran. She would have wanted this, for now at least. Nothing has to be permanent."

"What do you mean 'for now at least'?" asked Mehran.

"Mehran, there may come a time when we would need to let her go. It's too early to make that decision, but the time may come."

"Walter!" Amandine snapped.

Walter looked at her, but she knew that he was right. The time may come to say goodbye to Kirsten. How long would be sufficient to keep Kirsten in a coma, waiting for her to regain consciousness? A year? Two years? Five years?

Mehran wondered how matter of factly Walter, Kirsten's own father, could state that such a decision may have to be made. Mehran couldn't even fathom the idea of ever letting Kirsten go. Yet, he felt, if Walter, as a father, could talk about the possibility, a father who had loved his child for 30 years, that Mehran should also be able to consider the same.

Walter and Amandine decided to stay at a hotel near the hospital for the weekend.

Chapter Fifty-Seven

Mehran went home that night and the first thing he did was knock on the door of the apartment below him on the first floor.

A woman opened the door.

"Oh, hi!"

"Hi, Olga."

"Mehran, right?"

"Yes."

A man came to the door.

"Oh, hi Mehran."

"Hello, Pavel."

They stared at Mehran for a second.

"May I come in?"

Pavel and Olga looked at each other oddly. "Sure," Pavel said finally.

They opened the door and Mehran walked into their place for the first time, though they had been neighbors for over 10 years. Their apartment was simply adorned and with minimal furniture. It was the same size and layout as Mehran's apartment. He looked at the couple, who still appeared puzzled as to Mehran's visit. Olga was wearing a dress and had her hair in a ponytail. Pavel was in a T-shirt and a pair of jeans. Both appeared to be very fit, and that made sense when Mehran noticed two 10-speed bikes with professional pedals and handles in the corner of the apartment. He couldn't place their accent, but it was clear that they weren't born in the United States.

"This is awkward, so I won't beat around the bush. I would like to pay you for your apartment. You're probably paying $750 for rent. I am willing to pay for the rest of your lease for this apartment. I will also pay for your next place's rent for this and the next month, will have movers come in and move your belongings without you having to box a single thing, and I'll give you $5,000 on top of everything."

The couple looked at each other. "Why?" asked Olga.

Mehran knew he owed them an explanation for his intrusion and irrational behavior. "Remember the woman who was with me a few weeks ago when we all ran into each other?"

"The blonde woman?" asked Pavel.

"Yes. Her name is Kirsten and she is my fiancée. She was hit by a drunk driver last Saturday night and she's in a coma. She will be getting discharged from the hospital soon, and I want to get a hospital bed and a full-time nurse to care for her around the clock, except that I won't be able to do that in my apartment."

Pavel looked at Olga and said, "You might have simply asked before offering so much. Our lease is up in a couple of months anyway, and we were thinking of moving."

Mehran looked at them. "I realize that this will inconvenience you, which is why I offered what I did. Do you think you'll be able to find a place this weekend and move in the next week?"

The couple looked at each other and nodded their heads.

Mehran couldn't believe what he had just done. How rude of him, without an explanation he had blurted out commands to a couple he barely knew. What had become of him? He felt ashamed. "I am sorry," he said. "I must sound crazy."

"No, no. We are sorry to hear about Kirsten. We would love to help. We'll let you know tomorrow or Sunday when we have found a place," said Pavel.

Mehran put his head down. He didn't have the courage to look the couple in the eyes. "Thank you. I'll call movers when you let me know."

He turned around and headed upstairs. Once inside his apartment, he headed straight into the bedroom. He wanted to hold Kirsten's pillow so that he could smell her shampoo on it. He realized, though, that Walter and Amandine had slept in the same bed while he was at the hospital. Instead, he headed for the Laura Ashley box and picked up the shirt Kirsten had worn on the Friday before the accident. He passed out on the bed with the shirt held up to his face.

On Saturday, Mehran started receiving calls from potential nurses. He weeded a few of them out on the phone and set up interviews for Sunday at the hospital with a couple of them. He wanted to interview them with Walter and Amandine at his side. Kirsten's condition remained the same, although the bruise on her face had started to pale. The doctors had opted to put braces on Kirsten's arm and leg instead of casts since she was immobile and her chances of hurting the healing process were small. That way, once Kirsten was situated in a bed at home, the braces could actually be removed and the skin allowed to breathe.

Mehran told Walter and Amandine of his talk with the first-floor neighbors. He also told them that he had already set up two interviews for tomorrow at the hospital.

"Mehran, you made a lot of assumptions when you set these up," said Amandine.

"Yes, but I figured the worst you could say was no."

Mehran plugged in the radio cassette player he had brought with him from home, turned on the radio and tuned to WFMT, Chicago's classical station. The doctor had said all sorts of stimuli could benefit and bring Kirsten around; Mehran was willing to do everything possible.

On Sunday, the three of them interviewed two candidates in the hospital cafeteria. Mehran also heard back from several other nurses and set up two more for later in the day.

The first two candidates were young women, one who was married, another one divorced. Mehran cut the married woman since he didn't want her marriage and caring for Kirsten to interfere with each other. Walter and Amandine vetoed the younger divorced woman, since she had no prior experience caring for patients with Kirsten's specific needs.

The third candidate was an older woman named Greta who had prior experience taking care of her own comatose son. During his late teens, he had a cardiac arrest due to a defect in his heart; he slipped into a coma from lack of oxygen. She cared for him for 10 years before he died of complications from pneumonia.

Greta looked to be about 47 or 48; she had short silver hair that appeared well gelled. She had minimal makeup on her face and wore no jewelry besides a silver necklace. She was tall, perhaps a bit taller than Mehran, but not as tall as Walter. Mehran paid attention to her fingers and noticed that she had short, unpainted nails.

Mehran asked Greta some questions, mainly to determine her commitment to the job. He told her that, while taking care of Kirsten would be an around-the-clock job, there would obviously be periods of rest in between. He wondered what she would do in her free time, and worried that he may hire a person addicted to television. He decided to ask her outright what her plans were for those periods.

"I like to read a lot. I also make miniature furniture for dollhouses in my spare time and listen to a lot of music when I'm doing that," responded Greta.

Mehran was satisfied. Because of her experience with a comatose patient, they all agreed that she would be the right caregiver for Kirsten. They agreed on a salary for her, and she said she could start as soon as they let her know Kirsten was home.

Dr. Chand alerted them that they could release Kirsten into home care on Tuesday, or if Mehran wasn't ready yet on Tuesday, they'd be able to keep her at the hospital for a few more days.

After the interviews on Sunday, Mehran went back to the apartment to check with the couple on the first floor. They weren't home, so he went to his apartment. When he opened his door, he saw a note that Olga had slid under his door: "We found a place not too far from here. It's a bit bigger, which is what we were looking for, since we're expecting in 6 months. Here's the address."

Mehran was relieved. All the pieces were falling into place. He went back to the hospital and showed the note to Walter and Amandine.

"Since it looks like we may move Kirsten out this week, we'll stay in Chicago," Amandine said.

On Monday morning, Mehran called a moving company.

"We can send a group of movers who will pack everything and do the whole move in one day, but it will be expensive given the rush for completion," said the woman from the moving company.

"How much?"

"Probably between $2,000 and $3,000 for a single-bedroom apartment."

"Not a problem. So, you do it tomorrow?"

"I'll schedule it."

Mehran gave his address and credit card number to the moving company and went downstairs. He knocked on the door, but there was no answer, so he proceeded to the hospital.

When he went up to the room, Amandine was talking to Kirsten in French while Walter was sitting in the chair by the bed, reading a book. "The movers will be moving the first-floor occupants out tomorrow. It'll take a day to get a hospital bed and supplies in the apartment, so I think we should ask the hospital to discharge Kirsten on Wednesday evening."

Walter nodded.

"I should go and take care of getting everything ordered for the apartment," said Mehran.

Mehran stopped by the nursing station and asked to speak with the placement counselor. Corrien came up to the nurse's station.

"I have almost everything ready, but I need supplies and a hospital bed."

"Follow me," said Corrien.

They headed to her office on a different floor.

She reached into one of the cabinets and pulled out a piece of paper.

"This contains a list of items you should have to care for Kirsten. I also understand that you've hired a full-time caregiver. That's great. You should also ask her what additional supplies she'll need."

Mehran looked over the paper. It included items such as towels, rags, diapers, blankets, sheets, hospital gowns, I.V. equipment, catheters and needles. Big-ticket items, such as a hospital bed, a wheelchair, an oxygen tank and a pulse monitor/oxygen sensor, also were on the list.

"Can you direct me to where I get these?"

Corrien turned the paper over and several medical supply stores were listed.

Mehran left the building and took a cab to the nearest store on the list. While on his way, he called Greta and ran the list by her. Greta said that it'd be best for her to meet him at the store. Mehran waited for about 10 minutes outside the store until Greta showed up; together, they went inside and picked out their supplies. The only item he could not purchase was the oxygen tank, which required a doctor's prescription. Mehran told the clerk that they should include the tank in the order and that he'd have the doctor's office give them a call shortly.

Mehran stopped by his office to let them know that he would not be in for the rest of the week, but he would be able to resume work the following week.

By late afternoon, he figured that the couple on the first floor of the apartment would be home. He stopped by before he returned to the hospital.

He knocked on the door.

"Hello, Mehran," Olga greeted him.

"Hello. May I come in?"

"Of course."

"I read that you're expecting. Congratulations."

"Thank you."

"Have you signed a contract for the new place?"

"We put a security deposit down."

Mehran reached into his pocket and took out a check for $7,000, with an empty recipient. "I didn't know who you wanted the check made out to, so I left it blank. Please fill it in as appropriate."

Olga looked at the check. "This is more than we agreed upon."

"Please, take the check. You have done me a great favor. I wish I knew you better and could repay you in other ways."

"Thank you."

"Thank *you*. I have arranged for the mover to be here tomorrow morning. They will pack everything for you and move you to the new place. They have assured me that you will not have to worry about anything, including the contents of your refrigerator."

"They have people who do that?"

"Like I said, I wanted this to be the least disruptive to your lives as possible. I will keep all your mail separate until it gets forwarded. There'll be someone here 24 hours a day, so you should be able to stop by at any time to pick up the mail that still comes here."

"Thank you. You've thought of everything. How is Kirsten?"

Mehran lowered his head. "The same. She hasn't changed."

"I'm sorry. If there's anything we can do, let us know."

"Thank you." He stepped out of the apartment and out to the street. He hailed a cab and went to the closest furniture store, where he purchased a bed, table, couch, and a television stand. He paid for expedited delivery on Wednesday. Then he hailed a cab to go to the hospital. On the way there, he called his landlord and told him how he would be taking over the lease for the first floor and why. The landlord did not have any issues with Mehran's arrangement, since he had never received a late payment in the past decade Mehran had lived in the apartment. Mehran also called the phone company to set up new service for the first floor under his name. The last call he made was to Greta to confirm that she would start work on Wednesday. He needed her in the apartment to accept all the deliveries and have the hospital bed ready for Kirsten's arrival on Wednesday night.

At the hospital, Mehran took the elevator up to Kirsten's floor. On his way to the room, a nurse stopped him. "Mr. Noori, ER brought this bag up. It's unlabeled and they wondered if these were Kirsten's belongings." Mehran looked in the bag and recognized the engagement ring he had given her when he proposed only 4 months ago. The diamond had fallen off, probably due to the force of impact with the hood, the windshield or the ground.

"Yes. That's her engagement ring," he said.

"I'll label the bag. Do you want me to keep these for now, or would you like to take them?" she asked as she took a marker to write Kirsten's information on the bag.

"I'll take them," Mehran said. He waited until the nurse finished labeling the bag and then he went on to Kirsten's room.

He updated Walter and Amandine on everything he had done.

"You have been busy today," said Walter.

"I want everything to be ready for her. I don't want to cut any corners."

Walter looked at Amandine. "Let's go back to the hotel. The two of them can be alone for the evening."

Mehran turned the lights down and sat by Kirsten, holding her hand in his.

"Kirsten. I have missed you. We haven't been alone for a while. Last night, I was at home and listened to the nocturne you were going to play at our wedding. I miss the way you played it. I wish I had recorded you practicing it, so that I'd be able to listen to your version over and over. You know, I'm going to take you out of this hospital and take you home. I'll be able to spend every night with you. I'll be able to play all the same music we always listened to together. I'll be able to read you books, care for you, clean you, give you baths." He paused and held back his tears. "Please, baby. Come back to me. I need you. I can't go on without you. You need to be in my life. I want you to be happy. Right now, I don't know if you're happy or not. Please tell me something. Open your eyes. Move your finger. Give me a sign. Any sign that you care for me. This is me. I'm the same Mehran who has loved you for the past year."

He opened the plastic bag, took the ring out and continued. "I'm the same Mehran who gave you this ring," he said as he slid the ring on Kirsten's finger. He played with the ring on her finger, the two sides of the ring meeting in the middle to hold together nothing but thin air. "Remember when I proposed to you? In the middle of falling snow on Christmas? And you said yes?" He looked at her face.

Not a twitch of a muscle. Not a twitch of an eye. Not a twitch of her lips.

He gently put his arm under her and lifted her back, cuddling her head with his other hand, and brought her up to his chest. He held her in his arms and continued to talk to her for a couple of minutes before he set her down gently. He looked at her beautiful face and thought he should kiss her. He lowered his face in front of Kirsten's. He could feel the warm air she was exhaling with every breath. He put his lips on her upper lip and felt her warmth for a few seconds before he released her.

Not a twitch of a muscle. Not a twitch of an eye. Not a twitch of her lips.

He stayed the night in the hospital, sleeping on the chair a few feet from Kirsten.

Chapter Fifty-Eight

The next morning Walter and Amandine walked in early.

"Mehran!" said Amandine. "Have you been here all night?"

"Yes. I couldn't leave her."

Amandine looked at Walter and said to Mehran, "Kirsten is lucky to have you by her side."

"I'm not so sure; I believe I'm the lucky one. I'm lucky to have her by my side."

"We are all lucky to have her in our lives," Walter said.

Mehran left to check on the movers. By the time he got to the apartment, the movers had already packed most everything in boxes. Everything was going according to plan. He stepped inside and Olga greeted him.

"Hello, Olga."

"I can't believe how fast these movers work. They're doing in one day what would have taken us two weeks," she said.

"Anything I can do? Are they respecting your belongings?"

"They're fine. Everything is okay, except – "

"What's wrong?"

She reached into her pocket, brought out the check Mehran had written. "We can't take this check."

"Why not?"

"We talked about it, and we don't feel it is right for us to take any more of your money than this move may have inconvenienced us."

"Please, believe me when I say that you have done a great favor for me. It is the least I could do after the way I very insensitively dumped my problems at your doorstep."

"We understand your dilemma and want to help as much as possible. We were going to be moving in a few months anyway, so it's not like what you asked put us completely off. We calculated and we believe the right amount would be just the extra month's rent for the new place, plus you have already paid for movers to move our belongings, which is more than enough. If you could please rewrite a check for $850, that would make us very happy," she said as she extended the check to Mehran.

"You are very nice people. Your child will be lucky to have you as parents," Mehran said as he took the check from her hand. He took out his pen and checkbook from his pocket and wrote a new check for $850. "Who do I make this out to?"

The woman said, "Olga Netrebko."

Mehran looked at her. "You're Russian?"

"I am. Pavel is Ukrainian."

Mehran thought how he wished he would have gotten to know them better. They probably would have been able to share stories of their homelands. He handed Olga the check. "Thank you. Please let me know if you need anything. I'll be upstairs for the next few hours."

He went to his apartment and crashed on his bed. A few hours later, the ring of his cell phone woke him up.

"Hello?"

"Mehran, hi. It's Fallah. Everyone at work wants to know how you're doing, and I figured I'd call you and check on you."

"Everything's fine." He explained the plans to move Kirsten. "Kirsten will be coming back tomorrow night."

"Can I come and see you both sometime?"

"Let's not plan on anything yet. Maybe next week."

"Okay. Please let me know if you need any help."

They hung up. Mehran took a shower and headed back to the hospital.

"Anything?" he asked.

"No. We're just talking to her about her childhood," said Walter.

Mehran leaned against the wall by the window. It was a cloudy day, just the way he liked them.

Dr. Chand came to the room to talk to them, accompanied by a gastroenterologist.

"As you know, we're releasing Kirsten tomorrow. We are going to prescribe total parenteral nutrition packs for Kirsten to cover her for the next week, but she cannot continue to get her nutrition through an IV line for much longer. We will need to consider other options."

"What options do we have?" Mehran asked.

The gastroenterologist answered. "Ultimately, for long-term care, she will need a tube leading directly into her stomach. The tube will come out of her abdomen; a liquid nutrient can be fed through it. For the short-term, we can place a nasogastric tube through her nose and throat, that passes through the esophagus and into her stomach. We can leave that tube in for a few weeks, but it has to be inserted at the hospital because it requires the use of X-ray to ensure it is properly inserted into the stomach and not into a lung by mistake."

Mehran looked at Walter and Amandine. "Let's start with IV and move to the nasogastric tube. Who knows by then what may happen," Mehran said.

Walter looked at Amandine. Amandine nodded and then covered her face with her hand. It seemed now that Kirsten was close to being released from the hospital, the reality of the situation was sinking in on all of them. Nothing was normal about Kirsten, even though her body was functioning properly. Constant movement, constant diaper changing, constant feeding, around-the-clock care.

Mehran looked at Kirsten on the bed.

Not a twitch of a muscle. Not a twitch of an eye. Not a twitch of her lips.

"Another thing we'll need is for all the caregivers to be present tomorrow afternoon so that everyone hears the same instructions," said Dr. Chand.

"I will arrange that," Mehran said.

"Good. Then we will see you tomorrow afternoon at 3."

Mehran called Greta and asked her to come to the hospital on Wednesday afternoon instead. "Please bring what you'll need to stay at the apartment, since we'll be going to the apartment from here."

He hung up with Greta and turned to Amandine and Walter. "I was hoping that Greta would be at the apartment to accept all the deliveries, but I'll ask if Fallah could stay at the apartment instead." He then called work and asked Fallah if he could take a day off and stay at the apartment to accept the deliveries. They planned to meet at the apartment in the morning before Mehran went to the hospital.

"I need to leave now to take the keys from the neighbors on the first floor, but I will be back later," Mehran told Walter and Amandine.

He left for the apartment. When he entered, he saw Olga and Pavel sitting on the stairs, waiting for him.

"How is she?" asked Pavel.

"Unchanged."

"I wish I would have known her better," said Olga.

What if Kirsten and Olga had known each other? The whole accident may have been avoided. *We could have gone on a double date, the four of us, to the fado concert and things would have been different. Just any change to shuffle things a few seconds one way or another.*

"You would have liked her. She is an amazing woman," said Mehran.

Pavel extended his hand. "Here are the keys. The front door, the inner door and the mailbox."

Mehran took them. "Thank you. I do not know how to ever repay you for what you've done for me."

"No need. The movers were non-intrusive and everything went beautifully. In addition, you have already compensated us," said Pavel.

Mehran wished that money could solve all his problems. Unfortunately money was just a means to some ends, not all.

"I will be here every night and the nurse should also be here around the clock. Your mail will be sitting on a table."

"The post office has re-routed our mail to our new home, so we don't expect much to come here. This is our phone number. If you need anything, please do not hesitate to call," Olga said.

Pavel and Olga left the building. Mehran turned and walked into the first-floor apartment. The movers hadn't left anything in the apartment, except the stove and the refrigerator. Mehran made sure that the refrigerator was turned on before he left.

He went back to the hospital. Everything he had done in the past few days seemed to be running like clockwork. He had changed modes from the romantic, and then the reminiscent, to the realist. These were the facts of his life now. Kirsten needed help, and he would make sure that she got every bit of it. Where were the feelings that would cripple and debilitate him? Surely they lingered somewhere in the back of his mind. He simply didn't think he had enough time to tend to his feelings. It would be easy to dismiss his sense of duty and leave Kirsten's care to her parents. But would it be right? *At the end of the day*, he thought, *I wouldn't be able to live with myself.* But was it duty that he was thinking of? *This isn't a feeling of duty. It is a feeling of love. It is a feeling of "I want to be with her forever."*

At the hospital, Mehran, Walter and Amandine took turns reading to Kirsten. They all wanted something to change in these last hours of Kirsten's stay in the hospital. They all wanted a miraculous recovery. A Hollywood recovery, like they had seen in movies. They tried their darndest, sharing their most spectacular memories with Kirsten in an effort to wake her, to no avail. It simply looked as though Kirsten was ignorant of all that was happening around her.

Mehran stayed at his apartment that evening. In the morning, Fallah came to the building.

"Thanks for coming, buddy. This is a great help," Mehran said.

"Of course," said Fallah. "After everything you've done for me? This is nothing."

Mehran gave the keys to both apartments to Fallah. "The deliveries will be throughout the day. I'm expecting furniture and medical supplies." Mehran proceeded to tell Fallah where the large furniture and the bed were to be placed.

"I guess you'll get to see Kirsten when we come home tonight," said Mehran.

"I hope she gets better in the hospital before you bring her here."

Mehran said goodbye to Fallah and left for the hospital just after 9. Walter and Amandine were in Kirsten's room. Greta showed up at the hospital at about 2 in the afternoon.

They stayed in the room until Dr. Chand, the gastroenterologist, a neurosurgeon, a general practitioner and the placement counselor were all in the room. Space was a bit crowded but manageable. The doctors and the counselor each took turns to talk to Kirsten's parents, Mehran and Greta. They explained everything that was to be expected. They were pleasantly surprised to find out that Greta had already taken care of a comatose patient and that it had been her son.

After all the preparation, Walter and Amandine needed to sign papers to release Kirsten into Mehran's custody. Mehran saw that they were both emotional. Even up to the last minute all three of them were hoping Kirsten would show signs of consciousness.

Greta left the hospital to organize the supplies and prepare the bed for Kirsten.

Early in the evening a patient transport company arrived to move Kirsten.

Mehran again tried to ride in the back with Kirsten but was told that he could have a seat in the front. Patient transport brought Kirsten in the first-floor apartment and transferred her to the bed.

Greta got busy hanging an IV line, connecting the oxygen sensor to Kirsten's fingertip, adjusting the bed, making sure Kirsten's diaper wasn't soiled, emptying her urine drainage bag and covering her with blankets.

"Mehran," she said, "I actually like a warm room, but it is always easier to cover Kirsten than to take layers off. We should keep the temperature at 70 around the clock."

Mehran agreed and set the thermometer to 70 degrees. It was the beginning of May, and the temperature wasn't likely to dip much below 70 degrees or rise much above it for now.

Mehran took a look by the kitchen and saw Fallah standing by the kitchen door, trying to hold his tears back. Mehran walked over to Fallah and asked, "Are you okay?"

Fallah stuttered at first but managed to speak. "Why did this have to happen to her? Why to you? You both are the nicest people I have met here. This is not right."

"It is life, friend. Sometimes bad things happen."

That night, Amandine slept on the couch near Kirsten. She wanted to have that proximity before leaving her daughter to return home. Mehran laid in his bed upstairs, thinking about Kirsten and finding comfort that she was only a few steps away from him. He got up and walked to the closet where the Laura Ashley box still held Kirsten's blouse. He knew he could never wash Kirsten's clothes.

Mehran, Walter and Amandine had watched others in the hospital provide physical care for Kirsten, such as stretching her muscles, turning her and so on, but in the apartment they needed to do the work. Somehow it seemed different taking care of Kirsten in person as opposed to watching hospital nurses take care of her. For Mehran, it was the closest he could be with Kirsten. He loved helping to make her comfortable.

Alas, not a twitch of a muscle. Not a twitch of an eye. Not a twitch of her lips.

Mehran felt the need for feedback from Kirsten. He wanted her to tell him that she was comfortable and that everything was going to be all right. Greta had warned him about this. Having cared for her son for nearly 10 years, Greta said that the hardest part was forcing herself to realize that she was caring for a living human being, because the lack of any response from her comatose son had an adverse effect on her own psyche. Mehran would have to convince himself that Kirsten was as well as she was going to get, but he wasn't at the same stage Greta had been with her son. At least not yet.

Mehran realized early on that first full day with Kirsten at home that he wasn't sure what was driving him to care for Kirsten in this way. Was he doing this for Kirsten, or had he done this for himself?

He thought he knew Kirsten well. Kirsten probably would not have wanted him to take care of her for a long time. Certainly, she would not have wanted this to go on for years. As Mehran moved Kirsten's limbs to help her muscles, he remembered a conversation they had a few months ago, after they watched a documentary on euthanasia on PBS.

"If that's the life I would be doomed to have, I wouldn't want it," said Kirsten.

"But a life like that is surely better than not having one at all, isn't it?" asked Mehran.

"Not if it means that it burdens everyone around me for years and that I suffer through it."

"Why is it up to you to decide whether your life is burdensome to your loved ones?"

"Because it's my fucking life! I don't want people to remember me as someone who couldn't take care of herself. When all options are exhausted, I want to be put to fucking sleep."

"That's easy for you to say, if you're the one who won't feel anything after you're gone. It's the people around you that will hurt for a long time."

"You're right. It's easy for me to decide that. It's everyone else around me who would have to know to let go."

"That's really sticking it up to your loved ones."

Kirsten thought about it and finally said, "If I get an illness that is going to kill me, I wouldn't mind putting my head up on the chopping block. You'll just have to deal with it. You would have to deal with my death either way, so why make me suffer?"

Mehran continued stretching Kirsten's muscles by bending her knee, curling her toes and moving her foot upwards.

"I'm not sure if this is good enough. I think I should hire a physical therapist for you," he said to Kirsten as though she might have an opinion.

But she said nothing.

"I think I will. I don't want to take any chances," Mehran said. "At least I'll have someone who can show me what to do."

Greta walked into the living room, put her hand on Mehran's shoulder. "Mehran, I have done plenty of this before. We'll be fine."

Kirsten's parents, Mehran and Greta spent the day at the apartment. They took turns reading stories to Kirsten and playing music for her. Mehran called the movers and scheduled them to move the piano downstairs. He took a cab to Best Buy and purchased a television set and a stereo system for the first floor. He put the television in Greta's bedroom, while he put the stereo in the living room with Kirsten. His objective was to pump as much familiar music into the atmosphere as he could, in the hope of stimulating Kirsten.

On Friday, Anja flew in to be with them. Mehran drove to the airport in Kirsten's car and picked her up.

"I remember when Kirsten bought this car," Anja remarked.

Mehran laughed. This was the first time he had laughed since the accident. He remembered how he and Kirsten had made love in the car in the cemetery.

"You're laughing! That's a good sign."

"A good sign of what?"

"Obviously what I said reminded you of something."

Mehran thought for a second. "Kirsten was trying to teach me how to drive a stick shift in a cemetery. I already knew how to drive, except she didn't know I knew. It was funny when I floored the gas pedal and popped the clutch."

Just as quickly, sadness came over him. That memory seemed so long ago, never to be repeated again. Tears collected in his eyes, but he checked himself before they fell.

"Mehran, it's okay. You can cry. You should cry."

"I want her back," he said as a tear escaped and rolled down his cheek.

His cry broke. He pulled over to the side of the highway. "I want her back the same way she was. I want her to talk to me. I want her to hold me. I want her to make love to me."

"Those times are passed for now. Now you'll have to do everything by yourself. *You* are going to have to talk to her. *You* are going to have to hold her. The end result is the same. You still love each other. You're still spending time with each other."

Mehran thought for a second. "No, it is not. It's not the same."

He looked at Anja. Her eyes were full of tears. When she saw his eyes, she broke down as well and started to cry. "Don't listen to what I'm saying," Anja said. "The words are the right thing to say, but they can't compensate for what you're going through. The feelings behind them are genuine, though. I know life's not going to be the same. All I can think of is her in her white wedding dress, and how that's never going to happen. And how she always protected me when we were growing up, whether it'd be from a bully in school, or from a boyfriend who had broken up with me."

"I just want her to come back to me," he said just before the sobs came. Anja put her hand over his neck and pulled him toward her.

She wept, too, along with Mehran. She held him until he pulled away. "I'm sorry. I don't mean to be a basket case." He wiped his nose with his sleeve like a first-grader might.

"Mehran, do you realize what you and Kirsten had?" Anja managed to say.

"A beautiful life. That's what we had."

"Do you know how many other people in this world go without having even a shred of what you shared with Kirsten?"

Somehow the thought wasn't comforting Mehran.

Anja stopped crying, reached in her purse and took out a bag of tissues. She took a couple and gave a couple to Mehran. "Let me ask you a question. If you knew of the accident ahead of time, knowing that at some point a bad accident would happen to Kirsten no matter what you did, and you had a chance to back out of your relationship with her, would you have? Would you have done *anything* differently?"

Mehran thought and then shook his head. "Not if I couldn't change things to avoid the accident. No. Our time with each other was perfect."

"Would you rather not have had the love you had for each other?"

"I would never want that love to not have happened."

"Then look at the positive side of things. You and Kirsten shared something so profound that, even in her death in your relationship, you still cherish it. That is something to be proud of. That is something to remember forever. You shouldn't remember Kirsten in her current state. You should cherish what you and she were able to achieve. That's the eternal love. That's the magic. That's something to remember her by, not the vegetative state she's in now."

Mehran looked at her and wiped his tears with the tissue.

"It won't be easy," he said.

"No, it won't."

Mehran put the car in gear, waited for an opening and pulled into traffic.

Anja stayed for the weekend and, on Sunday, the Hostetler family returned to Denver.

Once everyone left and only Kirsten, Mehran and Greta were left, Mehran realized that this would be his life for the foreseeable future. He would spend every night with Kirsten and possibly Greta. He wasn't upset about it; as a matter of fact, he looked forward to being with Kirsten at home – or close to home – again.

Chapter Fifty-Nine

Mehran woke up early on Monday morning. He showered and shaved off the two-week-old beard before heading downstairs. Greta was changing Kirsten's diaper. Mehran walked over and helped by rolling Kirsten to one side.

"She's pretty easy to care for when it comes to things like this. My son was 6' 2" and weighed over 200 pounds. Rolling Kirsten around is nothing."

Mehran looked at Kirsten's face.

Not a twitch of a muscle. Not a twitch of an eye. Not a twitch of her lips.

As they finished, Mehran asked Greta to make a list of everything she'd need to make her stay more comfortable, and everything else they would need to care for Kirsten. "I'll be back at 4 o'clock and will make a shopping run."

"Actually, I already thought about that and have a list."

"Good!" Mehran looked over the list and there were things he expected: silverware, plates, garbage can, dish towels, etc.

"I will stop by the store and pick these things up before I come back. You have my cell phone number if you need to get a hold of me. I'll check in as well."

He kissed Kirsten on the forehead and left in her car.

Greta walked back to Kirsten's bed and looked at her. She then cupped Kirsten's cheek in the palm of her hand. "You're a lucky girl. And he must be a lucky guy."

Everyone was happy to see Mehran back at work, but they wished it was under better circumstances. They told him how sorry they were of what happened. In the short time he was gone, Victor had retired and Fallah was now in charge of the stock room.

Joe showed up at his doorway. "When I told Niloofar about the accident, she wept. She and Kirsten had hit it off at the party and she is very sorry, as we all are. But she wanted me to personally relay to you her sympathy."

"Thanks, Joe. Tell Niloofar I appreciate it."

"Let us know if there's anything we can do."

Mehran called Greta to check in.

"How's everything?"

"Just about the same. I'm reading the newspaper to Kirsten."

"She likes the letters section."

"I'll read her some of those as well."

Now what? thought Mehran. "I suppose some work is in order," he said aloud. He tried to concentrate on his work and looked over all the memos from the past two weeks. He sent an email to the team of engineers, asking for an update meeting that afternoon.

He had lunch with Fallah.

"Can I come over to see Kirsten?"

"How about tomorrow night?"

"Okay. It's been so long since I have been with you both, besides the other night," said Fallah.

Mehran was pleased to find that his staff had managed well in his absence. They talked about a few projects that they put on hold for Mehran's input. It was a busy meeting that helped take Mehran's mind off the tragedy of the accident.

At the end of the meeting, Mehran laughed. "It looks like you can do well without me. I don't know why they'd ever need me here."

One of his engineers piped up. "Short-term, anybody can survive. It's the long-term that'd be of concern. We couldn't do this without you long-term."

A couple of engineers nodded their heads in agreement. Mehran felt good to hear that.

Back at his office, he thought about the engineer's words. "Can I survive long-term in coping with what has happened to Kirsten?"

At the end of the day, he left work to buy the items on Greta's shopping list. He also bought some groceries to stock the kitchen.

At home, Mehran and Greta unloaded the supplies. Mehran realized the television was still in the box.

"Greta, would you like me to set up the television for you?"

"I've already done it," she said.

"Really? That's great." Mehran walked to the stereo box and unpacked it. "Do you watch a lot of television?"

"Actually, I don't. I'd rather read. I just unboxed it because I didn't have anything else to do."

The phone rang. Walter was calling to check on Mehran.

"How are you, son?"

"As good as can be expected. We're just setting the place up. I'm unpacking the stereo, and Greta is organizing the kitchen and things."

"How is Kirsten?"

"She'll well. I suppose."

"Can you put the phone near her ear for a few seconds?"

Mehran put the phone near Kirsten's ear. He could hear that Walter was speaking in German to Kirsten. He didn't want to know what Walter was saying. It was private. He held the phone until he heard Walter stop talking.

"I think I'll get a speakerphone tomorrow so that you can call and talk to Kirsten any time you'd like."

"That's a good idea."

"How is Amandine? How are you?"

"Going through the motions here. We're just numb from all of this. What can we do?"

"I'm lost without Kirsten," Mehran said quietly to Walter.

"I know, but you'll find your way. Everyone will find a way to cope with this tragic situation."

"Does Amandine want to talk with Kirsten?"

Mehran heard Walter call Amandine before saying, "She's not in any shape to talk right now."

She probably had been crying in the seclusion of her own home. When Mehran wanted to cry, he never cared who was around, but he had barely seen Amandine or Walter cry when they were in Chicago. Mehran thought how strange it was that he had cried way more in his late teens and as an adult than he had ever done as a kid.

"How late will you be up?" asked Walter.

"Probably around midnight."

"If she feels like it, we'll call back later."

"Okay. Don't hesitate to call."

"Will do. Stay strong."

Mehran returned to setting up the stereo. "What kind of music do you listen to, Greta?" he asked.

"I can listen to anything. Nothing bothers me."

"Yes, but is there a particular type of music you would choose to listen to? What's your favorite station on the dial?"

"I suppose WCKG. My favorite genre would be hard rock, but not all of it. I like the 70s and 80s hard rock. You know, Zeppelin, The Who, Pink Floyd. I listen to a lot of NPR, too."

"I like those bands."

"What did Kirsten listen to?"

"We listened to a lot of classical and jazz. I have an extensive collection of jazz LPs upstairs."

"Like I said, I can listen to anything."

"Good. One of the things I am going to do is play pieces Kirsten and I have listened to together in an effort to stimulate her."

"That's a good idea."

"Tomorrow the movers will be here to bring down the piano from my apartment. I am going to leave you with my key so that you can let them in."

"Sounds good."

Mehran left for work early the next morning. On his way back he stopped at a used bookstore to pick up a couple of books to read to Kirsten. He had read "The Count of Monte Cristo," as he was sure Kirsten must have read it, too, but he picked up the book anyway. He also picked up Pearl Buck's "The Good Earth," even though he had read that as well. To these, he added a collection of classic short stories. On his way home, he stopped at the grocery store to pick up ingredients for fesenjoon.

On his way upstairs, he stopped by the first floor and found that Greta had tuned the radio to WFMT. That brought a smile to his face.

"Greta?"

"In the shower. Would you please close the bathroom door now that you're here?"

He closed the door, walked over to Kirsten and kissed her on the lips. "Fallah is coming over tonight, and I'm making fesenjoon, your favorite Iranian dish."

He walked over to the kitchen and started to organize for cooking.

Greta walked out of the bathroom with wet hair and said, "Sorry. I left the door open so that I could hear if the oxygen monitor went off for some reason."

"Thank you. How was she today?"

"We listened to the radio, and I read the letters section of the newspaper. She's changed and clean, and I've put a new IV nutrient up. She's doing well."

"I brought a few books. Have you read any of these?"

Greta looked over the books and indicated the "Count of Monte Cristo," but not the others.

"I will read her the Count. Do you mind reading her 'The Good Earth'?"

"Not at all. It's about time I read books like these. What's 'The Good Earth' about?"

"It's a great novel by Pearl Buck about the life of a peasant family in China." He paused. "What do you normally read?"

"Cheesy romances, like Harold Robbins."

Mehran chuckled. He had read a couple of those in Farsi and knew exactly what Greta meant.

His cell phone rang.

"Mehran, this is Greg."

"Hi."

"Hey, I found out when the arraignment is scheduled. June 3 at the courthouse, downtown Chicago."

"Is it open to the public?"

"Yes."

"I want to be there."

"It's at 10 in the morning. Come to my office by 9 and we'll leave from here."

He hung up and turned to Greta, "Fallah's coming over for dinner tonight."

"Do you want me to retire to the bedroom?"

"Not at all. I am making Persian food tonight, Kirsten's favorite dish. You should join us to eat."

"I've never had Persian food. Is it spicy?"

Mehran laughed. "Not at all."

As he prepared to begin cooking, Mehran thought to open a bottle of wine, but he didn't have any wine in the first-floor apartment.

He ran upstairs, grabbed four wine glasses and a couple bottles of wine.

"Do you like wine, Greta?" he asked when he returned.

"I do."

He opened a bottle and poured three glasses. He put one of the glasses on the nightstand by Kirsten's bed, hoping that the smell of the wine would reach her nostrils. He gave one of the drinks to Greta and kept the last one himself.

Mehran continued to cook until Fallah arrived, holding a bouquet of flowers.

"Come on in, Fallah," Mehran greeted him.

Fallah came into the apartment and saw Kirsten on the bed. He murmured something in Arabic under his breath and went toward Kirsten. He gave Mehran a look that didn't require words. Fallah's shoulders and back slumped and his face held a hint of a frown.

"Hi, Fallah," Greta said.

"Hi, Greta,"

"You know you can talk to Kirsten," Mehran said to Fallah.

"Hello, Kirsten. This is Fallah. I'm here to see you. I have brought you flowers. They are beautiful, full of colors."

He smelled them. "But they don't smell like good flowers." He walked up to Kirsten and wanted to lay his hand on hers, but his upbringing stopped him from doing so.

"Why do bad things always happen to the nicest people?" Fallah asked.

"I wish I knew my friend," Mehran sighed.

Greta took the flowers from Fallah and realized they didn't have a vase. "Do you have anything upstairs I can put these in?"

"Yes, in the cabinet by the refrigerator. The door is open."

Greta headed upstairs.

Mehran looked at Fallah's teary eyes and opened his arms up. They hugged each other.

As Greta returned, Fallah separated from Mehran, holding his head down and away from Greta so that she wouldn't see his tears. Fallah walked toward Kirsten and grabbed a tissue out of the box on her nightstand.

"Fallah, will you drink wine with us tonight?"

Fallah turned back, looked at the empty fourth glass and nodded conflictingly.

Mehran poured. "Have you ever drank wine before?"

"Never."

"This is one of Kirsten's favorite Cabernets."

They raised their glasses together, to one another and to Kirsten.

Not a twitch of a muscle. Not a twitch of an eye. Not a twitch of her lips.

"So, how do you like wine?" Mehran asked.

"Not sure yet."

Mehran got back to his cooking.

"So, what about the driver who hit her?" asked Fallah.

"He's got a hearing on June 3. I am going with my lawyer to see what happens to him."

"I would like to come with you."

Mehran thought it odd, but he agreed.

"Honey, do you smell the fesenjoon, your favorite?" yelled Mehran from the kitchen.

"We're trying to use as much stimulation as possible with her, hoping that something might trigger her consciousness," Mehran told Fallah.

"Then, in that case, you should play the piano for her."

"The movers are coming tomorrow to bring the piano downstairs. Not that I know how to play much piano."

"Good. She loved to play that piano."

When the food was ready, they moved the table close to Kirsten's bed to eat.

Greta was hesitant with the food at first, but after she tasted the sweet and tangy fesenjoon, combined with the taste and aroma of the rice, she liked it and asked for more.

"Kirsten, the fesenjoon tastes really good," said Fallah.

Mehran took a small bowl of fesenjoon and sat across from Kirsten. He held the bowl in front of Kirsten's nose and gently blew on it, hoping that the scent would make it through to Kirsten.

Not a twitch of a muscle. Not a twitch of an eyelid. Not a twitch of her lips.

Mehran took Thursday off to go to the hospital with Kirsten. He had arranged for a patient transport company to take her to the hospital and back. Kirsten was admitted and taken to a hospital room. A doctor took out the staples from her scalp and another doctor placed the nasogastric tube through her nose. They took an X-ray to confirm the path the tube had taken, since there would be massive complications if the tube ended up in one of Kirsten's lungs. The doctors checked her other vitals and declared that everything was okay. Since she would be receiving nutrients through the tube, the doctor taped over the IV line for the time being. This meant that they could give Kirsten a full bath as opposed to just wiping her body with sponges. Kirsten was discharged and the patient transport company returned her back home.

On Friday night, Walter and Amandine came back to Chicago. Mehran asked Greta if she would like a day off, and Greta agreed to take Saturday off. On Saturday night, Mehran made dinner for Walter and Amandine at Kirsten's apartment. Again, they sat around the table near Kirsten. They talked to each other and to Kirsten from time to time as well.

"What stimulation methods have you tried?" Amandine asked.

"I'm reading to her. We play classical and jazz music. I have rubbed her feet, her shoulders, her hands. I make sure she smells the wine I drink and the food I eat."

Walter got up and went up to the piano. The sheet music on the piano was the nocturne Kirsten had been practicing. Walter started to play. Mehran looked at Kirsten.

Not a twitch of a muscle. Not a twitch of an eye. Not a twitch of her lips.

Walter stopped at the end of the piece and quietly moved to the bathroom.

"Have you tried any other stimulation?" Amandine asked.

"I don't know what else to try."

"I have been talking to a friend of mine who is a neurologist. I told her that Kirsten's brain functions seemed to be intact and how the doctors had seen the increased neural activity in her brain when they played her the music Walter just played." Amandine hesitated before she said, firmly, "My friend suggested that Kirsten be sexually stimulated."

Mehran looked at Amandine in shock. "I can't do that."

"Nobody's saying that you should have sex with her. Now that you can give her baths, you should try to sexually stimulate her while she's bathing. This is not for your good but for hers. She may be so close to snapping out of her coma that something like this might just push her out."

"I don't know. It seems wrong," Mehran hesitated.

"For God's sake, Mehran! If she was living with me, I would already have tried it, and I'm her mother. I'm sure she would rather have you do it to her than me."

Mehran was desperate. He would have tried anything to bring Kirsten back. This seemed a bit over the top, though. They dropped the conversation when Walter returned.

Walter and Amandine flew home on Sunday. Before they left, Amandine hugged Mehran and whispered, "Don't forget what we talked about. She needs this, and we need to do everything we can for her."

Mehran thought about it all afternoon. Finally, he decided that the benefits outweighed the feelings of guilt he would have. The possibility of Kirsten coming out of her coma outweighed everything. After all, if this worked, what guilt would there be? He told Greta about what Amandine had said.

"I suppose you have to look at the purpose for which you're doing something like this," said Greta. "If your purpose is self-satisfaction, then that changes things. If you're doing this as a possible stimulant for Kirsten, then there's really nothing wrong with that."

That night Greta filled the tub. They replaced the braces over Kirsten's leg and arm with plastic ones meant for use in showers and baths. Then they removed her gown. Greta removed the catheter and Mehran picked up Kirsten, while Greta brought Kirsten's right arm over Mehran's shoulder.

He knelt by the bathtub and slowly lowered Kirsten into the warm water while Greta held her arm.

Kirsten kept slipping down in the tub, so Mehran had to keep his left arm behind her and hooked under her armpit to keep her upright.

"Do you need any help?" Greta asked.

"No. But would you please play the cassette I have in the stereo? And please keep the door open."

Greta started the music. Mehran grabbed the sponge with his free hand and began to wash Kirsten. He started with her face.

Because of the way he was holding her, his mouth was near Kirsten's ear. He started to whisper.

"Kirsten, honey. I have you in the bathtub, and I'm washing your face. I'm here, baby."

He continued to sponge Kirsten's arm, then her shoulder and up over her graceful neck. He dipped the sponge in the water and brought it up, squeezing it so that water dripped on Kirsten's chest. He put the sponge back in the water and started to wash her breasts. He ran the sponge underneath her breasts. He tilted her forward a bit and held her with his right arm while he ran the sponge over her back. He leaned her back again. He moved the sponge between her legs and washed.

He put the sponge aside and started to run his hand over Kirsten's face.

He still hadn't come to grips with what he was about to do. Finally, he asked himself, "Would Kirsten want this?" He tried to come up with a reason why she would *not* want this and he couldn't. His face was still near Kirsten's ear. He started talking with her.

"Kirsten, I love you." He moved his face in front of Kirsten's and kissed her on the lips, just a gentle kiss. He couldn't fully kiss her anyway with the tube coming out of her nose.

"Please don't be mad at me or upset for what I'm about to do." He moved his hands over her breasts and cupped them. He started crying. "I don't know if this is going to help or not, but I would do anything to get you to come out of your coma. Please, make this easy for me and wake up."

He continued to move his hand down Kirsten's body.

Not a twitch of a muscle. Not a twitch of an eye. Not a twitch of her lips.

He reached Kirsten's vagina and fumbled with his fingers, feeling for Kirsten's clitoris. He began moving his index finger in a circular motion, all the while crying and talking into her ears. "I'm sorry. I'm sorry. I love you. Please come back."

He felt ashamed of what he was doing to her, even though there was no shame in it. He wasn't doing this for his own gratification. He wasn't even doing it for Kirsten's gratification, although had he known that she would receive pleasure and would have wanted him to do this, he would have gladly done so. And it wasn't like they had never pleasured each other this way. They had.

He continued to rub Kirsten's clitoris with his index finger. Just when he was about to give up, he thought he saw a twitch, ever so slightly, of her leg.

He stopped and pulled his hand out of the water. Had that just really happened?

"Greta!"

Greta came into the bathroom.

"She had a twitch."

"What were you doing?"

"I was rubbing her clitoris."

He put his hand back underwater and began to stimulate Kirsten's clitoris again. A couple of minutes later, Kirsten's leg twitched again, this time noticeably.

"I saw that!" Greta said.

Mehran had stopped crying.

"Kirsten," Mehran said while continuing to rub her clitoris, "You just had two twitches. You must be feeling me. It must feel good. You can do this. Come out of wherever you are. You can do this."

Mehran continued to talk and stimulate Kirsten for the next 10 minutes. There were several more twitches of her legs, but eventually it seemed to stop happening.

Mehran stopped. He wasn't sure whether he was excited or disappointed. He looked at Greta in despair. "With things like this, you never know. We'll continue to try different things," Greta comforted Mehran. "I think we should wash her hair and get her out for tonight. The water's getting cold."

Mehran held Kirsten while Greta washed Kirsten's hair. He lifted Kirsten from the tub and moved her to the bed. Together, Greta and Mehran dried Kirsten, dressed her and removed the plastic braces. Kirsten looked and smelled clean.

Mehran sat down at the table with Greta.

"Now what?" he asked.

"You should let the doctors know."

Mehran thought for a second and picked up the phone. He let Amandine know what had happened that evening. She said that she would talk to her neurologist friend and get back in touch.

The next night, Amandine called Mehran.

"What did the neurologist say?" he asked.

"She's here. I'll let you talk to her."

Amandine handed the phone to her friend.

"Hi, Mehran. I'm Anna."

"Did Amandine tell you what happened last night?"

"She did. I'm afraid I don't have any good news for you. The twitches in Kirsten's legs are completely involuntary. It is not likely that she had any control over them."

Mehran's entire hope was deflated. For him to have put Kirsten through what he had with no true result was humiliating. "But you have known of cases like this happening before? Of sexual stimulation bringing patients out of a coma?" he asked, grasping for anything positive.

"What you saw was most likely an orgasm. There's no way to be sure, but that's most likely. The fact that she can get an orgasm from stimulation is a good sign that her limbic system is functioning. As with any comatose patient comparable to her, ones with high-functioning brains, the important thing is to continue stimulation of all senses."

Chapter Sixty

On June 3, Mehran and Fallah met Greg at his office. Together they headed downtown and to the Cook County Court, where Daniel's arraignment was scheduled.

They sat down and shortly before 10 o'clock, Daniel, his father, and their lawyer walked in. Daniel and his father were wearing yarmulkes.

"They're Jews?" asked Fallah.

"I suppose so, if they're wearing yarmulkes. I didn't know."

Fallah seemed agitated.

Soon the judge walked in.

"All rise. This court is now in session. The honorable Judge Thompson presiding."

The judge said, "Please be seated." They sat down. The court clerk stated, "This is case number 97-TR-32768, The People of the State of Illinois versus Daniel Newberg, for arraignment. Counsel, please state your names for the record."

"Good morning, Your Honor, Ron Watkins and Jackie Feldmeier for the State of Illinois," said the public prosecutor.

"Good morning," said the judge.

"Good morning, Your Honor," said Ms. Feldmeier.

"Good morning, Your Honor. Yona Smoler with Mr. Newberg, who is present," said Daniel's attorney.

"Good morning," said the judge. "Is the state ready to proceed?"

"Yes, Your Honor."

"Is the defense ready?"

"Yes, Your Honor."

"Mr. Newberg, if at any time during these proceedings anything confuses you, please stop me so that your attorney or I can clarify it for you. I understand that there is a change of plea in this matter?"

"Yes, Your Honor," said Watkins.

"Mr. Watkins, will you please state the proposed terms for the sentence and your reasons for the recommendation?"

"Yes, Your Honor. The defendant, Daniel Newberg, agrees to plead guilty to Counts Two, Three, Four and Five of the indictment and not guilty to Count One. Count Two charges the defendant with refusing to submit to a field sobriety test in violation of Illinois Code 623 ILCS 5/11-501.1. Count Three charges the defendant with refusing to submit to a breathalyzer test in violation of Illinois Title 20 Section 1286. Count Four charges the defendant with reckless driving in violation of Illinois Code Section 625 ILCS 5/11-503. Count Five charges the defendant with driving down the wrong way on a street in violation of Illinois Code Section 625 ILCS 5/11-708. The maximum penalty for the violation of Count Two is one-year suspension of driving privileges. The maximum penalty for the violation of Count Three is one-year suspension of driving privileges. The maximum penalty for the violation of Count Four is one-year of imprisonment and/or a fine of $2,500. The maximum penalty for the violation of Count Five is $120. The defendant is aware that, pending sentencing in this matter, he will not seek release from detention. At sentencing, in this case, the Government will move to dismiss Count One. The Government proposes maximum penalties in Counts Two and Three. The Government recommends the maximum fine in Count Four due to the defendant's status as a juvenile on the date of the violation. Furthermore, the Government recommends the maximum fine in Count Five."

"Mr. Watkins, what is the charge on Count One?"

"Your honor, Count One charges the defendant with operating a motor vehicle under the influence of alcohol or a controlled substance."

"Mr. Smoler, do you concur with the terms of the plea?"

"Yes, Your Honor."

"Mr. Newberg, do you understand what the charges are against you?"

"Yes, Your Honor."

"Before I take your plea and issue a sentence, you must understand and agree to give up your constitutional rights. You have the right to a jury trial …"

Mehran looked at Greg. "That's it? Those are all the charges?"

"Sshhhh."

The judge continued to question Daniel, making sure he knew what he was doing.

"Have you discussed these rights with your attorney?"

"Yes, I have, Your Honor."

"Do you have any questions about what I have just explained to you?"

"No, Your Honor."

"Mr. Smoler, do you join in those waivers?"

"Yes, Your Honor."

"Does the State join?"

"Yes, Your Honor."

"Mr. Newberg, other than what has been stated here, has anyone else made any promises in connection with the penalties to convince you to plead one way or another?"

"No, Your Honor."

"Before entering your plea, do you have any questions?"

"No, Your Honor."

"Mr. Newberg, are you prepared to enter your plea?"

"Yes, Your Honor."

"Mr. Newberg, you are charged with a misdemeanor violation of Illinois Section 623 ILCS 5/11-501.1. To that charge, what is your plea?"

"Guilty, Your Honor."

"Mr. Newberg, you are charged with a misdemeanor violation of Illinois Title 20 Section 1286. To that charge, what is your plea?"

"Guilty, Your Honor."

"Mr. Newberg, you are charged with a misdemeanor violation of Illinois Section 625 ILCS 5/11-503. To that charge, what is your plea?"

"Guilty, Your Honor."

"Mr. Newberg, you are charged with a misdemeanor violation of Illinois Section 625 ILCS 5/11-708. To that charge, what is your plea?"

"Guilty, Your Honor."

"The court finds that the defendant has expressly and intelligently waived his statutory and constitutional rights. The court further finds that the plea was freely and voluntarily made with an understanding of the nature of the charges pending as well as the consequences of the plea. The court accepts the plea and finds the defendant guilty. I would like to proceed with sentencing. Any objections by the State?"

"No, Your Honor."

"Mr. Smoler, any objections?"

"No, Your Honor."

"Very well. Mr. Newberg, please come and stand at the lectern with your attorney."

Daniel and Mr. Smoler went up and stood before the judge.

"Mr. Newberg, you have the right to address the court prior to the imposition of your sentence. Is there anything that you wish to state to the court this morning?"

"No, Your Honor." Daniel kept his head down.

"You were found not guilty on Count One. You are now discharged on that count. However, you were found guilty of counts Two through Five. I am now going to impose the following sentence: For Count Two, I shall punish you with the suspension of your driving privileges for a period of one year starting with the date of the violation. For Count Three, I shall punish you with the suspension of your driving privileges for a period of one year starting with the date of the violation, to be served concurrently with Count Two. For Count Four, I shall punish you with a fine of $2,500 and 300 hours of community service. For Count Five, I shall punish you with a fine of $120 and mandatory appearance at a driving school. I will now state on the record the reasons for making the downward departure that I have just made in regard to Count Four."

"This court in no fashion condones what you have done. From what I understand, you hit a pedestrian who was crossing the street before you plowed your vehicle into another vehicle that had already entered the intersection. The pedestrian, according to the police officers familiar with the case, suffered grave injuries and has been in a coma since the accident. I considered giving you some of the prison term afforded to me by the law on this count, but, as a juvenile, I cannot determine if it will do you any good. From what I have seen here, your conduct has been exemplary. I also understand that you have been accepted into Northwestern University and that you will be attending in the fall. I thus cannot condone a prison term for you. Know that your actions have devastated a family and destroyed the future of another human being. That is something you will have to live with for the rest of your life. You may stand aside now. Court will stand adjourned."

"All rise. The honorable Judge Thompson."

"That's it? That's all he gets?" asked Fallah.

"Without a DUI, the prosecutor doesn't have a case. He sought the maximum, with the exception of prison," Greg explained.

Mehran put his head down into his hands.

"This is fucking bullshit. The fucking Jews," said Fallah in a loud voice.

"Shut up! This is a court! You can't swear here," said Greg.

The three left the courtroom and the building.

Chapter Sixty-One

Greg told Mehran that he had another case, and he'd have to go back in court. He apologized to Mehran for the outcome and said to call him if he wanted to pursue a civil lawsuit.

Mehran and Fallah began walking toward the lake.

"This is such bullshit. Fucking Jews. They get away with everything," Fallah exclaimed.

"I will talk to Kirsten's parents. We'll get Daniel and his dad on civil charges."

"What are civil charges?"

"Well, when you do something wrong, you can face two different groups in the court. The first is the State, which comes after you because you deprived someone of property or life or violation of State codes. Take, for instance, robbery. They come after you for that. Another thing is murder."

"Murder? What about Kirsten?"

"Well, technically, she's not dead. When it comes to the law, it's all about technicalities."

"What about the part that he was drunk?"

"The prosecutor decided to drop those charges, probably because he couldn't make them stick."

"What? Either he was drunk, or he was not."

"Or he was drunk, but the prosecutor couldn't prove that he was."

"Wouldn't the fact that he refused to take a breathalyzer mean that he was drunk?"

"Technically, no. That just means we don't know if he was or not."

"This is bullshit."

"It probably is. But that's what we have to live with."

"Is there nothing we can do?"

"The State can appeal, but the fact that the state made a plea bargain, meaning they settled for less, means that they won't appeal. Which brings us to the civil court. In a civil court, anybody can sue anybody. The punishments are always monetary, meaning if we sue him in a civil court and we win, all we're gonna get is money. He'll never serve jail time."

"That's better than nothing. Take all their money and watch him rot."

"Maybe. I don't know. I'll have to talk with Greg. In the end, I cannot sue him in civil court because I'm not related to Kirsten. It'd have to be her mom or dad."

"That's it? I hate this country!"

Mehran looked at him. "Actually, I think this is the way things should be."

"Why? So someone like that can get away with murder?"

"That's a price we pay for having a whole bunch of other amenities."

Fallah couldn't understand. Rage was filling his head. *Why should someone as nice as Mehran, someone as nice as Kirsten, suffer because of the stupidity of an asshole, and a Jew on top of it?*

"You may want to believe what you want, but I believe they're a menace to our environment. They're a menace to everything I stand for."

"Who are you talking about, Fallah?"

"Jews. They're the termites of society. They shot my brother in front of witnesses. They always get away with murder."

"You have to let this go. Thanks for coming with me today. Go to work. I'll see you there this afternoon."

Fallah walked away from Mehran. Mehran could understand why Fallah would think this way. He was raised in Palestine. His people had been bombarded and abused by the actions of the State of Israel. It was just unfortunate that Fallah couldn't separate Jews from the actions of an unjust occupying regime.

Mehran sighed and walked to the corner to hail a cab.

When Mehran was about to walk into the apartment, he suddenly felt panicked. How could he talk to Kirsten about what had happened at the courthouse? He decided that he needed to keep the events of the day to himself.

He walked into the first-floor apartment. "Honey, I'm home!"

Greta laughed. Mehran looked at Kirsten. There was no laughter. He wasn't disappointed, though, since he was getting used to no reaction from Kirsten.

"And how are *you* doing, Greta?"

Greta looked at him funny. "I'm doing fine."

"And how are *you* doing, Kirsten?"

He put his head by Kirsten's and listened.

Not a twitch of a muscle. Not a twitch of an eye. Not a twitch of her lips.

"Yes? I know. The first half of my day has been great, too!"

Greta looked at him again.

"How would you like to go to a movie tonight?" he asked Kirsten.

Greta wondered what had flipped Mehran. He wasn't himself and all that he was saying was out of character for him. She wondered if he was starting to lose sight of the situation. "I don't think that's a good idea. What has gotten into you? What happened at the court?"

Chapter Sixty-Two

Later in the week, Mehran received a call from Nawal while he was at work.

"This is Nawal."

"Nawal? Oh, how are you?"

"I'm well. How is Miss Kirsten?"

"She's okay."

"Good. I need to ask you. Do you know what is going on with Fallah?"

"Fallah? No, why? I think he's been at work every day, no?"

"He's not been coming home until late hours."

"I'll check on him and make sure everything is all right."

Mehran took a walk to the stockroom and called out to Fallah.

There was no answer.

"Fallah!" he called more loudly.

"Yes?" Fallah came around the corner.

"Fallah! What's going on? I called for you."

"I'm sorry, I was exhausted in the back. My finals are next week. I've been studying."

Finals? Thought Mehran. *Finals should have been finished by now.* But he didn't say anything.

"Fallah, Nawal called me and she is worried about you. She said you have been going home late. What have you been doing?"

"I have been at the library studying."

"The exams should have been over by now, though. No?"

"Yes, but don't forget we're on quarters. The exams don't finish until the middle of June."

"Ah!" said Mehran. "Well, make sure you tell your family what you're doing, so they don't worry about you."

"I understand."

"Okay. How's work going?"

"It's going well."

"Good. Let me know if you need anything."

Mehran left for his office.

On June 13, Mehran was in his office when Fallah came to see him.

"Fallah! What's going on?"

"Nothing much. How are you?"

"I'm okay."

"How's Kirsten?"

"The same. We started acupuncture therapy with her, but it didn't seem to do any good. She looks excellent. But we'll probably have to take her to get the feeding tube implanted directly into her stomach."

"That's good."

"That's good? I don't know. I suppose you can look at it like that. I don't think that's particularly good."

Fallah nodded his head. "That's not what I meant."

"Mehran, I know I had said this to you before, but I don't think I have ever really appreciated what you've done for me, until now. Getting me this job has been a blessing for my family and me."

"Fallah, don't mention it. I'm glad everything is working out for you."

"Yes, I thank you for that." He paused. "You know, I have the utmost respect for you. I am grateful for what you've done for me."

"I realize that, but you don't have to kiss my ass, buddy. We're in this together."

"I know. I just wish there was something I could do for you and Kirsten."

Mehran got up from his seat. Fallah looked like he could use a hug.

"It's okay. We're doing fine." Mehran hugged him.

Fallah wiped a tear. "I know. You've been like a brother to me."

"Well, thanks, Fallah! That means a lot to me."

"I'll never forget you. And you never forget me."

"Okay," Mehran said.

Fallah left. Mehran thought the conversation was a bit weird, but he attributed it to the Middle Eastern culture he and Fallah had been raised in.

The next day, Mehran was massaging Kirsten's feet, listening to the *Nocturne in E minor*, the very piece Kirsten was to play at their wedding that very day.

The nocturne was a beautiful piece, as it was every time he heard it. Greta had heard it many times over, too. It was the one piece Mehran continued to play in the hope of waking Kirsten.

"Greta, did you know Kirsten and I were to be married today?"

"Really? Today?"

"Yes. Saturday, June 14, 1997."

"Well, congratulations. You're here together. We should celebrate."

"We should bake a cake. Wait! The wedding cake is already paid for. We can pick it up and eat it here."

"I think Kirsten would really appreciate that."

Mehran found something to be happy about. He began humming along with the nocturne. He kissed Kirsten on the cheek, humming the tune in her ear. Kirsten's finger twitched, but neither Mehran nor Greta saw it. Mehran grabbed Malak's doll from the stand by Kirsten.

"Kirsten, honey, your doll is lying on the bed next to you. You know, we were supposed to get married today. It's a gorgeous day outside. Nice and cloudy, just the way you know I like it. I'm going to pick up our wedding cake and bring it here. It'll be beautiful.

Her finger twitched again, but, again, neither Mehran nor Greta saw it.

"Do you know how much I love you? I love you more than I love this nocturne. I love you more than I have loved any piece of music I have ever listened to. I love you more than Bach. I love you more than Dizzy Gillespie loves his trumpet. I love you more than Sonny Rolling loved the saxophone. I love you more than Chopin loved the piano."

He stayed near her ear. "I love you more than electricity loves wires. I love you more than electrons love protons. I love you more than moths love light."

The fingers in her left hand twitched, but still neither Greta nor Mehran saw.

"I love you more than fleas love dogs. I love you more than butterflies love flowers. I love you more than submarines love water. I love you more than Mehran loves you."

His cell phone rang.

"Mehran, this is Nawal."

"Nawal! How are you?"

"I was wondering if you had heard from Fallah?"

"No, why?"

"Nothing. He didn't come home last night. We've never had a time when he didn't come home for the night."

"Did he say anything to anybody?" Mehran asked.

"No. He went to work yesterday, and he never came back."

"I talked to him yesterday. He was fine. I'll see what I can find out."

"Okay. You will call us back?"

"Yes, I will."

They hung up. Fallah didn't have a cell phone. Mehran didn't know where to start. He decided to go to work first.

"Greta, I have to go to work for a bit. Would you please take over? I'll pick up the cake on my way back."

Mehran kissed Kirsten on the lips and said, in the voice of Arnold Schwarzenegger's Terminator, "I'll be back."

Greta laughed.

Mehran drove Kirsten's car to work. He went to the stock room, looking for Fallah.

"Hello? Fallah?"

He knocked on the door. "Fallah?"

No answer. He walked back to the receptionist area. He entered his code into the safe on the wall; the safe opened, and he took out the master key. He returned to the stock room.

He opened it with the master key and walked in, but he saw no trace of Fallah.

Mehran was about to turn back and walk out, but something on the desk caught his attention.

A soldering iron? Why? he thought. He looked at the other items on the desk. Wires, electronic schematics for a high-voltage amplifier. "What the hell."

He looked under the desk and found a container labeled "Lead Azide."

Lead Azide? he thought. *That's a detonator. What the fuck is Fallah doing with lead azide?*

He looked around further. In the chem lab at the back of the stock room, Mehran found several other containers. A bottle of toluene, a bottle of sulfuric acid, a bottle of oleum and a container of aqueous sodium sulfite.

He mixed and matched the ingredients in his head, and suddenly panic set in. It added up to TNT. But to stabilize the TNT, liquid nitrogen would be needed.

He hurried to the stock room inventory logs. "Liquid nitrogen, liquid nitrogen." The stock room was not designed to store liquid nitrogen, since it would quickly evaporate over a couple of days and be a hazard. However, liquid nitrogen could be stored in a container for a brief period of time. He looked over the inventory and the orders from their chemical supplier. "Eight liters of liquid nitrogen, delivered on Friday, June 13."

The ingredients all added up. They would have, with some processing, produced TNT. *Why? Why would Fallah be making TNT?*

Mehran's stomach began to tighten up as thoughts raced through his mind. He hurried back to the desk with the soldering iron. He remembered seeing a piece of paper on the desk. He found it, picked up the phone on the desk and called the number that was on the paper. After a few rings, a boy answered. "Shalom Northbrook Synagogue." His heart dropped as he hung up.

He dialed 411.

"411 directory assistance."

"Address for Shalom Northbrook Synagogue, please."

"That is 10739 Brookstone Boulevard, Northbrook. Would you like me to connect you?"

Mehran hung up and ran to the car. He floored the gas pedal and headed north out of the city to Northbrook.

He can't be doing this, Mehran thought. *He's not that stupid. I am mistaken. There must be another explanation for this.*

The ride to the synagogue in Northbrook was full of terror. Mehran switched from lane to lane as he sped down the highway. He stopped at a red light at the exit and took a minute to look at the map, trying to figure out the address for the synagogue. The light turned green and the person behind him honked the horn. Mehran floored the M3 again and took off. He arrived at the temple a few minutes after getting off the highway. Looking at the perimeter of the building, he didn't see anybody around. He got out and headed toward the entrance. The Saturday service was in session. He entered the building without noticing the taxi sitting in the parking lot.

At the synagogue, he looked inside. The congregation was peaceful and the rabbi was taking the Torah scroll around and letting people touch it with their books and shawls. Mehran stood at the doorway when the outer doors opened, and Fallah walked in.

"Mehran, what are you doing here?"

"Fallah! I know what you're about to do. You don't need to do this."

The congregation turned to look back at the two whose voices were interrupting their service.

A man came toward Mehran. "May I help you?"

"No. Go back inside," said Mehran.

"Sir, I am going to have to ask you to leave."

"Please go back inside."

A couple of more people came toward Mehran. One grabbed him by the shoulder. "Sir, please step outside. We are in prayer."

"Don't lay your filthy hands on him!" Fallah yelled.

The men backed off. "Please leave peacefully. We don't want any trouble," one said.

"You don't want trouble? It's coming your way anyway," Fallah shouted.

"No, Fallah."

One of the men turned toward the congregation. "Call 911."

"911! That won't do any good for you. You're all dead," said Fallah, taking his backpack and holding it in front of him.

The men stepped back. Mehran could hear the touch-tone noises from a phone in the distance.

"Fallah! What are you doing?"

"These Jews destroyed your life."

"It wasn't them. They had nothing to do with it."

"They killed my brother, and they killed Kirsten."

Chapter Sixty-Three

Greta heard Kirsten's oxygen sensor go off. She rushed to the other room to find Kirsten pulling on the tube in her nose, which was taped to her cheek.

"Oh my God!"

Kirsten started to cough. Greta rushed to her.

"Oh my God! Kirsten!"

Gretta hurriedly undid the tape and pulled out the tube.

"Mhrn!" Kirsten whispered.

"Take it easy! Take it easy!"

Kirsten had her eyes open. She took a deep breath a few times and said again, "Mhrn!"

Chapter Sixty-Four

"They killed Kirsten!"

"Fallah! Kirsten's not dead. She's in a coma."

Fallah approached the inner doors. He was clutching the backpack. "They destroyed your life."

"It wasn't them. It was a stupid boy who was drunk. He hit Kirsten."

The crowd stirred toward the door.

Fallah saw Daniel through the crowd in the aisle behind Mehran.

"It was him! It wasn't just a person. It was him!" Fallah pointed to Daniel. "And what did he get for it? All he had to do was pay a fine."

Mehran looked over his shoulder and saw Daniel and his dad; Daniel's dad's face had gone white.

Someone near Mehran screamed, "He's got a bomb."

The crowd panicked. People began running toward the inner sanctum of the synagogue, screaming.

"Fallah, put the backpack down. These people didn't do anything to you."

"They killed my brother, they killed Kirsten."

"It wasn't them. They didn't kill your brother. The Israeli government killed your brother. Kirsten is still alive. They didn't kill her."

"Yes, but she's dead. She can't hear you. She can't respond to you. She can't argue with you about going to strip clubs for your bachelor party. Today was supposed to be your wedding day."

Mehran put his head down for a second, thinking about beautiful Kirsten in her white gown on their wedding day, walking down the aisle, accompanied by Walter.

He raised his head. "Fallah, put the backpack down. These people are innocent. They don't need to die."

"Look at them! Look at him! He's cowering behind the crowd. He doesn't even have the guts to come forward."

"He's stupid. He's just a boy. He has much to learn. But this is not the way to go about it. Put the backpack down, and let's sit down. We'll talk to them."

The crowd had moved away from Mehran.

"Come on, buddy. Put the backpack down. Nothing good is going to come out of this."

Fallah started to cry. "I'm tired of being pushed around."

"Nobody's pushing you around, Fallah. It's how things are. Bad things happen, we deal with them."

Fallah put his hand on a string that looked to be protruding from the side of the backpack.

"Fallah, you don't want this on your conscience. Think about your family. Think about Nawal. She has a bright future."

Fallah didn't say anything.

"Think about your mother. Think about your father."

"They've lost one boy to Israel. They have to lose their other one now."

"No, they don't! Do you think this is what your mother wants?"

Fallah hesitated. "No."

"Do you think this is what your father wants?"

"No."

"Do you think this is what Kirsten wants?"

"No."

"Do you think this is what I want?"

"No," Fallah said. His fatigue began to set in, perhaps because of the late nights working on this.

"Then put the backpack down. We'll sit down and talk. I'll cook you fesenjoon, and we'll sit and talk."

They could hear the police sirens from afar.

Fallah clutched the backpack to his chest. "I can't. This is the end for me."

"No! This is just the beginning. You'll start to see things differently."

"In what way? In a jail cell?"

Mehran looked back at the congregation. He saw Daniel and his father together. Mehran pointed at them and said, "Is that who you want to be? The destroyer of lives? Someone who buys the law with his money and doesn't pay the consequences? Because by you pulling that trigger, you bring yourself down to their level. You chicken out of living the consequences of your life. If you pull that trigger, you're no better than Daniel Newberg."

Fallah noticed the congregation turn to look at Daniel. "But that Jew ruined your life."

"Yes, he did. I hate him. I hate his father. But that doesn't mean that I want to blow up a whole bunch of innocent people. Look at these people behind me. They're scared. They didn't do anything to you or me. They're here just to worship their book and their God."

The police sirens were getting louder.

Mehran's cell phone rang.

"Come on. Put down the backpack. I have a lot of money. I'll fight to make sure you don't get incarcerated. You haven't done anything wrong. You were just thinking of doing it."

Mehran's cell phone continued to ring.

"I can't. There's no way they are letting me go after this," Fallah said. "Get away from the door. I have to do this."

Mehran looked back at the congregation. By now they had moved a good 50 feet away from the inner door. Mehran raised his arms to his side, started walking toward Fallah, and whispered in a low voice, so that only the two of them could hear him. "You're going to kill me? After everything I have done? You realize this is going to kill me with you, don't you?"

Fallah was still clutching the bag and crying. He closed his eyes and started moving toward Mehran. Mehran's thoughts slowed. He remembered Bahar, and the moment they had shared in his back yard. The moments they had shared in the streets of Tehran. Naghmeh and the fire on the beach. His first day in college with Parisa. The news of the death of his parents and the night he had made love to Naghmeh. The horrid experience with the prostitute. Coming to Chicago and being on his own. His graduation. His first job. Loving Naghmeh and watching her die. Asking Kirsten out and getting to know her better. Reading her Turkish coffee fortune on their second date. The Art Institute trips with her. Making love to Kirsten and adoring her naked body lying in bed next to him, pleasuring Kirsten on the hood of her car, her moving in with him, meeting Walter and Amandine, spending the only Christmas he had ever had with Kirsten and asking her to marry him, and her saying yes, the planning of their wedding, Kirsten practicing Chopin's nocturne on the piano, and the awful accident that had taken Kirsten away from him. He wasn't bitter. Having had Kirsten in his life, even for the short while they were together, had made his life worthwhile. Without Kirsten, his life was meaningless. He was ready to go. Had the accident taken Kirsten away from him? He didn't want to admit it, but it had. He didn't have a single reason to live.

Mehran lunged toward Fallah. They met in the middle and Mehran grabbed Fallah's hand. They looked into each other's eyes for an instant before Fallah pulled the string with force.

The explosion shook the whole building. The shock wave knocked down the first few rows of people behind Mehran. The others scrambled away from the explosion, screaming frantically. The police arrived in the next minute, and the sound of ambulances and fire trucks followed shortly.

Ariel pushed the person above him off and looked for Daniel.

"Daniel!"

He looked and found Daniel underneath the person who had been standing in front of him. He hugged Daniel. "Thank God."

Surprisingly, the only injuries sustained by the congregation were minor scratches. Mehran's body had shielded much of the explosion and since he had held Fallah away from the congregation, only the shock wave and the scrambling of people after the blast had caused injuries. The ambulances and medics tended to the injured. In less than a half hour, the FBI was at the scene, questioning witnesses.

Chapter Sixty-Five

"Honey, I called him. He's not picking up. Let me call your father," Greta said.

She hung up and dialed Walter's number.

"Walter, it's Greta."

"Greta! Is everything all right?"

"Yes! Very all right. Kirsten is lucid."

"Lucid? Are you sure? Where is Mehran?"

"I cannot get a hold of him on his cell phone. He left about an hour ago to run an errand."

"Can Kirsten talk?"

"Not really. But I can tell she's asking for Mehran."

"Can you put me on speakerphone?"

Greta put Walter on the speakerphone.

"Kirsten?"

Kirsten managed to utter "Dada."

"Oh, Kirsten. This is a miracle."

"Whrs Mhran?"

"He's all she asks for," said Greta.

"Greta, we will get on the first flight. Kirsten, honey, we will be there as soon as we can."

After they ended the call, Greta tried talking with Kirsten.

"Kirsten, my name is Greta. I'm your caregiver. Can you tell me your name?"

"Krstn"

Kirsten lost consciousness every 30 seconds or so, going between wake and sleep states.

"Kirsten!" snapped Greta.

Kirsten opened her eyes.

"Good. Very good! Do you know where you are?"

Kirsten looked around. "My pino."

Happy tears started to roll down Greta's cheeks. "Yes. That's your piano. Are you thirsty?"

"Ys."

Greta rushed to get a cup of water. She held it to Kirsten's lips. "Not too much, honey. Just a little."

Kirsten drank a sip of water.

"Mhrn."

"Honey, I don't know where he is, but he is going to flip out when he sees you."

"Woo r you?"

"I'm your caregiver honey. My name is Greta."

"Hw lng?"

"How long what?"

"Hw lng?"

"How long have you been out? About a month and a half, sweetheart."

"Mhrn."

"I don't know where he is. I'll call him again for you."

Greta called Mehran's cell phone number.

"No answer. See, no answer."

Greta continued to talk with Kirsten during her periods of wakefulness and tried to repeatedly answer the question Kirsten had: "Mehran?" A couple of hours later, they heard a loud bang in the hallway. Greta opened the apartment door to see what was going on.

"Stay in your unit please, ma'am."

"What's going on?"

"FBI! Do you know the man who lives upstairs?"

"Mehran? Yes! What's happened?" she asked as she tried to step out of the apartment.

"All clear," yelled someone from upstairs.

"Please stay in your unit."

Greta went back in, closed and locked the door. *What the fuck is going on?* she thought.

A few minutes later there was a knock on the door.

Greta opened the door.

"You said you know the person who lives upstairs?"

Greta stepped into the hallway and closed the door behind her.

"Yes, I am a caregiver and he has hired me to care for his comatose fiancée."

"He has a comatose fiancée?"

"Yes, except she just came out of her coma a couple of hours ago."

"We need to search this apartment."

Greta barricaded the door. "You can't. She just came out of a coma. She's extremely fragile and scared. You will freak her out."

The agent looked at the agent standing behind him. "Ma'am, we need to search this apartment."

"Do you have a warrant?"

"No, ma'am."

"Then fuck off. I will let one of you in as long as you're not intrusive and do not question the girl in the hospital bed. Or you can go get a warrant from a judge."

The agent looked at the other agent and said, "Okay. One agent."

Greta opened the door and the agent looked inside. He saw the hospital bed from the entrance as he stepped in, his hand clutching his sidearm.

Greta tried to close the door behind him, but the other agent put his foot inside the threshold to keep it open.

The agent walked over to the bed, looked into Kirsten's scared face and nodded. He went into the bedroom and looked inside the closet and under the bed. He walked into the bathroom and opened the closet there. He pushed the shower curtain to the side and checked the shower before walking out. He checked the refrigerator and the kitchen cabinets. He then walked toward the door and nodded to Greta. "Thank you, ma'am. May I speak with you outside?"

Greta stepped out and closed the door behind her.

"You said you know the man upstairs. What can you tell us about him?"

"Like I said, he hired me to care for his fiancée."

"What was he like?"

"What kind of question is that?"

"Was he – suspicious?"

"Suspicious? No. He was a regular man."

"Did he have a lot of guests?"

"No. The only guests I have seen are the girl's parents who live in Denver and his friend, Fallah."

The agents looked at each other. "Any other friends?"

"Not that I know."

"What is your name?"

"Greta."

"Greta?"

"Greta Van Holsten."

"How long have you been in this building."

"Listen guys. Like I said, I have a patient inside the apartment who just came out of a coma, and I have to go back inside to tend to her. I haven't got time for this Mickey Mouse bullshit. So you guys can either speed this up or fuck off."

"When would be a good time for us to come back?"

"I just called her parents, and they're on their way from Denver. They should be here in a few hours. You can ask me all the questions you want then."

"Yes, ma'am. We'll be upstairs."

Greta walked back in the apartment and locked the door behind her.

"Mhran. Whrs Mhran?"

"Honey, I don't know. I am trying to get a hold of him."

"The car?"

"Yes, you were hit by a car."

"Hw long?"

"It was a month and a half ago."

"Wht s today?"

"It is June 14."

"Wht?"

"June 14."

"I suppsed to gt mrrd day."

Greta's eyes welled up. "Yes, sweetheart. You are supposed to get married today."

"I cn't gt mrrd lik tis."

"Mehran pushed the wedding back. Don't worry. Nobody is going to the church today."

"Whrs Mhran?"

Greta wished she knew. She did her best to keep Kirsten busy all afternoon until her parents arrived. The FBI agents outside the apartment stopped Walter and Amandine. Greta stepped out and interrupted the agents. "They are here for this apartment not the one upstairs." She dragged them in.

"What's going on?" asked Walter.

"I don't know. They just showed up and started asking questions about Mehran."

Walter and Amandine rushed to Kirsten's bed as their tears flowed.

"Mmm! Dd!"

Kirsten's parents did their best not to disturb her broken limbs as they hugged her.

"Oh, sweetheart. This is a miracle," Amandine said finally.

"No. I Kirstn."

"Yes, you are," Walter cried happily.

After Greta made sure that Kirsten was secure in her bed, she stepped out of the apartment and closed the door. Two FBI agents were posted in the hallway. "Okay. You can question me all you want now."

During their line of questioning, the FBI agents asked what she knew about the friend Mehran had, named Fallah.

"He came over once or twice for dinner. He seemed like a nice guy. He seemed to care a lot about Mehran and Kirsten, Mehran's fiancée."

"What about Mehran. Can you tell us anything about him?"

"He seems like a very decent man. He is head-over-heels in love with Kirsten."

"Can you tell us why he may have had a friend like Fallah?"

"Not really. Can you tell me what has happened?"

The agents looked at each other. "Have you been watching the news, ma'am?"

"Not today. Like I said, I have been busy with Kirsten coming out of the coma. Why? What's on the news?"

"Earlier today there was a bombing at a synagogue in Northbrook. Two people were killed. They have been identified as Fallah Kataan and Mehran Noori."

The color vanished from Greta's face and she almost fell over. How could this be? But, worse, how could she tell Kirsten?

"Mehran couldn't have had anything to do with the bombing. Could he?"

"From interviews with the people at the synagogue, it looks like it was the younger man, Fallah, who had the bomb, and Mr. Noori tried to diffuse the situation. When Mr. Kataan was ready to blow the bomb, Mr. Noori covered him to make sure nobody else would be hurt."

Greta didn't know Mehran that well, but during the month that they had practically lived together, she found him to be a gentle, kind man. She held her face as tears rolled down her eyes.

"We do not believe there's any reason for us to hang around here. Nevertheless, we have to close the apartment upstairs since that's where Mr. Noori lived. We will place a police line at the entrance of the apartment."

Greta nodded numbly as she headed back inside.

Kirsten's talking was improving by the minute. When Greta walked back inside, Kirsten asked "Is Mehran outside?"

"No honey. I just found out that Mehran had to go on an emergency trip to the company headquarters in California. He will not be back for a couple of days."

Walter and Amandine looked at Greta in confusion.

"How are you doing? Do you want any more water?"

"Yes, please."

Greta gave Kirsten water. "How about you keep your mom company while I have a talk with dad."

Walter was confused, but he followed Greta into the bedroom anyway. Greta closed the door. Several minutes later, Walter worked to keep himself upright as he walked out of the room.

"Kirsten, honey, would you like to try to walk?" asked Walter as he motioned for Amandine to go to the bedroom.

"Dad, I believe I have a broken leg."

Walter smiled. "Of course you do. How silly of me."

"Dad, what happened to me? I know that I was in an accident. I recall Mehran talking to the doctors about it."

"You could hear things around you?"

"Some things. I remember Mehran whispering in my ear that he loved me. I also remember —"

"You remember what?"

"Nothing. I remember other things, like the Chopin preludes. I remember hearing it on my piano, too."

Walter's eyes watered. "That was me, sweetheart."

"You were good. I was supposed to play that today at my wedding."

Walter couldn't hold it together any longer and started weeping, weeping for a wedding that wasn't to happen. "Would you like to talk to your sister?"

"Why are you crying?"

"Because I love you, sweetheart. Because I love you."

He picked up the phone and dialed Anja. He held the phone to Kirsten's ear.

"Oh my God! Kirsten!"

Kirsten laughed hoarsely. "Yes, it's me. I'm God!"

Anja broke into tears. "This is a miracle. You have no idea how much I've cried in the past couple of months. How are you feeling?"

"Okay. Groggy."

"Where's Mehran?"

"I don't know. I think he is in California."

"California?"

Walter took the phone back to talk with Anja. "Yes, he is in California for a business trip."

"How is she? She sounds good."

"She's doing well. She needs to get used to talking again."

"I am going to get on a flight."

"That's a good idea."

"Okay. I'll see if I can get out tonight. If not, I'll get out first thing tomorrow morning."

They hung up as the bedroom door opened. Amandine looked like a ghost as she walked out.

"Mom, are you okay?"

"I'm fine, sweetheart." She spoke a couple of French sentences to Kirsten, and Kirsten responded in French.

"Good! You still remember French."

"Kirsten, do you remember now where we are?" Greta asked.

"This is our apartment." She looked around a bit. "Although it looks a little different."

Greta looked at Walter and Amandine. "This is actually the first floor. Mehran rented the first floor so that you could live here."

"Is he upstairs?"

"No, sweetheart. We don't know where he is."

Kirsten seemed confused. "He loves me. He wouldn't leave to go anywhere without telling you where he was going."

"Sweetheart, he left for California," Walter said.

"I don't remember their company having any business in California. No, they don't operate in California."

There was no fooling Kirsten. She knew too much and remembered everything.

"That's where he told us he was going, Kirsten," Amandine said.

"Did he go to see his family in L.A.?"

"Yes, that's what he did," said Walter.

"Why didn't he tell you guys that?"

"He did. It just slipped our minds," Greta said.

Kirsten looked at the three of them. Something about the story and the way they were acting didn't seem right.

"How are you feeling, Kirsten?" asked Greta.

"My body's sore. I think I need to move around."

"We don't have any crutches," said Greta. "All we have are these plastic braces."

Greta proceeded to put the plastic braces on Kirsten.

"Someone help me," Kirsten said. She tried to push herself up. "I can't."

"You've been getting therapy to keep your muscles from atrophying, but you're still weak. You need to get your strength back," Greta explained.

"Help me." Kirsten was adamant. She wanted to move.

Greta and Amandine helped her to sit up straight. She held on to the rails on the bed and lifted the covers to see herself in diapers with a catheter tube running out to the side. "You've got a catheter in me?"

"Yes, we had to."

Kirsten reached down and tried to pull the catheter out, but she couldn't.

"Lean back, honey, and I'll take it out," said Greta.

Walter excused himself to the bathroom.

Kirsten leaned back. Greta removed the diaper and the catheter from Kirsten.

"Help me go to the bathroom."

Greta and Amandine helped Kirsten sit up again and then held her underneath the shoulders to have her stand. At first, Kirsten could not stand on her left leg, but she straightened her knee and was able to hold it locked. The breaks had happened more than 6 weeks ago and were mostly healed by now.

"See! It was that easy," said Kirsten.

Amandine smiled. "Good!"

Walter walked out of the bathroom. Amandine and Greta walked Kirsten to the bathroom and helped her sit on the toilet. Amandine stood over Kirsten.

"Mom, go. I'll be fine."

"Okay, Kirsten."

Greta was hesitant to leave Kirsten alone.

"You can stay. What's your name? Oh, wait. It's Greta."

Greta smiled. "Yes."

Kirsten sat on the toilet for a few minutes, but her bladder was mostly empty except for a small tinkle.

"Ahhhhhhh."

Greta laughed.

Kirsten whispered to her. "Greta, where's Mehran?"

Greta looked at her. "I don't know, sweetheart."

Kirsten seemed disappointed.

"Why won't you tell me?"

"I really don't know, Kirsten."

Kirsten was silent for a minute. She looked for the toilet paper.

"Are we done?" asked Greta.

"Yes, I'm done."

Greta tore a few pieces of toilet paper and handed them to Kirsten.

"I know that he held fesenjoon in front of my nose."

"Just how much do you remember about what happened around you when you were in a coma?"

"I don't remember everything, everyday. But there are *things* I remember."

"He tried everything to awaken your senses."

"Of course he did. He cried in my ear. He kissed me on my lips. He combed my hair."

"He loved you."

Kirsten thought for a second. "Loved? What do you mean, loved?"

Greta corrected herself. "I mean he loved you when you were in a coma."

"And what now? He doesn't love me anymore?"

"Of course he does."

"You said 'loved.'"

"You know what I meant."

Kirsten dropped her gown down over her front and said tersely, "No, I don't."

She tried to get up, but she fell forward. Greta caught her before she hit the ground.

Amandine opened the bathroom door as Greta was trying to lift Kirsten up.

Kirsten tried to yell, but she only sounded like she was barking. "Tell me where Mehran is."

"Honey, we don't know."

Greta and Amandine helped Kirsten to stand. Kirsten lunged forward, only to fall forward onto her arm.

"Owwwwww."

"Kirsten. You're going to kill yourself," Amandine said.

Kirsten held her right arm with her left hand and began to cry. "Where is he? Where is he? Where is my Mehran?"

Walter looked at her through the bathroom doorframe and started to weep.

Amandine walked out of the bathroom while Greta got Kirsten back up to her feet. She walked over to Walter. "We cannot tell her!

She'll slip back into a coma," she whispered before looking back at Kirsten.

Walter turned away from the bathroom toward the front door.

"Dad, stop! Walter!"

Walter froze in his tracks.

"Dad. What happened to Mehran?"

Walter turned around. Amandine turned and looked him in the eyes, her head shaking side to side.

"Kirsten. He loved you to the end of the Earth, but he's no longer with us."

Greta bowed her head while holding Kirsten in place.

"What do you mean? Did he leave me?"

"No. He was in an accident. He didn't make it."

Kirsten's right leg gave away and she went limp. Greta did her best to hold her up. She grasped Kirsten under her arms and dragged her to the bed. Together, the three of them, laid her on the bed.

Kirsten had lost consciousness.

For the next few hours, Walter, Amandine and Greta watched and waited until they couldn't stay awake any longer. At two in the morning, Kirsten opened her eyes.

"Dad," she whispered hoarsely.

Walter raised his head from his slumped position on his chair.

"Yes, honey?" he whispered as he moved to her side.

"How did he die?"

Amandine and Greta stirred with the sound of Kirsten's voice.

"We don't know. He was involved in a bombing."

"A bombing?"

"It seems like Fallah was about to bomb a synagogue when Mehran tried to stop him," Greta said. "At least that's what the FBI agents told me. They said they didn't think he was involved because he was trying to stop Fallah."

"Why would Fallah want to blow up a synagogue?"

"I think it may have had something to do with the boy who hit you," said Walter. "He was Jewish. He got off with no criminal charges, just fines and community service. We were preparing to file a civil lawsuit against him."

Kirsten finally understood all that had happened while she was unconscious. She lay awake for hours. Tears fell from the sides of her eyes, soaking her pillow, as she mourned Mehran.

Chapter Sixty-Six

When Kirsten woke up at 10 the next morning, her parents and Greta were hovering near her bed.

"What's going on?" she asked sleepily.

"Sweetheart, it's just that after you've been in a coma, every time you fall asleep, we worry whether it's the coma or just sleeping," Amandine explained.

Kirsten grabbed the side rail with her strong arm and pulled herself up. "I'm fine."

"Why didn't you tell me?" Kirsten asked to no one particular.

"We didn't know how you would react," said Amandine. "You have just come out of a coma. We couldn't give you bad news like that."

"He was the love of my life."

The others remained quiet.

"He loved me more than anyone has ever loved me."

Walter looked at Amandine.

"He was supposed to marry me. He was supposed to give me children. He was supposed to love me for the rest of my life."

Kirsten broke into tears. "How can I ever love again like that?"

"Maybe you can, maybe you can't," said Greta, "but you'll never know until you've lived a long life."

"I've lived enough."

"Don't say that," Amandine said.

"Leave. Please leave me."

"Kirsten."

"Mom. Please leave. Leave me for a few hours. Let me dwell on the horridness that is my life."

Walter took a crying Amandine out of the apartment. Kirsten heard the door shut behind them.

Kirsten stared into space.

"Greta!" She called a few minutes later.

"Yes, dear?"

"I need to ask you for a huge favor."

"Yes, what is it?"

"In a dresser upstairs, in the top drawer, there's a frame. Would you please bring that to me?"

"The FBI closed off your apartment. It's off-limits. There's a police line in front of the door."

"Are they here now? No. I really need this frame from upstairs. It's the only thing I need."

Greta seemed conflicted. Kirsten looked at her.

"Greta, the man who loved me, the man who I adored, is dead. The least I can have is something of his that we shared in our lives."

Greta nodded and left to go upstairs. In a few minutes, she returned with the frame.

"What is this?" Greta asked.

"It's called the 'True Lovers' Knot,'" Kirsten said. "See the way the lines intertwine to form a symmetry? It's because the lines separate and then join together. It's harmonious."

"Yes, I see that."

Kirsten sat up on one elbow to look around the apartment. "Greta, you see Mehran's gym shoes over there? Can I have them please?"

Greta was hesitant. She didn't understand why Kirsten wanted them. Cautiously, she brought the shoes over.

Kirsten untied one shoelace and pulled it from the shoe. She put the frame in front of her. Looking at the knot in the frame and back at Mehran's shoelace, Kirsten tried several times to reproduce the same knot. After several attempts, Kirsten held her own True Lovers' Knot.

Greta smiled.

"I did it. This knot with Mehran's lace is the symbol of my love for Mehran."

"That's very special, Kirsten."

"Yes, it is."

Kirsten looked at her and gave a small nod as she clutched the knot in her hand.

"I feel sleepy."

"Lay back and rest. I'll give you some space and retire to my room. I imagine your parents will return soon."

"I hope so. I owe them an apology."

Kirsten laid down and pretended to fall asleep while Greta went into her bedroom and started to read her book. After a few minutes, Kirsten opened her eyes. She pushed against the railing and flipped herself on her side. She reached out to the nightstand next to the bed and quietly pulled open the drawer, stopped and listened for Greta. She looked in the drawer and took out a syringe without a needle. She looked at her left arm with the IV line still in it. It was intact. She carefully removed the plastic covering from her IV line and pulled the syringe plunger to the top of the tube without removing it, filling the tube with air. She then screwed the tip of the syringe into the IV line hookup.

Kirsten paused as she looked at her arm with the syringe hanging and images began appearing in her mind: Mehran at Marie's desk, him bringing chocolate to her office. The defeated look on his face when he asked her out and then the restaurant incident, the limo ride, reading his Turkish coffee fortune, the Art Institute trips, making love in her apartment, Mehran pushing her against the wall at Baja Beach Club, Mehran pretending he couldn't drive stick. She smiled to herself. Mehran pleasuring her on the hood of her car, the trip to the Alps and giving herself entirely to him. She remembered Ravinia with Anja, moving into Mehran's apartment, meeting Fallah, finding out about Mehran's other children, meeting Nawal and Malak, getting robbed on the street, their first trip to Orchestra Hall, Mehran giving her the piano on Christmas, and then his proposal to her in the snow at the park.

Tears rolled down her cheeks and she grabbed the syringe.

Greta heard Kirsten crying and walked into the room.

"Kirsten, stop!"

"Go away."

"Kirsten! You can't do this."

"Please, go away. I don't want you to see this."

"Kirsten! Stop!"

"I can't. I have no reason to live this life."

"Yes, you do. You're a wonderful woman who was and is loved."

"You don't know that. How could you know that?"

"Because Mehran told me so, and because he loved you."

"What?"

"Because he loved you. He was a beautiful man. He never did anything to make me question his love for you."

"That just means that he was a beautiful man. And he was. I miss him. I want to be with him. There's nothing for me to live for in this life."

"If he was a beautiful man and he loved you, do you think that he would have loved someone who wasn't equally as beautiful as him?"

Kirsten was quiet.

"Doesn't that make you beautiful?"

"I don't know," Kirsten cried. "I just want to be with him."

"My son died after I cared for him for 10 years. There's not a day that goes by that I don't remember him, how much he loved me, and how much I loved him." Tears were rolling down Greta's cheeks. "But by me living on, his memories live on. I continue to talk about him and his memories make my life worthwhile. I want to be with him, too, but I continue to celebrate the life I did have with him."

Kirsten continued crying and whispered, "He loved me."

"I know. I could feel it, too. Now you have a choice. You can imagine that now that he's gone, so is his love for you, or you can imagine that even though he is gone, his love lives in you. In who you are."

Kirsten's fingers were shaking on the syringe. She let go. "I miss him," she sobbed. "Why did he leave me?"

Greta walked over to her and pulled Kirsten into her chest. "Not everything works out our way all the time."

Chapter Sixty-Seven

Walter and Amandine helped Kirsten get into the rental car to drive her to the hospital.

"They have a lot of questions for you. They want to know how you heard everything, and they want to perform some tests on you," Walter explained.

"Whatever," Kirsten said, uninterested.

They arrived at the hospital. The neurologists were waiting at the entrance.

The medical staff ran myriad tests on Kirsten, looking for something unique in her brain that would have led to the experiences she had in the coma. In the end, they couldn't determine anything different in Kirsten's brain versus any other patient.

The tests lasted 24 hours. Kirsten spent the night in the hospital.

The next morning, a gentlewoman walked into her hospital room. "Good morning, Kirsten. I'm Dr. Shelley Glenn, your ob/gyn doctor."

"Hello," Kirsten said.

"How are you feeling?"

"I'm fine."

"Any morning sickness?"

"No. Why would I have morning sick – " Kirsten stopped.

"Did you know you were pregnant?"

Kirsten's eyes widened. "What?"

"Yes, you are into your 10th week."

"How?"

Dr. Glenn chuckled. "Do you need me to tell you how?"

"I can't be. I was on birth control pills."

"Well, you know what they say. They don't work 100 percent of the time, especially if you weren't strict about taking them."

Kirsten was shocked. "What does that mean? What about everything I went through? The anesthesia, the other drugs? The surgery? The coma?"

"The anesthesia could have had an adverse effect on your fetus in the first trimester, specifically with potential loss, but here we are seven weeks after surgery and you're still pregnant."

Kirsten set her hand on her abdomen and looked at the doctor.

"Everything is going to be okay?"

"Kirsten, you had massive trauma to your head, and then you were in a coma. There's no telling how everything is going to turn out. But based on everything I know right now, I believe your baby is doing well."

Kirsten thought of Mehran. A part of him was growing inside her belly.

Chapter Sixty-Eight

In the middle of September, the weather in Martinique was extremely fair, with only the occasional threat of a hurricane. Kirsten stepped out of the Jeep, took a deep breath and sighed.

It was early in the morning, a Tuesday. Kirsten looked toward the east side of the island. The sun had started to come up. She waited until the sun was full in the sky and then walked into the school.

She began by talking with some of the adults, meeting some of the teachers who were coming into school to start the day. She struck up a conversation with a young, pretty teacher.

After some casual conversation about Kirsten being from the States and the weather, Kirsten asked, "Do you speak French?"

"Oui."

Kirsten switched to speaking French as she continued her conversation.

"I'm sorry, and I don't mean to be intrusive, but how long have you been teaching here?"

"Oh, about 12 years."

"That's wonderful."

Kirsten paused.

"When are you due?" asked the teacher.

Kirsten caressed her belly. "Around January 1."

"How fortunate! You'll have a new year baby."

"I may," Kirsten smiled.

She thought of Mehran and of his baby growing inside her. If it was a boy, she'd name him Mehran; if a girl, she'd name her Naghmeh.

She thought about Mehran, his kind face. She looked at her ring finger on her left hand, a ring without a diamond. Where was he now? She looked at the sun that was now well above the horizon, shining its light on the people of the planet. Surely that was him. He was the sun in the east. He was the love of her life. She could never love someone as much as she loved him.

With one exception – their child.

She remembered Mehran's 23 other children, children he had put through school in the hope of making this world better. That is, after all, why she was in Martinique. She wanted to keep his efforts going and continue his tradition.

"Can I ask you a question?" Kirsten asked. "Please think carefully about your answer. The answer you give me will last a lifetime."

"Oui."

Kirsten wiped away a tear. "Which child, in your opinion, has the greatest potential to make an impact on your society if he or she were to attended college but won't get a chance to make that impact because he or she can't afford college?"